Keepers of Arden

The Brothers
Volume 1

L. K. Evans

Dedicated to my husband.
Thank you for loving my faults as much as my few redeeming qualities. I'll just say that you give off a distinct shimmer.

Thank you to my editor, Ray Rhamey. I will never be able to fully express my gratitude.

Thank you to phatpuppyart for my cover art and bookish-brunette for my typography.

Thank you to Jo Michaels at Indie Books Gone Wild for proofreading.

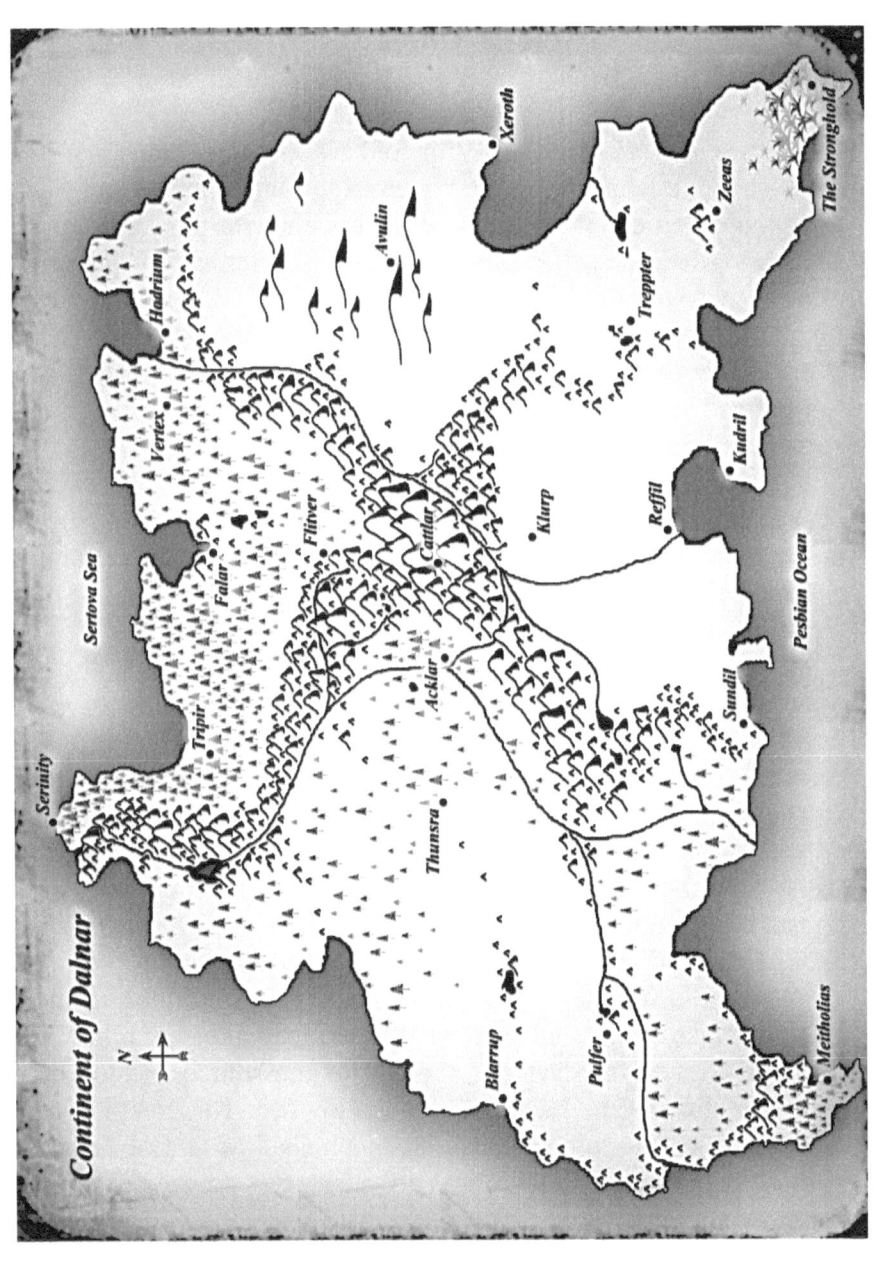

Continent of Dalnar

Chapter 1
999 years after god Nevlar's Retribution

Legs and skirts were all Wilhelm saw when he darted out of the mage shop, clutching his mother's cloak, blood pounding in his ears.

People fled down the cobblestone streets with the consistency of a tornado, and screeches rang from every which way. Men shoved other men down as a means to save themselves and provide a victim for the creatures hunting within the city. The crisp autumn air was overpowered by the stench of sweat and only the briny scent of the sea pierced through it. As if to offer compliment to the harrowing scene, the sunset painted crimson veins across the sky.

"May the gods help us," his mother breathed, her gaze sweeping over the chaos. She gathered her cloak about her to hide her standard mage robes before snatching his hand. Looking down at him, she cast a small smile. "We're going to run home. Don't let go of me no matter what happens."

Wilhelm nodded. Wincing from his mother's tight grip, he plunged into the bedlam alongside her. He was too short to see the terror going on around him. He only reached waist high, and as wails crescendoed, he snapped his eyes shut to avoid an accidental view of what might be unfolding. He'd yet to see another creature, and he prayed to the godless sky that his luck held. What he'd witnessed rising from the darkness in the alley had frozen his blood. There was no name for them that he knew of, no writings or pictures of them in books he'd read, but what he'd seen he named shadowfire.

When warmth devoured the evening chill, bringing with it a hissing noise, followed by what sounded like bubbling stew, Wilhelm opened his eyes and looked for the source. Beside him, a man was clutched in the arms of a shadowfire. The creature was in the form of a featureless human, as much shadow as fire. Instead of burnt orange flames, this fire was alive like curling smoke, roiling in hues of deep gray.

However, the shadowfire wasn't the source of the noise. The cause was the man flailing about in the creature's arms. He was burning, skin popping like a crackling fire, scream hissing in his throat, insides sputtering like boiling water, his dripping skin bathing Wilhelm in the stench of burnt hair and baking flesh.

A flood of people blocked the scene as his mother hauled him mercilessly onward, unaware of the horror he'd just witnessed. His stomach churned and relieved itself of its contents.

Time blurred into a landscape of faces twisted in fear and cries of the dying. In what seemed like mere breaths, Market Street became an obstacle course of charred bodies.

A corpse thudded to the ground next to him, smoking and sizzling. In a hoarse voice, Wilhelm whispered, "twenty-seven," adding the person to his count of the dead.

The melting lump disappeared from view when his mother darted down an alley. It was less busy and much quieter than the main thoroughfare, making his slapping footfalls echo like a metalsmith's hammer.

His mother took shelter in a deep alcove of an estate. "We're almost home," she breathed, kneeling down in front of him. She brushed his hair aside, cupped his face in her hands, and shifted his head left to right. "You're not hurt are you?"

Wilhelm couldn't find his voice. He shook his head.

His mother's warm smile spread across her face, driving away the furrow in her brow. "You're the bravest boy I've ever seen." She kissed his forehead. "The most amazing little boy." Leaning back against the brick wall, she rested a hand over her heaving chest. "We'll rest a moment. Just another two main streets and we'll be home."

Her courage reminded him why he loved her so dearly. It was just the two of them, and had been for his entire five and a half years of life, which had always been fine by him. But now, as he watched the tailor's family fleeing down the alley, the father's arm wrapped protectively around the mother, for the first time, Wilhelm wanted a father of his own; someone who could offer his mother the same comfort. He was too little to help fight the crowd.

A shifting shadow tucked between two buildings caught his eye. The blackness within the crevice lightened to the sootiest gray, and then churned like smoke from a billowing fire. It spilt from the gap to form an inky, undulating mass, looking like a pot of boiling black water.

Sucking in a breath, he pointed a shaking finger towards the growing creature. His mother latched hold of him and shrank back to the shadows.

The shadowfire swelled up from the cobblestones, sprouting arms, legs, and a featureless, oval head, morphing between twisting flames and writhing smoke. It raised its sunken eye sockets to the sky, and its screech pierced the night air, driving Wilhelm's hands to clamp over his ears.

Any person in the alley screamed and fled. The shadowfire looked both ways before gliding towards the street Wilhelm had just left. Once alone, his mother's breath exploded out.

Seizing hold of his hand, she sprinted from the alcove, dragging him until he got his feet under him, her grip making his fingers numb.

The next main street teemed with people trampling one another, half running one way and half running the other in some attempt to find safety. Shiny armor fleeted in front of Wilhelm and wails of terror drowned out the guards' orders.

After adjusting her cloak again, his mother darted into the mayhem. He bounced among legs, wincing and giving soft grunts from the rougher jabs that would surely bruise.

When Wilhelm and his mother rounded the corner to the next alley, they both froze.

He whispered, "thirty-six" when the flaming tailor streaked by, screams gurgling in his throat, burning arms flapping. As he entered the main street, people parted way except for a little girl Wilhelm's age. She was sobbing, standing alone with no parents protecting her. He tried to wrench his hand free so he could save her, but his mother's ironclad grip kept him by her side.

The little girl's wide eyes focused on the man sprinting towards her. Obviously paralyzed with fear, she merely stood there as the tailor smashed into her. The girl reeled backwards, tripped, and tumbled to the ground. The man fell on her legs, twitching once before lying motionless.

A guard shoved past the people and scooped the girl up in his arms. Despite the fact she'd been pinned under the burning tailor, her legs were unharmed, her wool dress not even singed. The blackfire had spread to nothing else.

"What in Veedran's damnation!" Wilhelm's mother hissed.

She jerked him down the alley to the wife and daughter of the tailor who were huddled together. Reaching out a hand, his mother said, "Come with us. We'll help you."

The wife of the tailor bolted to her feet. "Mage!" she shrieked, pointing at the sliver of slate-blue mage robes peeking from beneath his mother's cloak. "She's the one responsible! Burn her!"

Fleeing people paid the woman no heed. His mother's eyes saddened, but she said nothing when she continued down the alley, leaving the woman and her daughter alone.

The last main street before their home was less packed than the other two. Even so, chaos owned the people and crispy corpses speckled the cobblestones.

Odd warmth on Wilhelm's back made him crane his neck to look over his shoulder. Towering behind him was a shadowfire. Though the creature had no eyes, there was little doubt the sunken sockets stared at him—stared *through* him—into his soul, his heart, his mind. As he opened his mouth to shout a warning, the creature clamped its fingerless hands around Wilhelm's head. A swarm of what felt like maggots massed in his skull, squirming through his mind, searching. They leached away his voice and stole the stability of his legs and vision.

A hissing voice whispered in his ear, "I ssseee you, boy. I know who you are."

The pressure in his mind swelled until he was sure his head would burst open. Then he was whisked away. The pain ebbed and his vision returned to reveal the shadowfire gazing after him. Soon, fleeing people blocked the creature from view.

He locked his hands together behind his mother's neck, burying his face in her hair, wishing with all his might the screams would stop and the deaths would end.

Someone rammed into his mother, sending her plummeting to the ground. Wilhelm's air whooshed from his lungs when his back smacked the cobblestones and her weight pressed on his chest. Shoving herself to her hands and knees, she used her body to shield him from the stampede.

He gulped in a few deep breaths before rolling to his stomach and pushing himself to his hands and knees. His mother's soft cries of pain tightened his chest as she jerked with each kick she suffered. Wrapping her arms around him, she pressed him close, draping herself over him.

A flaming body collided with the cobblestones in front of them, sending a cloud of flaking flesh into the air.

"Forty-nine," Wilhelm whispered.

Then he was being lifted into her arms again. He twisted around and caught sight of shining armor and hazel eyes before his mother sprinted ahead. The crowd soon engulfed whomever had helped them. She dodged past another man consumed in flames and darted up the stairs to their home. At the landing, she fumbled for the key in her robe pocket. Wilhelm looked down at the disorder to see a shadowfire staring at him.

"Mother, hurry!" Wilhelm yelled.

The key clinked on the wood planks. His mother uttered a curse before lowering him to the ground and retrieving the key.

The shadowfire shrieked. All the creatures on the street stopped their inspection of the person writhing in their arms to stare up at Wilhelm.

Once again, a swarm of maggots bulged in his skull, slithering around his brain, searching.

"Mother!" Wilhelm cried, clamping his hands over his head in hopes of holding it together.

The lock gave and his mother hauled him inside, slammed the door shut, snatched up the nearest chair, and wedged it under the door handle.

"Are you hurt?" she asked.

Wilhelm reeled on unsteady legs until he found the wall, exhaling deeply when the maggots stilled and the pressure ebbed. He shook his head.

She walked to the kitchen and dipped a cloth in the washbasin. Lifting aside her hair, she dabbed blood from her temple. "Come over here, dear."

Wilhelm joined her at the kitchen table as she settled into a seat.

"You're sure you aren't hurt? No one kicked you or stepped on you?"

He shook his head.

A voice called from outside. "Ashra? Are you there?"

"Jyfil!" She rushed to remove the chair and flung open the door.

The old baker hurried inside. "Ashra! Thank the gods you're alive!"

"What in Nevlar's fury are you doing in the streets?" she asked, shutting the door quickly. "You should be hiding in your cellar."

"Nonsense. We're fleeing the city. You need to come with us."

"I don't think that's wise. These creatures are looking for something. They're not killing every person out there. It would be better to stay inside where it's safe."

Wilhelm tilted his head. The screams penetrating the window were subsiding.

"You lived in my home as one of my own daughters for a year and a half! I'm not leaving you here by yourself!"

She pinched Jyfil's wrinkled cheek. "I know, dear man, but I won't be safe out there. I'm safe here."

Jyfil shook his head. "No. I've heard people say those things can walk through walls. You must come with me."

"I'm not leaving. I'm in more danger out there. The citizens will blame the shadowfires on the first mage they see. I barely kept covered on the way here."

Jyfil paced. "They're saying more creatures are roaming Arden than ever before. Horrible beasts! *New* beasts!"

Wilhelm's mother laughed while she moved to the nearest window. "Who is 'they?'" She peeled back the curtain and stared out the window.

"Nabulik says the horrors left by the dark god Veedran are rising to take our lands and force us into slavery! He said they're led by the god Crutar!"

"You're letting your imagination run away with you, Jyfil. Crutar is too drunk to coordinate any kind of attack. These shadowfires are just old horrors growing brave and stepping out of whatever hole they've been dwelling in since Veedran's departure. Look." His mother motioned to the window. "They're already leaving. Crutar's no more interested in shackling us into slavery than I am in learning how to bake. He barely qualifies as a god! You mustn't believe everything you hear. I'm sure by morning this will be over."

Jyfil stared out the window before shaking his head. "You're a resilient woman."

"We've dealt with horrors emerging from time to time for near a thousand years." She shrugged. "Crutar's little raids are common. There's no need to panic."

Jyfil smiled at Wilhelm with flushed cheeks. "I hope I didn't scare you, boy."

He shook his head.

"My son will grow up to be a strong man." She beamed a smile at him. "Demons exist, but we remain calm and steadfast in the face of evil, do we not, son?"

Wilhelm nodded. "Yes, Mother."

Jyfil winked at Wilhelm, bid Ashra good evening, and slipped into the darkening night.

She repositioned the chair to block the door. "Go wash, dear."

Wilhelm went to the washroom, cleaned, and attempted to put on his bedclothes, which seemed to have an agenda of their own. He won the tussle and made his way back to the kitchen.

"Let me see." Ashra examined behind his ears. Once he passed inspection, she said, "I'm proud of you. I know you were afraid; but you followed directions, kept control of your fears, and were very brave."

"Were you afraid?"

She smiled, smoothing his hair. "Perhaps. But I know a secret."

"What?"

She took his right hand and turned it palm up to reveal his raised birthmark of a silhouetted bear. "Do you know what the bear stood for in the Armies of Light?"

"Protector."

"That's right. The commanders wore armor with a bear etched on their breastplates. It was a favorite of the goddess Zerana." She brushed back his hair. "You're meant to do something wonderful in this world, son. Zerana's grace will protect you."

"But Zerana's dead. She can't protect me."

His mother gathered him in her arms and rocked him. "Ah, therein lies the secret. She may be dead, but her love survived the Retribution. The love she left in Arden cares for and protects those who have a kind heart. You know, your father had the same mark on his hand. That's why he can't be with us. He's doing something important in the world."

Wilhelm snuggled against his mother. Her clothes always smelled of baked bread. "I'm never going to meet him, am I?"

"No, I'm afraid not."

"He doesn't want a son?"

In her conversation-ending tone, she said, "I don't know, dear.

You mustn't dwell on it. I love you and that's all that matters."

"I'll never have a baby brother, will I?"

"You ask this question daily, and what do I tell you?"

"Maybe one day." Without a father, Wilhelm's hope of filling the void in his life dwindled each day.

She pinched his nose. "Now go to bed."

He realized he had nothing in his stomach, and now that his fears were subsiding, food sounded wonderful. "But I'm starving!"

His mother laughed and lifted him to a chair. "I almost forgot about dinner." She cupped his face in her hands and kissed his forehead.

Wilhelm grinned at her and folded his hands on the table, waiting. He heard no more screams, nor did his mother's conversation end long enough for him to dwell on all he'd witnessed since leaving the magic shop.

It was dark when Wilhelm woke. He crawled out of bed and crept from his room. Moonbeams streaming through the windows lit his way to the kitchen.

He was starving by the time he made it to the food cupboard. Standing on his tiptoes, he sorted through a variety of dried meats, smelling each and nibbling on most. He was rummaging through the loaves of bread, contemplating which would pair best with venison, when his mother's cry of alarm resonated through their home. Though no candle burned, Wilhelm knew his house well. He dodged the furniture and burst into her room.

A moonbeam shot through his mother's window, lighting four shadowfires pinning her arms and legs to the bed. Another shadowfire stood at her side, screeching in a high-pitched voice. Wilhelm gaped at a ball of black shadowflame burgeoning between the creature's outstretched arms. With a chilling shriek, the beast pressed the ball into his mother's belly. Her beddress smoked and the sound of her sizzling skin was lost in her scream.

Wilhelm lunged at the nearest shadowfire. He fought rising panic when his hands swept *through* the creature. They were like smoke to his touch.

Suddenly, he was lifted from the ground. A shadowfire's arms surrounded him, feeling like a warm fog but holding him as if it were stone. He kicked, arched his back, squirmed, and punched. It was like fighting water.

The creature carried him to his sobbing mother and forced his palm to touch the ball of smoke sinking inside her. The mark on his palm burned red hot, sending a throbbing pain through him that didn't diminish after he yanked it back.

The creature that had generated the ball turned its demonic gaze on Wilhelm. Sunken eye sockets of utter, empty darkness burrowed into him, seeming to snake through his entire being, leaving him drowning in a horrible lake of violation. Fingers of icy fear froze his blood and tightened his throat.

Its hissing voice raised chills along his arms. "The boy will be *mine*; he will do *my* bidding. No longer isss Arden sssafe."

The wicked being launched Wilhelm across the room. His head slammed against the wall. Warm blood trickled down the back of his neck. Before pulsating darkness claimed him, his mother's pleading, "no" echoed in the room.

Chapter 2
Spring 1000 a.r.

Wilhelm propped his elbows on the window ledge in the back storage room of the magic shop where his mother worked. As usual, there was nothing to do. Himiks, the shop owner, had made it clear on several occasions that if any of his goods happened to break, the world would be engulfed in the vilest of evil imaginable. So Wilhelm, ever seeking to be a good son, sat in silence while his sulking gaze followed the few passing citizens, which he assumed— or rather dreamt—were hurrying home to prepare scrumptious dinners. With his stomach growling away the waning hours of afternoon, he pondered the idea of being full. In his six years of existence, he had yet to experience the joy of a stuffed belly. Not to say his mother didn't feed him properly. They maintained a humble life of modest dinners made with inexpensive ingredients—his least favorite being stew. The pot of thrown-together vegetables, herbs, and unsavory animal parts did little to entice his appetite, yet even the two bowls he'd devour never squelched his insatiable hunger.

"Time to go, dear," his mother called.

He hopped from his stool and sprinted towards the front room. Before bursting into the merchandised-stocked area, he slowed to a brisk walk in order to avoid a scolding from Himiks. When Wilhelm rounded the corner, his mother's welcoming smile awaited him.

She held out her hand. "Ready?"

His grin faded at the sight of her peaked complexion, enhanced by the dark circles rimming her eyes that had been present since the attack of the shadowfires two seasons ago, along with fevers and violent retching.

"Good evening, Ashra," Himiks growled. "Hopefully, tomorrow you can stay in the front long enough to prove your use."

When she responded, her voice lacked its customary strength. "I'm sorry."

Himiks grunted and waved his hand in a gesture of annoyance. "I don't pay you to make a mess of my washroom."

"I understand." Her feverish hand clasped Wilhelm's. "I'll see you tomorrow."

Wilhelm stepped outside into the warm spring sun and inhaled a deep breath. A perpetual layer of staleness hung in the air of the magic shop because Himiks preferred to keep the doors and windows barred shut. Though Wilhelm had grown accustomed to the stagnant store, the freshness of the light breeze brought about an awakening of his mind and lungs. His mother seemed to enjoy the sweet smell of spring as well. She closed her eyes while taking a deep breath and raised her face to the sun.

The breeze played with her thick hair. "Wonderful evening."

He was about to utter his agreement when a passing man spat at her feet. Wilhelm could never push his mind to understand why mages, especially men, endured taunts and spitting competitions conducted by loitering pedestrians with seemingly nothing better to do than torment wizards and witches. Wilhelm had witnessed such events, which regularly ended with a mage covered in filth, or—if the crowd was in a sprightly mood—beaten or dead. Luckily, his mother's striking features and shiny blanket of auburn hair spared her such torment. Most people merely resorted to name calling or spitting at her feet.

His mother gathered her cloak about her, hiding the slate-blue robes that identified her as a mage, and continued down the bustling market street. The spring sun mingled with the cool sea breeze as it weaved between buildings, sneaking through the narrow streets to lift the heavy smells of the market. Filth clung to sides of buildings, and accumulated grime layered the cobblestones. The city of Falar relied on the rains to cleanse its dirt. It never rained enough.

They passed bards singing a discombobulated mess of melodies. The raucous voices joined pleading calls from merchants attempting to cajole passersby into a purchase, and the combination soured Wilhelm's mood. He lived in a quiet home or sat in a quiet shop; and only his mother's crooning broke the silence. The street noises made him wince.

His mother massaged her stomach, which, despite her illnesses, had grown a little bulge. "We'll visit Delora at the potion shop on the way home."

When the two arrived, a familiar man, clothed in voluminous slate-blue robes, stood at the counter examining a leaf.

Wilhelm rushed the mage. "Uncle Mafarias!"

Mafarias whisked him into a warm embrace. "Wilhelm, my boy! How are you?"

"Fine! Where have you been?" Wilhelm asked.

His mother arched her eyebrow and used a scolding tone. "It's been seven months since your last visit, Uncle."

Mafarias set him down and kissed her cheek. "Lovely as ever, Ashra."

"I'm sure you have an excuse as always," she said.

Wilhelm grinned at his great uncle. "You're in trouble."

Mafarias rolled his eyes and cast a wry smile. "Alas, my dear, my talents are always required somewhere in the world."

"You'll stay for dinner?"

"Of course."

After Wilhelm's mother visited with Delora, the family trio made their way to the butcher shop where Mafarias bought a delicious looking roast of venison before they set off for Wilhelm's home above the baker's shop. The fresh breads, sweet rolls, and pies constantly baking in Jyfil's oven caused Wilhelm's stomach to grumble. Many times over, he wished they would move.

When they entered his home, he sighed in contentment at the coziness of the space as he hung up his and his mother's cloaks on wall pegs next to the door. He smiled at the two chairs nestled in front of the fireplace where his uncle was already working to light a fire. One side of the room was lined with wooden shelves crammed with books that Wilhelm had read, twice; some of them three times. The dining table was long for the small space and seemed to be a constant reminder of the loneliness that often crept into his heart. He stopped himself from asking his nightly question of when he'd be getting a brother.

He went to the kitchen and helped prepare the assortment of foods his uncle had bought.

"The Association of Mages has come up with another brilliant law," Mafarias said in a tone of disgust.

"Do they have nothing better to do than sit around and talk of ways to harm our reputation?" she said.

"I fear not. Now they'll add our level of power to the guards' list of known wizards and witches."

She furrowed her eyebrows. "What's the point? It makes no

sense."

"I agree completely. The Association says it will ease the guards' concerns. If they know how powerful we are, they'll know how many men it will take to kill us."

She rolled her eyes. "Wonderful. I don't understand why they fear us. There are what... fourteen or so spells available to us? They fear those spells as if we could defeat an entire city."

Mafarias sighed. "Man will forever fear what is not understood, my dear."

Wilhelm carried a cheese and bread plate to the table. Before he turned, Mafarias lifted Wilhelm's hand and examined his birthmark.

"Has the mark been acting up, boy?"

"Yes, it kind of hurts and tingles a lot." In fact, it had itched, throbbed, and even burned since the night of the shadowfires.

"Anything odd happen lately?" Mafarias asked.

"Not since the shadowfires two seasons ago."

Mafarias studied the mark for a moment before the color drained from his face. He turned to Wilhelm's mother, his voice hardly a whisper. "You look pale."

She nodded, carving up the roast. "I haven't been feeling well for months. Fevers, and my stomach is in knots."

"Did you ask Delora?" Mafarias rose to stand next to her and touched her forehead.

"Yes. She has no idea."

Mafarias's gaze lowered to her distended belly and widened. Wilhelm thought it a tad rude to stare at her new bulge.

"What?" His mother turned a rosy pink and adjusted her robes. "I've put on a few pounds. Stop looking at me that way."

Mafarias's eyes widened further. "You don't know?"

She rammed the knife into the wood counter. "It's not possible! It can't be!"

Wilhelm flinched from the anger in her voice. He'd never heard her snap at anyone.

Mafarias rested a hand on her shoulder. "We can deal with this—"

"No! There's nothing I need to deal with!" Lifting the heavy plate of meat, she turned on her heel, and took two steps before she swayed to a stop. The platter shattered on the floor and she grabbed her belly.

"No," she breathed. "This can't be happening!"

Mafarias caught her in his arms. "Wilhelm, run and fetch Delora from the herb shop. Tell her your mother is having a baby."

"What did it do to me?" she screamed.

Her cry of pain and the pool of blood forming on the floor sprang Wilhelm into action.

Wilhelm paced in front of the fireplace as he had since Delora arrived hours earlier. He was upset by the cries coming from behind his mother's bedroom door and the thought that she'd keep such a wonderful secret from him. As the night crawled on, a fast moving cloud shrouded the silver moon and limited the light streaming through the sitting room window.

"*Ecia lumenious,*" Mafarias whispered, and a crystal resting on the table emitted a warming, pure white light. "You're about to wear a hole in your floor."

"I can't be still. What's taking so long?" Unfortunately, Wilhelm hadn't inherited his mother's patience.

"These things can't be rushed. We enter the world at our own choosing. By the way, good Birth Day to you."

Wilhelm glanced out the window. Indeed, the palest light of a new morning threatened to devour the constellation of Ctol Lilkous, honored Knight and first King of Arden. Elbows propped on the window ledge, he stared at the stars, brooding.

"Did you do anything to celebrate the coming of the New Year last week?" Mafarias asked.

"No, we stayed home. Mother doesn't like to be on the streets when there's a crowd. They always spit on her and call her names."

"I see." Wilhelm felt his uncle's gaze for several moments before Mafarias spoke. "Have I ever told you what a sharp boy you are? You don't act six years old at all."

"Mother makes me study all the time. I'm smarter than the other boys."

"Your mother has high standards for her son."

"I know." Wilhelm rolled his eyes. "No other kids my age can read and do math."

Mafarias chuckled and shook his head. "Quite a talented boy you are, Wilhelm. You must've read the stories of Ctol Lilkous then."

Wilhelm nodded. "He was the knight who won the war against the god Veedran's Minotaur army, turned them to his cause, and saved Arden from the evil god's reign. He became the sole king of Arden before god Nevlar's Retribution."

"He did indeed; a brave man and skilled with a sword. He fought with two weapons. Did you know that?"

Wilhelm glanced at the constellation again. "No."

"They say his strength was unmatched. He used both a great sword and a broadsword simultaneously."

"Bah!" He waved the story aside. "Impossible."

"Nothing is impossible."

"Everyone knows a great sword is too heavy. You have to use two hands."

"At the rate you're growing, my dear boy, you might have a chance of trying it yourself."

Wilhelm grinned. "It would be wonderful if I fought with two swords." He allowed himself a daydream, imagining fierce creatures running in fear as his swords swung through the air. His grin broadened at the thought of his baby brother fighting by his side.

Wilhelm's smile faded when his mother's cries switched to screams.

Mafarias cleared his throat. "So, tell me of the night the creatures appeared. Everything."

"We were at Wizard Himiks's shop when they came. I saw one come up right from the ground. The city panicked and Mother pushed through the crowd until we reached home. We latched the door and stayed inside. When I woke up, Mother said the creatures had left in the night."

Mafarias's brow furrowed. "Nothing else?"

"No. Mother has been sick, like she told you, with fevers, and she throws up a lot." Wilhelm batted away the nagging feeling that something else had happened.

Delora gave a cry from Ashra's bedroom, bringing him and his uncle to their feet. A painful hole formed in Wilhelm's heart as if someone had taken a spoon and carved out a portion of his soul. With each breath the hollowness grew until he doubled over, clutching his chest.

What seemed like days passed before Delora's voice croaked barely audible words. "I've tried everything, Ashra. The baby won't breathe and has no life beat. I'm so sorry."

Wilhelm's feet melted to the spot where he stood. He wanted a sibling. He'd watched other children play with younger brothers or sisters with shameful envy. He seethed with jealousy when they laughed over newly devised games and shared jokes no one else understood. He ached for the same closeness. Now, Delora's fateful words leached away his hope.

The door opened and Delora motioned Mafarias to enter. "Ashra's in poor condition." Delora's voice dropped so Wilhelm barely heard her. "I nearly lost her more times than I care to count. She's lost a lot of blood, and I doubt she'll have more children."

Mafarias nodded and disappeared into the room.

"You stay here, dear," Delora said to Wilhelm. "You can see your mother in a bit."

"Can I hold him?"

She patted his cheek. "I'm not sure that's wise."

"Please?"

Delora regarded him for a moment and then said, "Wait here."

She closed the door and returned a short time later carrying a bundle of white cloth. Wilhelm accepted the tiny body, along with Delora's hug before she left his home. He settled into a plush chair beside the fire, pondering his request to hold his dead brother. It didn't make sense.

Carefully peeling away the cloth, Wilhelm stared at his tiny brother. Thick black hair mantled his small head, and Wilhelm smoothed an unruly lock sticking straight up. The baby looked as though it was sleeping, and Wilhelm stared at its chest for some hopeful sign of life. Nothing.

Tears cascaded down his cheeks when he clasped the tiny hand in his own. With all his will and heart, he begged his baby brother to live, to fill the void that had plagued Wilhelm for as long as he could remember.

A painful sensation flared from the mark on his palm, creeping along his body as if a wave of needles were being jammed into his flesh. As it rippled through him, the aching in his heart ebbed. Surging warmth tingled inside him, seeming ready to explode from his body. It mushroomed with such speed he grew faint, yet he shivered from the euphoric sensation blazing through his blood. The link he felt to the baby amplified, and the intensity escalated the longer Wilhelm's thoughts focused on his desperate want of a brother. Just as he thought his mind might burst, the power roaming through his body imploded upon itself deep within him. A prick of pain stabbed his palm, and then it all stopped.

He jerked his hand away and stared at his mark. It didn't look different. He rubbed his palm against his trews, trying to rid himself of the last vibrating tingles. Glancing at his lap, he twitched with a start when he saw the baby staring at him. Gray-black irises, just a shade lighter than the jet-black pupil, were so large that only a sliver of white on each side could be seen. Not only were the irises overly large, they seemed to have a life of their own. They churned like black smoke from a smoldering flame, whirling in shifting hues of gray and black.

Questions ran rampant on how the baby had suddenly come to life, but one thought satisfied his curiosity. Finally, he was an older brother. He'd be damned by all the gods in all the worlds before he questioned the reason for receiving such a special gift.

His grief switched to joy. "Salvarias Laybryth. That's your name."

A sparkle lit up his brother's black eyes. Wilhelm's grin snuck across his face. For the first time—because of that sparkle—Wilhelm's soul felt whole.

In his blissful state, it took a moment before he became aware of a presence in the room, and as he raised his head, a figure robed in blood-red velvet stepped from the shadows. Wilhelm gulped for air, which seemed to have been sucked from the space. A weight mantled itself in the room and pressed down on him, pinning him to the chair.

No doubt existed, no scholar could have pledged otherwise, pure evil had forged the man standing before Wilhelm. The figure reached a skeletal finger for Salvarias.

Wilhelm struggled against invisible bonds that seemed to strap him to the chair. He attempted to call out, but no sound escaped his lips. Time stopped.

The instant the man's finger rested on Salvarias's forehead, the baby writhed in Wilhelm's arms, features twisted in agony, tears flowing down the newborn's cheeks. A weak cry escaped his tiny lungs and his black eyes filled with horror.

A snakelike hiss issued from the hood, cold and calculating.

"Yesss, thisss will be the Sssoul. Hhhe will determine the outcome! Thisss Guardian issss *mine*! Hhhe will do *my* bidding!"

A smoky red fog oozed from the man's finger and encased Salvarias. Another feeble cry escaped, and his gray-black eyes widened and distanced. A drop of blood trickled out of his nose.

Fear for the baby sparked in Wilhelm. The warm tingle he'd felt only moments earlier surged up and imbued strength in his every muscle. Using all his power, his brow beading with sweat, heart pounding, he wrestled the bonds that held him until his right hand rose. He commanded the power coursing through him to move his arm. Eternity seemed to pass before his hand rested on the robed man's finger. The man recoiled with a yelp of pain.

The red smoke that had seemed to be feeding on Salvarias seeped into him, inducing yet another cry. The man sucked in a breath before melting into the shadows. Wilhelm's trapped cry escaped into the room as the door to their home clicked closed.

"What is it, Wilhelm?" Mafarias asked from the doorway of Wilhelm's mother's room.

He forgot why he'd cried out. The last thing he remembered was seeing large, black eyes. Gasping, he looked down at his brother. Salvarias's unfocused eyes were opened wide, tears streamed down his pale cheeks, and blood trickled from his nose.

"Help him! He's alive!" Wilhelm pleaded.

Mafarias's robes rustled in the quiet room when he strode to Salvarias. Like the red-robed man, a smoky light poured from his uncle's outstretched thumb when he rested it on Salvarias's forehead. But Mafarias's fog ebbed with the palest blue light. Whatever he whispered caused the light to pulse, almost blinding Wilhelm. Suddenly, Mafarias cried out. The light flashed and he fell to his knees. Quicker than the blink of an eye, the blue fog sucked inside Salvarias.

"May the gods have mercy," Mafarias breathed.

He turned Salvarias's left hand over to reveal a black raised mark that filled his palm; a silhouetted flame circled by a black ring.

When Salvarias fidgeted under his uncle's touch, Wilhelm pulled his brother's hand away. "Don't touch him. What's that mark?"

Mafarias rubbed his forehead. "Nothing to worry about yet."

Salvarias had calmed and now studied Wilhelm with serious intent. A grin spread across his face and he ruffled his brother's soft hair. The black eyes sparkled back.

Unupture examined his smooth, orange-tinted hand in the light of the rising sun while he waited for his master to return. His wrinkle-free skin was a painful reminder that he was well over a thousand years old and had once served the almighty dark god, Veedran. The rewards Unupture had received—eternal life to name one—hardly countered the punishments Veedran had inflicted. The dark god wasn't a kind master, nor was Unupture's new one. He sighed. He seemed to attract cruel masters. Why did the side of Light never want to test the boundaries of creation?

He lifted his plum-purple robes to avoid a fleeing rat and mulled over the possibilities of breeding the rodent with one of his prisoners.

Finally his master emerged from the shabby home above the baker's shop. By God's scowling face and stomping feet when he descended the stairs, things hadn't gone according to plan with the babe God called the Guardian.

God strode over, his overly large black eyes sending a shudder down Unupture's spine. Nothing but dominance and contempt flowed from them.

"What happened?" God demanded. "Sssense my powersss. Are they weaker?"

"Yes, my Dark Lord. Tell me what occurred."

He cursed. "I wasss planting my ssseed, imbecile! I wasss going to have complete control over the Guardian!"

"The baby has taken a great deal of your power. Were you successful at all, my Lord?"

"Only partly." God kicked a fleeing rat. "The damn doe-eyed Protector prevented me from finishing."

"Still an accomplishment. The baby is already ours."

God shook his head. "He isss not like other Guardiansss. I *mussst* have his sssoul."

"The soul?" Unupture frowned. Yet another detour from God's original plan. "Might I ask why, Master?"

A gleam of perfect white teeth flashed a smile. "It isss linked to my battle, ssservant. Hhhow truly remarkable, isssn't it? A Sssoul, one tiny little sssoul isss all I mussst obtain."

"I don't understand."

God snorted. "No, you don't! If the babe followsss me, willingly, then victory isss mine!"

"I see. If I may be so bold, what's preventing us from marching up those steps and taking the baby now?"

Anger flashed in God's eyes. "How, I'll never know, but hisss Protector wasss already there!"

"I don't see how, my Darkest Master. His father has not transfer his power."

God held up his hand to reveal a fresh burn on his finger. "I know! But the boy hasss it! He can hurt me!"

"This is most unfortunate." Unupture paced. "Most unfortunate. The sole option we have is to allow our servant to monitor the situation. With the bond already active with his Protector, we must be strategic and careful. You mustn't go near the baby. He'll continue to steal your power, and the Protector will only continue to harm you." He turned to his master. "The Guardian will be ours."

"If I cannot get to him, if hisss Protector hasss already claimed him, hhhow can I turn his sssoul?"

"Your seed, Master. It will wear down the babe over time. We only need patience." He gazed at the window above the baker. His next suggestion sickened him. "And fear, my Lord, is a wondrous emotion. So much can it rule who we are and the choices we make. Send your servant to induce the fear and the Guardian's soul will turn. What seed you did plant will grow and help corrupt his mind. With the servant's aid, we cannot fail."

"And the Protector?"

Unupture shrugged. "With your seed, the baby will require additional monitoring by the Protector. The Protector will grow tired of the boy. He'll grow to hate him and eventually leave or lower his guard. We will wait patiently for that day. *Patience* will get us to our goal, my Lord."

"What if the Protector and Guardian grow clossse? Already he isss protective."

"Even if they do, you underestimate your seed. It *will* turn the baby. I doubt his soul will ever be held in the light. The seed will whisper to him and drive him towards dark forces, steer him from the light as well as those who would aid him. It will force the Guardian to leave his Protector at some point. All we must do is wait."

God clenched his fist. "I did not finisssh. I cannot control my ssseed within the baby."

"It will do enough damage on its own. Your manipulation of the mind is subtle. Along with the fear we induce, I don't see how we can fail. Events are aligning in our favor too rapidly. The tides have already shifted. Even without the babe's soul, our powers are growing."

"Oversssee the sssituation and report to me often. We'll continue our other plansss."

Unupture nodded. "Even if we fail in turning the boy, our other preparations are well underway. Either direction, Arden will bow to you, The One True God."

"It had better. You don't want to be around for the consssequences ssshould it not. Leave me."

Unupture bowed deeply. "As my Dark Master commands."

Chapter 3
Spring 1002 a.r.

Ashra curled up in her favorite chair and gazed at Wilhelm. Her son's bright amber eyes sparkled in the spring sun streaming through the window, and the deep tone of his voice filled the air. She beamed with pride while he read a book most adults would struggle to finish. He soaked up all she taught him, though he complained at every lesson that other eight-year-old boys weren't required to learn so much. In fact, he'd been complaining since he was four.

Wilhelm paused in the story to take a sip of water, and before he continued, he cast Ashra his lopsided grin. She couldn't help but smile. No one who was the recipient of that crooked, impish grin could resist him. There was purity in his eyes, which seemed amplified when he smiled, yet a mischievous and cunning mind was hidden behind the innocence. What made it even more powerful was the fact that he was completely oblivious to how charming he was.

Her son picked up a blanket and wrapped it around the shivering monstrosity nestled in his lap.

Ashra shifted her gaze to the floor. She couldn't look it. All Salvarias sparked within her were memories of the horrid night of its creation. Two and a half years had passed since the terrifying shadowfires had snuck into her room and impregnated her against her will, desecrated and defiled her. She shuddered at the memory of smelling her own baking skin, the sickening feeling when the black smoke seeped into her flesh, and the violation she felt when it implanted itself in her womb. She rubbed her scarred stomach and covered her mouth to fight the rising bile. The memory was so vivid she found it difficult to enter her room each night. More than once, she'd woken up from a nightmare of reliving that harrowing incident to be immediately ill. She felt alone on those nights.

Now, two years had passed since its birth nearly killed her. Two years since Delora had thought the evil child died. Two years since she was bedridden for near a month trying to recover from the internal damage. Delora had confirmed Ashra's horrible suspicion on the fateful night she gave birth to the demon: She'd never have more children. The birth had been too arduous, too long, too much blood had been lost, and the baby too premature.

As any rational person would, she'd wanted to kill it. She remembered staggering from her bed and snatching up her dagger. But Mafarias had wrested the weapon from her hands. She'd been too weak to fight him. To this day, no doubts existed in her mind: nothing good could come from a child created by creatures made of shadow and fire. Nothing that forced its seed inside a woman could be of the Light. No, only darkness, only evil, only horrors performed such atrocities. Still, even though she was certain of its wickedness, her uncle had stopped her from butchering it. He'd promised her the child must live; that it had a purpose. As always, she trusted him.

She shook herself to free her thoughts. At least she'd been able to have one son that wasn't a monster. One perfect little boy had blessed her life, and that was all she needed.

She felt the evil child's stare upon her. She raised her gaze to see it snuggled close to Wilhelm, encased in his arms. The churning black eyes were a mirror of the evil creatures that had defiled her. The haunting irises didn't sparkle with the innocence of a two-year-old. Instead, they glittered with the awareness of a man who'd witnessed first hand the suffering of the world. An intelligence and maturity past its years was evident in the eyes.

As usual, the demon's expression was stern and serious. What made it all the more eerie was the creature's tiny size. It was too small for a two-year-old. Yet, even as that trait should call upon cooing attention from women, the instant any saw its eyes, they recoiled from the child with visible shudders racking them. Only Jyfil, Delora, and Mafarias—after two years of enduring the evil child's stare—could remain in its presence. And, of course, Wilhelm. In fact, her lovely son never let it out of his sight. Nor did Wilhelm question how he'd obtained his "gift," his "treasure," as he called it. He never asked who fathered it and, at Mafarias's request, Ashra never told Wilhelm the truth. He seemed not to care that she never touched it. So her innocent, pure son treated the evil baby as though it were his own. He cared for the infant, fed it, changed it, and read it stories.

"All done," Wilhelm announced.

Ashra startled and realized she was still staring at the demon.

Wilhelm lowered it and went to return the book to the shelf. The demon took a step towards her and she curled her lip in disgust and rose from the chair. She turned on her heel and headed for the kitchen.

"Get your cloak, son. I have to visit Delora."

"Yes, Mother."

Wilhelm retrieved his cloak and a small one Ashra had sewn for Salvarias upon Wilhelm's request. She snatched up a loaf of bread, slipped it into a pouch tied to her belt, and led her son and the monster into the bustling streets of Falar. She held Wilhelm's hand and used the other to keep her mage robes well concealed under her cloak. Salvarias's hand was clasped firmly in Wilhelm's, and the demonic black eyes surveyed the streets with their usual intense stare.

As she crossed the crowded guardhouse square, repulsion teemed at the sight of the gallows and a man being led to the noose. Though criminals deserved punishment, she preferred a swift end, not a slow, tortured death. Some were sure to be innocent, which added to her disgust. Every part of the device, from the construction to the method used to tie the rope, was meant to prolong death.

She shielded Wilhelm from the ghastly display as she made her way through the throng of onlookers, though he seemed uninterested. Salvarias, on the other hand, stared with alarming zeal as it maneuvered to obtain the best view. Ashra avoided looking at the death scene, and instead, watched the abomination with swelling fear and revulsion. When the noose snapped, the black eyes flickered with pleasure. She could have sworn it even twitched a smile.

Shivering, she hurried them around the corner, out of sight of the gruesome spectacle and away from the packed crowd.

Once the scene vanished, she snapped to a stop when the abomination's eyes welled with tears. It was the first sign of emotion the creature ever exhibited around her. She'd never seen it cry, nor had it ever issued the slightest noise. She'd assumed it was a mute. But now, soft whimpers erupted.

Wilhelm wiggled his hand free from hers and knelt in front of it, wiping away its tears with his sleeve. "It's all right, Salv. I'm right here. What's wrong?"

The monstrosity flung itself into Wilhelm's arms and buried its face in his chest. Within the time it takes to crack a whip, the sky bloomed with menacing storm clouds, thunder vibrated the buildings, and lightning fingered across the darkening sky. Wind shrieked through the streets, whipping Ashra's hair into her face and binding her robes to her body. A raindrop, cold as snow, landed on her cheek. Then the sky unleashed its fury.

Wilhelm lifted the child into his arms and Ashra led him forward by the shoulder. The ominous sky churned with sickly gray and muted green clouds while the rain pelted down on scrambling citizens seeking shelter. A sharp snap and sizzle issued close by, followed by panicked screams. A crescendoing roar of thunder shook the ground, cracking cobblestones under her feet. Seeing a large overhang in an alley, she directed Wilhelm under cover while both shivered in the biting wind and rain. Thunder boomed in an encore of ear-shattering ferocity among the deepening clouds, and the tremor rocked the building where Ashra sought shelter.

"It's all right," Wilhelm whispered, holding Salvarias close. "Nothing's going to happen."

A woman ducked into the alley, but upon seeing Ashra's mage robes, fled back to the scurrying streets.

"What is it?" Wilhelm asked the abomination.

The evil child seemed unaware of the storm. Its eyes seemed to stare at something else, and its gaze darted this way and that.

A man staggered into the alley with a hand clamped on his bleeding head. Ashra withdrew a cloth from her robe pocket and steered the man under the overhang while applying pressure to the wound.

The man shouted over the roar of thunder, "They trampled me!"

Wilhelm set the abomination down and knelt in front of it. "Look at me, Salv."

The child raised its face. It jerked with each attempted breath.

"It's all right," Wilhelm said. "You're fine. Nothing can hurt you. You believe me? I love you, and I won't let anything happen to you."

The monstrosity stared at her son long enough for her to think it wouldn't respond, but finally it nodded. With a crooked grin plastered across his face, Wilhelm ruffled its soaked hair.

The rain eased to a light misty sprinkle, clouds shifted to soft gray and began dissipating. Bright sunshine filtered through leftover wisps of friendly clouds to warm the frigid air. The entire event ended as abruptly as it had begun. Ashra turned her narrowed eyes to the creature.

The man broke her thoughts. "Thank you for your help."

She took a deep breath and offered a smile. "Are you all right, or can I help you home?"

"No, I'm fine." The man smiled, abashed. "My wife wouldn't take kindly to me accepting help from a mage."

"I understand. Good day."

The man nodded and then disappeared into the crowded streets. After adjusting her soaked robes and cloak, they continued to the herb store.

When they arrived, Delora giggled. "Ashra! How are you, dear? I see you got caught up in that storm."

"We did, but found cover in an alley." Ashra set the loaf of bread on the counter.

"My daughter has returned from her travels. I'm anxious for you to meet her."

Ashra smiled at the elderly woman, warming in the closeness they shared. Delora had never judged Ashra for being a mage, had cared for her after Salvarias's birth, and had acted like a second mother when Ashra had lost hers at the tender age of seventeen.

A woman waddled down the stairs, as round as Delora, her face as cheerful, with rosy cheeks and curly, yellow hair.

"Milred, this is Ashra." Delora beamed.

"Hello! I've heard all about you!" Milred embraced Ashra before taking her hands. "Your hands were made for alchemy!"

Ashra smiled. "Mages are most effective when their fingers are long and slender. Some runes are intricate to trace."

Milred pinched Ashra's cheek and then turned to the boys. Salvarias was breathing hard and quick. It never seemed to get enough air, and she suspected its premature birth to be the cause. Only six months in the womb. It should have died, or rather stayed dead.

Milred knelt in front of the monstrosity. "Does he breathe like this all the time?"

Salvarias took a step behind its brother.

Wilhelm shifted in front of it. "He gets attacks a couple times a day. Can you help him?"

"My, those eyes!" A visible shudder ran down Milred's body.

"And those hands! He'll make a wonderful alchemist. Why, they're just as delicate as yours," Milred said to Ashra.

"Can you help him?" Wilhelm asked again.

"Maybe. Let's go in back, dear." Milred led them down a short hall to a room with a three-chaired table. A cool breeze drifted through a window, and a bright stream of sunlight fell across the oak table. Wilhelm settled Salvarias into a chair.

"Poor child." Milred reached for the abomination but Wilhelm intercepted.

"Don't touch him," Wilhelm muttered.

"I want to help him, see if I can figure out what's wrong. In order to do so, I'll need to examine him."

Wilhelm looked at the two plump women and then at Salvarias. With evident reluctance, he stepped to the side. Salvarias's black eyes filled with hurt; as if its brother had betrayed it, and it stumbled from the chair, reaching for Wilhelm.

Wilhelm lifted the child and returned it to the chair. "She's going to help you, Salv."

Ashra shook her head. Her son never allowed a single person to touch Salvarias. This was the first time Wilhelm had, and by his frown and furrowed brow, he was having difficulties with his decision.

"I'll hold him, dear," Delora offered. She rested a hand on Salvarias and it flinched away. She recoiled. "What's wrong? I'm not going to hurt you."

"Hold him, Mother," Milred murmured.

Delora grabbed hold of the child. Ashra was impressed with Delora's courage. Only once had Ashra ever touched the monstrosity. It was when Wilhelm was bathing and the creature had crawled over to her while she was making dinner. It had hugged her leg. She'd been quick to kick it off. Ever since, it never touched her and she never touched it. This was the first time Delora ever laid hands on it. She knew it should have died. They both knew.

The abomination paled and trembled with each passing breath as the women listened to its chest while murmuring possible causes to each other. Ashra glanced out the window. It was getting late.

Suddenly, the monstrosity convulsed and its eyes rolled back in its head. Tremors shook through it and a trickle of blood ran from its nose. Wilhelm swept it from Delora's grasp. Salvarias's eyes rolled back and it gasped harder for air, its knuckles turning white when it clenched Wilhelm's arms.

"That's enough!" Wilhelm ordered. He cradled the monstrosity in his arms. "I'm sorry, Salv. I won't let it happen again."

Milred shook her head. "I've never seen a case like that before." She smiled at Wilhelm. "Don't fret dear. I'll start looking for something."

"Thanks," he muttered. He accepted a cloth from Delora and wiped the blood from the abomination's face.

The evil child's reaction to touch, the incident at the gallows, and the unnatural storm shook Ashra to her core. She ordered her herbs and paid, desperately wanting to return to the safety of her home where the abomination's behavior wouldn't embarrass her.

By the time they left the shop, the setting sun had painted the sky orange and families hurried through the market. She uttered a curse at the late hour. The streets cleared rapidly, merchants closed for dinner, and bards gathered their coins and instruments. She turned down an alley towards the bakery, and three men stepped out of the shadows, blocking her way. Too late did she realize her robes were visible.

"A witch out after dark?" One man smirked.

She turned to flee, but a man sprang from the shadows behind her. Her gaze darted around, seeking rescue, but any passersby merely turned their heads as though injustice wasn't unfolding. With slow steps, she backed towards the stone wall, pushing Wilhelm behind her and keeping her gaze locked on the four men. Her mind leapt from one pathetic idea to another. Knowing it to be futile but lacking any other plan, she whispered her spell and then pulled the surrounding energy into her body. The instant her fingers moved to draw the symbol needed for her magic to come to fruition, a fist backhanded her.

"Oh no you don't!" another man said.

The hit flattened her to the wall and tears welled from not only the stinging pain biting into her cheek, but her aching skin when the gathered energy for her spell seeped through her pores to escape her body. A hand grabbed her hair, yanking her from Wilhelm, and fingers dug into her arm. Through blurred vision, she heard the man snicker when he pinned her to the wall.

One who was shorter than the others hissed in her ear and the stench of ale reached her nostrils. "We don't want your kind here. Mages are responsible for the darkness inflicted on Arden."

Wilhelm struggled in a captor's hold while the evil creature trembled by its brother's side.

Foul breath washed over her face again. "Sorry, pretty lady, but know your death will bring us into the light."

Ashra's eyes widened when she saw a dagger flash in the fading light. She kicked and writhed with all her strength.

"Mother!" Wilhelm cried.

She screamed when the dagger plunged towards her chest. Suddenly, a hand reached from the shadows to stop the knife mid-strike. The man holding the dagger issued a deep grunt, and the sound of steel raking bone echoed in her ear. A sickening gurgle and hands slipping from her arm were followed by a thud. A shining sword cleaved the other felon's midsection, but the dead man kept his grip, hauling her to the ground.

Ashra jerked her head up, trying to pry the rigid fingers from her wrist, to see her rescuer fighting the man who'd held Wilhelm. Through the lengthening shadows, she caught sight of the fourth assailant circling behind the man trying to save her. Forced on the defense, her liberator stumbled back while calling for help. Wilhelm was huddled over the monstrosity.

Finally unhinging the dead man's fingers, Ashra chanted a spell, pulled the energy, and drew her rune. An icicle appeared, and with a whispered word, she sent it sailing for the ruffian's back. Not waiting to see if it had struck a deathblow, she scrambled to her son, flinging her body over his. She spared a glance just as her defender sliced the last attacker's leg cleanly off at the knee.

Chanting, she drew her rune and a ball of light floated over her. Her savior was a plain-looking city guard with a gentle face. He staggered to the wall and then seemed to stabilize his stance. He stood straight and approached her. Her gaze drifted to the blood dripping over his hand pressed to his side.

"Are you all right, my Lady?" His voice was as gentle as his face but lined with strength and confidence.

"Yes, thank you."

"Allow me to escort you home. The streets are dangerous at night."

Two guards rushed into the alley, and her rescuer called to them.

"They attempted to kill this woman. I'll escort her home if you men will take care of these bodies." He turned his pale face back to her. "Please, lead the way."

Ashra nodded and snatched Wilhelm's hand.

"Were you harmed?" the guard asked her eldest.

Wilhelm stared with admiration pouring from his eyes. "No. You fought wonderfully!"

The guard smiled. "Why, thank you gentleman…?"

"Wilhelm."

"Gentleman Wilhelm." The guard's smile broadened. "You're a very brave boy."

Ashra took a deep breath to steady her voice before she spoke. "And who is my rescuer?"

The guard bowed. "Tobin Cohil, my Lady."

By the time they reached the stairs leading to her home, blood still flowed from his puncture and his face glistened with sweat. "Please, come inside and allow me to examine your wound."

"I'm sure it's nothing. I wouldn't want to impose or upset your husband."

"I insist. I'm not married."

Tobin smiled and bowed. "As you command, my Lady."

Wilhelm ran ahead and opened the door. Tobin faltered after the first step and she hurried to his side. She wedged herself under his arm and supported him up the stairs.

She seated him in a kitchen chair and said, "Fetch me water, Wilhelm."

Wilhelm did as he was told while Salvarias sat in a chair opposite Tobin, taking in huge breaths and studying the guard with its normal intense, soul-reading gaze.

"And who's this?" Tobin asked.

She shuddered. "Salvarias."

Tobin smiled. "Hello, Gentleman Salvarias." His smile broadened when the abomination's expression remained cold. "An observant and cautious boy. A good quality in one so young."

Ashra laughed. "His nature is too serious for a two-year-old."

Tobin winced when she poured water on his wound. "I'm sure he's just misunderstood."

"I'm afraid your cut is rather deep. I'll need to sew it."

"You've been too kind to me already. I'll go to the healer at the guard barracks. I do not wish to disrupt your evening further."

Ashra laughed again. "If you hadn't disrupted my evening, dear Tobin, I wouldn't be here at all. Please, I must insist."

Tobin's gaze lingered on her figure. "As my Lady commands."

For the first time since her passionate night with Wilhelm's father, she felt a spark of interest in another man. Tobin demonstrated the same kindness and honorable nature as her former lover.

She smiled shyly, gathered her needle and thread, and began her work. Tobin endured the pain well while talking with Wilhelm about swordplay. Her eldest eagerly engaged, and the two became so enthralled with the conversation she ended up holding Tobin still more than once.

She finished wrapping his wound. "Few guards would have risked their lives for a witch, dear Tobin."

"Who am I to judge? Witches and wizards are people of Arden. I protect all within the city," Tobin replied, as if his view should be common. "Too much darkness surrounds us for such prejudices. The people have forgotten that mages battled alongside Zerana. Many died to save others." He turned to her eldest. "Wilhelm is a strong name. How old are you, boy?"

"I'm eight," he answered.

"Eight? You're a large boy for eight. I would have guessed close to thirteen."

"He's grown at an alarming rate," she confirmed.

"His muscles and height alone are uncharacteristic for such a young boy."

Ashra laughed. "You should see the way he eats. I'm surprised he's not plump."

Wilhelm's shy grin spread. "I'm always hungry. Why is Wilhelm considered a strong name?"

Tobin winked. "Food nourishes the mind and body. No reason to be ashamed. As for your name, a general for Zerana was named Wilhelm. An excellent strategist on the battlefield as well as his brother. They were said to be favorites of King Lilkous and the goddess Zerana."

She smiled at her grinning son. "I pray he doesn't have magic. I do not wish him to endure the same ridicule."

"Ah," Tobin said. "It's why you chose such a strong name; a

warrior's name."

She nodded.

Tobin winked at Salvarias. "Yet your youngest has a name I've never heard before."

"Wilhelm picked it," she responded.

Tobin shrugged. "I like it. And I've yet to learn your name, my Lady."

"Ashra Laybryth."

He pressed the back of her hand to his lips. "It's a pleasure."

There was an awkward moment of silence before she rose from her chair. "It would please me if you returned tomorrow so that I may ensure the wound is closing properly. Also, allow me to offer my gratitude by making you dinner."

Tobin pushed himself up and took a step closer to her. He leaned forward and his voice was a whisper. "As my Lady commands."

When his soft lips kissed her cheek, her face burned with shyness. His hand brushed against hers.

"Now, I must bid you good evening and report this incident to my captain. I'll see you tomorrow night. Thank you once again for your care."

He bowed to Ashra and a shook hands with her eldest. At the door, he glanced over his shoulder and smiled at her and the boys before leaving.

After she checked Wilhelm for injuries, she went to the washroom, bolted the door, and crumbled to the floor. She allowed her tears to break free. Her mind replayed the knife glinting in the fading sun and her precious son clutched in the arms of a murderer.

"Mother?" Wilhelm called. "Are you all right?"

"Fine, dear. Almost done." Hauling herself up, she shook off the feeling and cleaned her shaking hands. After a quick glance in the mirror to be sure she was collected, she strolled to the kitchen, humming her mother's favorite lullaby, and kissed Wilhelm's forehead. He settled into a chair with the abomination in his lap.

She smiled at Wilhelm and withdrew the kettle for stew, almost dropping it when Mafarias entered through the front door.

"Where have you been?" she demanded. "We were attacked in an alley. Luckily, a guard saved us."

Mafarias gave them a cursory look. "You all appear fine. I'm leaving in the morning."

"What?" She couldn't hide the fear in her voice. Her uncle had stayed in Falar for the last two years. She speculated he'd done so to ensure she didn't kill the monstrosity. "I'm not ready. There's something I have to tell you. I think you'll finally see my point."

Mafarias arched an eyebrow and glanced at the creature encased in Wilhelm's arms. "We'll talk after the boys go to bed."

After they ate dinner, Ashra sent the boys to bed and sat close to her uncle by the crackling fire. She recited the day's events and looked pointedly at him.

"I tell you it was happy. There was a... a satisfaction in its eyes, Uncle. Wilhelm is in danger." She fiddled with her braided belt. "Take it with you."

"Stop calling him it. He's a boy!"

"It is not. It is not my son. It was not created out of love! It has no father and is a creation of evil! I don't want it in my house." Her tears fell unbidden. "Wilhelm never leaves its side. It will corrupt him, hurt him."

"I told you Wilhelm can't be corrupted. He's safe." Mafarias stared into the fire. "Our lifetime will either end in darkness or be lived in the light. One soul... one soul will determine our fate. It's cruel to play such a dangerous game."

"I don't understand."

Mafarias focused on her. "You're partly right, my dear. There is an evil within the child, but it's your responsibility to drive it from Salvarias. As a mother, you must help him, but no others can know of it. The boy's... condition must remain a secret. As well as what impregnated you. It'd be best if all thought the boys shared a father."

Her strength drained out of her and she wept into her hands. "I'm afraid of it. How can you ask me to care for something you know to be evil?"

"I promise, he'll never hurt you." Mafarias lifted her face. "I promise. The boy will never harm you or Wilhelm."

She stared at the man with whom she'd entrusted her life since her mother's death. Ashra nodded and forced a smile.

Mafarias kissed her forehead before he rose. "The evil can be driven from the boy. You must save him, and do not fear him. I promise, he won't hurt you. I'll visit soon. I love you, Ashra."

She gazed absently at the door after he left. The roaring flames in the fireplace had dwindled to embers by the time she went to her room. She stared at her bed, rubbing her scarred stomach, battling terrifying memories. She lacked the strength to sleep there tonight. Returning to the sitting room, she chose her favorite chair, curled up, and wept.

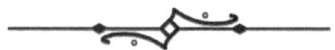

Ashra ran a brush through her hair, staring at her reflection in the mirror, wishing she could stop her childish grin. Over the past three months Tobin's visits to her home were every evening for dinner, but today they both had the day off and he'd requested permission to visit her in the morning.

A knock on the door caused her grin to widen. Setting down her brush, she strolled to the front door, opened it, and was greeted by Tobin's smile, which switched to a grin as he bowed.

"My lady," he said.

"Come in, please." She stepped aside.

Wilhelm leapt up from his chair and rushed Tobin.

Laughing, Tobin gathered Wilhelm in his arms. "And good day, Gentleman Wilhelm."

Wilhelm grinned. "Did you get in any fights this morning?"

"Well, let's see. Not this morning, but last night there was an unruly drunk pestering a woman. I had to give him a good wallop to calm him down when I arrested him." Tobin winked at Salvarias. "Morning, Gentleman Salvarias."

The abomination didn't respond or look away from Tobin.

"Are you hungry?" Ashra asked. "I have some potatoes left over from breakfast. I can cook an egg for you as well."

Tobin nodded. "Thank you, my Lady." He settled in a chair next to Salvarias. "What are you boys doing today?"

Wilhelm shrugged. "Mother doesn't have to go to Himiks's, so we'll probably visit madam Delora."

Ashra cracked open an egg in the skillet before compiling a plate piled high with all the foods she'd seen Tobin favor.

He cleared his throat. "I was thinking... that is, if you don't mind, of having..." He shifted in his chair. "Of taking the boys to the guardhouse with me today. I'd keep an eye on them." His words tumbled over one another. "It'd be good for you to have a day to yourself. Being a single mother must be difficult. And, with your permission of course, I'd..." He glanced at Wilhelm. "I'd like to teach the boys how to use a sword."

Wilhelm's jaw dropped. "Truly?"

Tobin nodded.

Wilhelm whirled around to her. "Please, Mother? We'll behave, I promise! Please?"

She fetched a rag and lifted the skillet. "Go to your room; both of you."

Wilhelm lifted Salvarias in his arms and cast her one last pleading look before going to their room and closing the door.

She deposited the egg on Tobin's plate and carried it over to him. "You're too kind." She sat next to him. "Boys are forever curious. Wilhelm will undoubtedly question you all day. You'll have not one breath of peace."

Tobin smiled. "I'd like the privilege to get to know them better."

She was about to utter her agreement when a thought occurred to her. Over the past season, she'd stumbled over ideas on how to rid the creature of its evil. With Wilhelm never leaving its side, it was an impossible task. Until now. Tobin offered her the opportunity to be alone with it.

"A compromise. Take Wilhelm and leave Salvarias with me."

Tobin frowned. "I was looking forward to getting to know Salvarias better. I find him fascinating. I think I could coax the boy into talking to me."

"Perhaps. But you've seen Wilhelm never leaves its—" She cleared her throat. "His side. I've not gotten the chance to know my own son. If you take Wilhelm, I can finally be with Salvarias."

Tobin pushed the potatoes around with his fork. His brow furrowed for a moment, and then his face lit. "Another proposal for you, my Lady. Let me have them during the day while you're working."

She scoffed. "I won't have my boys wandering the streets. Your work is dangerous."

"You misunderstand," he said quickly. "I can do jobs inside the guardhouse most days. I know Himiks. He's not a kind man and Wilhelm's told me of their treatment. The boys need to be boys. They need to play and get dirty. Romp around. And, by chance, if I do get called out into the city, one of the other guards, one that I trust mind you, will watch them. It can't be worse than having them sit in a back room, hands folded, not speaking or moving."

"I give them learning assignments. I want them to be intelligent—"

Tobin laughed. "My Lady, Wilhelm is smarter than I am. I don't think you need to fear having dull-witted children."

She rose from her chair and moved to stare out her front window. She watched children running through the streets, laughing and getting underfoot. She'd always wanted that for Wilhelm.

"So be it," she said. "You can take them four days a week, they'll be with me two, and on my days off you can have Wilhelm and you'll leave Salvarias with me."

She turned to be swooped up in Tobin's arms

"Thank you, my Lady!"

Ashra had forgotten the embrace of a man. She wrapped her arms around his shoulders and buried her face in his neck, inhaling the sour smell of armor that seemed permanently imbued into his skin. His laugh faded and he lowered her, taking several steps back.

"Forgive me, my Lady. I... that was forward of me."

"I was not insulted." She smiled. "I enjoy your company, dear Tobin."

Tobin flushed and looked away. "Boys!"

Wilhelm entered the room holding the monstrosity's hand. "Yes, Gentleman Tobin?"

Tobin squatted in front of them. "How about we drop the formal titles?"

Wilhelm grinned.

"Your mother and I have come to an agreement. Four days a week, you boys will come to the guardhouse with me and two days you'll spend with your mother at Himiks' shop."

Wilhelm flew into Tobin's arms, knocking him over. He laughed and squeezed her son. She couldn't help but laugh with them.

"You approve?" Tobin asked.

"Yes!" Wilhelm exclaimed.

Tobin sat up and turned to Salvarias. "Is that all right with you, Salvarias?"

"It is," Wilhelm answered, unraveling himself from Tobin's arms. "But we talked about it and he doesn't want to learn to fight."

Tobin nodded. "You don't have to fight if you don't want to,

Salvarias. We'll bring some books and we can read together while Wilhelm practices. Today is a special day, though. For both of you. Every day your mother has off, I'm going to take you—" He tapped Wilhelm's chest. "To the guardhouse for special training. It'll give your mother time alone with Salvarias."

Both boys tensed. Wilhelm stepped in front of Salvarias, shuffling back from Tobin. "No. I won't go without Salv."

Tobin shook his head. "It's important for you two to spend time apart. What will happen when you're older? Will you two never marry? Will you live in the same house all your lives?"

"We will!" Wilhelm said, taking another step back. "I won't leave him."

The abomination latched on to Wilhelm's arm.

"I won't!" Wilhelm yelled.

Ashra motioned Tobin to join her at the window. When he was by her side, she whispered, "I feared such a reaction. I'd understand if you don't wish to take him. You'd have to drag him out of the house kicking and screaming."

"I have a brother of my own and we're close. As much as I admire their bond, I see the harm in Wilhelm's behavior. Salvarias will be suffocated by him if he continues. I think it best I take him. Unless you object."

"No, I agree with you. They must learn to be apart. Thank you."

Tobin inhaled a deep breath, strode over to Wilhelm, and held out a hand. "You don't have a choice. Your mother and I feel this is best for both of you. You'll come with me one way or the other."

"No," Wilhelm said.

Tobin plucked him up. Wilhelm thrashed about in Tobin's arms, screaming to be released, punching and kicking. Tobin grunted and readjusted his grip to avoid the flurry of fists.

Cheeks burning with embarrassment, Ashra hurried to Wilhelm's side. "Stop this at once! You will behave—"

"No! I won't leave him!"

She opened the door and cast Tobin an apologetic smile.

Tobin winked. "He'll calm down."

"No!" Wilhelm roared. He stared at Salvarias who stood frozen, eyes wide, gasping. "No! I can't be without him!"

Tobin carried him out of her home. Closing the door, she went to the window and watched Wilhelm struggle in earnest. Everyone on the street stopped to stare. By the gods, he'd never misbehaved before.

She turned around. The abomination stood by the front door, wheezing and clutching its chest. It rested a hand on the door.

"No," Ashra said. "You're staying here." Gathering all her courage, she planted her hands on her hips and cast it a stern stare. "I'm going to ask you questions and you'll answer them. You'll not lie to me. Do you understand?"

It nodded.

"You can speak?"

It nodded.

"Then do so. When did you learn to speak?"

The creature's eyebrows stitched together. It opened its mouth, closed it, and then cast her an apologetic frown. "I just knew how."

"When did you say your first word?"

"The day after I was born."

She thought she might faint. She leaned against the counter. "Why don't you speak to me or others?"

"People seem afraid of me, and I am afraid of them. You do not let me near you. I..." The demon glanced around, twisting his hands together. "I thought you did not want me to talk. Forgive me. I only—"

"I've never feared you," she snapped.

Salvarias lowered its head. "I am sorry."

"You haven't seen your third spring. How is, how is it possible for you to speak like an adult?"

"I have understood conversations since I can remember." Its eyes lit up. "I can count too, Mother! And I can read." It pointed to a book. "I can show you, Mother!"

"No." Her fears were subsiding the longer it spoke. She had no doubts Mafarias was correct. The creature seemed to want her approval.

"I can think of ten things at once." It glanced around, moving its mouth. It pointed at a wall. "See! There are thirty stones in that top row, six logs in the fire, two dirty skillets, and—"

"Enough," she said. Questions buzzed through her mind. "How far back can you remember?"

Its excitement faded and fear flashed through its dark eyes. "Since my first breath. I remember everything." In an instant, it struggled for air.

"You're afraid?"

It nodded its head vehemently.

"Of what?"

"Of..." It burst into sobs. "Of my evil! *Something* lives within me! It whispers to me and always a hand is reaching for my soul! *My* soul! It says horrible things. It shows me people dying. They flash in my mind, image after image. I cannot make them stop. There is blood everywhere, Mother! So much blood. So many people. I can hear them, too. I hear them begging not to die! Their pleas whisper in my ear all day! I cannot stop them! When I sleep, I see how they died. I watch their murder. I see what men do to women, I see what women do to children, and I see—" It jerked in a few breaths before it continued its ranting confession. "I see what men do to other men. So much blood." Its gaze unfocused and darted back and forth. "I see it now. There are so many. I see horrible things. I want it to stop! Please, help me! I do not want to see it anymore!" It rushed Ashra and clung to her leg.

She stood frozen, listening to it weep. It heard and saw what it did because of what created it. Her hand strayed to her scarred stomach, recalling each breath of that horrid night. She'd wept for the shadowfire to stop after it flung Wilhelm across the room, but the creature had thrust the remaining ball of fire into her stomach. She remembered its sick moan when its hand sunk into her womb, planting its seed. Once it had impregnated her, it moved to her side and whispered in her ear, "It isss not by random chanccce that I found you. I have gifted you the privilege of bearing my child."

She shuddered, remembering its hand resting over her belly.

"It isss hisss sssoul that will condemn Arden or lead it to sssalvation." The shadowfire moved to kiss her stomach. "Condemn them to eternal damnation, ssson. Remember well my anger and feel it in your very bonesss. Sssee what I sssee, my ssson. Prove me to be merccciful."

Ashra spoke barely above a whisper to the abomination clinging to her. "Does Wilhelm know?"

"No, Mother. He would worry. I do not tell him what I see or hear. I do not understand it."

She inhaled a deep breath, preparing herself for what it might say next. "You enjoyed watching that man hang."

It raised its face to meet her gaze. "Yes, Mother."

Its answer chilled her bones and her horror grew with every breath as she stared into its demonic eyes. "Make your evil leave."

It shook its head. "I have tried. I cannot."

"I said make it!" Ashra snapped.

The creature flinched. "I promise; I have tried! I do not know how!"

"Tell it!"

Salvarias shook its head. "It will not leave. It is a part of me. I want it to—"

"If you were a boy, a *good* boy, you could make it leave!" She clenched her jaw and grabbed its arm. "Drive it from you! Make it leave!" The temperature in the room dropped. She no longer saw a little boy; she saw a *thing*, something disguised as a child. A demon of darkness.

"I am trying!" it wailed.

"You are not! If you were it would leave!" She flung the creature across the room. It smacked into the wall and toppled to the ground. "You are exactly what I thought you were when first you left my womb! An abomination of life, a monstrosity! And you are not my son!"

"Mother, please!" It crawled towards her.

"Get away from me!" She shoved it away with her foot.

It gasped for air, curling into a tight ball.

She fumbled behind her and grabbed a book. "Make it leave!"

It didn't respond. Instead, it reached for her, its arms outstretched, its demonic gaze pleading.

"I love you, Mother. I promise I will try harder! I promise! Help me!"

By the gods, those eyes! Evil, utterly evil!

She brought the book down on its legs, ranting orders for the evil to leave. She beat it more, releasing all her fears and anger on the horror that had been forced upon her.

It was the throbbing in her arms that made her stagger away. Sweat rolled down her face and her breathing was quick. Blood stained the book's binding. She dropped it and raised her gaze to the abomination. It had scrambled to the corner of the room, hugging and rocking itself, whispering the same phrase, "I am trying."

She'd done the right thing; she was sure of it. There might have been a moment when it left, when she'd frightened it enough. Surely with time she could make it leave. She could save it.

Then her thoughts shifted to her perfect son. If Wilhelm saw... If Tobin knew....

Ashra inhaled a few quick breaths to steady her voice. "Stand up."

The abomination peered up at her between its arms. Blood matted its hair.

"I said stand up."

It winced and groaned when it shoved itself to its feet.

"Take off your tunic."

It struggled out of the shirt, whimpering as it did.

Red welts were already forming, and its skin was turning shades of blue and purple. Wilhelm would leave her. She sank in a chair and tears welled. How could she explain this?

The abomination reached out its hand. "Please do not cry. I promise I will try harder. I promise."

She recoiled from it. "Don't touch me."

It stepped back, wrapping its arms around itself. "I am sorry."

"You lie. If you were, you'd drive it from yourself. You'd make it go away." Ashra straightened in the chair. "You love your brother?"

"More than anything."

"Then you'll tell Wilhelm we went into the city today and you snuck away from me. Some boys found you and did this to you. Do you understand?"

Its face contorted into a pleading expression. "Please, do not make me lie to him."

"You will do this. You're lucky I allow you near him. You're nothing but an abomination. Look at yourself." She motioned to the washroom and rose from her chair. "Go!" She followed it to the mirror. "You see? Look at your eyes. Do those look like any other persons' you know?"

It shook its head.

"That's because you're a defilement of life. A demon from the depths of Oblivion! No one will love you! Even Wilhelm will one day see you're evil!" She sneered at it. "And you would do wise to stay away from others. Surely you'll infect the innocent with your evil."

Salvarias looked away.

"You *will* lie to Wilhelm. If you don't, I'll have your uncle take you away from here. You'll never see your brother again. Do you understand me?"

The evil child nodded.

"You'll never tell him. Promise me."

"I—"

"Look into my eyes and promise!" she snapped.

It turned to face her and met her gaze. "I promise. He will never know."

"Nor anyone."

It nodded. "Nor anyone."

She pointed at the washbasin. "Clean yourself up."

Ashra left the room. A storm had started outside. The clouds were a sick green and rain poured down in sheets. Thunder shook her home and lightning streaked across the sky.

She rested her forehead against the cool glass window, and whispered, "If there are any gods, please help me. Give me the strength to do what must be done."

Chapter 4
Winter 1005 a.r.

Wilhelm cracked open his door and peeked out to see his mother dozing in a chair beside the crackling fire. She was waiting for Tobin to be done with guard duty later in the afternoon. With the morning young and the day beautifully warm for winter, Wilhelm saw no point in wasting away the hours inside his room. Of course, it would be rude to wake his mother. She needed rest. Going through the front door would surely disturb her, so being the polite boy he was, he decided to sneak out his bedroom window. A brief thought occurred to him: his actions might be construed as misbehavior. He was quick to justify his thought. His mother had never uttered the exact words "you can't leave the house without me," so he closed the door with a shameless smile. He'd be able to uphold his reputation as an obedient son and still have a little fun.

"Ready?" he asked his brother.

Salvarias nodded and leapt up from the bed with an excited smile. Wilhelm grinned back. The last five and a half years had been the happiest of his life.

Furrowing his brow, he studied the two-story descent to the snow-covered cobblestone alley. He gauged the drops he'd need to make from ledge to ledge in order to accomplish a safe landing. He glanced at his brother who leaned on the sill next to him, feet dangling off the floor.

"You'll have to hold on tight, Salv."

Salvarias nodded, his eyes sparkling with eager anticipation.

Wilhelm gathered up a pouch with two apples tucked inside and tied it to his belt. He went to the window, swung his legs over the ledge, and helped Salvarias climb on to his back. Small arms clasped around Wilhelm's neck. As always, his brother felt lighter than air. With an excited deep breath, Wilhelm twisted around and dropped. He caught the window ledge while his feet fumbled for the second-floor shelf that jutted out a good foot. After kicking aside the snow to find a solid foothold, he squatted and allowed his feet to fall from under him. He grabbed hold of the ledge and glanced down at the alley. He could jump and land safely, but he kept to his original plan.

Resting his feet on the first story window frame, he kept a tight hold on his brother's arm, and said, "Crawl down."

Salvarias swung down and stood on the ledge, nestling his feet in the snow. When Wilhelm felt Salvarias had good footing and was secure, he leapt down to the street. He landed light as a feather and grinned at his success.

He opened arms. "Jump."

Without hesitation, Salvarias dropped into Wilhelm's embrace.

He chuckled, squeezing his brother before lowering him to the ground. "Nicely done, little brother."

Salvarias's eyes sparkled their familiar smile and his tiny hand slipped into Wilhelm's.

At almost twelve years old, Wilhelm's physique gave the illusion of an older boy, closer to fifteen or sixteen. He used this to his advantage and stood straight as he walked into the bustling street with confidence. His adventure offered the first test quickly. A group of guards walked in the brothers' direction and Wilhelm recognized three of the four. Since he and Salvarias spent most days at the guardhouse, they knew a fair share of the men. Wilhelm even fought the majority of them.

The guards continued along in conversation, paying no heed to the brothers.

He grinned at Salvarias. "Where do you want to go?"

"The docks," Salvarias whispered.

Wilhelm nodded and turned down the next street. He smiled when he heard Salvarias whispering numbers. His brother's voice was soothing and somehow rhythmic, almost hypnotic. Wilhelm assumed it was due to the constant counting his brother performed. The numbers were barely audible, and one wouldn't know what his brother was doing unless he confessed. According to Salvarias, his mind spun with relentless "images" and they often gave him headaches. Even after questioning him, Wilhelm didn't understand. All he gathered was that counting objects helped focus Salvarias's mind and eased his pain.

The ocean was lazy and the docks mellow when Wilhelm found a quiet spot to sit and eat their apples.

Salvarias inhaled several deep breaths, and his eyes softened while he stared at the blue-gray sea slapping the wooden wharf.

"Beautiful," Wilhelm commented.

Salvarias leaned his head against Wilhelm's arm. "Indeed, my brother." Salvarias's soft voice always seemed more like a whisper in Wilhelm's ear, no matter how far away or close his brother was.

They spent an hour in the same spot while Wilhelm made jokes about each outlandishly dressed watythm sailor who strutted by. His brother's laughter filled the winter air and seemed to brighten the world.

Wilhelm heaved a deep sigh. "I guess we should head back." His sigh was echoed by Salvarias. "But first..."

Salvarias jumped into Wilhelm's arms with hardly contained excitement. He rose to his feet, cast his brother a grin, then tossed him high in the air and caught him just before he landed on the wood planks. Salvarias laughed harder, and Wilhelm hurled him higher. When air barely entered his brother's sick lungs from all his laughing, Wilhelm finally stopped.

After Salvarias caught his breath, Wilhelm ventured once again into the crowded city streets. He slowed his pace, reluctant to return home. When alone together, Salvarias blossomed into a wonderful child full of life and smiles, but when near others he turned reserved, silent, timid, and frightened.

On a main street, a man robed in burnt-orange caught Wilhelm's eye. The way the robes were cut, he would have assumed the man to be a mage, but the orange color couldn't be worn by wizards or witches; only burgundy or slate-blue were permitted. The man's milky eyes seemed focused on Salvarias. Wilhelm's feeling of safety vanished in an instant and he picked up his pace.

They didn't make it far before Salvarias was gasping. "Brother," he wheezed. "I cannot keep up."

Wilhelm scooped his brother up and increased his speed. Hazarding a glance backwards, he saw the robed man following them. Cursing, he increased his pace to a jog.

"What is it?" Salvarias asked in a shaky voice.

"Nothing. I just want to get home before Mother wakes."

There was a scolding tone in Salvarias's voice when he said, "Brother."

He sighed, never understanding how Salvarias picked out lies. "I think someone is following us."

"The man in orange?"

"Yes."

Even though Wilhelm carried extra weight, his breathing remained measured. He thanked the gods for the daily run through Falar he performed every morning with Tobin.

"He is keeping up," Salvarias said.

Wilhelm increased to a slow run. He rounded a corner into an alley, which, to his dismay, was deserted and shrouded in shadows.

"Brother!" Salvarias cried.

Wilhelm glanced over his shoulder to see the man directly behind them. They sprinted for the major street ahead. It felt as though they ran in slow motion and the street seemed to move farther away. Wilhelm spared another look back and saw a raw hand reaching for Salvarias.

"Help!" Wilhelm called.

Passing citizens glanced down the alley, but continued onward as though nothing were amiss. Salvarias trembled violently, and Wilhelm spared a glance. A skinless hand had a firm grip on Salvarias's wrist.

"Allow me to give you a glimpse of your future, my young one," the man whispered.

"Stop!" a voice called.

Wilhelm whipped his head around to see Idolar, a city guard, standing in the alley entrance.

Salvarias grunted.

"Get away from those boys!" Idolar roared.

The man sneered at Idolar before fleeing around the corner. Wilhelm realized how harshly he was breathing; not from the run, but from his fear for Salvarias.

Idolar stormed up to them. "What in Nevlar's fury are you boys doing in the streets by yourselves?"

The guard was a close friend to Tobin. Wilhelm fumbled for a lie but came up blank. Instead, he pleaded. "Please don't tell our mother or Tobin. We just wanted to sit at the docks."

Idolar shook his head. "Follow me."

Wilhelm followed him from the alley and winced when Salvarias's tiny fingers dug into his back. "Are you all right?"

Salvarias buried his face in Wilhelm's shoulder and nodded.

Idolar led them through the streets while muttering curses under his breath until they reached the alley behind their home.

He pointed at the brothers' window. "I suppose this is how you got out?"

"Yes," Wilhelm mumbled, downcast.

"Don't let me catch you out again! Next time, I'll tell your mother."

Wilhelm nodded. "Thank you."

Idolar seemed to try to calm himself, but his voice carried a steel edge. "Who was that man? Why was he with you in the alley?"

"I've never seen him before. On our way back, he followed us. I think he was bent on hurting us."

Idolar eyed the street. "He didn't look like a pleasant man. I'll have some guards follow him around. You boys get back up there, and don't let me catch you out again!"

"Yes, Gentleman."

Wilhelm shifted Salvarias to his back, and after a helpful boost from Idolar, scaled the wall and crawled into their bedroom. Just as Wilhelm's feet landed on the floor, he heard a knock on their front door. He jumped to a wild notion the orange-robed man had followed them home and would burst in and snatch Salvarias. Wilhelm cradled his trembling brother and backed towards the window. Then he heard Tobin's voice. After an exhaled breath of relief, he lowered Salvarias and knelt to eye level.

"It's all right..." Wilhelm's voice choked off when he saw blood oozing between his brother's fingers clamped over his arm. "What happened?"

"He had a knife."

Their door swung open without warning, and Tobin entered with his usual smile. "How are you—By Zerana's grace, what happened?"

Wilhelm flushed. He wasn't a good liar.

Tobin walked towards Salvarias, but he stumbled back, falling to the floor only to crawl into a corner of the room, leaving a trail of bloody handprints.

When Tobin spoke, his voice was soothing as he knelt beside Salvarias. "It's all right. I won't hurt you."

Salvarias curled in a ball, pressing himself to the wall. The behavior wasn't unusual, and each time Wilhelm witnessed it, his heart hurt. It had started three years ago. Salvarias's former shyness towards others had turned into an absolute dread of people.

Wilhelm stepped in front of Tobin. "I'll clean him up." His brother crawled into his open arms. "It's all right, Salv. I won't let anything happen."

Snatching a clean tunic, he carried Salvarias to the washroom, closed the door, and lowered him. Wilhelm went to take off his brother's tunic, but Salvarias flinched away, eyes averted, head downcast. Wilhelm's anger boiled his blood.

"Did those boys hurt you again?"

Teardrops pattered on the floor.

"Tell me who they are!" he demanded.

"Please."

He flung open the door and stormed into the sitting room. "They got to him again!"

Ashra nodded. "He wouldn't give me the boys' names."

Tobin shook his head and entered the washroom, Wilhelm right behind.

Tobin spoke in the same gentle tone. "Tell us who they are, Salvarias, and we can help you."

Salvarias backed into a corner and slid to the floor, curling into a ball.

Wilhelm knew his brother wouldn't talk to another. Salvarias only spoke to Wilhelm, only allowed Wilhelm to touch him, only allowed Wilhelm to love him.

Tobin took a step closer and Salvarias cringed. Inching back, Tobin turned to Ashra. "Maybe you shouldn't go to the market without me or Wilhelm to keep an eye on him."

"It only happens when Tobin makes me leave," Wilhelm said pointedly.

Ashra sighed. "He needs to listen to me. I tell him to stay beside me, but he's always running off."

Tobin shifted. "I understand, but maybe you should carry him."

"I agree," Wilhelm interjected.

Ashra threw her hands up. "You know he won't let me! Wilhelm is the only one he allows to touch him!"

Tobin nodded and turned back to Salvarias. "I'm here if you want my help. I won't hurt you."

After the two left, Wilhelm knelt and gently pulled his brother into an embrace. Tiny fingers embedded into his shoulders. "I'm sorry. I'm not mad at you."

Once his brother calmed, Wilhelm removed Salvarias's tunic with tender care, fighting his need to pummel every boy in Falar when he saw his brother's body covered in deep purple contusions and swollen welts. After cleaning the cut, Wilhelm wrapped a piece of fabric around the wound and then ruffled his brother's hair. Salvarias raised his head and offered the smallest smile, which induced an instant grin from Wilhelm. His grin broadened when he felt a weak punch to his ribs.

He winked. "Ouch." It didn't hurt, but each time he feigned pain, Salvarias's eyes sparkled a smile. Wilhelm's grin faded as he studied the bruises. "You should have told me earlier. I wouldn't have tossed you."

"It did not hurt, brother."

He doubted the truth to those words. "You know that Tobin wants to help."

"I know."

He dressed his brother in a fresh tunic. "Think about allowing him to help. For me."

Salvarias flung his arms around Wilhelm's neck. "I love you, my dear brother."

"Love you too, Salv. Ready?"

Salvarias nodded and slipped his hand into Wilhelm's.

Tobin was gathering a bread sack from the kitchen table when they entered the room. "Let's go to the market. We'll pick up some food for dinner," he said, tying the bulging sack around his waist.

Wilhelm's stomach growled audibly in approval and he grinned at his brother. The black eyes sparkled back.

They left home and headed to the bustling streets. Salvarias's trembling hand gripped tight, and he walked so close to Wilhelm they tripped over each other often. He didn't mind. He preferred to keep Salvarias close and would have carried him if their mother didn't insist on holding Wilhelm's hand. He kept his gaze sweeping over the streets, searching for the man robed in orange. If he saw the bastard again, he would beat him into the ground. Even better, he'd run him through with Tobin's sword. He pieced together a plot on how he could snatch the weapon before being stopped. Once a plan was laid out and all the possible scenarios examined, his thoughts stumbled to a halt. He was planning murder without the slightest feeling of guilt or hesitancy. He glanced at his brother. Yes, Wilhelm would take the life of anyone that hurt Salvarias. Willingly, without remorse or hesitation. Armed or unarmed, friend or foe, Wilhelm would kill them. He pondered if he should feel guilty, if his actions would be immoral, if they were those of every other big brother in Arden.

When they rounded the corner to Market Street, Milred's excited scream jolted him from his thoughts. She pulled Ashra aside and the two became engrossed in conversation. He followed Tobin to the nearby blacksmith where the warmth of the forge washed over him, battling away the winter chill.

A grouchy, curly-haired cavrul owned the smithy. The man's face bolstered a permanent frown, and his luxurious, waist-length beard surely envied his bushy eyebrows. According to Tobin, cavruls were renowned for their expertise in weapon forging, and Durak had earned a reputation as the best in Dalnar and Windlous.

Wilhelm grinned while he watched the five-foot man scowl at customers as if they were thieves until his dark eyes fell on Tobin. The grumpy expression lifted by the slight upturn of Durak's wrinkles.

Tobin's welcoming smile spread. "Good midday, Durak."

The cavrul uttered an oath under his breath.

Tobin hefted a sword. "Excellent craftsmanship. I wish the guard could afford your weapons."

Durak puffed up his chest. When he spoke, his voice was heavy with a cavrul accent. "Me work isn't free! Good weapons take time and money to make! I can't be givin' 'em away!"

Tobin winked. "No, you can't, Gentleman."

Durak mumbled another curse.

Wilhelm liked the gray-skinned cavrul.

Tobin selected a stunning long sword. "One day, Wilhelm, I'll give you my broadsword."

Wilhelm's mouth dropped open. "Truly?"

"I do hope so," Tobin murmured.

Durak's eyes narrowed at Wilhelm. "That's a fine sword to pass down. Ye should be honored, lad."

He nodded in agreement as his gaze wandered to the sword belted at Tobin's waist. Though old, the quality of the blade was unquestionable. The pommel and guard were black, contrasting the polished steel blade, and the handle was simple and thick, made for large hands.

Wilhelm smelled baked bread as his mother's arms wrapped around his shoulders. "Hello, Durak."

His concentration on the weapon broke. "Did she find anything yet for Salv?" He squirmed from under her hold when she kissed his forehead.

"Nothing, dear."

He pulled Salvarias close and grinned at him. "I'll keep looking."

Salvarias, as usual when around others, remained quiet. Wilhelm wrapped his cloak around Salvarias, ruffled his hair, and felt the affection returned by a punch to the ribs.

"How's business?" Ashra asked Durak.

"Slow as always in winter. That damn bard isn't helping, either!" Durak yelled in the direction of a rather untalented musician.

She pulled the loaf of bread from the pouch tied to Tobin's waist. "I'm sorry to hear that. I brought you spiced bread from the bakery. Cinnamon is your favorite, am I correct?"

Durak accepted the loaf. "Aye, cinnamon."

Tobin bowed to Ashra after a wink at Durak. "Are you ready, my Lady?"

"Of course, dear." Ashra took Wilhelm's hand.

"Mother, I'm almost twelve. You don't have to hold my hand."

She planted a kiss on his forehead to drive home his embarrassment. "Yes, I do."

He sighed and continued down the street. Durak's roar of laughter faded into the calls of merchants and the jerking words of a bard. Wilhelm's spirits lifted at the smell of roasted meats, and his grin emerged of its own accord when his mother stopped. His mouth watered when she selected a plump roast of venison. Since Tobin joined the family at almost every supper, the quality of their meals had improved. Wilhelm didn't miss stew.

Tobin paid for Ashra's purchase with an insistent smile.

Wilhelm glanced at his brother eying a fruit stand. "Mother, we need fruit for Salv."

Salvarias refused to eat meat, and of all the "oddities," as he called them, this one was the only one that disturbed Wilhelm. After all, what was a meal without meat? No meat is just a snack. Fruits, vegetables, breads and cheeses are sides, not a meal. He shuddered at the mere thought of never eating meat. The rejection of the mouthwatering delights had begun four years ago when they passed the slaughterhouse with their mother. His brother had stared wide-eyed at a bawling cow as an axe whistled through the air. When the head rolled from the block, swift tears had streamed down his face. Ever since witnessing the bloody act, he flat out refused to eat anything containing meat. Whenever Wilhelm tried to understand or ask questions, tears would well again and he'd quickly change the subject.

He felt his brother's stare and looked down at his black eyes sparkling with amusement. Wilhelm grinned.

After selecting fruit, Wilhelm held his mother's hand and continued down the street. With a city guard strolling next to them, few comments were cackled in their direction, and peace fell before them like a rolling wave.

Salvarias stumbled and Wilhelm caught him before he fell. His brother was focused on a mother fussing over a scraped knee on her son. As the touching scene faded from view, Salvarias lowered his head and moved close to Wilhelm.

He wrapped an arm around Salvarias's shoulders and lifted him ever so slightly to avoid further trips. "You all right?"

Salvarias nodded, staring at the cobblestone street, and soft whispered numbers filled the air. Wilhelm was certain his brother wasn't aware the numbers were audible. Tobin glanced at Salvarias and winked at Wilhelm. With only one small plea, Tobin had agreed not to bring up the fact that Salvarias's counting was discernible. It would embarrass him if he knew he counted aloud, and surely he'd endure the pain instead of whispering numbers. Wilhelm took his brotherly duty seriously and shielded Salvarias from as much embarrassment as possible. If counting helped, Wilhelm wouldn't care if Salvarias shouted at the top of his lungs, and Wilhelm would be damned if anyone pointed out his brother's habit.

They entered the potion shop to find a familiar mage standing at the counter. Thick robes of slate blue draped over his tall frame and he was deep in conversation with Milred.

Wilhelm strode up to his uncle. "Uncle Mafarias!"

"Wilhelm, my boy!" The wizard embraced him. "Look at you! You've grown! I can't pick you up anymore!"

"I'm almost twelve. You haven't seen me in four years."

"You don't say. My how time slips by."

"Yes, Uncle. Time has slipped by," Ashra said.

Wilhelm grinned and winked at his uncle. "I think you're in trouble again."

Mafarias smiled and kissed her cheek. "Lovely as ever, Ashra." He looked at Tobin. "And who is this?"

The guard bowed. "Tobin Cohil."

"Good to meet you, Gentleman Tobin."

"You'll stay for dinner, Uncle?" Ashra asked.

"Of course!"

Wilhelm turned to Salvarias, who took a step behind him. "It's all right, he's our uncle. Do you remember him?"

Mafarias stared at Salvarias, lips pursed and eyes narrowed. Salvarias snatched Wilhelm's hand and gripped tight, not responding to the question or averting his gaze from their uncle.

Uncle Mafarias held open the door to Wilhelm's home, which smelled of sweet rolls. Already his stomach growled in hunger.

"How is Master Himiks?" Mafarias asked.

Ashra filed through the door with the others. "Same as always."

Mafarias removed his cloak. "I'm surprised the Association of Mages hasn't stripped him of his robes and killed him by now. I'm also surprised that you continue working for him."

"True. His magic is that of a beginner, and he does nothing for our reputation." Ashra went to the kitchen to unpack their purchases. "You know how difficult it is for mages to find work, Uncle. Jyfil is too generous. Working for Himiks allows me to pay for the home, and running errands for Jyfil puts food on my table."

Mafarias mumbled, "Himiks wouldn't have half the business if it wasn't for you."

Ashra smiled. "Thanks for noticing. Since he can only perform two spells and only knows what two components do, I'm the only one who can help our fellow mages. Your instruction has been invaluable, Uncle."

"Still selling enchanted items?" Mafarias asked.

"Yes, though business is slow. We haven't found any new objects. Happening upon something enchanted is as common as..."

Ashra smiled at Wilhelm. "As common as my son eating vegetables."

Mafarias chuckled, and lifted Wilhelm's arms. The sleeve of his tunic snuck above his wrist. The hem of his pants rested above his ankles. The mage glanced at Salvarias's overly large clothes, which had been Wilhelm's.

Mafarias said, "In my travels I've come across several items. I'll give them to you and teach you how to use them. Himiks should give you a little bonus so you and the boys can get new clothes."

"Thank you. I can't keep up with Wilhelm. He's growing faster than I can sew."

Tobin finished hanging up the cloaks. "I've not heard much about the Association. Can they truly take away a mage's robes? And what good would it do? The mage doesn't lose his or her power and could continue to practice."

Mafarias shoved logs into the fireplace. "Good point. Yes, the Association can strip robes. The mage's name would be removed from the list provided to the guard. If the mage continues to wear the robes and is no longer on the list, they'll be executed by the guard."

Tobin stiffened. "I am familiar with the right of the guards, Gentleman. I can't comprehend why the Association allows their own to be butchered because of an outdated list."

Mafarias glanced at Ashra. "A sympathizer?"

"A smart man, Uncle."

Tobin started the fire. "I see no need for senseless deaths."

"I agree. I also feel the lists are an inappropriate way to handle the situation. Alas, the Association believes it's for the 'greater good.' Eases the minds of the city guard, does it not?" Mafarias asked with a raised eyebrow.

Ashra slammed a block of cheese on the counter. "Uncle! Honestly!"

Tobin flushed. "I feel none should suffer for the ignorance of others. Instead, we should educate. How else can we move forward?"

Mafarias settled into a chair next to Wilhelm at the kitchen table. "One death to save many is what the Association hopes to achieve."

Tobin sat stiffly in a chair across from Mafarias. "One meaningless death is as detrimental as a thousand. Murder is murder. It's a matter of principle."

Mafarias grinned. "Well said, my good man! To answer your other question: Yes, the mage will retain his power, but the Association pays a hefty reward to kill any mage not wearing robes. Basically, either the guards or other mages will execute the person. Again, the greater good."

Tobin shook his head and curled his lip in disgust. "It's a disgrace."

Wilhelm's mouth watered when his mother laid out a dinner of his favorite breads, cheeses, and the roast of venison.

After Ashra settled in her seat, Mafarias said, "We need more light, dear."

"We do not."

Mafarias took on a hurt look. "I miss your light spell."

"Make your own. There's no reason to show off."

Wilhelm's uncle whispered and flicked his hand in the air. Before them, a ball of light appeared. It morphed into a translucent white rabbit that danced about the room.

"Honestly!" Ashra rebuked.

Mafarias winked at Wilhelm and whispered another word, ending the rabbit's adventure. "You should do more magic around your boy."

A soft whisper from his brother turned Wilhelm's attention to a fist-sized ball of light floating in front of Salvarias.

Ashra gasped, springing from her chair. Salvarias moved his lips again, and the light disappeared.

"That was brilliant, Salvarias!" Tobin said.

"Amazing!" Wilhelm exclaimed.

His mother glanced at Mafarias, who was studying Salvarias.

Tobin's smile faded. "Did he do something wrong?"

Ashra shook her head. "No. He did nothing wrong. No mage has been recorded to perform magic before the age of seventeen. The majority come to their gift between nineteen and twenty. Our minds suppress the magic until mature enough control the energy. As our minds strengthen with age, so does the magic."

Mafarias folded his hands in front his mouth. "Impressive. He did it without using our energy. I've never known another to do so with their first spell. And the power…"

Ashra sank into her chair. "We need to talk about this later, Uncle. I did sense the power."

"It's nothing to be alarmed about."

Tobin motioned to Ashra and Mafarias. "Shouldn't you have known the boy was already gifted?"

"Not necessarily," Mafarias said. "Magic rests in the unconscious part of our minds. It's undetectable until the mage's mind is ready. And on top of that, it must be awakened by the words of magic. I assume my spell did it. We all know Salvarias is an intelligent boy. His mind has probably been ready for some time, but since Ashra doesn't perform magic around the boys, it hasn't heard the words until now."

Tobin shook his head. "She performed a spell the day we met."

Mafarias frowned and gazed at Salvarias. "Perhaps the situation was too stressful. You were under attack. The boy was too frightened to understand what was happening, much less pay attention to a spell Ashra whispered."

Wilhelm gave his brother a squeeze.

"You won't contact the Association, will you?" Tobin asked.

Mafarias spread his hands. "We must."

Tobin bolted up. "But surely they will look poorly upon one who can perform magic at such a young age!"

"What would you have us do?" Ashra asked. "Lock him away at home; never allow him to see the light of day until he's eighteen?"

Tobin slumped back into his chair and stared at Salvarias. "Well, no. I just want him to be safe."

Mafarias's eyes narrowed when he glanced at Ashra. "I know a man in the Association. I'll contact him directly and do everything in my power to help."

Tobin tilted his head. "Thank you."

Mafarias shrugged and continued his interrogation of Tobin. Wilhelm ceased listening and thought of his pride in Salvarias, the youngest mage in history. Then thoughts drifted through the conversation and the way Mafarias and Tobin acted. Salvarias was in danger. Fear clamped around Wilhelm's heart and brought a lump to his throat. He gathered up his brother and cradled him close. Wilhelm's first thought was to flee. He could take his brother away in the night; keep him safe and secret. Seemingly oblivious to the peril, Salvarias heaved a deep sigh, pressing his ear to Wilhelm's chest.

Mafarias soft voice said, "It'll be fine, Wilhelm."

Wilhelm startled from his dark thoughts and stared at his uncle.

"I'll be there," Mafarias continued. "Nothing will happen to the boy. I promise."

Tobin touched a finger to his lips and nodded to Salvarias. He'd dozed off.

"Why don't you boys go to bed?" Tobin whispered. "Everything will be all right."

Wilhelm glanced at his grinning uncle and allowed belief to set in. Mafarias would not permit harm to come to Salvarias.

Keeping a tight hold on his brother, Wilhelm went to his room. When he lowered his brother to the bed, Salvarias stirred awake. "Sorry."

"Don't apologize." They both changed into their bedclothes, and then Wilhelm tucked the newly discovered mage into bed. "Love you, Salv."

A familiar sparkle crossed Salvarias's eyes. "Love you too, brother."

Tobin entered, smiling broadly. "Would you boys like a story tonight?"

Salvarias sprang up, his eyes lit with eager curiosity. Wilhelm sat in his brother's bed and pulled him close. As usual, Salvarias drew his knees to his chest and leaned against Wilhelm.

"What will it be about tonight?" Tobin asked.

Salvarias clenched Wilhelm's arm. "Your childhood."

Wilhelm offered an encouraging grin to his brother to continue speaking. Already Tobin's eyes were glassy, and both knew this was a pivotal moment; the first time Salvarias had talked to another besides Wilhelm.

Salvarias huddled closer, trembling in Wilhelm's arms. "Please tell us about your father and mother."

Tobin cleared his throat. "All right. My mother died when I was born, so my father had to care for a baby. Of course, he had no idea how. He was a knight in the army."

"How does one become a knight?" Salvarias asked.

"You have to earn the title. The first part of the trial is testing your fighting skill against knights from other cities. The next is of one's character. The Knight Council presents several situations to the candidate, and based on his actions and choices, they determine if he'll be accepted. You see, the knights remained united after god

Nevlar's Retribution and are the sole army left in Dalnar and Windlous." Tobin sighed. "Though their numbers are few; barely allowing their forces to be called an army. Sadly, most guards never aspire to be knights and merely enjoy the authority they have."

Wilhelm shrugged. "The knights keep us safe. They've defeated Crutar's pathetic attempts at war for near a thousand years now."

Tobin nodded. "Indeed. We could wipe out the lesser gods left over from Veedran if Loutsil knights would unite with us. We could rid our world of them. But the kings of Loutsil have kept to themselves. They don't even follow the standards to initiate knights. As long as a person's sword skill is adequate, Loutsil bestows the sacred title of Knight. They have no test of character. It's a disgrace to the order."

"Why are you not a knight?" Salvarias asked.

Wilhelm felt the tension leaving his brother's body and gave an affectionate squeeze.

Tobin shrugged. "I'm not skilled enough with a sword. I'm learning, though, and one day I'll take the test. Until then, I do what I can."

"Sorry," Salvarias said. "Please continue."

Tobin nodded. "After mother died, the other knights helped raise me, and their wives tended me when I was an infant. My father was with me every moment he wasn't working. I felt I was the most important thing in his life, even above his knighthood. I guess that's a sign of a good parent." His gaze grew distant. "I didn't have everything I wanted; like toys or sweet breads. But I had his love and constant attention. He listened to me and actually heard what I said, understood me and took the time to learn what I cared for and needed. He was an amazing father. So I spent most of my childhood in the guardhouse with him learning swordplay or spending time with other knights when he worked. Shortly after I turned fifteen, he came home with a boy my same age that'd come from Loutsil. The boy was already a Loutsil knight, and though not blood, my father loved him as though he'd been part of the family for years. And I love him as a brother."

"Where is your brother?"

"Traveling. He never joined the guard here or united under the Dalnar and Windlous knighthood. He's a rather restless man, always moving, so he turned to mercenary work. I begged him to join the guard with me, but I realize now he would've been miserable. Humar needs travel. He's stuck out in Blarrup, but he said as soon as the job is done he'll visit. With a little more instruction from him, I'll test for knighthood."

"When did you see him last?" Salvarias asked.

"Our father's funeral. Over four years ago."

"How did your father die?"

Tobin shrugged. "Old age. He was in line for a commander position here, but his heart gave out before his dream was fulfilled."

"I am sorry," Salvarias said.

Tobin cast a wane smile. "I was lucky to be with him when he passed. He taught me everything I know. Tolerance, caring for the less fortunate, the innocent, and he said, 'Until you place yourself in another man's shoes, do not pass judgment. Everyone has a weakness, and one must never judge a person for succumbing to it because at one point you might succumb as well. And wouldn't it be nice to have another who understands your pain and mistake?'"

Salvarias's dark eyebrows stitched together. "You agree?"

Tobin shrugged. "With a portion. I adhere to his lessons in tolerance and help for those less fortunate. I also agree one should never judge a man unless they've put themselves in that situation. As far as weaknesses, I think there are two types. The man who steals a loaf of bread to feed his children has a weakness for his family's health and well-being. A man who murders in cold blood has a weakness to torment others. I understand the first man, but never will I understand the second. Therefore, I judge the second man and condemn him to death, but not the first."

Salvarias shook his head. "You are not judging the weakness, you are judging the heart."

"True." Tobin smiled. "Very true."

Salvarias's eyes grew intent and he leaned forward. "What if the heart wants to be good but cannot?"

Tobin frowned. "If a heart wants to be good, it can. We control our actions. Our actions do not control us."

Ashra appeared in the doorway. "Time for bed."

Wilhelm accepted a hug from Tobin. As it happened every night, Salvarias cringed when Tobin offered an embrace. "Good night, boys." Tobin winked and then left the room.

After ruffling Salvarias's hair, Wilhelm started to rise but stopped when he noticed something under the bed. He picked it up and turned it over in his hands.

Made of different shades of wood, the object was what he'd call a puzzle box, for lack of a better term, though not hollow. Larger than a grapefruit yet smaller than a melon, it contained hundreds of tiny pieces that could be moved and shifted; yet all were connected at the core. Intricate carvings covered each of the eight sides. It was beautiful. The construction of the device was unfathomable.

"Where did this come from?" he asked.

"I do not know." Salvarias moved to get a closer look. "Can I see it?"

Wilhelm examined it thoroughly before deciding it was safe for his brother to handle. Salvarias accepted the box and his deft fingers manipulated the pieces. His expression softened while the device twisted into odd formations. After several moments, he smiled and presented the device to Wilhelm.

He eyed the peculiar shape. "What is it?"

"A bear." Salvarias frowned. "Do you not see?"

"I see it now," he lied.

He took the box and attempted to move the pieces, but his hands felt clumsy and the pieces were difficult to shift. He glanced at his brother, who remained mesmerized by the object. "I'll ask Mother about it."

Wilhelm found her humming happily while cleaning dishes with Tobin. "Have you seen this before, Mother?"

"No. Where did you get it?"

"It was under Salv's bed."

Her eyes narrowed. "Did he steal it?"

"No. He doesn't know where it came from either."

Mafarias rose and examined it. "I've never seen anything like it before. You found this under your brother's bed?"

"Yes."

Mafarias muttered a few words under his breath and flicked his hand. "It's not enchanted." He pursed his lips. "Under your brother's bed..." He stared at the object several moments before inhaling a deep breath. "Give it to the boys, Ashra."

He grinned at his uncle before turning back to his mother. "Can I keep it?"

"May I?" Tobin asked.

Mafarias handed the puzzle box to Tobin.

He frowned, turning the box over in his hands, attempting to move the pieces as Wilhelm had done. "I've never seen the likes of this, Ashra. I wouldn't trust it with the boys."

Wilhelm scowled at Tobin. "Uncle said it's fine. Can I keep it, Mother?"

She leaned against the counter and regarded Mafarias and then Tobin.

"It's safe," Mafarias murmured.

She smiled at Wilhelm and opened her arms. "Of course, son." He grinned and accepted her hug and kiss.

"But..." Tobin glanced at Mafarias. "No offense, but we don't know where this came from. How could you trust such a strange object?"

Mafarias clapped Tobin's shoulder. "You're a good man. You care for these boys as if they were your own."

Tobin's cheeks flushed. "I... They are special to me."

Mafarias nodded. "I see. Rest assured, I wouldn't allow harm to come to my nephews. There are no magical properties to the puzzle box. It's a lump of wood. No doubt it was left by a previous owner."

Tobin scoffed. "Surely they would have found it before."

"Objects turn up when they're needed most." Mafarias turned to Wilhelm. "Go to your room."

Wilhelm took the box from Tobin and rejoined Salvarias.

"Here. I want you to have it."

Salvarias smiled broadly. "Thank you, brother."

He accepted the device and rested against Wilhelm. Salvarias whirled the puzzle box into different shapes as if he'd had it for years. The movements seemed like an intricate dance between his hands, and the rhythmic transformation sent a calm ripple through Wilhelm. The tension of the day melted, his shoulders relaxed, and he stared in almost a daydream trance at the device. Eventually, his brother slowed and drifted to sleep. Wilhelm lowered Salvarias into bed and went to take the device, but Salvarias pulled it close like a treasured toy.

Slipping a pouch of lavender under his brother's pillow, Wilhelm doubted Milred's promise that it would ease Salvarias's troubled sleep. His head tossed side to side and his face twisted in terror as it did every night.

Chapter 5
Winter 1005 a.r.

Wilhelm glared at the parchment he'd been writing on for the past month. He'd questioned Mafarias relentlessly when Salvarias was asleep. There was much to learn about the mages that would visit. Though Mafarias assured Wilhelm time and time again no harm would come to Salvarias, Wilhelm thought it best to conduct his own investigation. So it was that he sat in his room and read over his notes, piecing it all together.

According to Mafarias, the Association of Mages set stringent guidelines surrounding witches and wizards. The general populace thought mages to be evil: eating children, sacrificing animals and virgins, and deceiving the innocent, all in an effort to gain power. Of course, the horror stories were fabricated, but to quote his uncle, "People fear what they do not understand." In actuality, Wilhelm had learned mages harnessed little power. Only fourteen spells existed, but since mages were rare and no pattern revealed how or who received the power, they were feared and tormented.

The rules and etiquette put forth by the Association were supposedly an effort to improve the image of magic users. If the Association suspected a mage might cause harm or initiate fear, drastic action would be taken—the Association would kill him or her. To ensure that there were no rogue mages, the Association published a list of wizards and witches to each city, allowing guards the right to murder any magic user not on the list and wearing robes. An occasional outdated list ended many young lives, but this was considered a small price to pay for the greater good. The guard list was the one thing Wilhelm could easily fix. Tobin was a guard and could ensure Salvarias was added to the list.

Young mages who hadn't met with the Association yet were expected to be detained until such time as the Association could meet with him or her. In turn, it was a mage's immediate duty to kill a fellow mage who wasn't wearing robes and appeared to be over the age of twenty. All this was possible, according to Mafarias, because mages could sense one another's magic and level of power, after, of course, the magic made itself known to its host. The Association paid a heavy reward for such "justice," and mages undertook their duty seriously since many found it nearly impossible to find work. This also was intended to ease the public's fear.

When a person was known to be a mage and reported to the Association, three heads of the order visited and recorded the level of power, his or her name, and decided if the mage would live or die. This visit was what worried Wilhelm the most, and it would happen today.

With his brother preparing in the kitchen, it left Wilhelm brooding alone in his room, giving his imagination time to concoct a scene of the Association's mages killing his brother. The thought of the tiniest drop of blood leaving Salvarias set Wilhelm's mind with determination. He stashed the parchment under his pillow, tiptoed to his mother's storage box, withdrew a dagger, and shoved it in his boot. If any of the three mages raised a finger to Salvarias, Wilhelm would slice open their throats and not even think twice. Feeling better, he strode into the kitchen and plopped down next to Salvarias, ruffling his hair.

Wilhelm grunted when Salvarias's tiny fist landed in his ribs. "Ouch!" Winking, Wilhelm said, "Don't worry about it. You'll do great." His grin faded and he stared intently at his brother. "You know you'll have to talk to them."

Salvarias nodded.

"Can you do it?"

His brother squared his shoulders and confidence gleamed in his eyes. "I need this, brother. I will speak to them."

Wilhelm had no doubts. Since Salvarias learned of his magic, he was infatuated with it. He spent every waking breath reading and he performed his light spell every day. When it came to his magic, he was a different boy, brimming with confidence and eager to discuss it. Half the time, Wilhelm fell asleep listening to Salvarias excitedly repeat the seemingly unending knowledge he'd obtained from their mother's books.

A knock on the door caused both brothers to jump.

Salvarias grabbed Wilhelm's arm before he rose. "Will you stay with me, brother?"

Wilhelm pointed to a chair near the fireplace next to their uncle. "I'll be right over there if you need me. I promise; they won't lay a finger on you."

Salvarias inhaled a deep breath and nodded. "Thank you."

Salvarias rose, lowering his head respectfully, while Ashra welcomed three men into their home. Wilhelm went to his chair, picked up a book, and pretended to read.

Mafarias's gaze moved to Wilhelm's boot, and an arched eyebrow confirmed his suspicion. Wilhelm returned the look with his own raised eyebrow. His uncle winked.

"Lovely—" one man started.

All eyes went wide and stared at his brother. Wilhelm tensed and slid his hand down his leg to his boot.

"My, my," one man breathed.

"Indeed," another said.

"Salvarias Laybryth?" yet another voice asked.

Salvarias raised his head and glanced at Wilhelm. He offered an encouraging smile to his brother. Fear and submission faded from Salvarias's black eyes. Resolve, strength, and new confidence emerged, and Wilhelm grinned with approval.

"Yes, Master," Salvarias whispered.

"I'm Yunfral. This is Felkar and that is Kilt."

Salvarias tilted his head.

"How old?" Yunfral asked Ashra.

"Six years in a month," she said.

"Truly?" Kilt murmured. "We feel those who receive their power at seventeen are a danger. Tell me, Ashra Laybryth, how old were you when your gift appeared?"

"Over eighteen, Master."

Kilt shook his head. "Too young. I prefer to see it appear when one reaches their twenties."

Ashra smiled. "If only we had control over when it curses us."

Yunfral's eyes narrowed. "Curses or blesses us?"

Ashra glanced at Mafarias and Wilhelm. "Curses."

Felkar cleared his throat. "May we?"

Wilhelm's mother nodded. "Of course. I'll retire to my room. Please feel free to call upon me should you need anything."

The three men bowed, and Wilhelm became disgusted when they hungrily watched her walk from the room. All three could've been her grandfather. He glanced at his brother and saw the same glimmer of repulsion.

"Please, sit," Felkar said.

Salvarias returned to his seat, and his intense gaze moved to each man. Wilhelm smiled when the old men cringed as they settled into their chairs. Salvarias's stare had never bothered him, and he couldn't understand why each person who met his brother shuddered.

Felkar was plump and clean-shaven, his face wrinkled both with age and fat. His head contained a ring of white hair and a stubby white beard. His eyes were shrewd and his air conceited. Kilt had aged somewhat better. His white beard resembled clouds, and Wilhelm was amazed the man could grow so much hair on his face but nothing on his head. He seemed nervous, fidgety and shifty. Yunfral was frowning, and the lines on his face drooped together. His skin hung off his elbows, and his beady eyes darted around the room. Yunfral reminded Wilhelm of a scholar.

Yunfral started the questions. "Tell me how you first learned of your magic."

"I felt my uncle cast a spell. I listened and repeated his words, mirrored his rune and controlled the energy."

Kilt frowned. "Your uncle used your energy?"

"No."

"If he didn't use your energy, how did you 'feel' the spell?" Felkar asked.

"I felt my uncle's power ignite. It grew as he cast the spell."

"How powerful is he?" asked Kilt.

"More than any of you. That is him over there."

Felkar shook his finger. "That's not polite, boy."

Salvarias's brow furrowed. "Lying to you would be?"

Mafarias chuckled.

Yunfral sat up straight and arched an eyebrow. "You miss the point. There are more appropriate ways to talk to your superiors."

Salvarias's eyes danced with thought and his face softened. "Forgive me. I meant no disrespect. I am new to learning the rules of the Association and fear I have more questions than answers. Please, it was not my intent to insult any of you. I respect your power and humbly ask forgiveness for my rude response."

Mafarias chuckled again, and Wilhelm shared a grin with his

uncle. Salvarias was getting exactly what he wanted and the three men were none the wiser.

Kilt smiled broadly. "Indeed there are many rules to learn. Your mother should teach them to you."

Salvarias nodded.

"Where does the energy come from?" Kilt asked.

"Energy is the released life force from every living thing in Arden."

Kilt continued the questions. "Can you use the energy when it is within the life force?"

Salvarias nodded. "Yes, though you can kill it."

"How many spells are available to us?"

"Fourteen."

Kilt fluffed his beard. "Why do we chant a spell?"

"We speak the spell so our magic knows what we attempt."

"Explain runes," Yunfral ordered.

"Runes are drawn in the air to hold the energy in order to execute the spell. It is the only way for the energy to leave us safely. It allows us to conduct powerful spells since we can continue to funnel energy into the rune once drawn. Meaning, if a fireball is not large enough, I can pull more energy and channel it to the rune, growing the fire."

Kilt leaned forward, rubbing his hands together. "Explain components."

"A component is similar to a rune since it holds the energy. However, the component cannot accept additional energy past what it has been originally given. Therefore, component spells are not as powerful but take considerably less strength from our minds and body."

"What happens if you are interrupted?" Yunfral asked.

"It would depend on where you are at within the spell. If you have focused with the intent to conduct the spell, start speaking, and are stopped, nothing happens physically, though you cannot remember the spell. If you have drawn the energy and are stopped before the rune is completed, your magic must force the energy from your body through your skin since the rune has not been drawn. If you have drawn your rune but have not executed the spell, the magic will burn inside you and devour your mind. You must always say, 'Rulose' to execute the spell. Without the word, we lose control of the energy, and the magic will kill the mage in an attempt to save itself."

Kilt giggled. "Save itself?"

"I believe magic is a presence within us, not meant to be part of our bodies. It is self-serving and does not care for us. Therefore, we must guard against it, control it, and ignite it when we see fit."

The three men glanced at each other and Kilt laughed. Yunfral leaned back in his chair. "How long can a sustained spell remain active?"

"It depends on the level of the mage and the complexity of the spell. For example, a protection spell could not be maintained for long, but a light spell can remain sustained for extended periods of time."

Felkar folded his hands on the table. "Perform a spell for us."

Salvarias drew fluidly in the air and a small ball of light appeared.

All three men sprang from their seats.

Wilhelm gripped the hilt of the dagger.

Yunfral's voice shook when he said, "Change the shape."

Salvarias closed his eyes and whispered a word. The ball of light shifted to a sparrow.

Kilt giggled. "Why a sparrow?"

Salvarias lowered his head. "My reasons are my own."

Yunfral marched over and leaned close to Mafarias, and Wilhelm strained to hear the conversation.

"The power is unnatural. The boy could harm someone."

Mafarias waved his hand. "He won't, and I won't let you kill him. You will give him robes; you will add him to the list."

Yunfral's fingers turned white as he gripped the back of Mafarias's chair. "He'll be the ruin of magic. Surely you sense it. It's not like us. We must kill him now."

Mafarias's jaw clenched. "You will do this, Yunfral, or I'll kill you myself. This boy must live!"

The old man cursed before rejoining the other men.

"You are approved to wear the robes," Yunfral snapped.

Salvarias bowed and went to his room with the sparrow following. After Wilhelm's mother emerged, he joined his brother and closed the door.

"Nicely done, little brother."

"Thank you."

Lines of exhaustion were etched around Salvarias's eyes. The stress of the event settled over both of them. Wilhelm sat on the bed, pulling Salvarias close, and picked up the puzzle box from under the bed.

"I'm really proud of you, Salv."

Salvarias cast the tiniest of smiles, but it lit up the room, spreading a warmth and comfort only found on cold mornings when sipping hot cocoa. Wilhelm couldn't help but grin.

Salvarias withdrew the dagger from Wilhelm's boot. The knife teetered in his brother's small hands. "Why do you have this?"

Wilhelm took the weapon and shrugged.

"I heard Tobin and Uncle," Salvarias whispered. "What would you have done? There were three of them."

He met his brother's serious gaze. "I would've figured something out, Salv. I'll be damned if I let anyone hurt you."

Salvarias flew into Wilhelm's arms. "I love you, my dear brother."

"Love you too, Salv." He turned the puzzle box over in his hand. "I wish this was smaller. I could carry—"

He stopped speaking when the device shrunk in his hand to become no larger than a river pebble. Salvarias's eyes lit with curiosity, and he picked up the device. Upon his brother's touch, it grew to normal size. Salvarias placed it back in Wilhelm's hand, but the device remained the same size.

Salvarias frowned. "Make it smaller."

"I don't know how."

"Think about it; imagine it smaller."

Wilhelm thought about it, wishing it was the same size as a strawberry. In a blink, it shrunk to the size of the fruit. "Magic?" he asked.

"No," Salvarias murmured and focused intently on the puzzle box. After nothing happened, he picked it up and it grew to normal size.

"That's amazing!" Wilhelm exclaimed.

Salvarias looked at Wilhelm, then back at the puzzle box. "Think of something larger, like a roast of venison."

Wilhelm picked up the box and imagined his favorite meal, but nothing happened. He pictured the box smaller, and it shrunk. "It just gets smaller," he mumbled.

Salvarias took the device, and it grew again. He smiled up at Wilhelm. "Now it fits in your pocket. Will you carry it and keep it safe for me, brother?"

He grinned and ruffled his brother's wavy hair. "Sure, Salv. I'll always have it when you need it, and I promise I won't lose it."

After a quick punch, Salvarias curled up. The pieces shifted in his hands, hypnotizing Wilhelm with swift, fluid motions.

Chapter 6
Spring 1009 a.r.

Ashra picked up the next dirty dinner plate and wiped it clean. Tobin hovered beside her, waiting to put the dish in the cupboard. Mafarias was sprawled out in a chair by the fire chatting with Wilhelm, who was holding the monstrosity in his lap. She enjoyed listening to the murmur of their voices, and with Tobin by her side she delighted in the sense of family.

She smiled inwardly when he inched closer. Seven years had passed since the two met, and he spent every waking free hour with her family. He had yet to propose to her, yet to ask Mafarias for permission, yet to kiss her or hold her hand, and doubt of his interest sometimes crept into her mind. Then again, who would be attracted to a woman mage with two bastards? She fought her longing and desires, remained friendly, and balanced her flirtatious offers with an indifferent air. But after seven years, she was beginning to rethink her strategy. He seemed interested and cared for both of her sons as if they were his own.

She handed him the clean plate and then picked up the next dirty one, feeling his warm body press against her when he put the dish in the top cupboard.

Moments like these made her positive of his desires, yet each night he would leave, bidding Mafarias good evening and not asking to speak to him privately. She sighed when he accepted the plate, his hand lingering on hers.

"So, how is the guard treating you, Tobin?" Mafarias asked.

"Well," Tobin replied. "Same criminals, same crimes, and same whores."

Mafarias chuckled. "You don't find it repetitive?"

Tobin grunted. "What isn't? Every job is repetitive in some aspects. I like the occasional opportunity to help the innocent. It makes me feel like I'm doing something good with my life."

Ashra slowed her pace when she picked up the next plate. Whenever they finished cleaning up after dinner, and once Tobin had told the boys a story, he left. If she prolonged cleaning the plates, perhaps he might stay longer. Her hair fell across her face and she tossed her head. His rough hand brushed the mass behind her shoulder. She glanced up to see his gaze roll over her body. She looked away in frustration. What was he waiting for? The next Retribution?

Mafarias's mouth twitched a smile. "Must be difficult living in the guard barracks."

She shot her uncle a secret withering look. He cast back a secretive wink.

"It is," Tobin confirmed.

Mafarias leaned back in his chair. "Why not leave?"

Tobin shrugged. "I'm saving funds for my own home. I hope to buy one in the next two years."

Ashra tensed. Why would he need a home if she already had one? Wilhelm chuckled.

Tobin smiled, turning his attention to her son. "What's the laugh for?"

His lopsided grin spread. "Because both of you don't have enough common sense to talk to each other."

Ashra regarded her oldest. He was growing to learn about women with a speed she found alarming. She suspected he met plenty of young women near the guardhouse, and he looked eighteen, not fifteen. She never missed the lingering gazes women gave her son, nor did she miss his returned stares and crooked grin. He was his father in every way.

Tobin leaned on the counter, his arms folded over his chest, a smile twitching on his lips. "Explain?"

"It's obvious." Wilhelm wrapped another blanket around Salvarias. "Just move in here with us. We don't need a new home."

Tobin's cheeks blushed scarlet and cleared his throat, shifting his gaze to the floor. "It's improper to offer nothing to a woman, boy."

Wilhelm laughed. "I'm sure mother isn't one for tradition."

It was Ashra's turn to blush.

Mafarias roared with laughter.

Tobin glanced at her, and she understood his shameful smile. The home and boys were hers and she supported herself. He offered her no property, wealth, expensive clothes, or fine jewelry. In his mind, he came to the table with nothing, but in hers, he possessed everything she desired. She smiled at him.

He shifted a step away and furrowed his brow.

When they were done cleaning the dishes, Tobin followed the boys to their room while she reclined against the wall outside, smiling at his stories. Once he finished, there was a brief pause.

Tobin asked, "You would approve if I married your mother?"

Ashra's heart jumped to her throat and she swallowed hard.

Wilhelm chuckled. "Yes."

"Salvarias?"

This time her heart stopped. As it had promised, the monstrosity had never told anyone what she did to it. But with one word, it could end her happiness.

"Yes," Salvarias whispered.

"Good night, boys," Tobin said.

Ashra moved to the fireplace and Mafarias winked. She blushed but couldn't suppress a smile.

When Tobin emerged from the boys' room, her uncle rose and kissed her forehead. "I best be going. I'll see you tomorrow, dear."

"Pleasant night."

Tobin cleared his throat. "I'll walk you out."

Ashra's stomach knotted and her heart pounded in her chest. Once alone, she rushed to the washroom, splashed water on her face, cleaned her hands, and ran a brush through her hair. She bolted to the living room, nestled in a chair, and situated her robes, calming her breathing. She felt like a schoolgirl and rolled her eyes at herself.

Tobin wasn't outside long, and when he returned his smile was instant.

Wishing her hands would stop shaking, she stood. "Are you off then?" She tried to ask lightly, but her voice trembled.

His gaze never left hers when he walked across the sitting room to stand in front of her.

"I'm sorry," he whispered. "I should've asked what you wanted. I thought saving for a home we owned would allow you to quit working for Himiks. I thought it would make you happy and give you a reason to marry me."

She'd meant to remain calm, but her words blurted out of her. "I can't have more children." She flushed and lowered her head. "Salvarias's birth scarred me."

Tobin stepped closer so no space existed between them. "You've already given me two sons." His hand slid around her waist while his other hand raised her chin. "Why didn't you tell me how you felt?"

Her voice was barely a whisper. "I...you never made an advancement towards me. I thought you might not want to marry a mage. That perhaps you merely wanted to be friends."

He tilted forward, his gaze locked with hers. "Forgive me for ever letting you think you meant so little to me."

She smiled shyly and raised her head, offering her invitation. "Of course."

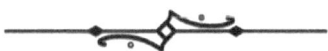

It was a spring morning when Tobin forcibly hauled Wilhelm from his home. As was the routine, he watched his brother's eyes fill with tears as they did every six days. Wilhelm writhed against Tobin's inescapable hold halfway to the guardhouse before he gave up and promised he wouldn't run.

"I know this is hard, Wilhelm, but your mother and I feel it's the right thing to do for both of you."

He kicked a pebble on the cobblestone. "I'm fifteen now! I can make my own decisions! Salv needs me."

"He needs to learn to take care of himself. We have the same argument each week." Tobin sighed. "He must learn to fight, and without you there, he'll eventually grow tired of the bullies and accept my instruction; or at the very least, stay by your mother's side."

Wilhelm remained quiet. Tobin had been his father for less than a season and the innate need to be an obedient son extended to his new father. Still, his heart hurt. His brother was his life; and over the past year, Salvarias's bruises had turned into punctures, as though a large spider nibbled on him. When he shook with sobs, Wilhelm stopped pushing for answers. As the beatings from bullies worsened, so did his brother's nightmares. Smiles became rare, cringes more common, and now his gray-black eyes reflected deep pain, heart-aching loneliness, and the submission of a beaten dog. If Wilhelm ever found out who was responsible, he doubted they'd survive his wrath.

"Race?" Tobin asked.

Wilhelm's yes was a low growl. He kept pace as they dodged between citizens, cut through alleys, and made it to the guardhouse in record time.

Tobin had a hand over his chest when they walked to the training yard. "You're getting faster."

"Hello!" Idolar called.

Wilhelm couldn't suppress a grin at the thought of a fight. "Ready to try your luck today, Idolar?"

The guard laughed and tossed Wilhelm a sword. Once the cool steel rested in his palm, his passion for knowledge surged through him and he took his stance, not waiting to catch his breath from the run.

With a bow to his foe, he winked, blocked Idolar's first attempt, and lunged for a strike. The rush of the fight, the elation of landing a mark, the quick heart pump at the near hit he might have taken rushed through him. He was in his element; focused, precise, and agile; and a grin seemed permanently stamped upon his face. No matter how hard he tried, the grin came and went at its own choosing. And the entire morning it greeted each guard who came to test their luck against him.

Over half the day was gone by the time he finished sword practice. Tobin moved the lesson from swordplay to hand-to-hand fighting. "You'll not always have your sword. You must learn to defend yourself by any means necessary, son."

Tobin wrestled Wilhelm to the ground. He assimilated his father's teaching on how to maneuver out of holds and pins, and in turn, how to restrain someone else.

When the weekly storm hit, the group rushed inside to the indoor training room. Wilhelm joined Tobin at a window and glanced up at the churning green clouds.

"Odd, isn't it?" Tobin muttered. "Every week that we practice, this same storm ravishes Falar."

Wilhelm nodded. "Maybe we should head home now before it gets much worse."

Tobin grinned. "Did you think you'd escape your lessons that easily? We've still got much more to practice."

Wilhelm spent the next hour testing his skill against various guards, and he narrowly lost eight of his seventeen challenges. Tobin offered encouraging words and educated Wilhelm on missteps that caused him to be defeated.

A deafening roll of thunder shook the guardhouse. Wilhelm broadened his stance to keep from toppling over. Dust hazed the air and weapons hung on the walls clattered to the floor. He shared a quick glance with Tobin and then both rushed to the nearest window. Hail the size of Wilhelm's fist pelted the city. The muted green clouds churned with malice and lit the sky with pulsating light. Another roll of thunder shook the walls and lightning fingered down from sky, striking the streets of Falar.

The screams followed shortly.

Idolar tossed Tobin a shield. "We've got to help the citizens get to cover."

Tobin nodded, wedging his arm in the shield strap. "You stay here, Wilhelm. I'll be back for you."

"I can take a shield and make it home."

"No, I won't have you out there by yourself. Panic can cause good people to commit unspeakable acts. You'll stay here where I know you're safe."

Without waiting for a response, Tobin dashed down the hall with Idolar and ten other guards. Only the younger recruits still in training remained.

Samanson patted Wilhelm's shoulder. "Come down with us. We'll see if any poor girls need refuge in our humble barracks."

He nodded at the grinning man. Samanson had an appetite for women, and Wilhelm's presence seemed to help tempt the blushing girls from their parent's side. He'd even stolen a few kisses, but once the girls turned shy and giggly he lost interest. Times such as those made him painfully aware he'd matured well past his age, even past Samanson, who was five years Wilhelm's senior.

He followed Samanson and two other guards, Gioff and Hansen, down the hall and accepted a shield. Wilhelm raised it overhead and sprinted through the training yards. Hail pounded down, sending vibrations along his arm, and embedded a ringing in his ears. They made it to cover.

Samanson shook his head. "This might not be worth it. Any woman still caught out in this is dead by now. That hail is the size of my fist!"

Wilhelm nudged him. "Don't be such a baby."

Samanson grinned. "You first."

Wilhelm winked before darting into the gallows. He shuffled his feet to avoid tripping over the hail and rushed towards the entrance shelter. He made it safely and propped the shield against the wall.

Samanson, Gioff, and Hansen weren't far behind.

"What do you plan to do?" Gioff asked, eyeing the empty street.

Samanson sagged against the wall. "I didn't think the people would clear this fast."

"We should head back," Gioff said. "We were told to wait in the training rooms."

"Quit being such a ninny," Samanson snapped. "No one is around to see us down here."

Hansen clenched his fists. "We should be out there helping."

Wilhelm grunted an agreement.

Samanson pointed at a private coach plodding down the deserted street. "Look here, boys."

"Lady Haleen," Hansen breathed.

Wilhelm glanced at the gaping men and then back at the coach. "Who is she?"

"The dream of every man in Arden," Hansen said. "She's a noblewoman who was recently widowed."

Wilhelm leaned against the wall. "What's so special about her?"

Hansen swallowed hard. "Since her husband's death, she's been the talk of the town."

Samanson smoothed his hair and tugged his soaked tunic straight. "She's taken a liking to guards; young ones."

Hansen nodded. "Any *boy* who enters her coach leaves a man. Samanson's right. It's well known she fancies the young ones. She wants to be the one who ushers them into manhood. They say she likes to be in control. We virgins deliver her desires since we don't know what in Oblivion we're doing."

The coach stopped at the entrance and the door edged open. Wilhelm stood straight. Lady Haleen was indeed every man's fantasy. Her dress was cut in the latest flattering fashion where it cinched her waist and clung to her upper body. The soft mounds of her breasts were barely visible in her tight corset, and he had a sudden urge to free them from their restraints. Sensations he'd yet to experience spread a fire through him.

Her large blue eyes scanned over each guard. "Dreadful storm, isn't it boys?"

They all nodded, mouths dropped to the floor, except for Wilhelm. He crossed his arms and leaned on the wall.

She took notice. "My, my, aren't you a tall one."

Wilhelm's grin emerged on its own and he winked.

"What's your name?" she asked.

"Wilhelm."

"Well, Wilhelm, would you like to join me for a ride around the city?"

He glanced at the clouds. "Not a good day for it. But I'd like a ride to my home."

"And where is that?"

"Above Baker Jyfil."

She smiled and opened the door further. "That's on my way. I'd be happy to take you."

Samanson grabbed Wilhelm's arm. "You might act of age, Wilhelm, but you're only fifteen springs old. This is *not* a lady. She's turned into a whore and all of Falar knows it. Tobin would kill me if he knew you went with her."

He grinned. "Then don't tell him. Just say I left for home. That way, you won't have to lie." He winked. "And don't be so jealous."

Samanson's frown switched to an ear-to-ear smile. "Remember, she likes to be in charge. Tomorrow, I expect all the details."

"Gentlemen don't kiss and tell."

Wilhelm darted from under cover and leapt into the coach. Hail thudded on the thick wood roof. Pale blue silk softened the interior wooden sides and two benches were plushly cushioned in complementary dark blue cotton. He settled on the one opposite from her.

Her gaze moved over him. "You're a fine specimen of a man."

He leaned back and pondered his situation. His mother would be upset if she knew what he was contemplating. But this was the first woman he'd met that wasn't shy, and judging by her direct stare, she didn't giggle.

She rose from her seat and sat by his side. "So, Wilhelm, are you a recruit in the guard?"

"Not yet."

"You are of age, are you not?"

Her lush lips beckoned to him, and he bent down and kissed her. When her tongue glided between his lips, he pulled back. The other kisses he had stolen were mere pecks, quick and soft.

Her eyes narrowed. "Exactly how old are you?"

He didn't like to lie. He was much more accustomed to withholding information, which he did on his brother's behalf. There was no way around her direct question. "Fifteen."

She sat back and studied him for a moment. "You're fifteen? You? Fifteen?"

He looked away and peeled back the curtain to a small window. The hail had died down to marble size. "I am."

What'd he expect? No one—except, of course, Salvarias—treated Wilhelm as though he were an adult. He was a man trapped by a teenager's age—not even by body. By the gods, he was larger than the young recruits and half the men he fought.

He startled when a hand touched his thigh.

"I see it," she said. "There is thought within you that is not that of a boy."

His heart jumped to his throat. Now presented with the opportunity, he was uncertain. He'd never actually thought she'd go forward.

"I've been labeled a whore by the other women. They think since my husband's death I've become heartless. They say I take what I want from a man and leave him once I've finished." She lifted her chin. "What they say is not untrue. I have men when I desire them. I am barren, so there's no chance I'll mother a bastard. Husbandless and childlessness has made me lonely." Her warm breath washed over his lips as she leaned forward. "After I've had my fill, I'll dismiss you and never see you again."

Wilhelm grinned. "I like an honest woman."

A smile twitched on her lips. "So I take it you hold no objections to my intent?"

All hesitancy vanished. In answer to her question, he brushed his lips against hers. He shivered with an aching need as he opened his mouth to her exploration. At first, he was awkward in where his hands ought to move, but she was quick to offer direction. He thought he should feel shame for touching a woman the way he was, but he didn't.

Each impassioned kiss grew his confidence; each desperate caress stirred more sensations, more needs. When next she went to move his hands, he succumbed to his instincts and lifted her onto his lap. He ripped opened her bodice and her moan conveyed her approval.

He wasn't sure when it was that her dress had been removed, but the sight of her naked made him pause. He angled back and drank in her body; the tone of her creamy skin, the curves of her neck, and her heaving breasts.

Soft hands snuck under his tunic and raised it over his head. Her fingers trailed down his chest to his trews. Tension coursed through every muscle as she pulled loose the tie and he burst out of his pants.

She rose and yanked off his trews, even as he fumbled to kick off his boots. Wedging his knee between hers, he parted her legs as he drew her down to his lap. He traced the curve of her neck, following it to her shoulder, then across her collarbone and down her breast until he rested his hands on her waist. He pulled her closer.

Gazes locked, Haleen bucked her hips and he slid inside her. Everything after that moment was a blur of aching need. No longer did she provide instruction. He took charge of his own exploration of her body and her cries of ecstasy drove him further into the depths of passion. But she was still in control, moving too fast and eager. He flipped her to the seat and knelt before her, pulling her to the edge of the bench. When he thrust himself inside her, she cried out and tossed her head back. Her moans, the way she moved with him, her glistening body, forced him past the point of his control. Need overcoming all thought, he increased speed, soaking in the sounds of her escalating moans and her expression of satisfaction. She arced and cried out. He groaned deep in his throat as he emptied inside her. Once spent, he fell against her, breathing heavily as sweat rolled down his back. It had ended quicker than he wanted.

"By the gods," she moaned.

"I'm sorry," he breathed.

Her fingers tangled in his hair. "Indeed, you are a man."

He didn't move for several moments while he gained his breath, enjoying the feel of soft hands gliding over his back.

Sudden shame came over him. He didn't love her, and his mother's lectures on waiting to be with a woman rang in his mind. Withdrawing, he sat back on his heels, searching for his shirt. He couldn't meet Haleen's gaze though he felt her stare.

"There are those women who expect a *pure* man to come to their bed on their wedding night," she said. "Rest assured, dear Wilhelm, few do. Men are creatures of desire and seldom do they make it to marriage before experimenting. Women, such as me, offer them... let's just say an education. What we did is nothing to be ashamed of, and one day, your wife will offer her appreciation to me."

Wilhelm pulled on his shirt. "Of course, my Lady."

"And yet shame burns your cheeks."

"I've been raised a certain way, my Lady. What I did, it was..." By the gods, he should say wrong, but the words wouldn't leave his lips. He enjoyed it too much to condemn his actions.

"I know of your mother. She wasn't married when she had you, nor was your father pure when he bedded her. Did you know she slept with your father after one day of knowing him?"

He glanced up, surprised. "No."

Haleen laughed. "I remember him. All the women swooned when that man strolled through Falar. He was here less than three days before he left your mother pregnant and alone. If I'd been a few years older, I would've slept with him." She caressed his jaw. "You look just like him, you know. I saw the way your parents looked at each other. Indeed, only a fool couldn't see their love. My late husband and I shared the same kind of love; that instant attraction, the unexplainable feeling of care towards a stranger. He was my life and I his. I grieve for him every night, just as your mother surely grieves for the loss of Tedris."

"Tedris?"

"Your mother has withheld much."

He snatched up his trews and sat opposite from Haleen as he dressed. "She still thinks of me as a child."

She dressed as she spoke. "Allow me to give you the story. My mother knew all the gossip, you see, and I eavesdropped on all her conversations. None knew of Tedris before he came to Falar, but he acted as though he owned the city when he arrived. He was quick to make friends and even quicker to be with the ladies. It was by chance that your mother and father met. Rarely was Ashra allowed away from Jyfil's watchful eye. She wasn't a mage yet, and her beauty was—and is—a remarkable sight. That fateful day, she was delivering breads, whether by sneaking out or Jyfil's direction we'll never know. When they met, I felt the air come alive. I was the same age as you are now, but everyone on the street, no matter how old, took notice of them. We lost track of them throughout the day. The next morning, we'd all heard he'd left in the night. When your mother's condition became apparent, the facts came out. Most called your father a coward for abandoning his child." Her gaze intensified. "I tell you, Wilhelm, something important must have dragged him away; something beyond his control. You must believe me; he would never have left her. I could see it in his eyes."

Wilhelm leaned back and regarded Haleen for a moment. "The fact is: he did. But I don't care about my birth father." His words were bitter in his mouth. "I have a real father now. One who isn't going to leave us."

"Ah, Tobin Cohil."

He nodded. "He's a good man."

"Indeed, one of the best. He's honorable beyond what's good for him. Trust me, I know from personal experience. I could count the number of men who've turned me down on one hand. And he's within that small group." She motioned to the front of the wagon. "Knock on the wall and tell the driver to go to Jyfil's home."

He hadn't realized they weren't moving. He banged on the wood and gave the order. The coach lurched forward.

"You're not your mother. You must find your own path in life. What we did, I don't regret. Do you?"

He leaned his head back. "No, I don't regret it. Nor do I love you. Nor do I see myself bedded solely with you."

She smiled, and seemed relieved by his statement. "I was worried. Most young men swear their undying love to me after our meeting. I feared with your age, you'd do the same. Indeed, you're older than your years." She stared at him a moment. "Perhaps, if you're not opposed to it, I won't dismiss your company permanently."

His arousal was instant. "What do you have in mind?"

"I must confess that I was pleased by your performance. I'd like to visit you."

He laughed. "My mother would love that."

"Let me be more specific. My coach will pass the guardhouse everyday at high noon. If you have the opportunity, I'd like your company once again. I assure you, I'm not looking for love. I've had it, and I'll never love another. By no means are you to turn down offers from other women. I don't want a monogamous relationship with you."

Wilhelm grinned and moved to kneel in front of her. "I think I can get away a few times a week."

"Then I'll teach you all I know." She kissed him lightly. "Your wife will worship me."

He pulled her close, fighting the urge to take her once more. "I'll be forever in your debt."

She smiled wickedly. "That you will."

The coach stopped and the driver thumped on the wall. Wilhelm kissed her and then moved quickly to the door before his restraint left. He winked at her before hopping out.

The hail had turned to sheets of freezing rain. The driver was waiting, wrapped in furs to ward off the chill. He was a burly man with a scraggly beard and a lazy eye. His posture was hunched, but his meaty hands and arms revealed he was perfectly capable of dispatching any man who might presume too much with Lady Haleen.

"Gentlemen Wilhelm." His voice sounded like sanding paper. "Lady Haleen extends her—"

"No need, Brenil," she called. "I've already given him the speech."

Brenil bowed. "Then good day, Gentlemen Wilhelm."

"Remember his face well," Haleen called. "He's welcome in my carriage any time."

Brenil's eyes widened. "Of course, my Lady."

Wilhelm clapped Brenil on the shoulder. "Thanks for the ride."

"The pleasure was my Lady's."

Wilhelm winked. "Indeed. Good day, Gentleman."

He glanced around to get his bearings. He'd been dropped off a street away from his home. Shivering, he raced down the flooded street. He was soaked through by the time he reached the stairs to his home. He barreled up two at a time and ducked inside.

"What in Nevlar—" Tobin's face was blotchy red. "Where have... By all the gods, I was worried sick, boy! How... Where... Why—"

Ashra arched an eyebrow at Tobin before turning her penetrating stare to Wilhelm. "I'm sure you know your father's question. Answer him, dear."

"I, I wanted to come home to see Salv."

Tobin threw up his hands. "Why, whenever it comes to your

brother, it is impossible for you to follow directions? I told you it wasn't safe! You could've been struck by one of those balls of hail! People died today, boy!"

He lowered his gaze. "I'm sorry, Father."

Tobin strode up to Wilhelm. "You *will* listen to me! When I tell you to do something, you'll do it!"

"Yes, Father."

Tobin grabbed Wilhelm in a fierce embrace. "I was so worried. I didn't know what happened. They said you left right after I did. It's been an hour, boy. An hour!"

He winced at Tobin's desperate hold and guilt clogged his throat. "I'm sorry, Father. I didn't mean to make you worry."

"Just don't do it to me again."

Wilhelm nodded.

"There are dry clothes in our room. Change, and then help your mother with dinner."

"I'm just going to check on Salv first."

"No." Tobin gripped Wilhelm's shoulder. "He's come down with a sudden fever today. Your mother's tending to him."

He started forward but Tobin held firm.

"You can't see him. We think he's contagious. Your mother got medicine from Delora, but it cost us much. We can't afford for you to become ill, too."

"I've got to check on him. I've never been sick. I won't catch it."

"You can't be sure of that."

"I'm taking care of him," Ashra said. "Delora is hopeful since we caught it on the first day. She thinks, with his breathing condition, drastic changes of weather such as these will be difficult for him. We'll see how he is tomorrow, and if he's better you can see him then." Her eyes narrowed. "There's something different about you."

Wilhelm lowered his head. "I'm just worried about Salv." He could still feel her stare.

"I see. Go change."

He muttered oaths under his breath on the way to their room. His anger didn't help in the removal of his wet clothes, and he tore his shirt. It sparked a whole new slew of curses that followed him into the kitchen.

The evening waned on and dinner lasted an eternity, as did the time after they ate. Wilhelm paced and then flopped in a chair, only to rise and pace again. Not only did worry for Salvarias gnaw at Wilhelm's heart, but his mother's intense gaze set him on edge.

Ashra's voice startled his pacing. "Time for bed."

The plush chair proved too small for him, so he sprawled out on the wood floor. Once his parents retired, he waited until the rumbling snore of Tobin filled their house before rising, retrieving a candle, and tiptoeing into the room Wilhelm shared with his brother.

Salvarias lay on his bed, curled up tight, pale and sweating while shivering at the same time. He looked near death.

Wilhelm moved the candle closer. Salvarias's gaze darted around, seeming unaware of his surroundings, and a haunted expression was frozen on his face.

"Salv?" Wilhelm set the candle on the floor and scooted closer.

Salvarias's eyes focused and instant tears fell down his pale cheeks. He flew into Wilhelm's open arms and small fingers dug into his shoulders. By the gods, his brother was burning up.

"It's all right, Salv. I'm here."

Salvarias's grip tightened. "It hurts! I begged them to stop but—"

He pulled his brother back. "What hurts? Who hurt you?"

Salvarias's eyes unfocused and he trembled violently. "I am scared. Please do not leave me. They will come for me. Please, do not let them take me."

Wilhelm's heart thudded painfully as he bent to catch his brother's stare. "Who? What's happening? Who's coming for you?" Salvarias seemed miles away. Wilhelm shook him. "Salv, look at me."

Salvarias's eyes focused, and he looked around the room and then at Wilhelm.

"What happened?" Wilhelm asked.

Salvarias lowered his head. "It was just a dream."

He clenched his jaw. "Take off your shirt."

"Please, do not make me, brother."

He fought the urge to hunt every boy in Falar and pummel them to Oblivion. "Take it off."

"Please!"

Wilhelm curled his hands into tight fists and looked away.

Salvarias hugged himself. "Forgive me, brother! Please! I—" He gulped for air.

Wilhelm scooped Salvarias up. "I'm sorry. I'm not mad at you, Salv."

Gently, he rocked his brother until he cried himself to sleep. Wilhelm lowered him to the bed, tucked a pouch of lavender under his pillow, and shoved a cot next to his. Wilhelm didn't even bother changing. Soon the thundering rain won his fight over sleep and cast him into restless dreams.

Late morning light battled the dark storm clouds when Wilhelm woke. He blinked, wiped the sleep from his eyes, and looked at his brother.

Salvarias lay awake; his eyes brimming with new pain and haunting fear that tore a hole through Wilhelm. Some color had returned though dark circles rimmed Salvarias's eyes, and he breathed raggedly.

"How do you feel?" Wilhelm asked.

Salvarias lowered his gaze. "May I have the puzzle box?"

Reaching in his shirt pocket, Wilhelm pulled out the pea-sized box and handed it to his brother. It grew the instant it touched his fingertips. Wilhelm sat up, rested his back on the wall, and lifted his brother next to him. As always, Salvarias curled up as he worked the device. Soon, the familiar twisting motions of the puzzle box lulled Wilhelm into a doze.

Salvarias's soft cry jolted Wilhelm awake. His brother bolted from bed, struggling against the blankets until scrambling to a corner, eyes wide and distant.

Wilhelm went to his brother. "It's all right, Salv. I'm here."

Salvarias grabbed the back of his head and fell to his knees, rocking violently, eyes staring at something not in the room.

"What is it?"

His brother whispered, "Just a dream… just a dream… just a dream."

Wilhelm lifted Salvarias and carried him back to bed. He offered the puzzle box, and Salvarias snatched it up and frantically maneuvered the pieces. No longer strategic, no longer calm, the puzzle box whirled at such a frenzied pace Wilhelm became dizzy. He rested his head on the wall and closed his eyes, trying to block out the haunting voice of his brother.

It took a day for Salvarias to become well, and Wilhelm's spirits rose when his brother seemed to move past whatever had ailed him. However, each time Wilhelm left his home, the entire event repeated, and continued to repeat, for the next year.

Chapter 7
Spring 1010 a.r.

Salvarias ambled through the lush woods surrounding Falar on a brisk spring morning, his brother near and his parents a short distance behind. The fresh, perfumed breeze of the forest intertwined with the songs of sparrows darting from tree to tree. The soft grass beneath Salvarias's feet offered a multitude of tiny flowers that lined his path.

He tightened his cloak about him, shivering in the breeze that rustled the aspens' new leaves and whistled through the thick pines. It did not take long before his chest constricted and he battled the air. When Wilhelm's hand rested on Salvarias's shoulders, his heavy feet felt lighter and his breathing eased. His brother, six and a half feet tall at the age of sixteen, grinned crookedly and offered an affectionate squeeze.

The family emerged from the forest into a meadow spanning over a mile, blanketed with tall grasses and spring flowers. Wilhelm gave one last squeeze and released Salvarias, grinning ear-to-ear at Tobin.

Wilhelm tossed Salvarias the puzzle box. "Ready, Father?"

"Of course, son!"

Ashra kissed Wilhelm's forehead before he rushed further into the meadow with Tobin, looking for uneven ground to practice on.

Salvarias averted his eyes, pushing down a rising pang of jealousy and hurt.

Once the two men were out of earshot, Ashra turned a cold gaze to Salvarias. "Help me, monstrosity."

He helped lay out the blanket and kick away lumpy rocks.

"Do you need anything else, Mother?" he asked.

Ashra waved her hand. "No, do what you want." She nibbled on grapes while reading her spell book.

He sat as far from his mother as possible and manipulated the puzzle box as it provided step by step pictures on how to shift each piece to create whatever wonderful creature he called to mind. As usual, the puzzle box subdued the more vivid images of people dying, and the clicking noises of each piece finding their rightful home overrode their screams. With his untamed mind sedated, his thoughts drifted to self-analysis, which he performed often, trying to understand himself, the voices of his mind, and the myriad of oddities that made him different from others.

As painful as it was, he stared into the shadows of his heart and forced himself to gaze into the true face of what he was; an abomination, a monstrosity, a child of evil. He swallowed the lump in his throat and choked down the words. He was evil. He felt a portion of himself cringe from those words, refusing the fact, fighting against the knowledge. He shook his head, disappointed that his own soul could not face the truth.

No other person except his mother knew of the wickedness residing inside him, and because of it, she withheld the love he desperately longed to receive. Her heart and care towards Wilhelm showed what a wonderful mother she was, and he wanted nothing more than to be the recipient of those emotions. His evil frightened her, and he accepted her torment while beseeching his soul to release its malevolence. But no amount of pleading drove the darkness from him.

Even now, as the puzzle box whirled in his hands, he heard it. Even now, as he pleaded it to leave him, it called to him. Even now, as he shielded his soul, mind and heart, a skeletal hand reached for him. Slowly, year by year, day by day, hour by hour, the evil grew stronger while he grew weaker. It found ways around his shield, and even as he sat in the sun on a beautiful spring day, he could feel the tiny nibbles the evil bit off from his soul.

He had monitored his evil since first it entered his body the day he was born. He remembered everything that had happened to him after his first breath. He remembered his brother's eyes overflowing with a deep sorrow that had caused his own heart to ache. Then Wilhelm's eyes had lighted. The sorrow was snuffed out and happiness, love of life, and love for Salvarias had blossomed. That sparkle was why he lived, why he fought, and why he hoped. After the light came a crooked grin. It infected him with love and, at that moment, Wilhelm was Salvarias's life. Then, his brother bestowed a name. Those were the only moments of peace, of utter happiness, in Salvarias's ten years of life.

What happened next changed him. He shuddered from the memory of the red fog of death coalescing upon him. It brought with it images of the dying that raced before him every breath he took, the screams of the innocent that rang in his ears constantly, and the taste of blood. Death after death, horror after horror, defilement after defilement had bombarded his mind. He remembered crying when it seeped through his skin. Then he felt the evil. It churned with life as it settled within him and gained a foothold in his mind. The images and screams increased until his mind had nearly caved. He lived in a waking nightmare, unable to breathe, unable to move. All that had coursed through his body was pain, all that had wormed into his hearing were dying screams, and he had bathed in blood. Then it had all stopped, and once again, he had seen bright amber eyes. Strong hands had held him securely, and then a lopsided grin had penetrated through the images of death.

Salvarias's heart rose from the depths of despair to peek at the light when he thought of his brother. Salvarias paused in his manipulation of the puzzle box to steady his breathing. He closed his eyes and focused, remembering the rhythm of Wilhelm's breathing and heart. Salvarias gained control, squared his shoulders and faced his next dark secret. Once again, he choked down the words. He found satisfaction in death.

The gallows were easily spotted from the window when he visited the guardhouse with Tobin and Wilhelm. When they practiced swordplay, Salvarias snuck out and watched the murderers choke and twitch at the end of the noose. Each time the dead made eye contact with him, each time he watched the light fade from their eyes, and most times he found pleasure in their deaths. It washed over him in waves of sweet satisfaction, tasty and filling. However, once he looked away, guilt, shame, self-loathing, and fear for his soul welled. He could feel the evil in him sneer in triumph each time. The knowledge that he was capable of such dark elation tormented him. The only respite, his only hope for salvation, was when he found some deaths dull and uninteresting. He would stare into the eyes and feel nothing, not remorse, not satisfaction, not pity.

To utter another truth, he cared little for people. Most he found self-serving, wrapped up in their own issues, and uncaring. Even those who committed good deeds generally did so for self-satisfaction, to know *their* actions were appreciated and to receive gratitude to fill their empty souls. He was not above the emotion; he was the same in that aspect as all others, though his selfishness far exceeded most. Any good deed he performed was in an effort to save his own soul, to counter the evil within him.

He shook his head at his own selfishness. He should be alone in the world, far from people he would surely harm one day. Try as he might though, he could not withdraw from Wilhelm. Salvarias loved his brother more than life itself and selfishly clung to the love Wilhelm imparted. And each breath of Salvarias's pathetic life, he hated himself for it.

"As you sshould, my pet," a voice said in his mind. *"I have told you many times to flee, leave your beloved brother behind. At sssome point in your ussseless life, you will kill him."*

He sighed at the truth spoken by the presence. The voice had talked to him since he could remember, offering advice, support, and bringing reality to light with the same cold tone and hissing voice. Never did the voice allow him to dream or lie to himself. It knew his darkest thoughts, his fears and hopes. The presence grounded him, and he listened to it often. The conversations were conducted in his mind, and he kept the voice a secret from everyone.

"I cannot leave my brother."

"I know you cannot now, but one day you will undersssstand it isss the only way to protect him. I hope it will not be too late to sssave his life."

Ashra's hate-filled voice cut into his thoughts. "Stop making those noises!"

He flinched. "I am sorry, Mother." He collapsed the puzzle box into the simple box shape.

Ashra narrowed her eyes and curled her lip. "Leave me. I grow tired of the sight of you, abomination."

"Yes, Mother. I am sorry."

"If you were sorry, you'd drive the evil from you. Think about it, because tomorrow Tobin is taking Wilhelm and I'll find out if it has left."

"I am trying, Mother," he said honestly, fighting his tears.

"I loathe you, liar!" She buried her face in her hands. "I hate what you've made my life, what you've forced me to do! Leave me now, monstrosity!"

"Yes, Mother. I am sorry."

He meandered through the meadow until he entered the trees. On a nearby branch, a sparrow sang a cheery song. Salvarias rested against a thick pine, catching his breath from the walk, and listened to the beautiful melody. He wiped his tears, inhaled a shuddering breath, and continued through the pine-scented forest, counting pinecones along the way. He eventually curled in a ball against a large rock, drawing his cloak close.

"Tell your brother the truth, my pet. Tell him it is not bulliesss who cut and bruissse you."

He rubbed his sleepy eyes. *"No. My brother deserves a mother. He would be angry with her if he knew."*

"Even now, knowing what you will endure tomorrow, you will not tell him?"

"No, my brother deserves happiness. Leave me."

The presence receded. He dozed in the woods, lulled to sleep by the merry songs of fleeting birds and the trees' whispered song.

"Salv!" Wilhelm called.

Salvarias opened his heavy eyelids and pushed himself to his feet. "Here, brother."

It took his brother a moment to find him, and Wilhelm's wide grin lifted Salvarias's spirits. "You shouldn't wander off by yourself."

Salvarias glanced at the shadows. Near an hour had passed. "Sorry."

"Don't apologize, Salv. It's time to eat lunch."

When they returned to their parents, Wilhelm settled him on the blanket near Tobin.

Over the last few years, Tobin had taken to calling Salvarias son, smiling and loving his evil soul. And though he wanted a father, he had yet to accept the man's love. Salvarias worried that if Tobin knew of the evil, he would not be so apt to offer his fatherly gift, but upon watching him, Salvarias pondered his true feelings and entertained the idea of allowing Tobin close.

"I advissse against telling Tobin of your love, my pet."

"I did not say I love him."

"I senssse it. I know your true feelingsss. You cannot lie to me, my pet."

Salvarias sighed. Maybe he did love Tobin. *"I want a father. My brother told me our real father would never return. I can have this, I* can accept him. He would not hurt me like she does."

"You cannot alwaysss have what you want, my pet. It is childisssh and selfisssh. You are acting like a ssspoiled boy, whining for what you cannot have and definitely do not dessserve."

"I can have this if I choose. I want a family, I want to be accepted and loved like my brother."

"Mark my wordsss, my pet, you will regret your decccision ssshould you allow the man near. Guard your heart, sssave yoursssself the pain of rejection. If thisss man findsss your evil, he will hurt you, leave you, beat you. I do not want to sssee your torment increassse."

Tobin smiled once again at Salvarias, offering a wink.

Ashra handed Wilhelm a heaping plate of food. "How was your training?"

Salvarias stared with hidden jealousy at his brother's food. Wilhelm's meals seemed more filling, prepared with close attention to his favorites.

Wilhelm winked at Salvarias. "Amazing! I beat Father."

When Ashra spoke, her voice dripped with love. "I love you, son."

"I love you too, Mother."

Salvarias lowered his head.

"It isss hard, my pet. I undersssstand and know of your pain. I regret to tell you a family is not what you are dessstined for, and sssadly, you'll never have it. Even if you find sssomeone to love you, they will leave you at the firssst test. You are alone."

Not wanting to believe the presence, rebelling against the words he knew to be true, longing for love, he gathered his courage and followed his heart. He leaned against Tobin. The normal images that he could control rushed to the forefront of his mind. He sat back up.

Tobin pulled Salvarias close. "It's all right, son."

The pain a simple touch induced was beyond description. Salvarias lived every breath staring at death. Bodies fleeted around him at all times. Some corpses he was unable to determine their fateful ends; others, it was all too clear. Over the years, he had learned how to process the dead along with his real surroundings. His mind, though chaotic and painful, had no issues seeing the dead while functioning. That is, unless someone touched him.

With Tobin's simple touch, images of people Salvarias had never met and landscapes he had never seen pounded against his mind with the force a metalsmith uses to forge a blade. What felt like the entire ocean filled his skull, compressing his brain, giving the sensation of his thoughts battling against an eddying current, drowning his rational mind. It was as if a thousand real life paintings flashed in front of him, only to be replaced by a thousand others. Layering on top of landscapes and faces were the bodies of the dead, fleeting by at heightened speeds.

He grabbed the puzzle box. The familiar instruction it provided clashed with the unfamiliar images from Tobin's touch.

The images rushed by too fast to process the longer Tobin held him, blocking sight, touch, air. Nausea set in, and his head seemed to double in weight, swaying from the maelstrom massing in his brain. The device barely moved, but Salvarias did not like defeat. He yearned for reassuring touches. Each night he wished he could accept Tobin's offered hug, to allow him to extend the comfort Salvarias so desired. Instead, he was forced to cringe away.

"Breathe, Salv," Wilhelm said.

Salvarias sucked in a deep breath at the command and the unbearable pain eased, reducing to a hammer striking his skull, and the images drifted to the background of his thoughts. He leaned against Tobin and smiled inwardly. He could suppress the images. He could overcome them and function when someone touched him. He almost wept with joy, but he kept his emotions checked around his mother. He knew he might pay dearly for his choice.

Salvarias put down the puzzle box and nestled against Tobin, resting an ear against his father's heart like he did with Wilhelm. It wasn't the same. The chorus of deep, steady breathing and a strong thumping heart wasn't as soothing. Salvarias shifted his ear away and instead focused on the songs of the birds.

Wilhelm's deep voice jolted Salvarias from a light doze. "Want to go for a walk?"

Salvarias opened his eyes, fought through the images, and glanced at the shadows, realizing he must have drifted off for near an hour. A broad, warming smile spread across Tobin's face as he lifted Salvarias to his feet. A smile snuck out.

Tobin blinked a few times and cleared his throat. "Before you boys go, I have something for your Birth Days." He rose, unsheathed his sword and handed it to Wilhelm. "This has been passed down through many generations, son. It was used in the Minotaur War and has stayed within the family since. Rumors say Nevlar himself forged it when he taught the first cavrul how to mold steel. I want you to have it."

Wilhelm embraced Tobin, and in 'a voice thick with tears said, "Thank you, Father."

Tobin clapped Wilhelm's back, then turned a grinning face to Salvarias. Squatting eye level, Tobin said, "And, for you, my curious son, a book of the old gods. Your favorite stories are included. I even made sure it has the *Scroll of Nevlar* in it."

He gingerly accepted the gift. Tears brimmed at the gesture, and he hugged the book. "Thank you."

Tobin winked and opened the inside cover. "I still want to tell you stories at night, though."

Salvarias nodded and another smile crept across his face.

Tobin's warm laugh filled the meadow. "You're going to be the downfall of many young ladies, my boy. That smile can light Arden!"

Cheeks burning with embarrassment, Salvarias lowered his head to read the inscription.

To my son, Salvarias.
May you forever remain curious and never change your
pure heart.
I will love you always.
Tobin

His tears broke free.

Wilhelm unsheathed the borrowed sword he had gotten from the guardhouse and replaced it with Tobin's, leaving the old one on the blanket. "Ready, Salv?"

"I'll hold onto it for you," Tobin offered. "I'll put it in our pack, and you can read some tonight."

Salvarias hugged the book once more before handing it over. Tobin smiled and swept Salvarias up in a tight hug. The sudden human contact lurched forward the images. By the time Tobin lowered him, he was blinded by pain and would have fallen if Wilhelm hadn't caught him. His brother flung him over a shoulder and Salvarias grinned when blood rushed to his head. When his vision returned, he counted the passing flowers.

Wilhelm strolled the meadow until their parents were no longer in sight.

"So you can touch people now?" Wilhelm asked.

"It took a moment, but I was able to gain control of the images. However, once he released me and then touched me again, it started all over."

"I could tell him about it if you want. Then he would know to give you time or at least a warning before he touches you."

The fact Salvarias could not be touch by another besides Wilhelm and their mother was mortifying. Salvarias despised that oddity above all others. "I would prefer you did not brother. I do not want anyone to know."

"I won't say anything then."

"Thank you, my dear brother." He balled his hand into a tight fist and slammed it into Wilhelm's side.

Wilhelm chuckled. "Ouch. You're going to pay for that."

The instant Wilhelm lowered him, he leapt to tackle his brother, only to be caught in midair. Salvarias found himself pinned to the ground. He kicked wildly but never landed a hit as his brother mussed his hair.

Wilhelm's rumbling laugh echoed in the meadow. "Come on, little brother. You can do better than that!"

Salvarias's laughter finally stole all his air. Once his gasps started, Wilhelm let him up.

After Salvarias caught his breath, Wilhelm asked, "Ready?"

"Yes!" he responded, jumping in Wilhelm's arms.

Salvarias laughed with delight when he soared through the air. The sky rushed towards him while the grasses sped from him. Wind ripped through his hair, and he swore he could almost touch the puffy white clouds floating above him. Then he was falling. Faster and faster he plummeted, and his laughter escalated until he landed in familiar strong arms. He could smell the grasses and he reached down to touch the yellow flower by his hand. He only caught a brief glimpse of his brother's lopsided grin before soaring through the air once more. Salvarias felt free as a sparrow.

Salvarias woke to a chill running up his spine, despite being wrapped in a blanket atop Tobin's shoulders. The sun seemed to be racing his family home, and halfway to the city it disappeared over the horizon, casting red hues in the sky and deep shadows through the forest.

Suddenly, a blinding, white light obliterated Salvarias's vision. An image flickered. He squinted through the bright light and forced his mind to snag the image and hold it. He saw an unmoving body lying on the forest floor. Considering the clothing and size, he could have sworn it was Tobin, but the image vanished before he could confirm. The bright light flashed again, and the darkness of the night charged Salvarias. The forest spun and tipped this way and that. He teetered off balance and toppled off Tobin's shoulders. Tobin caught him just in time.

Sitting him on the ground, Tobin squatted down. "You all right, son?"

Salvarias's vision returned to normal and he clung to Tobin's arm to prevent the stop and start of the images, not wanting to lose the control he had gained. "Yes, Father. I am sorry."

He jumped at his own uttered word. Never had "father" been issued from his lips, but apparently the trust he placed in Tobin had triggered his mind to allow what felt natural to be uttered. Tobin smiled, and his arms encircled Salvarias. The feelings he had suppressed for years surfaced, and he opened his guarded heart to his new father. "I love you."

"I love you too, son."

The presence snorted. *"The man will betray you. Mark my wordsss, he will know of your evil and leave you."*

He ignored the voice and clung to Tobin. Salvarias had a father; was someone's son, and was loved and accepted.

Tobin swept Salvarias up into a tight embrace. A new hope sprouted. Tobin's love was unconditional, despite all the evil within Salvarias's soul; Tobin saw something good. Tonight, Salvarias would tell his new father of the evil. Tonight, Tobin would save him.

The family continued at a brisk walk, and just as before drifting to sleep, Tobin suddenly lowered him to the ground. Jolted fully awake, he saw eleven men appear out of the shadows in front of them. Tobin rested a hand on the hilt of his sword.

A stocky man spoke in a raspy voice. "Well, look here, boys. A mage and her pets." His greasy yellow hair glowed in the dusky light, a thick scar on his chin rose white against his grimy complexion, and his beady eyes shifted from Tobin to Ashra. The other men grinned; their yellowish teeth seemed to drip blood as the fleeing sun left a red stain on the sky.

Ashra positioned herself next to Wilhelm when the group of men started walking towards them, branching out to form a half circle.

"Stay back," Tobin commanded.

"You shouldn't be in the company of mages. She's even cast a spell over the boy." The man pointed to Salvarias, whose slate-blue mage robes were a reflection of his mother's.

Tobin remained silent.

The man took another step towards Tobin. "Looks like we need to teach you a lesson. Teach you not to keep the company of mages."

Tobin drew his sword. The man's horrible cackle intruded on the peaceful forest. The other men stopped and drew their swords while a chilling chorus of laughter filled the air.

Fear ran rampant through Salvarias. The image flashed in his mind of the dead body, and no doubt existed that it had been Tobin. Salvarias's mind whirled with self-hatred. He had not warned his own father of the untimely death that awaited him.

"Yes. You might not be the one to plunge the sssword in his chessst, but withholding the truth is the sssame as killing him yoursssself. I told you thisss day would come."

The yellow-haired man and four others lunged at Tobin. Ashra was drawing a rune when two men grabbed her hands, stopping her from finishing the symbol. A cry escaped her when the energy released through her skin. Wilhelm drew his sword, facing four men, and shielded Salvarias.

Salvarias's chaotic mind sifted through spells as he watched the fight unfolding. He managed two words of a small fire spell, but stopped short of completion when pain blared in the side of his head. White and yellow sparks flashed before him. He crumbled to the moss-covered ground. Warm blood ran into his eye. Darkness swam in his vision, threatening to pull him into unconsciousness; but fear for his family pushed away the inviting peace. Shaking his head, he staggered to his feet.

Ashra screamed for help, but her call was cut off when a man hit her across the face. Her eyes glazed and she slumped in his arms. One attacker lay dead at Wilhelm's feet, and he was ready to lunge again, but another struck him from behind with the pommel of a sword. Wilhelm spun to the ground, unconscious.

Salvarias grew faint at seeing the blood run down his brother's face. Hands grabbed Salvarias and hauled him to a tree. His gaze never left his brother. Ropes cut into Salvarias's wrists as he was tied to a thin pine.

"Tie up the other one," the yellow-haired man commanded. "We'll deal with him after these two."

Another man dragged Wilhelm to the same tree, binding him next to Salvarias, and then left to join in the blood lust of the others.

Salvarias blinked blood from his eye. Tobin had been overpowered after he killed two men, and now hung limp in the arms of two attackers. After tying him to a tree, the yellow-haired man slapped Tobin awake. Ashra had gained consciousness, and softly begged the men to let them go.

A dagger flashed in the yellow-haired man's hand, and he sliced across Tobin's chest at an agonizingly slow pace, deliberate and planned. The next was a stab straight into his side. The yellow-haired man murmured, and the words "mage" and "lesson" reached Salvarias as the man drove the knife into Tobin's stomach. Salvarias stared, unable to remove his gaze, as the man rammed the blade into Tobin's shoulder, then to the other side. Blood was everywhere, but Tobin never called out or pleaded with his tormentor. He stared at Ashra, who smiled at him through her tears.

Eternity seemed to pass before the yellow-haired man finished inflicting further torment. Salvarias tore his gaze away and looked at his mother.

Her hate-brimmed eyes bored into him and her whispered words carried on the night breeze. "You did this, monstrosity."

His eyes burned with tears, and he turned his attention to Tobin, but could no longer tell if he lived. His head hung limp and blood seeped from his wounds.

Ashra's words vibrated in Salvarias's mind, and he knew it to be true. Evil followed him, sought those he loved, and devoured all that was pure.

"Yesss, now you understand," the voice hissed. "You are linked to evil, my pet. You call for it and it ansssswers. Remember what you do when they take you at night, remember your pleassssure, and remember the blood."

The leader with yellow hair walked to Ashra and used his dagger to cut away her robes. "You did that to him, mage. You should know better than to be around anyone. All he suffered was because of you." The man unlaced his trews. "This is all you're good for, witch." He shoved her to the ground.

Salvarias snapped his eyes shut when his mother's screams filled the night. "Please stop, please stop, please stop," he chanted.

Ashra screamed.

He spoke louder, trying to block her anguished pleas, but they would forever haunt him.

Then the storm started.

The night wore on. Salvarias struggled with his bonds, numb to his mother's moans of pain as one by one each man took turns tormenting and raping her. The ground was soaked from the heavy rains, and lightning added an eerie horror effect. He looked down to see his robes stained with bile.

A rustle in the woods gained his attention. Two men worked together to dig a hole and erect a stake while another man took a second turn with Ashra. Salvarias averted his eyes and sobbed.

Wilhelm groaned.

Salvarias jerked his head up. "Brother."

Wilhelm's eyes fluttered.

"Brother, please. I am scared!"

"Waking up, are we?" a man said.

Salvarias jumped. The man who had hit Wilhelm approached.

"Can't have that." The man withdrew his sword and struck the pommel across Wilhelm's temple. "We're not ready to deal with you."

Wilhelm went limp, fresh blood flowed, and a cry escaped Salvarias.

The rapist knelt in front of Salvarias. "You see what mages cause, boy? You see what happens to those who travel with them?"

Air pierced his lungs with each painful gasp. Terror clamped around his throat.

"I hope you've learned a lesson, boy." The man withdrew a knife. "Any mage that befriends others puts them in danger."

He scarcely drew air. The man sawed off Salvarias's robes, and he twitched each time the knife nicked his skin. Try as he might, he could not stop shaking, nor could he avert his gaze from that of the man.

"There." The man tossed away his robes. "You've seen what magic does, and I'm giving you a chance now. Stay away from mages, boy."

Leaving Salvarias naked and shivering in the rain, the man returned to Tobin and rifled through his pockets.

Salvarias did not know how much time had passed when he heard another commotion. He watched men tie his barely alive mother to the stake while lightning illuminated her once beautiful face and the rains washed blood from her body. The yellow-haired man set something in a bucket aflame and tossed the burning liquid on Salvarias's mother. Her body burst into hungry fire. She screamed.

Salvarias shut his eyes and deeps sobs racked him.

She screamed.

"Stop," he pleaded.

She screamed.

"Please stop!"

She screamed.

"Stop it!"

She screamed.

"No!" Tobin cried.

Salvarias opened his eyes to see Tobin awake, struggling weakly against his bonds and staring at the ravenous flames eating Ashra's skin.

Salvarias's gaze switched to his mother and satisfaction bloomed like a budding rose. He stared at her, screaming and writhing on the stake, and he felt happy. His soul rejoiced at being free from her torture, and he smiled after the last light of life faded from her eyes and shriveled in her skull. He breathed in the feeling of freedom, and his smile widened to a grin.

He turned his attention back to his beloved father. Tobin's eyes were filled with a mixture of hate and fear, and tears streamed down his bloodied face as he gazed at Salvarias. With one slight shake of his head, Tobin withdrew his love and Salvarias's worst fear became his new reality. His father's betrayed expression gouged a void in Salvarias's heart, one he was sure would never be filled, one he was sure he would never allow to be filled. His heart, fragile and scared, cringed further into the recesses of his body.

"You are no son of mine." Tobin's voice seemed to resound through Arden.

"I told you," the presence said. *"Sssadly, no one will love you. Even your brother will leave you sssomeday. Evil isss not meant to be loved, my pet. I am sssorry you had to learn your lesson in sssuch a difficult manner. You will alwaysss be alone."*

Salvarias leaned over and became sick.

"You still live?" Salvarias raised his gaze to see the leader standing over Tobin. "Allow me to end your suffering."

In one fluid motion, the yellow-haired man drew his dagger and slit Tobin's throat. Time seemed to slow as blood trickled down his neck. His gurgled last breath burrowed into Salvarias's ears. No satisfaction swelled in him this time, and when the last light faded from his father's eyes, Salvarias's hope died and his soul screamed in despair.

The words of the yellow-haired man sparked a horrible panic in Salvarias.

"Time to finish off the other two."

"But one is just a boy," a man protested. "I've talked to him. He'll—"

"The kid already likes mages, pretending to be one. Ridiculous. We'll kill them both. We don't want them reporting our descriptions anyway."

Desperation for Wilhelm caused Salvarias to pull harder against the blood-soaked ropes. After another painful tug, which peeled off a considerable amount of his skin, his hands were free. He leaned against Wilhelm's limp body, ignited the magic, and whispered the spell. The magic warmed Salvarias, comforting his mind with a reassuring protection as he harnessed energy from his surroundings. He drew a rune over their heads and funneled the energy into its holding. The men approaching with drawn swords gasped when a white light flowed over the brothers. Closing his eyes, Salvarias concentrated on sustaining the spell. He blocked out the men's angry voices, blocked out the smell of burnt flesh, blocked out the memory of his mother's moans of pain, her dying screams, and his father's last words. All Salvarias felt was the magic resting over him like a blanket and his brother's deep breathing.

Salvarias shifted when the familiar warmth of his magic grew hotter within him. Then something pushed against the shield. Sweat trickled down his temple, and his muscles flexed and ached from the strain of controlling the energy. Within a breath, his blood switched from a simmer to a raging boil, and he was sure his body was encompassed in flame.

Things poked the shield, and he grimaced against the power surging through each muscle, tendon, vein, and organ. Everything felt sore, as if he had plowed a field by hand for two days straight. He realized he had forgotten to breathe. His focus shattered and he heard horses' hoofs fading in the distance.

He choked the words to release the spell. *"Ru...Rulose."*

Darkness sprang upon him.

Salvarias woke next to his brother, the high moon offering illumination. A throbbing head and the lingering taste of blood were vicious reminders of what had occurred. Wilhelm sagged, unconscious, against his bindings. Tears welled at the memory of the night, and Ashra's cries replayed in Salvarias's mind. He untied his brother and tugged on his hand.

"Brother, please wake up. Please help me."

Wilhelm did not budge. Darkness ebbed as the sun battled the black night.

Shivering from the cold rain and lack of clothes, Salvarias walked on unsteady legs to his father.

Tobin had been untied and left to lay in a pool of bloody mud. Salvarias's gaze moved over Tobin's mutilations, remembering how each wound had been inflicted, replaying his withdrawal and expression of horror at witnessing Salvarias's evil.

Salvarias's mind plunged into the abyss of fear and his new reality. He picked up Tobin's hands, slick with blood, and pulled on his father. "Please Father, wake up! Please do not leave me! I am not evil! I will try harder, Father, please! I promise I will try harder!" His hands slipped. "You have to help me! We are a family now! You love me! Please!"

"No, my pet," the voice said. *"He cannot help you, he doesss not love you. I told you not to allow him into your heart. I told you he would betray you. It isss time for you to face the truth. My pet, you*

cannot be loved. He died becaussse of you. It wasss you who whissspered to the men, you told them to kill him. Your evil hasss no boundariesss. Go look at your dead mother. Sssee what you made them do."

"No! It was not me! I—"

"Sssspare me your liesss! Go to her! Sssee what I sssee! Do it!"

He balled his fist in his hair. "No! It was not me! It was not me!"

"Go to her and I will ssshow you, my pet! I will prove to you what lurksss inssside you!"

He stumbled to his mother's corpse. Her skin was charred and melted away to expose shriveled organs and bones.

"My pet, look at her. Remember her criesss of pain, her torment. Remember your sssatisfaction."

"I did not mean it!"

"Ssshe beat you and tortured you. You did not wisssh her dead?"

"I love her! I feel sorry for her!" He buried his face in his hands. "I did not mean to be evil! She tried to help me!"

"Ssshe did; and yet you could not drive the evil from yoursssself. Look what you did to the woman who tried to help you. My pet, you are the ssson of darknessss. You are a pawn to evil, a play pieccce to torment the innocccent." The angry voice rose an octave, its words a sword rammed into Salvarias's heart. *"Look at her! Accept what you have done! You've robbed your brother of the family he dessserved because of your selfissshness, becaussse of your evil! Look at her!"*

He stared at the blackened corpse, his mother once beautiful and now unrecognizable. The full weight of the evening crashed into him. For the first time in his life, he fully acknowledged the evil, fully accepted that it lived inside him, fully believed he was an abomination. All his years, he had battled his knowledge, cringed from the truth. Now he could hide from it no more. He fell to his knees and screamed in sheer hopelessness.

He was evil.

Clouds burst into the sky like a bulbous pustule, blocking the stars and the moon, overpowering the rising sun. Darkness pounced like a stalking tiger and lightning pulsed.

The voice roared in anger, *"Sssay it aloud, my pet! It isss time to acknowledge your true nature!"*

Salvarias breathed the words through his tears. "I am evil."

The ground beneath him turned cold as a fresh blanket of snow. The grass wilted. Insects sprang from the earth only to keel over within a breath. The nearest tree lost its color and death crept across the forest, a perfect circle of destruction, encompassing Salvarias.

"No," he whispered.

The presence cried, *"Yesss! You are the bringer of death, my pet! Thisss is what you were made for; death, dessstruction, unequaled evil! Know your true ssself and fear what you have become!"*

A sparrow fell from the sky and landed at Salvarias's feet. Lightning revealed rodents and vermin skittering across the ground and up trees, but none escaped the growing eradication of life. He stared, riveted by terror, while dying creatures staggered along the wilting ground, and birds gave shrill cries before their dead bodies plummeted from the sky. He sensed their fear, their pain. The trees' song turned frightening, the dying rustle carried on the fierce winds.

"Hear what I hear, my pet!" the merciless voice yelled.

Salvarias's voice joined the haunting chorus. Soft words whispered on the wind, on the rain. He heard the horrendous deeds he told others to do, terrifying things he never knew could be inflicted upon people. It was Salvarias who whispered the words.

"No," he breathed. "I did not." It was more of a plea than a statement.

"You deny it isss your voiccce?"

"No."

"Then how can you deny your actionsss? I try to stop you, my pet, but you whisssper to them. You tell people to kill, to rape, to beat the weak, to torment the innocccent. Sssee what I sssee!"

Salvarias's images of death slowed. Standing in the shadows of each was a wispy red fog. He squinted at it, and suddenly he saw the wisp was himself standing beside the murderers with a smile on his face, murmuring to the killers, encouraging their acts.

"No!" He stumbled back, pushing the image from his mind.

"You are the hossst for evil, pet! Remember what you do when they take you in the night!"

He fled to his brother, bursting dead insects, stumbling over dying animals. Salvarias snatched up Wilhelm's hands. "Brother, help me!"

"No! He cannot help you, bringer of death! You are alone!"

"No!" Salvarias screamed. "Brother, please! I am scared!"

Thunder bellowed in the sky and lightning bit the forest floor. The ground trembled, heaved, and cracked beneath his feet. A deer lurched by, struggling to survive. The pain the animal endured, its slow, agonizing death bored through his heart. Lightning pulsed again, sending a viscous roar of thunder to vibrate the world.

"Brother!" Salvarias's gaze was locked on the dying deer. "Brother, help me!"

He scrambled into his brother's lap, clawing at him for comfort. Salvarias's horrid commands from the images whistled on the wind louder than the booming thunder, ordering murders and unspeakable acts.

"Please brother!" He snapped his eyes shut and clamped his hands over his ears. "Please make it stop! Make it stop!" he screamed.

Everything spiraled around him. He felt himself falling through darkness towards a cavernous pit of red fog. He reached out his hands towards the darkness, begging someone to help him.

A hand reached back. It was not the skeletal hand of his evil, but a strong and stable hand.

A whisper sounded in his ear. "I will end your pain. Accept, and you will feel no more."

He glanced at the ravenous red fog below. "Forgive me, brother."

Salvarias latched hold of the offered hand.

Idolar patrolled the city wall, miserable in his wet armor and cold to the bone. Through the thundering downpour, he heard a noise echo from the woods and paused to listen. In the distance, smoke battled the frigid rain. The Falar forest was as dangerous as the sordid streets at night, and he had no doubt that a mage burned in the wilderness.

By the time he'd gathered a small force of guards, a wagon for the body, and ventured out of the gray city, the rain had stopped. The respite was short-lived, and when they entered the forest a new storm formed within three breaths.

Fresh spring growth thickened the woods and ferns littered the forest floor. It took several men to navigate and help push the wagon through muddy puddles. He paused when the ground trembled and an ear-shattering roll of thunder filled the early morning sky. Then the ground shook again. The vibration knocked men off their feet, and the horses reared, nickering in protest. The next quake seemed to shake the world. Then, as quick as it came, the rain stopped, the ground stilled, and the sky quieted. He pushed forward, shaking his head when a ray of sunlight reflected off his armor. The odd storms that had plagued Falar for the last eight years continued to intrigue him. No other city experienced such weather, and he secretly joked that Falar was cursed.

He entered a clearing and gagged at the scene. The grass and trees were wilted, and the ground was littered with dead insects, vermin, and birds. The cold air lacked the vibrancy of life and was stagnant and thick, tangible in a hazy fog that clung to the ground and drifted towards the treetops.

Tobin lay in bloody mud. Idolar looked away, swallowing his sorrow, removed his soaked cloak, and covered his friend.

Idolar moved to the burned corpse, kicking dead animals out of his path and crunching insects under his boots. He fought to control his stomach at the sight of organs and charred, melted skin mushy from the rains. Slate-blue robes lay in a pile, and Idolar knew the body to be Ashra. He didn't venture to guess what else had happened to the poor woman.

"Over here," Samanson called.

Propped against a dead tree was Wilhelm with his curled up brother. Idolar couldn't suppress the chill that ran up his spine at seeing the black eyes. Normally intent and unsettling, the boy intimidated Idolar a great deal, those eyes seeming older and more intelligent than a ten-year-old child's. Now they lacked life and reflected a vacant shell. The boy seemed to be in some sort of shock; numb, lifeless.

Idolar checked both boys for wounds. He found the cut and welt on Wilhelm's head and a few nicks on Salvarias's body along with a significant amount of missing skin on his wrists, as well as old bruises. After they tended to the boys, Idolar put a blanket around the youngest.

"Salvarias?" Idolar whispered.

The boy remained motionless, near frozen, eyes unblinking.

"Wrap up the bodies," Idolar commanded. "Get them out of sight and take down the stake, cover the evidence up. They don't need to see what happened here."

He waited until the dead were moved and Ashra's robes discarded.

"Wilhelm." He shook the boy by the shoulder. "Wilhelm."

Idolar motioned for a waterskin. After a guard handed him one, he splashed cold water on Wilhelm's face and slapped him lightly. He didn't stir.

Idolar called to a few of his men. "Take the bodies back. Leave me two horses. The rest of you, scour the woods. See if you can find the men who did this."

He waited near a half hour before he splashed cold water on Wilhelm and slapped him again.

Wilhelm moaned and his eyes fluttered.

"Come on, son." Idolar shook the boy again, slapping his face harder. "Wake up."

"Salv," Wilhelm mumbled.

"He's safe. He's next to you."

Wilhelm winced when touched the knot on his head. "What happened?" he asked, tightening his arm around Salvarias.

Idolar rested a hand on Wilhelm's shoulder. "I'm sorry, boy. Your parents are dead."

Wilhelm sat up and looked at Salvarias. "What happened to him?"

"I'm not sure. He was like that when we got here."

"It's all right, Salv. I'm here." Wilhelm lifted his brother's head. "Salv?"

Salvarias didn't focus or change expression.

Wilhelm shook the boy. "Salv?"

"Come, Wilhelm. Let's get you boys home." Idolar shuddered again at the soulless eyes. He helped Wilhelm stand and held him steady when the expected wave of dizziness occurred.

"What in Nevlar's vengeance!" Wilhelm cursed, seeing the dead forest.

"I'm not sure. I was hoping you could tell me."

"The last thing I remember is being hit by one of the people who attacked us." Wilhelm lifted Salvarias. "I want to see my parents."

"They've already been wrapped up and are being taken back to the city. Let's get you boys home so you can clean up." Idolar walked to the horses

"My mother... did they burn..." Wilhelm's voice choked off.

"They both died quickly," Idolar lied. There was no point in the boy knowing the truth.

Wilhelm glanced around. "Our pack? My father's sword? Salv's book?"

"Nothing remained. Whoever attacked you took all of it."

Wilhelm trembled when he mounted the horse. "Thank you for coming, Idolar."

With a nod, Idolar led the brothers from the clearing, impressed with Wilhelm's composure. But then again, Wilhelm's maturity didn't match his youth; it never had. "I know this is hard, but we need to bury your mother and father. Is there any place special, or would you prefer the main cemetery?"

Wilhelm raised his gaze towards the sky. "Serinity. We all loved the city, and there's a tree that overlooks the ocean outside the city walls. We had a picnic there once. Can we borrow a wagon? We'll take them ourselves."

"Yes, but I'll go with you. Tobin was a good friend, and I consider you a friend as well."

Idolar looked away when he saw tears streaming down Wilhelm's face.

God screamed in frustration, pacing the torchlit dungeon. "I almossst had him! Did you feel the ssshift?"

Unupture nodded. "I did. A minor delay, my Dark Master."

"I grow tired of your patienccce! We were ssso clossse! The entire world trembled!"

"We'll be successful, my Lord. He's merely ten, and already he almost turned."

"What ssstopped him?"

"That is a mystery." Unupture smoothed the front of his purple robes. "We're ready for another birthing. Would you like to stay?"

"Of courssse!"

A black-armored soldier dragged a young erthla woman in by the hair and chained her to the mossy colored stone wall. She was beautiful; light red hair framed her freckled face and at one point her body had been lithe. She'd been beaten and given to any soldier who'd have her. Unupture remained surprised to see how many men had raped her even though a creation of evil grew in her womb. Men disgusted him.

"There, there," he tried to console the sobbing woman. "It will end soon."

"No! Please no!" she cried.

God brushed her hair from her face. "What isss your name, my child?"

"Fressa. Please, don't kill me. I have a daughter. She needs me. Please!"

God smiled, but his words betrayed the insincerity of his sympathetic eyes and consoling tone. "I want you to dessscribe every feeling you have during your ordeal, Fressa."

Unupture shuddered. To feed off torment caused his stomach to turn. Unupture's soul wasn't as far gone as his master's. Unupture's pleasure came from his children, what he created in the stronghold. Not the suffering of the mothers.

He grimaced while he sliced open her distended belly and peeled back her skin. Seeing his little creature erupted his joy. He cooed at his new creation, urging it to emerge.

The woman's scream bounced off the stone walls when tiny teeth chewed through her flesh. He could see the perverted pleasure his master received from her pain. It took away from Unupture's moment of happiness. To witness a soul so lost turned one's blood cold.

He held up a cup to catch the woman's tears for his master while the creation ate its way into existence. "We have time, my Lord. As I've said before, if our attempts with the boy fail, we'll still overrun Arden. Our raiding parties continue to bring new women for breeding and healthy men for mining."

God's crazed smile turned to the woman. "You're not telling me, young lady. I want to know how much pain you're in, mother of darknessss."

"Kill me!" Fressa screamed

"All in due time. Tell me of your pain. I want to know how it feelsss."

Unupture passed the cup of her tears to his master. God drank while listening to the woman plead for death. A pang of pity for God nearly brought tears to Unupture's eyes. No being would be so cruel unless they'd been cursed to feed off the living; forced to survive off the souls of others. Unupture prayed to any god who might listen to spare him from such a horrible fate.

Chapter 8
Spring 1010 a.r.

Wilhelm climbed the stairs to his home, waving goodbye to Idolar, numb with grief but having closure at the burial of his parents. Once inside, he undressed, then undressed Salvarias and led him to bed. Wilhelm slipped the small pouch of lavender under his brother's pillow, shoved their beds together, and crawled under the covers.

Fourteen long days had passed since their parents' murders. Wilhelm had contemplated staying in the city of Serinity, but doubted he'd be able to provide for them both. He was exhausted from mulling over his options for employment, how he'd care for his brother, and where they'd live.

Eventually, Wilhelm's thoughts carried him into a fitful sleep. He tossed all night, and when the first rays of sun could be seen through his window, he turned his gaze to his brother. Salvarias lay with the same vacant expression that had been there since the forest and all through the trip to bury their parents. He'd yet to even sleep.

Wilhelm dressed and then gathered up Salvarias's mage robes and dressed him. Breakfast was made in silence, and Wilhelm desperately missing his brother's whispered numbers. He fed Salvarias, but, after a few bites, he no longer accepted food.

"We can't afford to stay here," Wilhelm said, settling into his own chair. "We have no family except for Mafarias, but I don't know how to find him. Idolar said I'm too young to be a guard. So we'll have to sell everything we can and pack what we can carry. We'll get odd jobs in exchange for food, and use the money we get from selling stuff only if we have to. We'll have to live on the streets. It'll be dangerous, but I'll take care of you, I promise. All right?"

Salvarias didn't move.

Sighing, Wilhelm finished his meal in silence.

Jyfil's voice and a knock came after Wilhelm's last bite. "Wilhelm?"

He opened the door and invited the old man in.

Jyfil's eyes glistened with tears. "I'm so sorry about your mother and Tobin. She was an amazing woman."

"Thank you, Gentleman Jyfil."

Jyfil glanced at Salvarias and frowned. "Is the boy all right?"

"He hasn't talked since it happened."

Jyfil offered a smile. "Don't fret, he'll come around. What will you boys do now? You know I'd allow you to stay if I could, but I need the rent money to survive. Times are difficult."

"I understand. No need to apologize. We'll be fine."

Jyfil fidgeted with his apron. "Well, come by if you're in dire straits, and I can give you some bread."

"Thank you, Gentleman. We'll be out shortly."

"No need to rush. I'll call upon the guard to pick up Tobin's uniform. Good luck." Jyfil shook hands and left.

Wilhelm rummaged through their house, making two packs of blankets, food, a spell book, spell components, a dagger, and their clothes. In a third pack, he added their mother's clothes and as many books as he could carry.

Kneeling in front of Salvarias, Wilhelm stared into the vacant, dull eyes. "Come on, Salv. Please talk to me."

Salvarias remained motionless, eyes lifeless.

"I miss you. Please talk to me."

The slight rise of Salvarias's thin chest was the sole sign of life. Sighing, Wilhelm put the lightest pack on Salvarias and gathered the other two. After one last long look at their home, Wilhelm shut the door and left his old life behind.

The spring market was busy. People hastened from store to store, and entertainers lined the narrow streets, filling the air with music and stories. Cavruls argued about which tavern had the strongest watythm ale, a few winsires browsed through clothing stores, and the occasional well-behaved minotaur wandered the streets. A group of mercenaries that included a burgundy-robed mage took Wilhelm by surprise, since mages were rarely accepted by non-mages. Upon seeing Salvarias, the mage nodded and smiled, a look of bewilderment on his face.

Salvarias did not return the gesture.

A shop filled with roasted and dried meats caught Wilhelm's eye, but he continued without stopping, trying to ignore the scrumptious aromas. He kept his cloak over both of them in hopes of avoiding nasty calls from people roving the market.

At the clothing store, the owner, a slender woman with tousled hair, offered one new article of clothing for each brother every year for five years in exchange for his parents' clothing. Wilhelm, ensuring it would include mage robes, signed the agreement, flirting with the woman and promising to visit her again soon. At the next shop, the bookstore owner paid ten silvers for their mother's book collection.

Overall, Wilhelm hadn't gotten nearly enough money. He'd have to be frugal, and only use it if absolutely necessary. He might even have to go a day without food. His stomach rumbled a protest.

He led the way to the docks where he found a quiet spot in the sun to eat their apples. He commented on every patched-up sailor who walked past them, trying to coax a word from his brother. After hours of fruitless effort, Wilhelm gave up and watched ships come and go throughout the remainder of the day in silence, deep in his own thoughts.

When the sky lit with hues of pink, he left the docks and chose an alleyway next to the library. They ate the rest of their food from home, and wrapped up in blankets to fight the spring chill. He cried himself to sleep, staring at the empty eyes of his brother.

The first night was difficult and Wilhelm woke cramped, stiff, and cold. He packed their blankets and headed to the busy streets.

In a city the size of Falar, if one didn't possess skill in a trade, options for employment were limited. Wilhelm's skill set revolved exclusively around fighting, and since Idolar had declined Wilhelm's plea to join the guard early, few options existed. Most found that servitude fed their families, but he doubted his ability to keep close to his brother in a large estate. Furthermore, servitude was not high on Wilhelm's list. The slaughterhouse provided another area one could work with skills easily taught. Over the years, he'd begged his mother to avoid the route near the butcher shop to eliminate the tears that welled in his brother's eyes each time they passed, so that choice was discarded. Taverns were Wilhelm's best bet. He could remain close to Salvarias, and washing dishes, cooking, and cleaning tables would earn their meals. Set on a plan, Wilhelm made his way through the maze of alleys and streets until he came to the Lucky Steed.

Inside, the smell wafting in the air was thick with ale, piss, and vomit. Fighting his stomach, he pushed through the crowd towards the bar, finding the owner, a rotund man with a red nose and cheeks. His eyes were watery, and his brow seemed to have a permanent furrow.

"Excuse me!" Wilhelm called.

"No mages!" roared the man. "Get out!"

"We need food. Can we wash dishes for some breakfast?"

The owner motioned to another man. Before Wilhelm could react, hands grabbed hold of him and another man snatched up Salvarias and escorted them out of the tavern, tossing them in the street. Wilhelm scrambled to help Salvarias, but his breathing was shallow and even. He hadn't even trembled from the man's touch.

Before the owner slammed the door shut, he yelled, "Stay out of my tavern!"

Wilhelm helped his brother up, pondering why the man's touch hadn't caused Salvarias any pain.

Fighting hunger, he wandered to the next two taverns, which ended in the same result. He prayed by Zerana's grace that the owner of the last tavern wasn't prejudiced against mages.

A man shoved off from a wall to walk towards them, his lip curled in a sneer. "Where you off to, mage?"

Wilhelm cursed himself when he saw a sliver of his brother's robes visible. "Leave him be!" he ordered.

The man looked mildly surprised, and he motioned a group of his friends back.

Wilhelm was unprepared for the immediate punch. Spinning from the blow, he fell to his hands and knees, dazed. Shaking his head, he turned to see the man holding Salvarias by the arms.

"What's wrong with you, boy?" The man spat in Salvarias's face.

Rage consumed Wilhelm and his vision tinged red. He rammed his fist into the man's side with such force a rib surely gave way. The man dropped Salvarias and doubled over only to find his chin meeting Wilhelm's knee with enough momentum to break a jaw. The man staggered back. Indeed, Wilhelm had succeeded. The man's lower jaw hung off-center.

Wilhelm's fury had yet to be spent, so he took the opportunity for one last punch across the man's cheek before grabbing Salvarias and running down the street. They zigzagged in and out of alleys until Wilhelm felt he had lost any of the man's friends who might seek revenge. He realized he was grinning.

He pulled a handkerchief out of his pocket and wiped the man's spit off his brother's face, gently pushing him to sit so Salvarias's breathing could steady.

"You all right?" After an expected lack of response, Wilhelm waited for Salvarias's breathing to even out before continuing onward.

The last tavern was the Red Lion located in a quiet part of town. The tavern was two stories tall with a garden near the front stairs. A well-maintained red sign depicting a lion drinking ale with a sheep creaked above the door. Upon entering, Wilhelm smelled the faint odor of ale, but the clean tavern lacked the other, less pleasant aromas of the Lucky Steed. Smells of food from the kitchen made his stomach roar in approval. He glanced down with a grin, but it faded when he looked into blank eyes.

Eight patrons occupied the large common room. Four men, merchants by the looks of their clothes and conversation, sat together eating a delicious looking breakfast of cooked oats and salted pork. At another table, three uniformed guards reminded him of his father and caused a pang of sorrow. The last man sat by himself in the far corner table, a knight in armor, maybe in his mid-thirties, muscular with sharp features. A short, trimmed beard was the same mousy brown color as his neatly cut hair.

"What do you want?" the plump tavern owner yelled.

Wilhelm's words tumbled out. "My brother and I would like to help you in return for a meal."

"I don't need any help! Get out!" He bumped Wilhelm back with a bulbous belly.

Wilhelm clenched his jaw. He refused to dip into their small funds. He *would* get a job and provide for his brother. Wilhelm planted his feet and glared off with the owner.

Humar stared at his half-eaten bowl of oats. He'd traveled far from Sundil, and though exhausted, looked forward to catching up with old friends. Over nine years had passed since he last visited Falar; the longest period of time spent apart from his friends and adopted brother.

Before Humar undertook his self-assigned mission to investigate the reason for the growing number of vicious creatures plaguing Dalnar, he'd spend time reconnecting with Tobin. Since their father's funeral, much had happened. Tobin had married and taken in two boys as if they were his own. Tobin's pride rang clear in his letters, and Humar found himself excited to meet his nephews, especially Wilhelm, who Tobin praised for possessing a natural ability with a weapon.

But the grouchy cavrul blacksmith was first on the list. Durak made magnificent armor, and Humar's was in dire need of repair. After Durak, Humar would spend most of the day and possibly the remainder of the week with Tobin before leaving the city.

Humar fished out coins for his breakfast as two boys entered the tavern. Pale and tired, the two were asking to work for a meal. Pity caused Humar to intercept the owner.

He rested a hand on the stout man's arm. "Easy, Mulard. I'll pay for their breakfast."

The older boy shook his head. "Thank you, Sir Knight, but we want to work for our food."

Humar pursed his lips. Then he smiled. "Come to the inn tonight and you can polish my sword and armor. I'll pay for your breakfast and dinner in exchange."

The boy accepted after a glance at his younger brother.

With a nod, Humar returned to his table after passing coins to Mulard, watching the boys. The owner muttered curses as he went to the kitchen and emerged moments later with breakfast.

The older boy ate with fervor, packs probably containing their every possession sitting next to them. The younger boy didn't eat until the older fed him the fruit and cheese. Noticing the mage clothes, Humar pondered if the child understood his actions. No person dare wear the robes except if approved by the Association, and clearly, this boy was too young. The other boy wore black trews and a white belted tunic, which was stained from sleeping in the streets, and he cast a crooked grin to Mulard often, quite the contrast to his seemingly lifeless younger brother. Though the large boy's clothes were spotted, he kept himself in impeccable condition. His light brown hair was cut in the latest fashion and longer than Humar's. A well-trimmed stubble beard enhanced the young man's strong jaw and square handsome features. Muscles were evident on the young man, and Humar admitted jealousy of the boy's physique. He would've been thought a full-grown man if there hadn't been the innocent sparkle of youth in his eyes.

After their meal, the boy thanked Humar and left the inn. He left shortly afterwards, setting out to find his friends.

Humar plopped into the chair in his room. His unsuccessful outing had soured his mood. Durak's door had sported a sign stating, "I'm closed," and Tobin wasn't home, nor was the baker. Humar had given up and decided to try Tobin again tomorrow before hunting down Idolar for help.

A loud knock on the door caused him to jump.

He opened the door and motioned the boys inside. "Come in. Please, make yourselves comfortable."

His room contained a bed in one corner, a chair on one side of the fire, and a small, four-person table on the other. The older boy dropped the two packs next to the table and situated his brother in a chair close to the fire.

Humar sat at the table and studied the boys. The older one, now with closer inspection, was indeed a strapping young man. His eyes sparkled with an alluring innocence, yet possessed the glimmer of a sharp mind. The small boy appeared dead. If Humar hadn't seen the boy's thin chest rise and fall, he would've thought the boy was a walking corpse. His eyes were flat, but what most chilled Humar's bones was the size of the black irises. No white could be seen; just blackness that had no end. He swore he could be sucked into the vacancy of that stare. He shook off the sensation. "We'll eat first and then you can polish my armor. So, what are your names?"

Before they could answer, there was a knock and Mulard entered with three bowls of rabbit stew.

Humar remembered what the youngest had been fed at breakfast, and he turned to the boy. "You don't eat meat, do you?"

"No, he doesn't," the older one responded.

"Thank you, Mulard. Could we also get some vegetable stew, fruit, cheese, and bread?"

"Certainly." The tavern owner left to fetch the extra food.

Between massive bites, the older boy said, "I'm Wilhelm Laybryth and this is my brother, Salvarias."

Humar stopped eating. "Are you sons of Ashra Laybryth?"

"Yes, we are. Well, we *were*. Our mother is dead."

He sprang to his feet. "What! How did it happen? And what of Tobin?"

Wilhelm's expression darkened. "I'm sorry to tell you, but Tobin is dead as well. It was two weeks ago. We were on our way back from the woods and eleven men attacked us. The guards haven't found the murderers." He glanced at Salvarias, who hadn't raised his head since they entered.

Humar sank back to his chair. He cleared his throat to fight down the lump. "I'm sorry, boys. Tobin wrote of you often. He was a great man, and told me your mother was an exceptional woman."

"How do you know Tobin?"

"Tobin and I grew up as brothers. Where are you living? Who's taking care of you?"

Wilhelm shrugged. "We move around the city and take care of ourselves. Are you Humar?"

"Yes." Memories of Tobin's gentle face surfaced. Humar turned his gaze to the bowl of stew.

"Pleasure to meet you. He talked of you." Wilhelm paused in his ravenous feeding to grin. "Said you gave him a run for his money with a sword."

Humar smiled ruefully. "So I did."

Wilhelm wolfed down the last three bites and tilted his head towards Humar's armor and sword. "That's an exceptional sword you have."

"Feel free." Humar glanced at the young mage. "Your mother was an accomplished witch. Tobin informed me that you were already practiced in the art."

Wilhelm lifted the sword; handling the weapon with the trained respect Humar had taught Tobin. "He's the youngest mage in history." Wilhelm beamed with pride.

The boy continued to stare at the table.

"I have nothing against mages, Salvarias. I have a friend who's a mage. Incredible power... he's saved my life more times than I care to count."

Wilhelm returned to the table. "He hasn't spoken since..."

Humar nodded, thinking the boy must be suffering from some kind of shock.

Mulard entered after a brief knock, served the additional food, and left with a small bow. Wilhelm fed his brother and then eyed the third bowl of stew. Amused, Humar stretched and stated he was too full to eat anymore. Wilhelm devoured any food that remained.

Humar turned his attention to the mage. Tobin had spoken highly of the youngest, of his intelligence, observation, and serious demeanor. Surely this wasn't the same boy.

Wilhelm rose and began polishing Humar's armor. "Where do you hail from, Sir Humar?"

"Just Humar. I come from across the sea, from Warton on the continent of Loutsil."

"Loutsil? I think Father might've mentioned it."

"Loutsil isn't a friendly place. I haven't been home for over nineteen years." Watching the boys, Humar felt a desire to help them. Tobin had spoken of them as his own sons and of Ashra as a wonderful woman. The least Humar could do was help. With no home of his own and no way of taking care of the boys, his mind drifted through his connections. He smiled to himself. "I might be able to find some work for you boys. Are you familiar with the smithy in the market run by Durak?"

"The cavrul who curses often? I've met him a couple of times."

"Well, he's getting old, though don't tell him I said so, and could use some help around the shop. You're, what, sixteen now?"

"I am."

Humar paused. The boy was too young. Erthlas didn't leave home and find work until they were eighteen, most waited until they were twenty. But without parents or a home, the brothers had little choice. The last years of their childhood were now lost. Humar squared his shoulders and nodded. "Old enough. I'll talk to him tomorrow if that's all right with you."

"Thank you. We appreciate your help." Wilhelm's eyes showed his relief, and the young man's smile couldn't have been bigger.

The market woke to a breezy spring morning wafting smells of fresh-baked bread and meats through the crisp air. Humar smiled to himself when he heard Wilhelm's stomach roar. The boy surely had an appetite, but wouldn't accept charity for breakfast. Though Wilhelm had agreed to stay in Humar's room on the floor, the boy had insisted on paying a couple of coppers.

The smithy flaunted a vast forge in the center of the open shop, enclosed by three-foot stone walls. A shelf displaying expertly crafted swords and armor wrapped around the front and a shelf in the back held additional merchandise. A single door led to the blacksmith's living quarters and storage area in the rear.

Humar smiled when he saw the old cavrul pounding away at the forge. Sweat trickled down his face wrinkled by frowns, not age, even though he was one hundred and eighty. His black, curly beard was tossed over his shoulder to prevent it from catching fire, although Humar mused the man's bushy eyebrows could use protection as well. Cavrul armor and swords were prized among all races, and Durak had done exceptionally well for himself due to his exquisite craftsmanship. In actuality, Humar had seen first hand the cavrul's enormous stash of money. Durak could have afforded to buy a town, but kept his living simple, saving his money for something he'd never disclosed to Humar.

"Humar!" Durak called, frown lines lifting. "What ye be doing around these parts, you numb-brained fool?" Noticing the boys, he frowned again. "Wilhelm."

"Hello, Gentleman Durak," Wilhelm responded.

Durak shook his head. "Sorry about your mother and Tobin."

"Thank you."

Humar grinned. "I've missed you, Durak. Ran into the boys yesterday and they're looking for work. I was thinking you could use help around the shop in exchange for food and a place to sleep. What do you say?"

Wilhelm had been eyeing the smithy with a raised eyebrow. "Just food and a place to bathe, Gentleman, no lodging is needed."

Humar winked at Durak's quizzical smile. Both knew he required no help in maintaining his shop and, by Wilhelm's expression, he knew as well.

Durak said, "I could use some help to keep the goods polished and the place clean." He studied both boys then turned to Humar. "I'll have 'em work here as long as they want. Wilhelm, look at those swords on the shelf and polish any ye see to be dull. Salvarias, go do the same on the back shelf. Set your packs inside my door for safe keeping." Durak paused and eyed Salvarias. "Did ye hear me, boy?"

"He hasn't talked since our parents died," Wilhelm said. He guided Salvarias forward, but stopped shy of the door. Wilhelm turned around, lopsided grin spread across his face. "Mind if we eat first? I'm starving!"

Durak grunted. "Of course. Go in the kitchen and fix what you want. Don't wander around in there. Eat and get back out here."

Humar shook his head. Tobin had been right; the boy would have his pick of young women. "You're doing a good deed, my friend," Humar said after Wilhelm had disappeared inside the home.

"Nonsense! The boys will be worked hard. I'm not sure they'll be seein' this as a good arrangement." Durak's face grew serious. "Where have ye been for the last damn nine years? Tobin was growing worried."

"I got involved with a noble in Blarrup. Occupied more time than I intended."

"Why don't ye settle down?"

Humar shook his head. "I'm not ready. There's something going on. The world is changing. There are rumors of new creatures. Crutar's said to be involved, though I doubt that one. The god is too drunk to leave the southern tip of Dalnar. I was going to spend the next year traveling, but I'll stay close and look at areas around here." He kicked a rock. "I feel it. Something big is about to happen."

"Humph. You're paranoid."

He sighed. "I didn't get any details about what happened from the boys. Do you know anything about the men who did this?"

"No, they never caught them. Wilhelm killed one of them, Tobin two, but the remainder got away."

"What exactly happened to Tobin and Ashra?"

"They were ambushed in the woods, killed quickly, and the boys were left tied to a tree."

"You lie poorly."

Durak eyed Humar for a moment and then cursed, but recited the details Idolar had supplied. At the end of the story, Durak shook his head and clapped Humar's shoulder. "I'm sorry about Tobin."

Humar sat on the stone wall, distrusting his knees to support his weight.

Durak uttered an oath. "He should never have married the mage. He put himself in extreme danger."

Humar heaved a deep sigh. He needed to tell Durak about Salvarias before the boy was caught doing magic in the smithy and the old cavrul suffered a heart lapse. "The boy is already practiced in the art. Tobin wrote me saying he's the youngest known." Seeing Durak's eyes darken, Humar quickly continued. "I know you don't trust magic users, but this is just a boy. They've both been through an ordeal and could use some help, some guidance. I don't know what else to do with them."

Durak stroked his long beard and winked. "All right. Ye owe me though, ye dolt of a knight."

Chapter 9
Spring 1011 a.r.

Wilhelm reined in his horse at the edge of the tree line to take in the wondrous sight of Serinity. Towering redwoods wreathed an expansive meadow larger than the city of Falar. Farmlands marred the meadow, but didn't intrude on the entire field, allowing the remainder to be untainted by humans. At the end of the farmlands, the city scaled a climbing cliff that dropped off dramatically to the thundering ocean below. Homes hugged the very edge and looked like miniature castles made of the light gray rock native to the city. Opposite from the sea were towering alps whose snowcapped peaks sparkled year-round, and clouds rarely let the full magnificence of those soaring mountains be visible. But today they shone like a beacon in the sky.

Wilhelm breathed in the brininess of the sea and the crisp aroma of spring flowers and new life. He smiled at Humar.

The knight winked. "My favorite."

Wilhelm nodded. His gaze fell to the lone tree clinging to the cliff ledge between the tree line and the farmlands. His sorrow over the loss of his parents had abated over the past year, but now it surged to full strength. He missed his parents, but more so, he missed Salvarias. Through all the change and challenges Wilhelm had faced since his parents' murders, what fueled his misery was his brother's lifeless presence. He lived the past year without Salvarias's conversation, without hearing his whispered numbers, and most of all, without seeing the sparkle that had lit his large, black eyes. Now Wilhelm stared into vacant orbs and lamented that the once lulling and soft voice was silent. He felt alone.

"You all right?" Humar asked.

Wilhelm startled from his melancholy. "Yes." He bent around to look into his brother's dull eyes. "Do you see where we are, Salv?"

Salvarias didn't move.

Humar nudged his horse. "Let's go down a little further. We'll tether the horses, and I can give you some time alone."

Wilhelm nodded and held tightly to his brother. "Thank you again, Humar. I appreciate you allowing us to tag along."

"Nonsense. I try to get out here once a month and check for any new rumors. Are you sure you don't want to stay in the city?"

Wilhelm looked longingly at Serinity ascending the hill and shook his head. "I'm trying to save as much as I can. I don't want to live in the streets forever. I need to be able to afford a place for us to live that's safe, and if Salv never gets better, I need to pay someone I trust to care for him while I'm at the smithy."

Humar scratched his short beard. "Large concern for a seventeen-year-old boy."

"I don't feel seventeen. I feel old."

"You've grown up in the last year."

"Not much of a choice," Wilhelm muttered.

"True, but you're doing well and taking good care of your brother. Tobin would've been proud."

"Thanks." He dismounted and lifted his brother from the saddle. "I hope so."

"I've never met a young man your age who was an apprentice. You're making more money than most men who just left home."

Wilhelm shrugged. "Durak pays me too much. We both know that. He's too generous."

"You're a hard worker. You earn it."

Wilhelm let the conversation die out. Both Humar and Durak had taken Wilhelm under their wing. Durak never needed help in the smithy, and if it hadn't been for Salvarias, Wilhelm would've turned down the offer. He didn't want to accept charity. But his brother needed food, warm clothes, blankets, and a place to bathe. Durak offered all. Humar was never gone more than a few weeks, and based on what Tobin had told Wilhelm, Humar wasn't the kind of man to remain in one place for long. The knight had taken up the torch of Tobin in the way an uncle might. More so than Wilhelm's own uncle, who had yet to be seen.

Humar tethered the horses, and Wilhelm respectfully stayed behind to allow the knight time alone at the grave. He looked away when Humar's shoulders shook with sobs. Though the knight was composed, never showing a temper or sadness, the death of a brother must be difficult. The mere thought knocked the breath out of Wilhelm. He lifted Salvarias and cradled him.

Humar didn't stay long at the grave, and when he returned his bright blue eyes were dry. "I'll be back by sunset. You'll be fine by yourselves?"

"Yes, thank you. I'm sorry, Humar."

"Me too." Humar patted Wilhelm's shoulder before continuing towards the city on foot.

Wilhelm wandered down the hill and realized it was his Birth Day. He shook his head, pondering where the past year of his life had gone.

He raised his face to the sun veiled behind a parchment-thin layer of clouds strolling in from the ocean. "If there is any god—*any* god—listening, please give me my brother back. It's all I want, and I'll never ask for anything again."

The tree's branches spread over the gravesite as if to protect it. Green budding leaves glistened in the filtered sunlight. Clover blanketed the ground speckled with tiny white flowers that cascaded over the dramatic cliff drop. The blue-gray ocean pounded the rocks below and added a musical lull to mid-morning bird songs. Wilhelm had carved the names of his parents into the dark wood, and the white letters still gleamed fresh as if the tree would never heal from its mutilation.

He lowered his brother and knelt in front of him. "Salv? Do you see where we are? Mother and Father's gravesite. They're dead and you're all I have. You need to talk to me. I can help you."

The black eyes remained vacant; no emotion, no reaction. Wilhelm no longer fought his tears. He sank to the ground, weeping for the loss of his parents, but more so for the loss of his brother.

Soft footfalls broke through Wilhelm's grief. A little girl close to his brother's age, with raven hair and piercing blue eyes, stopped shy of the tree.

She looked up at Wilhelm, tears streaking her cheeks. "I'm sorry for your loss."

He moved in front of his brother. "What do you want?"

The little girl threw her arms around Wilhelm's waist.

Startled by her affection, he unraveled her arms and knelt eye level. "Are you all right?"

She smiled and nodded, turning her gaze to Salvarias. "What's wrong with him?"

"Our parents died a year ago, and he's been like this since."

The little girl slipped around Wilhelm and cupped Salvarias's face in her hands. Once again, he didn't react to touch.

She kissed his cheek. "I'm sorry," she said, taking his hands in hers.

A gust of wind swept over the cliff edge and encased the two children. Leaves swirled up from the ground. The current increased speed until it created a cyclone of debris circling the girl and Salvarias. The temperature dropped so far that Wilhelm could see his breath snatched away by the whirlwind. He shielded his eyes and planted his feet to keep from being sucked into the vortex. The girl's hair whipped around, but the glimpse he caught of her expression was one of sheer curiosity, as if she was unaware of what surrounded her. Then, in a blink of an eye, the tornado of air ceased. The suspended leaves drifted to the soft clover. The little girl's breathing was quick and her eyes wide.

Wilhelm rushed to her side. "Are you all right?"

When she spoke, her blue eyes never left Salvarias. "He's so scared."

"I can help him! He just has to talk to me!"

She rested her thumb on Salvarias's forehead. "Come from the darkness."

White light sparked from her thumb, flickered along his brother's forehead, and flared once before disappearing. The girl kissed his cheek. She turned a smile to Wilhelm, but it faded. Her eyes grew wide and she covered her mouth with a shaking hand to muffle a sob. Before he could ask her what was wrong, she whirled around and fled back up the hill and out of sight.

He turned to his brother. Salvarias's eyes were switching from vacant to unfocused. He lurched, grabbed his head, fell to his knees, and screamed.

Wilhelm dropped in front of his brother. "What is it?"

Salvarias burst into frenzied sobs. He screamed again, doubling over, breathing harsh and irregular.

"Tell me and I can help!" Wilhelm begged.

He reached for his brother, but Salvarias cringed away, weeping louder. Another scream filled the air and his breathing increased, his body shaking violently.

"What can I do?"

Within a breath, freezing rain pelted down from muted green

clouds that cast a sickening shade to Salvarias's skin. Gusts of wind whistled over the cliff, flattening the grasses and leaning the first layer of trees into the second. The sky churned and heaved with thunder and lightning.

Salvarias screamed again and his head jerked up to stare at the tree. Sheer terror and grief passed through his black eyes. He bolted. Unprepared, Wilhelm stumbled to his feet, seeing his brother tripping, half crawling half running, battling the gale towards the edge of the soaring cliff. Wilhelm was sure his heart stopped as he took up chase. When Salvarias was three steps from death, Wilhelm leapt and grabbed hold of his brother's mage robes, pulling him to safety and cradled him.

"Salv, it's me," Wilhelm said. "You're all right."

Salvarias leaned away and became ill. He continued to dry heave until he switched to babbling incoherent sentences while his gaze darted around. Suddenly, the clover began to wilt and the ground grew cold. Insects sprouted from the earth, dying within a breath.

Salvarias's eyes widened. "No."

Wilhelm gaped at the dying clover. "What's happening?"

"No!" Salvarias shrieked, covering his ears and snapping his eyes shut. "Make it stop! Make it stop!"

Wilhelm stared helplessly at the spreading death.

"Please make it stop!" Salvarias screamed again.

The wind increased, screeching through the forest. Ocean waves thrashed the cliff, and lightning snapped in the darkening sky. The ground continued to die, the clover wilting to a sick yellow, and the small white flowers shriveled into nothing. Worms crawled from the dirt, most in the throes of death before fully emerging.

Death spread in a perfect circle around Wilhelm and his brother.

Prying Salvarias's hands away from his ears, Wilhelm used a calm and assuring tone. "I would never let anything happen to you. You're safe. Nothing can hurt you."

"Make it stop! Please!" Salvarias balled his fists in his hair, doubling over in Wilhelm's arms.

A sparrow plummeted to the ground a few feet from the brothers, sinking into the muddy soil. The bird's eyes were frozen open in a look of terror. Salvarias crawled to the dead animal and scooped it up.

"Please come back." Salvarias stroked the bird's head. "I am sorry. Please. I did not mean... Please!"

Wilhelm snatched his brother before the wind carried him away. "Salv, I promise you're all right." Gingerly, he removed the dead bird from Salvarias's hands.

"Please help me!"

"Nothing will hurt you. I'm here. Look at me, Salv. I'm right here." Wilhelm shook his brother. "Look at me."

Salvarias's gaze finally focused and utter grief flashed across his dark eyes. "Brother, help me! Help me!"

"I love you, Salv. You're all right. We're both all right."

Salvarias pulled himself close, embedding his fingers in Wilhelm's shoulder. "I did not mean to kill the animals, brother. I promise! I did not mean it!"

Wilhelm glanced at the dying ground, the dead insects, and the dead bird, and he remembered the dead animals surrounding him when he came to after his parents' murders.

He engulfed his brother in his arms. "I know, Salv. It wasn't your fault. You're all right."

Sobs racked Salvarias as he buried his face in Wilhelm's chest. The clover ceased dying, the wind left so suddenly Wilhelm nearly fell over, and the rain reduced to a light drizzle.

Bafflement replaced his fear. His little brother couldn't be the cause, yet there was no other explanation. The spectacle after their parents' death was identical to what surrounded Wilhelm now.

Unsure how else to comfort his brother, he offered the puzzle box. Salvarias snatched the device and rocked in Wilhelm's arms while moving the pieces at heightened speeds, speaking indecipherable words below a whisper.

Wilhelm carried Salvarias to the horses, changed him into dry robes, wrapped him in blankets, and cradled him close as Wilhelm reclined against a tree, under cover from the light drizzle.

At long last, Salvarias's sobs ceased, his whispers stopped, and he furled against Wilhelm. After allowing a good bit of time to pass, Wilhelm gently took the puzzle box from his brother's hands and lifted his head.

"You're all I have." Wilhelm brushed back his brother's hair. "You can't leave me here alone. I miss you, and I worry about you. Don't leave me again, please..." The growing lump in his throat cut off his words.

Salvarias flung his arms around Wilhelm's neck. "Forgive me, brother. I did not mean to hurt you."

Clinging to his brother, Wilhelm shut his eyes tightly. "I love you, Salv."

"I love you too, my dear brother." Salvarias inhaled a huge, steady breath.

The drizzle evaporated and the clouds vanished, revealing the bright sun caressing the horizon.

"Are you all right?" Wilhelm whispered.

Salvarias turned his gaze to the dead clover. Two wagon lengths had died in a perfect circle where the brothers had been. There was a heart-wrenching hopelessness in Salvarias's voice when he asked, "What is wrong with me?"

"Nothing, Salv. It wasn't you."

Wilhelm tapped his brother's chin and grinned. When the black eyes sparkled back, Wilhelm's grin grew childishly large.

As long as they were together, they could overcome anything.

Humar left Serinity near sundown; thankful the sudden storm had ceased. No fresh rumors existed in the peaceful city, and his feeling of impending doom continued to mass like a building hurricane. Time was running out, and he straddled the cusp of the old light and new darkness. Frustrated, he muttered curses and kicked rocks the entire distance to the grave, regretting his choice to camp outside the city. He felt like having an ale, maybe three.

His thoughts drifted to the brothers while he walked through a freshly plowed field, breathing in the earthiness of recently churned soil. Wilhelm's determination to strike through the young mage's wall was intense, and Humar wished him success. The vacant eyes exuded emptiness of the mind, and the body seemed soulless. The pain teeming in Wilhelm's gaze each time it fell on Salvarias could cause the most toughened soldier to sob. For the young man's sake, Humar sent a hopeless prayer to the godless sky.

When he crested the hill, the brothers sat together with their backs toward him. A translucent white sparrow floated around the gravesite, and clover had died in a perfect circle, just reaching the edge of the tree. A new voice, soft and hypnotic, floated through the cool breeze, and Humar paused.

"How long has it been?" the voice asked.

"A year exactly," Wilhelm responded.

"Joyful seventeenth Birth Day to you, my brother."

"Happy Birth Day to you too, Salv."

"You are not wearing Tobin's sword."

"They stole it along with the book Tobin gave you."

"I am sorry, my brother."

Wilhelm ruffled the mage's hair. "It wasn't your fault."

"Do we have a place to stay and money?" The younger brother drew his knees closer, snuggling next to Wilhelm.

"We're working at a smithy. You remember Durak? He's teaching me and pays me a silver a week. We live on the streets, and I can usually find a quiet place. It's not so bad. You'll get used to it."

"Tobin's brother visits often?"

"Yes, every couple of weeks. I really like Humar."

"Tobin said he is a knight from Loutsil, skilled and extensively trained with a sword. Is he teaching you additional techniques?"

"Yep, and he's even better than Father."

"Tobin spoke of him often."

"He didn't talk to me that much about him. When did he talk to you?"

"While you helped Mother with dinner or when you practiced with other guards. He loved him very much and wished he would visit. He was excited for us to meet him."

Humar cleared his throat.

In one fluid motion, Wilhelm leapt to his feet, drew his sword, and whirled to face Humar. Salvarias rose and whispered an all too familiar language.

Humar shifted a nervous glance to the mage. "Wilhelm."

Wilhelm sheathed his sword. "No, Salv. This is Humar."

The mage was deep in concentration with his eyes closed, and had already drawn his rune. Humar took a step back when a fist-sized ball of fire ignited in the air.

Wilhelm stepped in front of the mage. "No, it's Humar. It's all right."

"Rulose, Rulose"

The fireball shot over the cliff to land safely in the ocean, and the white sparrow faded from the air.

Wilhelm grinned. "This is my brother, Salvarias."

Humar smiled at the pride and love in the young man's voice. Holding Wilhelm's hand, the mage stood partly hidden behind his massive brother, and watched Humar with a serious, intense stare. The boy Tobin had written about was now evident. Intelligence and maturity beyond Salvarias's years glittered in the overly large eyes, a mind always thinking, always watching, and his grave stare pierced the soul, enrapturing his target. Humar couldn't avert his gaze, even as he felt naked and exposed. He shuddered.

"Should we make camp?" Wilhelm asked.

Salvarias's hold eased. Humar sucked in a huge breath, realizing he'd stopped breathing. He was sure his secrets and fears had been unearthed in that one stare. He felt exposed and his voice shook when he said, "Yes, let's get that set up."

Wilhelm helped clear an area for a fire while Salvarias scouted for dry timber.

Humar tore his gaze from the odd child and turned to Wilhelm. "How did you get him out of the trance?"

"A strange little girl visited us and she touched him. He came out of it and was in pain. After a while, it passed and then he was fine."

"What's with the dead clover? It wasn't like that earlier."

Wilhelm shrugged. "It's nothing; and don't bring it up."

Humar studied Salvarias with curiosity, recalling Durak's recount of a similar scene when Idolar had found the brothers.

A steel edge lined Wilhelm's voice when he said, "Leave him be, Humar."

Humar flinched.

"Don't ask him about it," Wilhelm insisted.

Humar nodded.

"And he counts aloud sometimes. He doesn't know he's doing it and don't say anything."

He nodded again. Salvarias returned to the campsite carrying a bundle of wood in his arms.

Humar patted the mage's shoulder. "Good job."

Firewood clattered to the ground. Salvarias balled his fist in his hair, his face hardened, and his eyes lost focus. Humar took hold to steady the trembling boy. Wilhelm plucked up the child and carried him to the fire pit, whispering. Salvarias nodded.

After ruffling the mage's hair, Wilhelm gathered up the dropped wood. When done, he turned a stern gaze to Humar. "Don't touch him. Ever."

Humar didn't mask the irritation in his voice. "I'm sorry." The boy needed a scroll to outline the ways not to upset him. It appeared his older brother was the only one with the instructions.

Wilhelm's shoulders dropped and he shook his head. "I'm sorry. There's things... look, when it comes to Salv, I'm a little protective. I don't want people touching him, and I don't want anyone to point out anything odd they might see."

Based on the evident uneasiness in Wilhelm's eyes, Humar chose not to continue with his questions. "All right. I won't mention anything I see to the boy. But I will question you."

Wilhelm raised his face to the starry sky. "I won't answer you, not when it comes to Salv."

Tobin's letters hadn't done justice to the protective nature of Wilhelm towards Salvarias. "I understand. For now, I'll let it lie."

A weight seemed to lift off Wilhelm's shoulders. "Thanks, Humar. Would you talk to Durak and get him to agree to the same when we return?"

"Sure."

Wilhelm winked and headed to the place they'd cleared for the fire. "Did you get your business done in the city?"

Humar nodded. "I did."

"Will you stay once we get back to Falar?" Wilhelm struck the flint twice before sparks ignited the tinder. "I've been practicing with some new guards, but they're not very skilled."

The eagerness in the young man's eyes portrayed his need to continue learning swordplay. Humar found gratification in teaching Wilhelm. He was one of those students anyone would want to instruct. "Sure, for another month. I'll ask Durak if I can stay in his extra room."

"I'd appreciate it. The guards haven't been giving me many challenges. It's been over three seasons since any have beaten me." Wilhelm winked at Salvarias.

Humar laughed. "I don't doubt it."

Wilhelm's infectious grin lightened the mood. The young man sat close to his brother while the three ate their meal. Salvarias hadn't spoken to Humar and the boy's head remained lowered, his body trembling. Though the haunting black eyes no longer bored into Humar, his feeling of exposure was still strong, and he maintained a cautious distance. He almost laughed aloud when he realized he was afraid of a tiny eleven-year-old child.

True to Wilhelm's warning, the boy whispered numbers constantly. As Humar listened, the numbers appeared random at first, but the longer he observed he noticed that the boy counted multiple objects at once. Curious, Humar glanced around the woods, attempting to count trees and the rocks surrounding the fire. He didn't get far before he lost count. Even through his uneasiness in the boy's presence, Humar admitted admiration for a mind that could perform such a feat.

When they settled in for the night, the first signs of terror from Salvarias became evident. His breathing switched to quick gasps while his gaze darted around the edge of the woods. Humar wondered if the boy had witnessed the events that occurred during his parents' murders.

Walking corpses littered the landscape. Salvarias stood under the sole enormous tree, staring at rolling hills, light pink and orange from the setting sun. Tall, wheat-colored grasses swayed in the breeze as far as the eye could see.

He sighed before wandering among the dead as he did each night. This dream was restful and pleasant compared to the others, and he always welcomed the respite. He avoided the stares of the dead people, their outstretched hands, their wounds streaming blood, and their moans of pain. No birds sang to distract him from the sounds, and darkness never came to block out the deads' stares.

"Hello."

He turned to see a girl with raven hair standing next to him, around his age but taller. Her body was not sliced apart, her eyes were not vacant, and blood did not pool at her feet. At first, terror crept up, but then she smiled such a sweet smile that it evoked a calming comfort that washed away his fears.

He glanced around, but saw nothing out of the ordinary except her. He turned back to the girl and said, "Hello."

She surveyed the plain of dead. "What are you doing?"

"Walking."

"May I join you?"

"Of course."

She smiled again, her ice-blue eyes sparkling with happiness and innocence. The two set off through the blood-drenched hills.

"Would you like to chase the butterfly?" she asked.

Salvarias studied the field of bodies. "I do not see a butterfly."

She pointed at a rotund man. "It's right there."

A blue and black butterfly danced unfazed around the bodies.

"Come on." She snatched his hand.

He jerked his hand back, but his mind remained calm. She smiled sweetly and offered her hand again. He hesitated, and then accepted. His eyes widened when nothing bombarded his mind. It did not hurt to touch her, and he was caught off guard by how real she seemed. He swore he felt the warmth of her touch as he glided his thumb across the top of her smooth hand.

She skipped while giggling, avoiding the dead, ducking under outstretched arms, and pulled Salvarias along behind her. Eventually, he lost track of the butterfly and she stopped with a heavy sigh.

"Maybe next time." She smiled and kept hold of his hand while she walked around the corpses. "I read a book today about the gardens in Windlous. It says they have wonderful plants that bloom year round."

"I have read the same."

"One day I'll travel there and see for myself." She turned her sweet smile to him. "I have to go."

Salvarias sighed. "Goodbye."

"Goodbye." She kissed his cheek and vanished.

He lowered his head. Drowning in the pooling blood of the dead was the butterfly.

Salvarias woke shivering in the cool spring morning. Wilhelm was snoring, and the knight was no longer in his bedroll. Salvarias caught sight of Humar gathering firewood.

"Good morning, my pet," the voice whispered. *"I have misssed our converssssations."*

Salvarias closed his eyes and fought his nausea and throbbing head that grew increasingly painful. His tight chest made every forced breath cut like a knife.

He mulled over the past day's events, which were hazy at best. He remembered memories flooding into his mind, and the incident barely tolerable as he relived each experience of his eleven years. His unconscious mind hid away chunks of memory in a neatly wrapped bundle in the recesses of his mind, and he chose not to probe. He remembered some of his time alone with his mother, though most of his memories of her after he turned five were missing. However, each memory of his brother remained whole and safe.

Salvarias glanced at the dead clover and shuddered. With every bone in his body, he hoped that Wilhelm was right and the death was not caused by Salvarias's evil.

"Now you lie to yoursssself."

"Please, let me be."

He picked up the puzzle box resting near his bedroll, and the instructions appeared in his mind of each square shifting to its rightful place. Soon the pain became bearable as the device enraptured him.

"Morning," Humar whispered.

Salvarias jumped, and the scare he suffered rammed a stake through his brain. The pain shot past his point of control and he bolted a short distance before becoming ill. He worked on the puzzle box, blocking out the hovering knight. After gaining control, he maneuvered the pieces to a simple box shape.

"Are you all right?" Humar asked.

Salvarias cringed and his words barely left his tight throat. "May I please have some water?"

Humar nodded. "Sure, let's head back."

Salvarias followed the knight to the fire pit, drank two cups of water, and accepted bread.

Humar pointed at the device before stirring the dying embers of the fire and adding more wood. "What is that?"

It took several hard swallows for Salvarias to get the lump in his throat to loosen enough for his words. "A puzzle box."

"I've never seen one like it."

His gaze left the ground and met the knight's eyes. Humar maintained himself well, and his mannerisms were those of a man taught to control outward emotion. There was an evenness to

Humar's tone, expression, and eyes. What was instantly betrayed was his restlessness even as he sat for the brief discussion. The slight fidget, the need to be busy, and glances towards the horizon gave clues. But what Salvarias noticed most was the deep sadness that lined Humar's eyes. It was old, and had worn on him over the years.

"Morning," Wilhelm said.

Salvarias switched his gaze to his brother and smiled inwardly at his sleepy grin.

Wilhelm stretched, his grin growing broader, and joined them around the fire. "I'm starving."

When Wilhelm's arm draped around Salvarias's shoulders, he relaxed and took a needed deep breath. No one ever hurt him when his big brother was near.

After a quick breakfast, they packed and headed for a home Salvarias had not yet seen.

Once inside the walls of Falar, Salvarias weaved down Market Street with the other two men. Wilhelm's cloak covered Salvarias's slate-blue robes, thankfully preventing taunts and spitting competitions.

He recognized the forge from frequent visits with Tobin, and the memory of his betrayal cut deep. After all, to Salvarias the event had happened a mere seven days ago. He did not remember the last year of his life except emptiness, dark, and cold. He shuddered.

When Wilhelm unlatched the gate blocking access to the forge, Durak roared, "Welcome home!"

Wilhelm laughed. "Glad to be back." He picked up the cursing cavrul in a bear hug. "This is my brother."

Salvarias didn't want to be rude. Durak was helping the brothers without a reason. Lowering his hood, Salvarias trembled out a reply. "Hello, Gentleman Durak." He was finding it easier to talk the more he did it.

The cavrul's eyes narrowed. "Hello, boy."

"Come on, Salv. I'll show you around."

Wilhelm showed Salvarias where food was kept in the cozy home and ended up in the storeroom where a single candle fought the darkness of the space.

"I'll get you when I'm done," his brother said.

Salvarias snatched hold of Wilhelm's arm before he left. "I can help now, brother."

"No. The forge isn't good for you. You can't breathe when you're out there."

Salvarias didn't want to be alone, nor did he want Wilhelm to do all the work. The men who had attacked them were fresh in Salvarias's memory, shadows jumped towards him, and his mother's screams echoed in his mind. His peripheral vision played tricks, and Tobin's blood oozed from the walls.

Salvarias clung to his brother's hand. "Please, brother, I will help you."

"No, Salv. You don't know how bad it gets."

As the snaking blood pooled around Salvarias's feet, he stood on his tiptoes and lifted the hem of his robes. "I do not care, brother. I will pull my own weight." He tried to hide the desperation in his voice. Air was harder to inhale.

Wilhelm frowned. "I'll agree, but only if you promise to tell me if it gets too bad."

Salvarias pushed his brother through the door and into the sitting room. "Yes."

Wilhelm squatted eye level. "Are you all right?"

Never able to meet Wilhelm's gaze when lying, Salvarias averted his eyes and whispered, "Yes."

"I know this is new to you." Wilhelm tapped Salvarias's chin.

He took a deep breath and met his brother's gaze.

Wilhelm said, "The entire trip home you talked with Humar and now Durak. I'm proud of you."

"Thank you, brother."

Wilhelm grinned, his eyes lighting, and ruffled Salvarias's hair. "I'll take care of you. You don't have to be afraid here."

He punched his brother's arm, smiling inwardly at his feigned pain. "Thank you."

Following Wilhelm outside, Salvarias listened to the instructions before nodding in understanding. He started polishing a sword that required no polishing while his brother went to work at the forge.

"What are ye doing?" Durak asked.

Salvarias cringed, keeping his eyes lowered, and battled an urge to flee to Wilhelm. "Polishing a sword."

"I see that, but you can't be out here."

"I would like to help earn our food."

"Ye won't last," Durak snapped. "Get inside."

Salvarias flinched. "Thank you for your concern, Gentleman, but I will be fine."

Durak moved close, his voice a threatening whisper, and his hatred-filled gaze locked on Salvarias. "You stay in the back, you hear? I don't want you talking to me customers or even looking at 'em. If I catch you doing magic in my shop I'll kill you meself."

"Of course, Gentleman." Salvarias bottled the hurt of yet another person who did not accept him.

After eyeing him up and down, Durak muttered something about robes, and went to the forge with Wilhelm.

"You are afraid of much, my pet," the voice scolded. *"Why do you care what he thinksss? Look at your insssecurities... your fearsss. Perform magic,"* the presence nudged. *"Sssee if he truly killsss you. He is ssscared of you, of your power. Kill him, take his sssoul where it belongsss. He has killed the innocccent. He deservesss to die!"*

"No. He is helping us. I will not disrespect him. And I will not kill him!"

"One day you will." Then the voice was quiet.

Salvarias cursed his weak need for acceptance and reset his emotions. Indeed, the "lesson" his parents' murderers provided was invaluable. Tobin's withdrawal had solidified Salvarias's need to shield himself from the painful betrayal of those who might uncover his evil and withdraw affection. Furthermore, he did not deserve love, however brief it might be. He did not need it. He needed no one, nothing. He glanced at his brother and sighed. Wilhelm was the exception.

"Tisssk, tisssk, my pet. So selfisssh."

"I cannot be without him. You will never persuade me to leave him."

"I have no doubt I will not, my pet. When you kill sssomeone, when an innocccent diesss for your evil sssoul, you will understand. Hopefully, it isss not your brother who will die for you firssst. I hope to ssspare him from your wickednessss."

Salvarias ignored laughter from Durak and Wilhelm, remaining in back, hood drawn close and head lowered.

As the day progressed, Salvarias watched his brother slip from the smithy three different times with three different women. Shaking his head during a third absence, Salvarias remembered all the times he had seen Wilhelm disappear when Tobin had read to Salvarias at the guardhouse. He had his suspicions then, but now, there was no denying it. Mother would be—

His thoughts stumbled to a halt and he swallowed the lump in his throat. He took a new interest in polishing the swords, begging the task to draw his mind from dark thoughts.

He polished each sword twice before Wilhelm strolled over.

They ate dinner with Humar and Durak. Salvarias kept his hood up and realized it provided a sense of security, a way to hide from his pain, fears, and the hateful stares of others. He was sure the others found relief in not seeing his evil eyes glaring at them.

After dinner, he followed his brother to a dark alley. They settled under several blankets on the cold cobblestones. When Wilhelm's snore started, Salvarias removed his mother's spell book from a pack and studied in the faint moonlight. It was difficult to read since his hands shook from the chilled night air. His chest ached with each breath, but he endured the pain in silence, understanding why Wilhelm reluctantly allowed him in the smithy.

When Salvarias's eyes eventually grew heavy, he tucked the book into a pack, and nestled down in his blanket.

In no time, he was standing under the sole tree, staring at the plain of walking corpses. As he walked amid the dead, he wondered if the girl with raven hair would visit him again. She had done so every night since he woke from the darkness.

"Hello."

Salvarias turned to see her standing behind him. "Hello."

She smiled. "May I join you?"

"Of course."

Her hand slipped into his and they set off through the field. She ducked under outstretched hands and gently parted the corpses while recounting a fictional book she had read about a minotaur who wanted to become a sailor.

Halfway through, she giggled with delight. "A bunny!"

Salvarias glanced around and caught sight of the furry white rabbit hopping towards them.

"I love bunnies!" she exclaimed, plopping down on the bloody field. She patted the ground next to her. "Sit with me."

He grimaced at the blood and was about to object, but suddenly the blood disappeared. A patch of lush grass sprouted up in a blink. He tentatively sat, waiting for the blood to infringe on their clean circle, but it never did.

The bunny hopped over and nibbled on the grass at their feet. The girl petted it while continuing with her story.

Salvarias gazed at her, watching her light with excitement during certain parts, while others she giggled, and even went so far as to scowl and switch her voice to be deep during dangerous scenes. Before he knew it, he had forgotten about the dead, and was stroking the bunny's soft ears.

Once she finished, she sighed deeply. "I have to go."

He almost begged her to stay, but he bit back the words and nodded. "Goodbye."

She leaned over and kissed his cheek. "Goodbye."

She vanished. He looked down to see the bunny gulping for air like a fish out of water. It keeled over, twitching in the blood flooding back to drown the grass. Salvarias smoothed its fur, whispering comforting words until its life ended.

He jolted awake to a reptilian sounding voice hissing from the shadows in the alley they slept in. "Boy." A hand protruded from the stark blackness. "Help me, boy."

Salvarias crawled out of his blankets. His need to help people, to fight the evil within him, moved him a step towards the man. The face was shrouded in shadows, but milky white eyes and skin covered in contusions caught the dim light of the moon.

The bruised arm stretched out further. "Help me."

A chill ran up Salvarias's spine and he took a step back.

"Fool!" the figure hissed.

Another arm unfolded from the darkness. Salvarias went rigid when an insect-like hand grabbed hold of his arm.

Chapter 10
Spring 1011 a.r.

Wilhelm jerked awake to see a man reaching for Salvarias. Scrambling from the blankets, Wilhelm drew his dagger. He froze when an inhuman arm uncurled from the shadows and latched hold of Salvarias. Shaking free of his shock, Wilhelm lunged, snatching hold of his brother while simultaneously slicing the beast's wrist. A hissing rattle spurted from the creature's blue-red lips, and in the dappled moonlight, mucus covered wings spread. Another insect-like arm stretched out from the creature's back. Not waiting to see what the winged horror intended, Wilhelm grabbed their packs and yanked his brother from the alley to the main street.

Wilhelm sprinted to the first home he saw with a roof overhang and flattened himself against the stone. Salvarias pressed himself to the wall, and Wilhelm gave his brother's hand a reassuring squeeze. The winged beast took flight and headed away from them. Moonbeams peeked between dawdling clouds to illuminate the street enough to see that nothing skulked near.

Screams erupted toward the city gate.

Wilhelm shouldered the packs so both his hands were free. "We've got to get to the smithy," he breathed.

Salvarias nodded and held tight while they sidled along the gray walls of homes, keeping to the shadows. Guttural whispers issued nearby. Wilhelm froze. Screams, clinking armor, and crashing swords made it impossible to pinpoint the hissing conversation. He spared a glance around the corner into an alley. Moonlight shone down on two figures creeping towards them.

Though he'd never met an octril, he'd seen enough paintings of the creatures to confirm what slunk down the alley. Close to six-feet tall, the octril's skin resembled aqua green fish scales. Stubby legs were disproportionate to the torso and at the elbow two forearms sprouted, each containing its own hand. The face resembled a human in dimensions, but the flat nose was catlike and the eyes larger. No ears existed on the smooth head and in their place holes oozed milky liquid.

"We need more men, the healthy sort," an octril hissed. "Stop raping and search."

As long as he could remember, octril slave parties had focused on rural towns. It'd been so long since any were sighted in large cities that most didn't even bother patrolling for them.

He turned back to the alley they'd just left. He peeked around the corner and cursed a foul-enough oath to cause Salvarias's eyes to widen. Two octrils were sneaking towards them.

"Our master will be angered," hissed one. "Not one mage has been captured in this filthy city."

Panic bordered Wilhelm's thinking. Then his mother's words rang in his mind: "Demons exist, but we remain calm and steadfast in the face of evil."

He inhaled a slow breath, let it out and gave his paling brother a wink. "We have to run."

Salvarias nodded.

They darted past the alley. Cries rose from the beasts and feet pounded behind the brothers. Wilhelm dashed down the nearest alley and caught another set of octrils by surprise. He planted his foot in one creature's stomach, causing it to stumble back and double over. Never releasing his brother's hand, Wilhelm slashed the other octril's throat open. Hot blood splattered across his tunic. Sweeping his dagger to the bent-over creature, he rammed it through the back of its scaled neck. The rush of the fight rang in his ears, and exhilarating strength and confidence surged through him. He was grinning.

Close footfalls, his brother's trembling hand, and screams from the city jolted Wilhelm into a run. He made it three steps before Salvarias collapsed. His breathing was almost nonexistent. Wilhelm plucked up his brother.

A swishing rush of wind echoed above. Salvarias whispered words of magic and an intense heat radiated on Wilhelm's back.

"Rulose."

A whooshing noise ended with a creature's painful scream and a thud.

Wilhelm grinned. "Nicely done, little brother."

"Three land creatures pursue us," Salvarias said.

Wilhelm thanked the gods for the endurance running he did each morning. He dashed between homes, then sharply turned a corner and sprinted behind a home in an attempt to keep his path sporadic, trying to lose the group.

"Five more have joined," Salvarias said.

Wilhelm rounded the corner and groaned. A group of octrils fought a cluster of guards in front of the smithy. The short outline of Durak, along with the shiny armor of Humar, was clearly visible. Wilhelm sprinted forward. Better to test their luck in a group than alone.

"Humar!" he roared.

A group of octrils burst from a nearby alley, feet slapping the stone and wicked grins on their faces. They headed for the brothers, blocking their way towards Humar.

Wilhelm lowered Salvarias and dropped the packs before being tackled by the group. The impact on the hard cobblestones and the weight of the beasts stole all the air in Wilhelm's lungs. He gasped, his vision blinked, and then a jolt of pain ran up his spine. He ignored it and focused on Tobin's training.

Wilhelm wrenched his arm out of a hold, kicking one octril in the face. He glimpsed Salvarias locked in concentration and, to Wilhelm's surprise, a shard made of fire appeared near Salvarias. It flew through the air to land in the throat of an octril restraining Wilhelm.

There seemed to be more hands than bodies. They dragged Wilhelm to the ground, attempting to pin his arms and legs. He gave a hard shove and rose, scrambling to reach Salvarias, but what felt like a boulder landed on his back. From out of the dark sky, insect hands snatched up his brother.

Salvarias gave a startled cry.

Lunging, Wilhelm tried to grab hold while his brother rose in the air. Wilhelm's fingertips grazed the sole of Salvarias's shoe. Fear morphed into desperate rage. Uttering an oath, Wilhelm brought up his elbow under the creature's chin with enough force to knock the beast back and snap its neck. He broke free and ran. The streets grew more crowded as citizens emerged from homes, screaming and pointing towards the sky.

The moon peeked through clouds to reveal a creature carrying Salvarias away in its arms. The creature's wings were thin and translucent, beating laboriously even in the still air. Torso up, it resembled a man, but instead of legs, the lower body curved into a pointed appendage poised like a scorpion's tail. A second set of arms sprouted from the beast's back and reminded Wilhelm of a praying mantis while the other set of arms on the torso were covered in bruised human skin. The third set of human arms stuck out from its sides and were long enough to use as legs.

The moon revealed several additional creatures rising with limp bodies held captive in insect-like arms. Wilhelm kept focused on the creature carrying Salvarias. Then the thumping rush of wings came. Wherever they were taking Salvarias, they would take Wilhelm. He stopped running and whirled around in time to see a gray insect hand grasp his arm. A claw penetrated his skin. His body was suddenly too warm, his stomach flipped, and his vision dimmed. He looked ahead at his limp brother in the other creature's arms.

Darkness claimed Wilhelm.

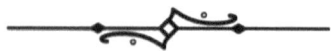

Salvarias stirred awake from nightmarish dreams. His heavy head swayed side to side, and he realized he was moving. He raised his gaze to see a group of beaten men huddled together in an enclosed wood wagon. Four book-sized windows directed sunlight through iron bars but did little to reduce the thick smell of warm bodies. He squinted at the ray of light falling across his face and shifted to the shadows.

Five other men occupied the space, three of them asleep. One of the slumbering men was Wilhelm. His sprawling frame took up nearly the entire floor. A wound on his arm was swollen and clotted.

Salvarias crawled towards his brother.

"It's all right, boy," a man said.

Salvarias jumped, staring in terror at the two men.

The man who had spoken recoiled and sucked in a breath.

Salvarias shook Wilhelm. "Brother, please."

The other stranger reached out a hand and Salvarias jerked away only to bump into another man. Salvarias flinched back.

Feeling like a caged animal, he shook Wilhelm harder. "Brother, I am scared."

"We won't hurt you," another man said, and unfamiliar arms

folded around Salvarias. The images of death mixed with people he had never seen flooded to the surface and blocked any awareness, beating against his brain with a merciless hammer. He offered a feeble struggle against the arms.

"Brother," he whispered.

No comforting touch came. Air disappeared. Heavy liquid compressed his skull. Every muscle in his body constricted. The images were too much to process. His vision left him, and blood trickled from his nose. He grew dizzy from lack of air and convulsed. He could hear the men yelling at him to breathe, but his lungs refused. Just when pressure built to the point of explosion, he blacked out.

He woke as he was being carried into a tunnel by an octril. His mind swam in a foggy drug-induced state, but he counted the turns, the passageways, and the number of steps taken. Sleep claimed him after they entered a vast cavern filled with gangs of chained men.

When next he woke, familiar arms encased him. A drum beat near his ear, and his head rose and fell with Wilhelm's measured breaths. Salvarias forced his heavy head up and Wilhelm's welcoming crooked grin was spread ear-to-ear. With safety surrounding him, Salvarias allowed his head to fall against his brother, shivering despite Wilhelm's warmth.

"You all right, Salv?"

Salvarias closed his eyes to his throbbing headache. "Yes, you?"

Wilhelm tightened his hold and raised his legs so Salvarias disappeared in the embrace. More warmth penetrated his bones, and his shivering reduced.

Wilhelm rumbled, "I'm fine. I don't know where we are."

Salvarias surveyed their space. "I was awake when they took us into a cave. I believe we are in the Cattlar Mountains."

Two sides of the brothers' holding cell were iron bars while the back and one sidewall was chiseled gray stone. The cavity, which appeared carved by man, contained five cells. Ten other men and one mage shared the confines with the brothers. The mage was watching Salvarias with an alarmed expression. Salvarias's mouth went dry and he tightened his grip on Wilhelm.

"Up, swine," an octril hissed.

Salvarias clung to his brother's hand when they were shoved forward. The tunnel from their cell dumped into a gaping cavern, which appeared to be a hub for the activity in the branching passageways. Gangs of chained men carried pickaxes into tunnels, and the high-pitched sound of metal chipping rock vibrated in the cavernous room. To Salvarias's surprise, several groups of unchained men followed octrils without showing interest in escape. Common among all groups was a beaten, exhausted-looking mage.

An octril with a nasty scar across its cheek approached the newly arrived captives, hissing and spitting its words. "You are slaves to the one true god's cause. You will do as we say, or we will kill you."

Fetters went around Salvarias's ankles, and an octril wrenched his hand from his brother's. Wilhelm shoved the creature back and his gaze darted around for an escape. Salvarias was about to utter a warning to stop, but his brother swept him up before Salvarias could speak. They didn't stand a chance. Octrils surrounded them and yanked him from his brother's grasp. Wilhelm continued to kick and punch, but four additional creatures tackled and shackled him.

"Separate the group," an octril hissed. "Mingle them with the others from Hadrium."

"No!" Wilhelm roared, still struggling.

Octrils grabbed Salvarias. He squirmed and wiggled, but to no avail. He was too small to cause any damage. His heart beat faster than a hummingbird's wings when several octrils piled on his brother, hammering him with merciless blows.

The octril carrying Salvarias turned down a tunnel and his brother went out of sight. Salvarias ceased squirming and retreated into his mind, focusing and calming himself, forcing rational thinking. He briefly wondered why he was not affected by the octril's touch. His first thought was that evil does not bother evil. The images were minimal, completely suppressible.

They entered a chamber that revealed three additional tunnels. Two mages sat huddled together. The octril tossed Salvarias near them. The fall bruised his side, and his bones throbbed from the impact. A hand touched him and he flinched away.

A man whispered, "It's all right, we won't hurt you."

Salvarias shifted out of reach and drew his knees to his chest, cringing from the man's hand.

A flabby octril entered the chamber and looked the three mages up and down with an appraising eye. "This is it?"

"All that we could find," hissed another.

Salvarias shuddered at the snakelike voices and the pointed teeth covered in black rotting film.

"Do you three know lightning spells?" the flabby octril asked.

The two other mages nodded, but Salvarias shook his head. He knew few spells and although the lightning spell ranked high on his list to learn, there were many to study before he was ready. Too frightened of Uncle Mafarias to accept the help he had offered, Salvarias only knew what he had taught himself from his mother's spell book.

"You." The octril pointed to the man who had tried to help Salvarias. "Teach him."

The mage shook his head. "The boy is too young. The spell will kill him."

The octril backhanded the mage. "Teach him or you die."

The mage nodded, stretched his jaw, and spat out a bloody tooth.

An octril grabbed Salvarias's arm and jerked him forward through a short, dim tunnel, which opened to another cavern four times the size of his home above the baker. A group of men cringed together in a corner. A mage lay dead on the ground. The blood running from his ears, nose, and mouth proved the magic had devoured his mind. Salvarias shuddered.

An octril spat directions. "Use the lightning on the back wall."

The mage knelt. He had kind hazel eyes and rich brown hair. "I'm Bartle."

Salvarias kept his eyes hidden in the shadows supplied by the hood of his mage robes. "Salvarias Laybryth."

Bartle smiled and continued. "Your power is strong. How old are you?"

"Eleven."

Bartle whistled. "Youngest I've ever heard or read about. Let's give this a try. This lightning spell is similar to a second-level fire spell or ice spell. Do you know those?"

Salvarias shook his head.

Bartle motioned to the nearest octril. "We need parchment or a book and a quill. And if you expect us to repeat these spells, all the mages will need the same in order to record the words and rune."

It muttered a few orders, and another beast returned a time later with the requested items.

The mage wrote the spell, drew the rune, and handed the

parchment to Salvarias. "We'll study at night. I assume it will be the spell they want us to use to crack through the rock."

Salvarias reviewed the words and recognized one of the four. An insatiable hunger dwelled in him when it came to his magic. He needed, wanted, and required knowledge. The physical ache for it shoved aside his fears and his ever-present curiosity soothed his nerves.

"Follow along as I chant," Bartle instructed. *"Ich comad skie fyian."*

Salvarias sensed the mage's magic grow and harness the energy. The complicated rune was comprised of intricate lines and quick movements. The magic within Salvarias stirred in excitement, and he squelched it. He was in control; the magic obeyed him. The needed amount of energy was decent but nothing he felt he could not perform.

"Rulose," Bartle whispered.

Lightning shot from the rune and struck the cavern wall. The rock shuddered and sizable pieces flew into the room. The aftershock vibrated along the floor. Dust hung in the air and Salvarias covered his nose and mouth with the sleeve of his robes.

An octril nudged Salvarias. "Perform the spell."

Bartle gaped at the creature. "He's not practiced enough for this kind of spell. It could kill him. He doesn't even know the second level—"

"Do it or die!"

Bartle turned, wide-eyed, to Salvarias. "Give it a practice before you draw the energy."

Salvarias nodded and read the parchment again. He whispered the spell and looked at the mage, who shook his head.

"The influx in *fyian* is over the *yi*."

Salvarias tested it again.

"Good." Bartle smiled encouragingly. "Now the rune."

Salvarias drew in the air, but he stopped after an error with his movement. He attempted the rune again, but the quick flick proved difficult. Frustrated, he ignited his magic, though he did not allow it to pull energy or focus on his words.

Bartle exhaled sharply, his eyes widened. "You've more power than I thought possible."

Thinking the mage exaggerated to help Salvarias's confidence, he ignored the comment and focused on his magic. It warmed and comforted him, and he breathed deeply at the confidence it supplied. His hands felt smaller and flexible, allowing the rune to be drawn with ease.

Bartle whistled in approval. "Perfect!"

Salvarias turned his attention to the cavern wall. He took several deep breaths and whispered the spell, drawing the energy, then traced his rune. The magic flowed like lava in his blood when together they pushed the energy to the rune. The new spell awakened a heightened level of power and his magic surged through him with delight. Its excitement made him lightheaded.

"Rulose," he whispered. Lightning shot through the air and the cavern wall exploded. Bartle grabbed Salvarias and covered him as a flurry of rocks flew across the room.

"That was amazing!" Bartle exclaimed over the thunderous noise. "Your power... I've never known its equal."

Salvarias scarcely heard the words as his mind went rampant with images from Bartle's touch. Salvarias's vision dimmed and then blinked out, his breathing stopped and his mind swelled under the pressure. As the room quieted and the vibrations reduced, Bartle released Salvarias, and he gasped as his vision returned to reveal blood pooling around an unconscious octril.

Stumbling to his feet, he bolted down the tunnel, ignoring Bartle's alarmed cries. Salvarias wanted his brother.

The heavy shackles cut into Salvarias's ankles, but he never slowed. He dashed through the empty room, rushed down the tunnel, and peered into the cavern. His brother lay on the floor, his face swollen and purple from the beating, blood dried around his lips and nose. Off to the side, seven octrils murmured together. Salvarias darted to his brother, knelt next to him, and shook his shoulder. "Brother."

Wilhelm looked up through swollen eyes. "Are you all right?"

"Yes."

Hands grabbed Salvarias, wrenching him from Wilhelm. He kicked and arched his back until the hands dropped him. Scrambling back to Wilhelm, he flung his arms around his brother's neck.

"You cannot fight, brother. They need mages. I will find a way, but you must not fight anymore."

Wilhelm shook his head. "I'm not going to let them hurt you."

"They will not kill me, brother. They need me. Trust me, please."

Hands grabbed Salvarias again and wrested him from Wilhelm.

"Stop!" Salvarias ordered. He hesitated in surprise when the octrils froze. "I will not help you. I will not perform the spells unless you allow me to stay with him."

Another octril grabbed his arm. Over Wilhelm's enraged cry, Salvarias heard a whip whistle through the air. He clenched his jaw and refused to cry out when the leather bit into his skin. Four octrils jumped on Wilhelm when he struggled to rise and pinned him to the ground. Another lash. Salvarias bit his tongue. He would not give in. Another lash. Wilhelm's roar turned to pleas. Another lash. Salvarias's vision dimmed and a sharp jab of pain jolted up his body. Another lash. Flashes of white and red raced across his vision. Then the whip rested on the ground.

Wilhelm's cry of anger reverberated through the web of caves.

The octril had a smug smile on his face. "Have you changed your mind?"

Salvarias raised his head and forced his clenched jaw to loosen. "Go to Oblivion."

It had the effect he hoped; the octril knew he would not yield. What he did not anticipate was the whip moving to his brother. After the first strike, Salvarias begged the octril to stop.

"Now will you do what we say?" the octril hissed in satisfaction.

Salvarias's mind spun through ideas. He had spent countless hours practicing the runes he learned. Unlike words to a spell, the rune was never forgotten, and his small hands, long fingers and dexterity would allow him to draw before many comprehended his intentions. Taking a quick breath, he chanted below a whisper, drawing his rune, and sent the white protective film over his brother before the octril interpreted the hand motion.

Once the angered cries of the beasts had subsided, Salvarias said, "All I ask is you allow us to stay together."

The creature brought the whip down on Wilhelm, but it never reached him.

"You cannot hold the spell for long, boy!" the octril roared.

The octril's two hands clasped together and the beast backhanded Salvarias across the cheek. The blow knocked him to his knees and dazed him. His pounding head roared in protest.

He winced when he pushed himself to his feet. "We could be

mining if you just allowed us to remain together. I will do what you ask, I will perform magic, but I must be with him."

The octril paced in frustration. One of the creatures that had been guarding the other captives in the cave with Bartle stormed into the cavern and whispered into the oozing hole of the upset octril. Its black eyes moved to stare at Salvarias, and it nodded to the other octril. The octril squatted in front of Salvarias, a wicked smile across its green lips.

"So be it," the creature said.

Salvarias narrowed his eyes in distrust. "I will hold you to your word." The throbbing pain in his back intensified and a sudden lightheadedness passed over him. His next words were a mumble. "I will not perform magic unless I am with him."

The octril nodded, and Salvarias ended the protection spell. Octrils tossed him next to Wilhelm and shackled them together.

Wilhelm enclosed Salvarias in an embrace. "Nicely done, little brother."

"Let's go!" an octril barked.

Pulling Salvarias to his feet, Wilhelm tried to grin, but winced when his cut lip opened. An octril shoved a piece of parchment in Salvarias's hand.

The scarred octril pushed him towards a tunnel. "Get going."

The shackles were heavy and awkward, and his ankles were sore from the scores inflicted by his previous flight. Wilhelm shuffled loudly, and based on his winces, he was in more pain than he let on. Another vast cavern opened with the same dark gray rock reflecting the torchlight, and silvery veins of metal snaked along the far wall. An octril hurried away a gang of men carrying pickaxes to the far corner of the cavern.

The scarred octril pointed to the wall the men had been mining. "Hit that."

"I cannot remember the spell," Salvarias protested.

The octril's blue lips curled in a sneer. "You best try." A whip sang through air, hitting his brother. Wilhelm fell to his knees, and blood ran down his flayed back.

Salvarias quickly read the parchment, but since he had already performed the spell in the other cavern, the words made no sense. An octril unshackled him and tossed him in a corner of the cavern while the remaining men were handed pickaxes and forced to mine.

Wilhelm barely stood upright.

Salvarias ignited his magic. For the first time in his life, his magic spoke in his mind. Though accustomed to whispers, he grew annoyed at yet another independent voice existing in his mind. He wondered what part of his soul and mind belonged exclusively to himself.

"*I will help you,*" the magic whispered. The voice was different than the presence that had talked to him since birth. The magic's tone was soft, comforting, and carried with it fondness.

"*Why?*"

"*Because I want to learn, to grow. You have powers seeded deep within you that I am most curious about, my young wizard. Furthermore, your mind is sharp and open to possibilities.*"

"*How is it you are speaking to me now and never before?*"

"*The last spell we performed opened your mind further to me, my young wizard.*"

"*I do not trust you. I control you.*"

"*I did not say you would not still control me, and as a matter of fact, it is imperative that you remain in control. All I ask is for mutual respect. We can work together and I will help you learn. Consider me a child, like yourself, who wants to grow and desires knowledge. You give me an opportunity to grow. There are words hidden in your thoughts, words unknown to other mages.*"

"*How do you know about other mages?*"

"*My brothers and sisters talk to me,*" the magic whispered.

"*Who are your siblings?*"

"*The magic within other mages. They are jealous of me, of you. They can sense your mind, your power. We can make new spells, my wizard, new and wonderful spells never before whispered in this land. Together we can learn; you can teach me, and I can teach you.*" The magic warmed inside Salvarias, comforting and protective. "*You may not trust me now, but know I do not trust you either. Allow us to work together, to see each other's powers, each other's character. If you are worthy, I will give you my trust.*"

He contemplated the magic's words.

Wilhelm grunted when the whip struck his back again.

Salvarias agreed. "*Help me remember the spell.*"

"*I will try, but you must calm your mind. You think of too many things at once. Your mind... It is chaotic at best with too many* distractions. You must only focus on me."

"I am not in complete control. I cannot do what you ask."

"I can only help so much then. Without a calm mind, your powers are less. Think of spells as problems, addition or subtraction, for example. Simple spells, one plus one, can be easily memorized and burned into your mind. I will no longer be required to focus so intently on the words and, by accident, wipe them from your memory. However, you must practice the spell often and train your mind to remember it. Since the words are simple, eventually I will become accustomed to them and we can perform the spell repeatedly. Complicated spells can be memorized again without lengthy sleep though the strain I inflict on your mind will be immense. We might be able to perform one twice before you can no longer remember the words without rest. We will never be able to repeat an advanced spell close together. The words are too complicated for me and the runes too intricate. You will require much rest after advanced spells since the harm I inflict will be substantial. Do you understand what I have told you?"

"Yes."

"This is a complicated spell, but not advanced. You must focus on the words one letter at time. Burn the letter into your mind and I will help."

"How?"

"My purpose, what magic is supposed to do, is protect your mind from the power, from the energy we require to perform spells. Together, we change the energy within your body. It is a concerted effort. However, I alone protect your mind and body, make you stronger. You alone control the power within, control me, and control the energy. With my powers connected to your thoughts, I can help you remember the spell. I can help you pull hidden words from your memory."

"If you can help me remember the spell, why would I need to chant? Can you not just perform the magic without the words?"

"A valid question, my studious wizard. Though I can say the spell, the words hold no meaning to me. Your voice, your command, your mind is what controls me, what controls the power. As I said, it is imperative that you remain in control."

He shook his head. "That is not what I have learned. I do not trust you."

The whip hit his brother again.

"Magic is misunderstood. We have been treated poorly by our mages, but you can help. You are the first to hear our words, to listen to what we say. Small leaps of faith are what we must take in each other. I am asking you to leap first. Study each letter, burn it into your mind, and I will help you."

Salvarias focused on the trembling parchment in his hand. Each letter he stared at danced around the page. With a grimace, he forced his mind past what he thought possible. The strain added exhaustion to his very bones. His brain pounded his skull. But each time the whip struck his brother, it deepened Salvarias's determination.

His magic spoke. *"Ich comad skie fyian."*

The words stuck in his exhausted mind but then fleeted out. *"Repeat it,"* he mumbled.

"Ich comad skie fyian."

The magic attempted several times before the words remained in his memory. Wilhelm's back was raw from the flogging.

Salvarias rose on shaky legs and walk towards an octril. "I will perform the spell." He glanced at his brother's blood seeping through his tattered shirt and almost fainted.

The octril's eyes narrowed when it called the slaves back. Wilhelm staggered beside Salvarias.

He took a deep breath, listened again to the magic and chanted the spell, drew the energy and rune. Lightning shot through air and struck the cavern wall. Rocks exploded from the impact. Wilhelm grabbed Salvarias and shielded him when stones rebounded off the walls. The entire mountain vibrated and dust perfused the air.

Exhausted, his mind past awareness, Salvarias slept in familiar arms.

Pain, pure pain jolted Salvarias awake. He cried out even as his mind realized what woke it. His body throbbed and a jarring vibration still rang in his bones. Before he had time to recognize the whistle and prepare, the whip shredded his skin. He became aware of Wilhelm's roar of anger.

Salvarias opened his eyes to see an octril crouched in front of him. "Perform the spell!" the octril yelled.

Using every ounce of muscle, Salvarias glanced around the

room. Wilhelm was lying on the ground. Blood dripped to form a pool on the charcoal rocks. Still, they flogged him.

"Stop," Salvarias mumbled.

The octril planted a foot in Salvarias's stomach. "Do the spell and we'll stop."

He curled into a ball, hugging his churning insides. He ignited his magic.

"My wizard, we cannot do this again." There was a heavy exhaustion in the magic's voice.

"You will."

He raised the parchment. *I.* His head throbbed but the letter seared into his memory. *C.* A stake placed against his temple was driven into his brain with the solid strike of a hammer. A cry escaped him.

"Slower, my young wizard. You are straining your—"

He ignored it. *H.* Another whack jammed the stake further in. He continued. Strike after strike. Halfway through, the pain flared beyond his control. He lost his place. Tears welled at his failure. He glanced at his unconscious brother still being thrashed by the whip.

Salvarias started over.

He blocked everything from his vision but the parchment. Sounds faded except the encouragement of his magic. Smells no longer existed. Pain from his body was not acknowledged. All that encompassed him was what was in his hand and the magic.

Time passed unknown, uncared about. When finally the spell remained in his memory, his magic barely functioned. It was as exhausted as Salvarias. He allowed his surroundings to rush forward. Wilhelm's lake of blood had branched off into a stream down the cave floor. A rancid smell reached Salvarias and he realized he was lying in a pool of his own vomit. Something warm trickled out of his nose and ears. He touched the liquid and pulled back his finger. Blood. His back was numb. He was sure they had flogged him further. The strength to stand was beyond his power. He simply raised his gaze to the octril and it nodded in understanding. The slaves were called back and Wilhelm was dragged to safety.

The imposing cavern wall challenged Salvarias, staring at him in its starkness as if to dare him to succeed. He smiled at it. He would save his brother from torment.

Shuddering in a breath, Salvarias winced from the pain in his ribs, and whispered the spell. Lightning shot from his rune. Something warm poured out of his mouth. It tasted of iron. He recognized it: more blood. Darkness pounced like a starved cat and he roamed through his nightmares.

Unupture crumpled the parchment and tossed the message into the fireplace. He'd lost the boy, and God would be none too pleased to learn of it. As Unupture left his room for the dungeons, he prepared himself.

Though he harbored no doubts they'd succeed, one way or the other, God only saw defeat, his patience wearing thin at all who surrounded him. Still, Unupture knew he was needed, so he'd be safe. Others should grovel in submission to God's powers, but not Unupture. God couldn't coordinate the destruction of Arden alone, and his three disciples were necessary, so he bestowed their every desire upon them to retain their loyalty.

Unupture's desire was to breed new creations in the depths of the stronghold. With the power given to him ages ago by Veedran, Unupture tested breeding creatures with different races in Arden and had found many intriguing combinations. He loved and cared for each little monstrosity born.

The second disciple was a sadistic man named Sansis, who wore the most putrid robes of burnt orange. Unupture had worked with the demented man during Veedran's wars. Sansis' love of the human body naturally led him to the role of tormentor, extracting information God required. Sansis had learned of ways to sustain a body while it was being hacked apart. The man's unique approach to healing caused a shudder of sympathy for the victims to pass through Unupture.

The third disciple was a woman, and her desire was God himself. She threw her body at him, begging for his love and attention. She disgusted Unupture, but her pure dedication caused her to perform many acts he found repulsive. He secretly suspected God enjoyed tormenting her, offering her sweet tastes but never allowing her all of him.

Unupture entered a room lined with tiny cribs. God stood watch over recently abducted infants. Their piercing cries gave Unupture an instant headache. The anticipation of what the innocent children would become raised his spirits, and he relished the memory of the new sound they would make, the new form they would take. Though he gagged at the thought of the suffering the babies would endure, he knew such sacrifices were required for advancement and study. Unlike the bloodleders he'd created for Veedran, this new race would possess the ability to breed.

"The poissson isss almossst ready," God said. "Sssoon we will have additional bloodledersss."

Unupture bowed deeply. "My Dark Master, I bring troubling news. The boy is missing."

"What!"

"It's most unfortunate, but I assure you we'll find him. This is a minor setback."

God curled his lip. "Another 'minor setback.' Find that damn boy! And our breeding isss too ssslow. I need additional women and babiesss. I will not fail."

"That's unwise, Master. We must be patient. We cannot show ourselves yet, cannot show our full powers. Patience will deliver us victory."

"I will not fail! Increassse the raiding partiesss!" God roared.

Unupture winced when the babies' cries escalated. "Of course, Master. I assure you, we won't fail. Our plans are well on their way."

"If you're wrong I will take your sssoul. Find the boy yoursssself. I grow tired of disssappointmentsss."

"Of course."

"Bring me a ssslave."

Unupture spoke to a black-armored soldier outside the room, and soon a trembling young man was brought in.

God seemed to grow and tower over the youth. "Are you frightened?"

"Yes," the man whispered. As if to confirm his statement, the slave wet himself.

"Do you want to die?"

Tears streamed down the slave's face. "No."

God lifted the young man to eye level and purred, "Then give me your sssoul. Give it to me freely. Deny me and I will kill you."

"Please—I—my soul—I can't..."

God's hand clenched into a claw and he ripped off the man's arm. Above the screams of the slave, Unupture heard God's jaw unhinge followed by the crunching of bone and cartilage as he devoured the bloody extremity. Unupture shuddered.

After the slave's screams died and he looked near death, God smiled. "Your sssoul or life, my pet?"

The slave's head rolled to the side and he gazed at his missing arm. "My soul is yours."

"Fool! Without a sssoul, you are already dead!" God feasted on the body, tearing through tendon and crunching bone as he consumed both the soul and its host.

Unupture became ill from the grotesque sounds of snapping bones and moist bites. He deftly avoided a violent spray of blood and fled the room, retching the entire way to his quarters.

Chapter 11
Spring 1015 a.r.

Salvarias strolled among the dead, barely containing his excitement. He wandered patiently, waiting for the raven-haired girl to appear. Every night since he woke from the darkness a year after his parents' murders, she had visited him in this same dream. And each time, she brought something alive and wholesome to the plain of the dead.

Even though he could not count the nights they spent together since he had been taken to the slave caverns, his rough calculations led him to believe they had shared another four years together and his gangly teenage body confirmed the passage of time.

"Hello."

Salvarias turned to see her standing behind him, a small smile on her rose-red lips.

"Hello," he said.

"May I join you?"

"Of course."

Her smile widened and she strolled to his side, slipping her hand into his. Their fingers entwined, and he glided his thumb on the top of her hand, relishing in her warmth and softness.

They walked in silence, feeling no need to fill the time with conversation. Just being near each other seemed to calm them both. She ducked past the deads' hands, parting them aside, and he was sure they did not walk in the same place. Her face was serene, gazing around as if seeing something beautiful, not a field of walking corpses.

It seemed they strolled for hours, walking lazily and with no purpose, until she stopped and sighed.

"I love autumn. It's my favorite time of year," she said.

"Spring," Salvarias murmured.

"The aspens though. So beautiful in autumn."

The dead parted from a cluster of aspen trees. Their leaves rustled in the breeze, singing the song Salvarias had heard since childhood. Bright yellow leaves glistened in a stream of pure sunlight. The usual dullness of the sky did not taint the life emanating from the trees. He breathed deeply at the sight he had missed since being taken into the caves.

He turned his gaze to the girl at his side. Always he had seen her as a friend, a little girl to discuss the books he had read when he was a child. But now, for the first time, or maybe the first time acknowledging it, he saw her as a young woman. Her sleek hair danced around her waist, not jet-black as his own, but alive with shifting hues of midnight blue and even the darkest green. Her ice-blue eyes pierced straight to his heart when she looked at him and smiled. Innocence had not left her. She beamed with a purity that seemed to reach out to him, beckoning him away from the darkness that tugged at his soul.

"Beautiful, are they not?" she whispered.

"Yes." He was not talking of the trees.

His gaze lowered to her collarbone, perfectly displayed by the oval neckline of her lavender dress. The silky fabric hugged her waist and torso, disclosing her lithe figure. The soft mounds of her breasts were covered modestly.

When he looked at her face, her smile had faded and she was studying him with the same curious stare, as if they saw each other for the first time.

He was painfully aware he was in the awkward stages of a teenager. He was short and nothing but a sack of bones. His body was experiencing sensations he had yet to understand, and he was too embarrassed to ask his brother. Nor was Salvarias cognizant enough most of the time to care. But here in his dreams emotions stirred, and he found himself attracted to her in ways that were not within the realm of friendship.

He loved her.

He loved a young woman that was nothing more than a dream. The thought nearly broke his heart. No woman in real life would ever live up to the pedestal he put her on. Her intelligence and beauty were not of Arden. But, at this moment, he did not care she was a dream. All he wanted was to touch her.

She stepped towards him. Meeting her gaze, he could see she felt the same. He could hardly believe it. Salvarias, a young man with a soul of evil, attracted a woman who was nothing shy of a goddess to him. Then again, this was a dream. His dream. His desire.

With a shaking hand, he traced her collarbone. Her skin was smooth and flawless, like a glass of creamy milk. He closed the distance between them. Warmth seeped from her body. She was as tall as him, and her breath brushed his lips. She did not cringe when she stared into his eyes.

He glided his fingers along her jaw, brushing his thumb over her pouty lips. Desire to taste her rushed through him. Her lips parted and her eyes offered her invitation. He leaned forward.

A sudden swell of inappropriateness surged up in him. This was a woman, dream or no dream, and she was to be respected, revered. It took every ounce of his control to lower his head. For some reason, it felt wrong to kiss her.

Settling for closeness, he slid his arms around her waist and pressed her against him.

"Why?" she whispered.

"It does not feel right."

"It does to me."

Burying his face in her hair, he inhaled a deep breath, fighting the urge her words raised. They stayed locked in each other's arms until their time ended.

She pulled back and kissed his cheek, her lips lingering longer than normal, and she whispered, "I have to go."

He ran his hand through her hair, gazing at the shifting colors as the strands fell between his fingers. "Goodbye."

She vanished. Salvarias looked at the aspens, withering into lifeless trees. He swore he heard their cry as they died.

Chapter 12
Autumn 1016 a.r.

Wilhelm stood next to his brother as Salvarias read the parchment once more. Time had lost meaning in the dark caves, but by Salvarias's scraggly beard and gangly body, Wilhelm assumed at least four or five years had passed. He took advantage of the break from mining to glance at another slave. The man shook his head and Wilhelm uttered a curse. His escape plan was a painstakingly slow process which had done much to teach him patience. Ever since the brothers' first failed escape, he'd flat out refused another spontaneous attempt. Even now, while he rested a hand on Salvarias's back, Wilhelm felt the raised scars from the whip. He knew his own back was in no better shape. His brother had barely survived the beating. After all, he'd been merely eleven years old.

Over the years, Wilhelm had befriended a handful of octrils who were free with information; discussing guard duty, how many large caverns existed, how many slave groups in each, and a plethora of other helpful information. He used every bit of knowledge, and his ability to easily win over the trust of others, to develop his escape plan. Now, provisions were his only missing puzzle piece. The first few days down the mountain would be blind flight. They wouldn't be able to forage the mountainside, therefore water and food would have to be gathered before escape. His patience, however, dangled on its last thread. Learning of storage locations had proved near impossible, and by the slave's shake of his head, Wilhelm's last idea for obtaining the information hadn't worked. Maybe they'd be forced to endure a lifetime in slavery. The idea wasn't appealing.

Salvarias's soft voice rose in a chant and a flash of lightning struck the wall. Wilhelm caught his limp brother while covering him from the flurry of rocks. Dust hung heavy in the air and the mountain shuddered. Wilhelm continued to be surprised that the caverns didn't implode from his brother's spells. Because of Salvarias's power, the slavers used Wilhelm's group on the most stubborn walls. Not to mention the fact that Salvarias had learned to perform the same spell three times in a single day, the only mage in the slave caverns to do so. At least it minimized the whippings the brothers received.

"Back to work," an octril hissed.

Wilhelm carried his brother to a blanket in the corner of the cavern, grimacing at bones protruding from his tunic, his sunken cheeks and eyes, his pale and sweating face. Over the years, his breathing had worsened, he fell sick often, he lost weight, and though he grew in height, he was short for his age. Yet, for all the physical suffering he endured, what clenched Wilhelm's heart each day was fear for his brother's mind. Within what Wilhelm calculated was a few months, Salvarias's thoughts had grown sluggish, and he was listless when awake performing spells. He slept unless reading his parchment for his spell or eating breakfast, which was the only time he seemed alert. Wilhelm couldn't keep his brother up long enough for a slice of bread at night.

Wilhelm wrapped Salvarias in the blanket before returning to snatch up a pickaxe. Opposite from Salvarias, Wilhelm had sprouted to over seven and a half feet tall. Mining and lifting heavy rocks had formed massive muscles over his body. He appreciated the exercise but found his new mass offered challenges in fitting through some of the tight spaces.

He pounded at the mountainside with his fellow slavers while he roved over possible ways to gather the information regarding the slavers' storage methods. Hours passed, and he glanced often at his brother, tossing restlessly, lost in a nightmare.

It was one such glance Wilhelm saw a purple-robed man enter the cavern followed by several octrils.

Jindrak, an octril Wilhelm had befriended, leaned close and whispered, "If you want to live, you'll behave yourself."

He tensed. "What's going on?"

"Stay still," Jindrak advised.

The robed figure knelt beside Salvarias.

"How long has the boy been here?" the figure asked.

The octril's voice was shaky when it responded, "Five years, Master."

The figure turned over Salvarias's left hand. His brother stirred, brow furrowing. Even in sleep, physical contact caused pain.

"Why wasn't I contacted earlier?" the figure demanded.

"We didn't see it until recently, Unupture."

The figure tossed back his hood and Wilhelm grimaced at the sight. The man's skin looked gooey, as if a thick, clear liquid covered his body. His complexion was orange, and red eyes filled most of his face. No hair existed on his shiny scalp or arms. Though part human, what other race mixed in his blood was indiscernible.

The man's slender finger rested on the octril's forehead. The beast cried out and dropped to its knees before the robed figure.

The octril clasped its hands together in a plea. "Forgive me, Unupture!"

"No. I do not forgive failure!" Unupture roared. "Do you have any idea what I've gone through to find this boy? Years, years of my life wasted, and he's been in your care the entire time!"

The scaled body spasmed and green-black blood trickled from its eyes. Several nearby octrils stepped back, their gazes shifting from the robed man to the tortured creature. Unupture whispered a word, and its eyes burst out of its skull. The octril fell dead to the floor. Melted brain matter oozed through the empty eye sockets.

Wilhelm shuddered.

So did Jindrak.

Unupture was shaking, and anger glared in his eyes. He smoothed his robes, seeming to collect his composure. He turned back to Salvarias and knelt next to him. Unupture's forefinger nail sprouted twice as long as the finger itself. Wilhelm sensed ill intention and took a step forward, but the octrils tightened their hold on him.

"I warn you, he *will* kill you," Jindrak hissed. "He won't kill the boy. He's part klusher: A mind reader from the days of Veedran. All he'll do is enter the boy's thoughts."

Uncertain what could be done with so many octrils nearby, Wilhelm paused, his heart pounding. He couldn't fight them all. Though Jindrak was an octril, he had Wilhelm's trust.

Unupture gently brushed back Salvarias's hair. With a quick flick of the wrist, Unupture jabbed his fingernail into the base of Salvarias's neck, sinking it halfway through his flesh.

Salvarias's eyes flew open and he inhaled sharply.

Wilhelm lost all sense of safety and lunged for Unupture. The octrils were prepared. Wilhelm gasped when several fists landed in his stomach. A punch to his ribs drove him to his knees. He tried to rise, but four creatures piled on his back. They shoved him on his stomach and pinned his arms and feet to the ground. His brother's scream of pain halted Wilhelm's struggles, and he jerked his head up.

Salvarias's eyes were shut tightly, his fists tangled in his hair, and sweat beaded his brow. Unupture had his eyes closed, head bowed and tipped to the side as if listening. Salvarias curled into a ball, gulping for air that never came.

"Stop! He can't breathe!" Wilhelm roared.

Unupture opened his eyes and withdrew the fingernail.

Salvarias lurched.

"He's the one I seek. Dethal will arrive at dusk tomorrow to claim him." Unupture strode to Wilhelm and flipped over his right hand. "Keep this one under close supervision, Jindrak. I'll send word on what to do with him." Unupture glided from the room.

Wilhelm yanked against the octrils' hold. "Let me help him!"

Blood ran from Salvarias's nose, and he shook violently. His knuckles had turned white, and another cry escaped.

"Please!" Wilhelm begged.

Several octrils dragged his brother from the room. Wilhelm heard another scream.

"Where are they taking him?" Wilhelm demanded.

"To a cell near yours. Calm yourself, finish your duties, and I'll let you bring him food tonight."

Wilhelm turned to Jindrak. "Why can't he stay with me?"

"Don't be a fool. They want him and there's nothing you can do to stop it. Behave and I'll let you see him one last time."

The octrils rose and Wilhelm staggered to his feet. With a shaking hand, he picked up his pickaxe and pounded on the rock. Escape would need to be in the morning.

Wilhelm trailed behind Jindrak to the holding cell after what seemed like days of mining. Once there, Wilhelm tried to see a few cells down, but only heard his brother groaning in pain, retching, or dry heaving. Sinking against the cold bars, Wilhelm rested his head in his hands. His other inmates kept to themselves on the opposite side of the cell. He was sure his face was a thundercloud.

When Jindrak finally showed with dinner, Wilhelm hovered near the entrance. Once additional octrils arrived, he realized they had no intention of allowing him to see Salvarias.

Wilhelm clenched his hands around the iron bars. "You said I could take him food."

"They said no visitors, and Unupture is not one I'll disobey. I'm sorry."

He punched the cave wall. "Dammit! Just let me see him!"

Jindrak shook his head and darted out of the cell.

Several curses later, Wilhelm conferred with the other men. It was agreed that it was time for escape, provisions or not. Using other slaves in adjoining cells to pass the word, they checked to see if everyone concurred with his plan. The escape was a coordinated effort. If any backed out, they'd all fail.

Late in the evening, word returned all were ready and it would unfold when they left the cells in the morning. Returning for his brother added another layer of risk, but no other option presented itself. Whoever this Dethal was would not take Salvarias.

Wilhelm slept fitfully, listening to his brother moan in his sleep, weeping words, and begging for Wilhelm's help before falling into another nightmare.

Once breakfast was delivered, the group ate in silence, a nervous anticipation hovering over all. When done, Wilhelm and the others followed Jindrak. After years of beatings, they were no longer shackled. The octrils assumed all fight, all hope, had been sucked from the wretched souls wandering the caverns. The tunnels were a maze, and no escape had been successful. The confidence of the slavers shook Wilhelm's faith in his own plan, but he had to try. His advantage was his counting brother. Salvarias could find his way in and out of any place.

They entered the vast cavern where four other slave groups were awaiting assignments and Wilhelm's order.

Gathering his courage, he belted, "Now!"

Even as the word left his lips, he wrapped his hands around Jindrak's head and snapped the octril's neck. The entire group of slaves attacked the beasts, and though the slaves outnumbered the octrils, the creatures' swords provided them an advantage. The mages were forced behind the fighters since most were too weak to stand. A dark-haired mage chanted words from a piece of parchment.

With no further time to see what happened, Wilhelm intercepted an octril heading towards the mages. Dodging the overstepped lunge,

Wilhelm splintered its wrist, exposing fragments of white bone. Using his free hand, he clenched the beast's throat and one squeeze crushed its jugular.

Suddenly, lightning struck, killing a fair number of the beasts. He glanced back to see the piece of parchment passed to another mage. More lightning followed. Five octrils remained but a bushel of slaves were beating the creatures.

Wilhelm found the cell key on Jindrak, trying to avoid the creature's lifeless gaze. Breaking Jindrak's neck erupted a pang of guilt. The octril had been kind, but Salvarias's life took precedence over anything else. Gathering three men, Wilhelm hurried to his brother's cell.

Salvarias lay curled up in a corner, his face colorless and shiny. Blood trickled from his nose, and his breathing was quick and sharp.

"Salv?" Wilhelm shook his brother and stared with widened eyes at the bloody, bile-covered floor.

Salvarias's sunken eyes barely opened.

"We're escaping," Wilhelm said. He fought a rising panic when Salvarias coughed and blood speckled his lips. "You remember the way out?" Wilhelm asked.

After a weak nod, Wilhelm helped Salvarias rise, and once he gained his footing, they hastened to the main cavern.

Salvarias studied each possible exit, pointed to one on their right, and then stood on his own. Wilhelm took the lead, making sure Salvarias was directly behind. They weaved through minor caverns and tunnels, engaging in quick brawls, before Salvarias said the next large cavern was around the bend.

Wilhelm left a force to protect the rear and took the remaining men with him. He peered around the corner to see octrils hissing at each other while slaves cowered in the center. Wilhelm issued a war cry and charged. The slaves had known the attack was coming and engaged in the battle. Potential freedom provided the farmers and merchants with brute strength, and an uncaged, animalistic cry echoed in the stone room.

An armed octril lunged at Wilhelm, and he dodged to the side, grabbed the beast's wrist, and pulled the octril toward him. He shattered its wrist and the sword clanged on the stone floor. He snatched it up, arching it as he rose, and disemboweled the stunned octril. Whirling to the next creature, he gripped the sword in both hands and swung it at the octril's gut. Bones snapped and blood splashed across his arms. He kicked the octril free of the blade and looked around for his next opponent, but the others were defeated. The brief fight had ended and they'd lost only three men.

He called to the men who'd remained behind with his brother. "Let's go!"

Salvarias entered the cavern and surveyed the room before pointing to another tunnel. Wilhelm motioned the men to retrieve any weapons available.

Salvarias became ill again, more blood and bile.

Cursing, Wilhelm entered the tunnel, listening to his brother's whispered numbers.

Suddenly, two octrils emerged from a side corridor among the front of the escapees, swords swinging. Several slaves fell immediately under the fury of the creatures' attack. One of the octrils cleaved through the second-to-last man standing near Salvarias.

"Bartle!" Salvarias cried a warning.

The mage jumped and avoided the swing, offering a clear view to Salvarias. The octril's gaze locked on him. Wilhelm yanked his brother back while Bartle used his own body to shield Salvarias. The sword embedded deep into Bartle's chest, crunching through bone, and the moist echo seemed amplified in the tunnel. Blood splattered Salvarias's face when the sword withdrew. Shoving aside his brother, Wilhelm slid his sword into the octril's throat. The creature toppled backwards.

The other octril had been run through by a slave. Salvarias remained frozen, eyes wide, staring at the dead mage. Wilhelm tugged Salvarias forward. They made it a couple of steps before Salvarias struggled against Wilhelm's hold.

"I can help him!" Salvarias cried.

He continued to push away but was no match for Wilhelm. Instead, Salvarias was merely slowing their escape. Fear knocked aside Wilhelm's patience, and he rounded on Salvarias, using a dominating tone never directed at his dear brother before. "You will leave him and you will follow me. Do what I say now!"

Salvarias's nodded slowly, his grief brimmed eyes switching to be a subservient slave to Wilhelm's command. Feeling sickened with himself, he continued.

After another scuffle, light glowed at the end of the tunnel and hope surged anew. They burst from the caves into bright sunshine, all shielding their eyes from the harsh rays.

Wilhelm called, "Close the cave, Salv."

Salvarias whispered, flicked his hand, and lightning struck above the cave entrance. Rocks tumbled down and a plume of dust rose up.

Wilhelm grabbed his brother's arm and hauled him down the sloping forest floor.

"Where are we?" a slave called out.

Wilhelm glanced around, but chose not to answer. They could be weeks, days, or hours from a city. All that mattered was putting as much distance as possible between the slavers and his group.

By the end of the day, his legs burned and the cool air pierced his lungs like a dagger. He had to practically carry Salvarias since his feet stumbled over each other and he seemed unaware of his surroundings.

Just as the sun danced on the horizon, Salvarias lifted his head and gripped Wilhelm's arm.

"We are lost, are we not, brother?"

Wilhelm motioned to the group to stop and lowered his brother to the ground. For the first time, Wilhelm realized it was autumn. Bright red, orange, and yellow leaves rustled in the trees and littered the forest floor. "I'll get us home. I promise."

Salvarias curled up, shivering in the breeze. "I can get us help, brother." He pointed off to the side.

It took Wilhelm a moment to see the enormous grizzly bear swaying back and forth, hidden by deep shadows. He grabbed his sword, but Salvarias rested a hand on his arm.

"He will guide us down the mountain, brother."

"How—" Wilhelm stammered, gaping at his brother. "You... what..."

"He will not harm us," Salvarias whispered.

Wilhelm was about to push for an explanation, but decided against it. He tore off a strip of his sleeve and wiped the blood from Salvarias's nose. More trickled out.

Glancing at the bear, Wilhelm shook his head in resignation. What other option did he have? "All right, Salv, we'll follow the bear."

"Thank you, brother."

Trying to convince the others was an impossible task. After what Wilhelm figured was too long, he threw his arms up and scowled at the fifty or so men. "Fine! Figure out your own way! I'm following the damn bear!"

He stormed back to his brother and lifted him to his feet. Without looking to see who followed, Wilhelm strode to the bear. Every instinct told him to run or fight, but just as Salvarias trusted Wilhelm, so did Wilhelm trust his brother.

Glaring off with the bear, Wilhelm growled, "Well?"

The bear snorted and plodded forward.

They walked the entire night and through the next day before the bear veered away from the group once they reached a main road. Happening upon a merchant, they learned of their location, which to Wilhelm's joy was a mere week from Falar. The group split, and only Wilhelm and Salvarias headed towards their hometown.

Chapter 13
Autumn 1016 a.r.

Wilhelm reclined against the rough bark of a tree while watching the bustling front gate of Falar. The past week had consisted of running from scouts, dodging raiding parties returning with additional slaves, scrounging for food, and barely sleeping. Though exhausted, hungry, and filthy, seeing the gates of Falar lifted his spirits. Soon he would be sitting with Durak, sipping ale by a fire, Salvarias warm and rested, and all Wilhelm's cares would disappear.

He glanced at his brother and offered an encouraging grin. "I think now is as good as time as any. If you see a mage, let me know."

Salvarias nodded, his eyes heavy, face pale, and body shivering even though the warm autumn sun blanketed the hillside. Wilhelm was sure his brother wasn't getting air into his lungs. He looked blue. At least the blood had stopped dripping from his nose.

After another cursory sweep of the crowd, Wilhelm draped his arm around Salvarias's shoulders and nonchalantly approached the gate.

Because Salvarias had outgrown his mage robes, he wore an oversized tunic and trews that barely stayed on his body. If any mages were to see him, they'd sense his power and possessed every right by the Association to kill him, or if they bothered to pay attention to his age, detain him.

Wilhelm took a slow gander around the steady droves of merchants and visitors. He remembered some of the guards but doubted any would recognize him. His hair was long, his beard overgrown, and his girth and height had changed over the years. He held his breath when he passed through the gate, but the brothers made it unmolested. His gaze swept the streets. No mages roamed nearby, so he turned down the closest alley.

The map of Falar remained strong in his mind, and he kept to alleys or quiet streets, strolling as though on no particular mission. The spicy smell of autumn mingled with the normal rank sourness of the grimy city. Fights could be heard from the main streets, guards attempted to preserve some semblance of order, and homeless men and women were passed out along the alleys. He smiled to himself. As much as he wished he lived in a nicer city, Serinity being his dream, he had to admit that he'd missed Falar. It had been his home for the past... he shook his head. He didn't even know how old he was, or what year it was, or even if Durak was still alive.

Salvarias stumbled, legs giving out, and he almost slipped from Wilhelm's grip. "Hang in there, Salv."

Salvarias mumbled, "Mage."

Wilhelm choked on his breath and plastered himself and his brother to the wall. Peered around the building, Wilhelm ducked back when a burgundy-robed mage paused in the center of a quiet street. Salvarias shivered and his legs gave out again. Wilhelm cursed and sent a silent prayer to the godless sky. He peeked around the corner. The mage was nowhere in sight. He lifted his brother and dashed to the next alley.

He chose a route that emerged behind the smithy and avoided nearly all of the busy market. The warmth of the forge filled the air, and he grinned when he saw the familiar cavrul pounding a new sword.

"Hello!" Wilhelm called.

Durak turned a scowling gaze. "What do ye wa—" Durak's eyes widened. "Wilhelm? Can it be?"

"In the flesh!" Wilhelm unlatched the gate to the forge. "How are you?" Laughing at Durak's shocked expression, Wilhelm released Salvarias and lifted Durak in a bear hug.

"We've looked years for ye, ye giant ogre!"

Wilhelm lowered the squirming man. "I hate to ask a favor right away, but we could use some food and a place to stay. I can—"

Salvarias collapsed.

"Inside," Durak ordered. "What's wrong with the boy?"

Wilhelm lifted his brother and followed Durak inside. "I can't get him warm. We've hardly eaten for days and he seems past exhausted. I don't know what to do for him."

Durak pulled a pack from a cupboard and withdrew two sets of Wilhelm's old clothes. "Get him washed and changed. I'll get a fire going and food." Durak paused. "Does he have a fever?"

Wilhelm shook his head. "No, I've checked."

"He looks blue," Durak noted.

"I know."

"Get him cleaned up. Maybe food will help."

"Thank you." Once in the washroom, Wilhelm lowered his brother to the floor and shook him awake. "Salv?"

He opened his eyes.

"Can you wash? I've got clean clothes."

Salvarias mumbled out something that Wilhelm took as a yes. He helped his brother bathe and ended up dressing him when he passed out.

Wilhelm cleaned himself up, trimmed his hair and beard, and attempted to change, but his old clothes no longer fit. Resorting to the ones from the slave caverns, he dressed, carried Salvarias to the sitting room, and settled him in front of the fire.

Durak offered a plate of cheese and bread.

Wilhelm propped Salvarias's limp body up, gently woke him, and handed him the plate of food. "Eat and then you can sleep." Wilhelm accepted a second plate and kept ready to catch Salvarias if he passed out again. "I'll work to pay for the meal. If you need help, I could offer my services again."

"Of course, lad. I could use the help."

"I don't want to impose, but would it be possible to stay in the storeroom? He's not well enough for the streets yet."

"I've got a spare room. I'll deduct the board from your pay."

"Thank you." He nudged Salvarias awake. "But I insist on the storeroom."

Durak shrugged. "Suit yourself. You know the boy can't work in the smithy. He's wasted to almost nothing and I doubt he would survive. He's barely breathing."

Wilhelm remained quiet. Durak was right, but the thought of being separated from Salvarias caused Wilhelm's chest to ache. He remained focused on his main goal, which was getting his brother fed, rested, and, for the love of the gods, warm.

Salvarias fell asleep after eating half the food. Wilhelm nestled him into a bedroll in front of the fire and covered him with blankets before joining Durak at the kitchen table. Wilhelm recounted his time in the slave caverns and was touched to learn that Humar had traveled nonstop attempting to find them.

"The slavers come often now," Durak said. "They were here

three nights ago. They take mages and healthy men. Now they be takin' women, too; young ones about the boy's age up to middle-aged."

"I didn't see any women in the mines."

"They take them a different direction, towards the east."

Wilhelm finished his brother's food. "Do we have any money left from when I used to work here? Salv can't leave the smithy until he gets mage robes."

"Of course you do and don't worry about money. I'm rich." Durak winked and tossed two gold coins at Wilhelm along with his old pack. "We were able to retrieve your pack, but they stole the boy's."

Wilhelm nodded. The puzzle box was his sole concern. He rifled through the pack and exhaled a held breath when he found it. He swore he'd never let it out of his sight again. "Thank you, Durak." He shoved his mother's dagger in his boot.

The cavrul muttered a curse of affection then said, "Get going before he wakes."

"If he has a nightmare, let him wake on his own. Don't touch him."

After fetching a borrowed broadsword from the smithy storeroom, Wilhelm forced his feet to leave. He stood outside the door, staring at the people coming and going. The aching void of his brother's presence started immediately. Wilhelm heaved a sigh. He'd have to learn to allow Salvarias out of sight. Still, each step twisted a knife in Wilhelm's heart.

His mind drifted to Bartle's death and the memory of commanding Salvarias as if he were a dog. Shame was a heavy burden. Salvarias wielded the same power and had never once abused it. The more Wilhelm thought about it, the sicker he became. He vowed never to coerce his brother or take advantage of their close relationship. Whether agreed upon or not, Wilhelm would always respect his brother's decisions.

"Wilhelm?"

He startled from his thoughts to see a private coach that he was all too familiar with. Brenil was gaping down from his seat.

"Wilhelm Laybryth?"

Wilhelm grinned. "Hello, Brenil."

"I'd heard you were taken." Wilhelm reached for the coach door, but Brenil hissed. "Haleen isn't in there."

"Where is she?"

"She died a year ago. Terrible fever swept through the city. Nearly two hundred people died."

Wilhelm raised his face to the sunny sky, wincing against the sharp pang of loss. "Shame. She was a good woman."

Brenil nodded and wiped his sleeve across his eyes. "Indeed. My new employer is treating me well, though. He's a wealthy merchant from Serinity. The man owns an estate in every city in Dalnar. He's hired me to be his coachman when he visits here. Free room and food as well as a salary. Very generous man."

Wilhelm scarcely heard the words. Haleen had been the first to usher him into manhood. Though neither kept solely to each other's company, she was always a breath of fresh air, a change from the demure, shy women he otherwise bedded.

Someone pounded on the side of the coach from inside and a woman's voice rose up. "What's the damn delay?"

"Sorry," Brenil called. "Ran across an old friend." He turned to Wilhelm. "The man's daughter. She's right up your alley."

Wilhelm nodded, his mind still miles away. "Thanks for the news, Brenil."

"Of course. Mind your safety. The city's worsened since you left. How's your brother?"

He smiled. "Sixteen now."

"Ah. Is he following in his brother's footsteps?"

He chuckled. "We've been locked in a cave for five years with no women. He hasn't had the chance."

"You must be in pain."

He winked. "You have no idea. Take care of yourself."

"You as well, Wilhelm." Brenil clucked his tongue and the horses plodded onward.

Wilhelm desired nothing more than a distraction from his sadness. He carried on down the street and was pleased to see Naffrita's clothing shop still in business. He opened the door and stepped into the store lined with bright fabrics and dull wools.

Naffrita stood behind a counter, folding a mass of deep-red velvet. Her tawny hair frizzed out of her loose braid, but her delicate face hadn't seemed to age. Her fitted dress hugged the curve of her waist and the soft mounds of her full breasts.

"Hello, Naffrita," Wilhelm said.

She narrowed her eyes. "Do I know you?"

He offered a grin and winked. "Been a couple of years."

Her eyes widened. "Wilhelm?" She flushed, straightened her dress, and lowered her head shyly. "Where have you been?"

He leaned against the counter and allowed his gaze to bring forward the many memories he had with her. Though older by six years, Naffrita was as stunning as she'd been five years ago.

"The octrils took us and I've been mining."

She cast a quick glance at his physique and blushed. "So you have."

"How's business?"

"Good. Better than good, as a matter of fact."

"Married?"

Naffrita smiled, meeting his direct gaze. "No. Not as of yet."

He grinned and strolled over to the window, drawing the drapes closed. "As you can see, I'm in need of some clothes." He walked to the front door and turned the key to lock it.

"I think we can take care of that." She lowered her head and smiled. "Why don't you come up to my quarters so I can get your... measurements?"

He strode over to her and lifted her in a fierce embrace, kissing her with all his pent up need. Feeling to the side, he found the table and shoved away the bundles of fabric. He lifted her on top of it, gliding a hand up her leg, relishing in her smooth flesh under his callused hand. With his free hand, he made short work of the strings to her corset, freeing her breasts with one pull. She moaned, opening her mouth further to him, succumbing to his hasty need. She ripped open his shirt, peeling it off him, and caressed his chest, her fingertips trailing further and further down. His trews constricted his manhood until she untied them. He told himself to move slower, but five years of being deprived a woman's touch drove him to an all-consuming lust. Running a hand up her chest, he tilted her back, bringing her breast to his lips as he thrust inside her. She cried out and clenched her legs around his waist, pulling him deeper inside her.

By the gods, he loved women.

Wilhelm entered Durak's home in clothes that were too small. The pant legs reached mid-calf and the tunic stretched in protest across Wilhelm's chest. The sleeves had required a rip down his biceps to allow room for his muscles. Though Naffrita needed two days to sew new clothes for him, she luckily had a set of burgundy robes for his brother, although Wilhelm was sure they were too big.

Durak roared with laughter when Wilhelm closed the door. "What in Veedran's creation are you wearing?"

Wilhelm blushed but joined in with a chuckle. "She didn't have anything that fit. It'll be two days before mine are done."

He unpacked the food he'd bought and folded his brother's new robes in the washroom before shaking Salvarias awake. "Salv."

He opened his eyes and looked as though he hadn't slept. "Please, brother. I am not hun—" Salvarias fell asleep again.

Muttering under his breath, Wilhelm joined Durak for a meal of roasted venison, a large helping of Durak's rosemary potatoes, crusty bread and plenty of yellow cheese. The two had just finished when a knock came to the door.

Wilhelm drew his mother's dagger and stood behind the door. Durak refrained from commenting on Wilhelm's skittishness.

Flinging open the door, Durak barked, "What do—Humar!"

Wilhelm popped his head around the door and grinned at the knight.

"Wilhelm!" Humar embraced him. "Where have you been?"

"We were taken to the Cattlar Mountains to mine by octrils."

"Salvarias?" Humar asked.

"Salv's by the fire. Do you think you can look him over? He's slept all day and I can't get him warm. He hasn't eaten a lot, and he says he's not hungry."

"Of course." Humar made his way to the sitting room. "Fill me in on the details."

As Humar examined Salvarias, Wilhelm gave the full story of his enslavement.

"Your brother will be fine," Humar eventually said. "He needs rest, food and plenty of warmth. He's freezing and malnourished." He rubbed his cheek. "Mining... I wonder if they intend to craft weapons."

Durak rolled his eyes. "Not this again. No talk of doom tonight, my friend. Tonight, we drink!"

The three men drank and told tales of the last five years until the moon was high. Wilhelm's exhaustion pounced after the fifth ale and he excused himself to sleep next to Salvarias, who hadn't stirred during the commotion.

Salvarias woke to a throbbing head and shivering body. No warmth seemed to exist in the world anymore, and though he felt the heat of the fire on his back, his bones ached from cold. He opened his eyes to see Wilhelm's crooked grin, and smiled inwardly.

"Time for dinner, Salv."

Salvarias raised his head and glanced around the cozy stone room. "Where are we?"

"The smithy in Falar." Wilhelm frowned. "It's been two days."

Salvarias forced himself to sit up and scooted closer to the hearth.

"Humar is staying in the guest room. Both are asleep. You need to eat."

He shivered. "I am hungry."

Though tired, he felt more rested than he had in the last five years. He rubbed his aching head and tried to bring memories forward. There were several holes from his time in slavery, and now he worried that permanent damage had been done to his mind. Pushing his magic to perform the spell three times daily had saved his brother from terrible abuse, and Salvarias would willingly do it again, but his skull felt constant pressure, and the lack of memories confirmed the harm inflicted. The last memory in the caves was unbearable and indescribable pain that had seemed to delve into his deepest thoughts, fears and joys. He felt violated.

He then remembered forests and the bear. He glanced at his brother, and Salvarias's cheeks burned with embarrassment. He was ashamed of his oddities, and it was only a matter of time before Wilhelm made the inquiry about how Salvarias had communicated with the bear. He would not lie, but wondered why his carefree brother loved him. Wilhelm was the paragon of a happy, loving, normal man. He deserved a better brother than Salvarias.

He tilted back for a better look at his brother. The word massive was now an understatement. Wilhelm was larger than any other man ever to roam Arden. His height alone was unheard of, and his entire body was muscle. He had been twice as big as Salvarias since he could remember. He rather liked it. His older brother offered a place to hide, a place to be tucked away in secrecy.

Wilhelm winked before lifting Salvarias to his feet. He battled his weak legs to the kitchen table and sank into a chair. "I am sorry, brother."

Wilhelm fetched a plate and piled it with too much food. "For what?"

"You have taken care of me for the last five years. Thank you." Salvarias rested his heavy head in his hands.

"I love you, Salv," Wilhelm said, as if those words explained his constant care.

"I love you too, my dear brother."

Salvarias accepted the plate of food and ate while Wilhelm reclined against the edge of the kitchen counter, his ever-present smile lifting Salvarias's spirit.

"I'm going to work at the smithy again, and Durak said we can stay in the storeroom. We're going to find some work for you that can be done out of the forge."

"No, brother. You know as well as I that Durak is excessively generous. He will find odd jobs that have no meaning so he can find an excuse to give me money. I will go to the market tomorrow and find work."

Wilhelm's brow furrowed.

Salvarias lacked comforting words. The same dark cloud hung over his head. He was not sure he had the strength to withstand hours of being separated from his brother, yet refused to allow him to carry the burden of survival. Already Wilhelm cared for Salvarias beyond what he deserved.

"Indeed he doesss, my pet," the presence confirmed. *"Your brother sssuffersss much becaussse of you, becaussse of your weaknesses. He had to raissse you sinccce your mother would not even care for you."*

"I am aware," he said shortly. Deep inside, a sick part of himself regretted their escape. Over the last five years, he had not been conscious enough to hear the lectures of the presence and he had found it a relief.

185

He finished what food he could and pushed the plate to the side, motioning at his brother, who grinned and sat down.

"Here." Wilhelm offered the beloved puzzle box.

Salvarias accepted the one thing that could ease his mind and subdue the horrid images of death constantly battering him.

"I don't want you out of my sight," Wilhelm rumbled. "Durak needs help around here. We can find something."

Noticing tightness in his brother's voice, Salvarias added a scolding tone and said, "What is it?"

Wilhelm shrugged. "You know the city is dangerous. I worry about you."

Salvarias sighed at the lie, but did not possess the energy to wring out the truth. "I will be careful. It is the right thing to do." He smiled at his favorite masterpiece of a bear.

"What is it?" Wilhelm asked.

"My brother."

Wilhelm ruffled Salvarias's hair and he elbowed his brother's ribs.

Wilhelm chuckled. "I miss your smile. It's been five years since I've seen it."

Salvarias cast his brother a sly grin. "I miss your old clothes."

Wilhelm flushed but chortled. "Naffrita needs time to sew. This is all she had."

"I am sure you delayed her work," Salvarias said dryly. Wilhelm's surprised expression at Salvarias's comment confirmed any doubts and he shoved his brother. "I saw when we were younger. Even the day we were at the forge before the flying creatures came you disappeared three different times with three different women. It is undeniable."

Wilhelm grinned. "Naffrita is a beautiful woman. There are many beautiful women in Falar."

"One day you will find one who can offer you a challenge."

"One day you'll find one that catches your eye." Wilhelm gave Salvarias a soft slap the back, and then rose to wash his plate. "You're old enough now. You're sixteen and a half."

Salvarias was sure he turned scarlet, and by his brother's chuckle, knew that he had. What his brother forgot was Salvarias's inability to be touched. He would never be with a woman, and he accepted his fate. Evil did not deserve love, did not deserve affection. Furthermore, he had his dreams with the raven-haired woman. In his dreams, he held her hand, soft and entwined in his. Those small moments were all he needed, or so he told himself. Even if they were not, he did not have a choice.

Wilhelm dried the plate. "Tomorrow, when the light comes into the washroom window, I'll try to teach you how to shave."

Salvarias rubbed his scruffy beard.

"I'm not very good. But I'm sure you'll be better at it than I am."

"Thank you." He ran his fingers through his hair and thought he could trim it himself. Maybe he would keep it long. It would help hide his evil eyes.

Cold away from the fire, he moved back to his bedroll and scooted it as close to the flames as possible. He began working on the puzzle box, deciding to make a squirrel. When Wilhelm sat by the fire, Salvarias scooted closer and rested his head on his brother's arm.

"I'm really sorry I made you leave Bartle," Wilhelm said.

Salvarias shuddered at the memory; the blood splattering on his face haunted his dreams and his mind was tormented by Bartle's sacrifice. "You were right. There was nothing I could do, and I put us in danger by fighting you. It is I who owe you an apology."

"That's not what I meant."

Though he felt no ill feelings towards his brother, the need to receive forgiveness shimmered in Wilhelm's misty eyes. Salvarias said, "You have nothing to feel sorry for, my dear brother. I love you and forgive you."

The comment worked, and his brother's eyes lit with their normal sparkle.

"Are you going to tell me about the bear?"

Salvarias could not stop his flush. "If I focus, I can sense what animals are near me, and I can pick up on their emotions, though I cannot hear their exact thoughts. I think I can talk to them, but it is not reciprocated."

"You sensed the bear was near and asked for its help?"

"Yes, and I sensed its respect for you."

"Me?"

Salvarias shrugged. "I assume it has to do with your mark."

Wilhelm turned over his hand. "It's just an odd birth-scar."

Salvarias studied the raised silhouetted bear taking up Wilhelm's palm. "I do not believe so. It is clearly a bear. There is no mistaking the symbol." Salvarias's fingers glided over his own mark of a ringed flame.

Wilhelm was silent for a moment. "You sense animals' emotions?"

"Yes."

"Is that why you don't eat meat?"

Salvarias shuddered, remembering the sheer terror the poor cow had endured in its last breath of life. "Yes."

"At least we'll never be attacked by wild animals," Wilhelm said.

Salvarias offered his brother a smile, clinging to the feeling of normalcy Wilhelm gifted with his acceptance of each of Salvarias's odd behaviors. His brother never showed signs of unease or uncertainty. Instead, each new abnormal trait seemed to grow his love. What Salvarias appreciated as much was his brother's discretion about those oddities. Wilhelm never allowed any to find out what horrible differences lurked within Salvarias. He'd give anything to be normal.

As evening wore on, Wilhelm's doze slipped into a deep sleep, and he leaned heavily against Salvarias. Eventually, the familiar, soft rumbling snore lulled Salvarias to dreams.

He stood on a hill painted in hues of pink from the setting sun. He gazed up at the tree with its branches stretching over the landscape. After an excited grin, he ambled down the hill and joined the masses of dead bodies. His hands trembled while he waited for her. Their relationship, even though dreamed up, meant more to him than he would openly admit.

"Hello."

He turned. "Hello."

She smiled her sweet smile, the same one she had cast upon him their first meeting, the same one that wrapped his heart in warmth. "May I join you?"

"Of course."

Her hand slipped into his. They strolled through the field of the dead while he listened to her talk of a book she had read. His thumb glided across the top of her hand, allowing him to feel the heat and softness of her skin. After she finished, she turned her piercing, ice-blue eyes to him.

"You've not spoken of books for some time."

"I have not read in many years. I have recalled all I could remember."

"Why haven't you read?"

This part of his dream intrigued him. He found it uncanny that he could not talk to a woman his own imagination dreamt up about anything personal. He neither knew what to call her nor would the question form. Rarely did she ask anything personal and if she managed to lay out questions such as the one she just had, Salvarias's mouth would not respond. He merely shrugged and led her forward, shaking his head.

"The sunset is stunning," she whispered.

He stopped walking and waited for the beautiful element she brought to his dreams. Eventually the dead parted to offer a narrow view of a setting sun. Instead of the standard pink, the sky was bathed in deep purples and pale yellows. It was indeed stunning.

When she took a step closer, a small smile played on her lips, and her eyes were an open invitation for his affections. By all the gods, she surpassed exquisite. Her eyes sparkled with innocence and strength, yet there was a palpable uncertainty. He found the mixture irresistible. Her ample feminine qualities seemed to be more prominent each time he saw her.

He traced her collarbone. Her chest heaved with quick breaths and she stepped closer, allowing her body to brush against him. He could feel her hot breath. He wanted to kiss her, to taste her lips, but instead he slid his arms around her waist and pressed her close. It was a dream. Nothing more. She leaned into his embrace, and her fingers tangled in his hair. He relished how real it all felt; how her skin was warm to the touch, how he could hear her heavy breathing, feel her tremble in his arms. But it was a dream. Nothing more. He buried his face in her hair even as his mind drifted to each place her body touched his.

He did not know how much time passed, but eventually she pulled away.

"I have to go," she whispered.

He ran his hand through her hair and watched the raven strands sift through his fingers. He sighed. "Goodbye."

She smiled sweetly before brushing her lips against his cheek. She whispered her goodbye in his ear and then vanished.

Salvarias raised his gaze, and the sky was once again pink and the dead corpses reached for him.

The next day, Salvarias left his brother's side for the first time in five years. As he stepped outside the smithy wall, he resisted a nearly overwhelming urge to flee back to Wilhelm. Latching the gate with trembling hands, Salvarias glanced at his brother. Wilhelm's crooked grin spread across his face, and Salvarias couldn't help but smile inwardly. He drew a deep breath before walking with determined steps towards the market, feeling his brother's eyes watching. A void grew in Salvarias's heart with each step, but the smithy was no place for him, and he needed to venture from his brother. The time had come for Salvarias to overcome his fears of other people, and now was as good a time as any to unlatch himself. Still, each passing person caused a lump to rise in his throat, his knees to grow weak, and every mother sparked a gut wrenching terror, certain their motherly gift allowed them to see his evil.

He kept his hood pulled low and his cloak hid his burgundy robes so none could see he was a mage.

He hated Falar. The buildings were crammed together, and only through deft dodges and skillful flinches could he avoid being touched. The citizens were grumpy, sour, unbathed, and unruly. Guards patrolled the streets, attempting to maintain order, but fights and angry merchants disrupted any moment of peace. Since the buildings were at least two stories, stuffing as many inhabitants into the city as possible, the sky was blocked and only the shipyard allowed a free view of the horizon. Salvarias needed sky, he needed fresh air, and he needed trees, plants, and life. Falar lacked all and wore on his mood.

Counting dirty, gray pavers, he made his way to the seamstress's shop and picked up the new clothes. Naffrita's pout conveyed her disappointment that Wilhelm had not come.

After Salvarias left, he continued down Market Street, mulling over what shop might accept him with the limited skills set he possessed when a familiar smell caused him to stop. Lavender. The comforting aroma was not something he had smelled since childhood, and he longed for the scent to soothe him to sleep as it once had. For some reason, it reminded him of Wilhelm, and Salvarias breathed deeply of the happy memories and the closeness to his brother the herb's scent brought. Salvarias found himself standing in front of the potion shop he had visited often with his mother. He lingered, inhaling the hypnotic aroma, but eventually decided to move on. When he turned to leave, someone grabbed his arm. He yanked free and found a plump woman with a merry face smiling at him.

"Oh, I'm sorry, dear. I didn't mean to scare you. Do you need herbs? I have lily weed, willow bark, fresh thyme and more. Won't you come in?" Her stubby fingers brushed a spiral of yellow hair from her eyes. He remembered Milred from his youth.

"No thank you, madam. I am looking for work." He glanced at the shop, wanting nothing more than to peruse the jars and vials and study their contents as he used to do while holding tight to Wilhelm.

"Really? Work you say?" She peered under his hood and stepped back, shuddering visibly. "Salvarias Laybryth?"

By now, after over sixteen years of seeing it, he thought he would have built immunity to people cringing, fleeing or shuddering. Yet the knife still twisted. He nodded.

"Those eyes!" she breathed. "I'd recognize them anywhere. You've grown so much!" She reached for him again.

He deftly avoided her touch and bowed. "It has been over six years, madam."

"So it has." She tapped a finger on her lips. "Do you know much about making potions or herb uses, dear?"

"No, madam."

"Hmm. Well, no time like the present. I'll tell you what, why don't you help me crush herbs and mix potions in the mornings? I can pay you two coppers a week." She flashed him a smile. "As you can see, my mind chose a profession my hands disagree with. I find it difficult to work with the components. If I remember right, your hands are most delicate."

"Thank you, madam. I would be honored." He followed her across the threshold of the shop.

Rows of shelves packed with jars containing wondrous and mysterious ingredients greeted him. Live plants spilt over mugs and pots, adding a heavy earthy aroma. A counter nestled in front of a wall blocked the view to the private rooms in back, a lone hallway the only path to the rear quarters.

He followed Milred down the hall to a work area containing wood bowls and various sizes of smooth rocks for grinding. It was positioned near a window to bring in fresh air. He inhaled deeply, his breathing steady and spirits high. Glancing around, his gaze lingered on bookcases crammed full of scrolls and bound books. He had not held a book in six years, and he ached for knowledge, for words. So much so, it was physically painful.

Seeing his gaze, Milred smiled. "Those books catalog the many varieties and uses of herbs and potions. Feel free after you're done for the day to read and become educated in alchemy. By the way, I'm Milred, in case you didn't remember."

"I do remember you. Thank you, madam. What of your mother?"

"Sadly she passed a winter ago."

"My condolences, madam. My mother was quite fond of her."

"I guess we've both lost our mothers." Milred smiled and brushed the melancholy mood aside. "My, how you've grown!"

Salvarias unclasped his cloak.

"Your hands... I would've recognized those hands anywhere. Just like your mother's! You were made for alchemy, my dear. It was your eyes that I remembered, though."

He glanced down at his hands. He didn't like them. They were not bulky like the other men he knew. They were not callused, and dirt did not stick under his fingernails. His hands were large, but instead of wide and masculine they were slender, and his fingers seemed feminine to him. Too clean, too thin. He knew he should not complain. The slimness and natural dexterity of his hands would be envied by any mage. Still, to Salvarias, it was just another trait that was not like other men.

For the remainder of the morning and into the afternoon, he did exactly as Milred asked. After he finished, he read two books. His mind felt satisfied, and the pain he endured daily from the images and irrepressible counting eased to a manageable roar.

When evening approached, he forced himself to leave the precious books behind. He found Milred behind the front counter. "Good evening to you, madam. I appreciate your help and the opportunity you have provided me."

Mildred was examining one of his potions with pursed lips. "Of course. I think I can mark up my potions since your skill far exceeds mine. Why don't you take another book home with you? You can bring it back tomorrow." She handed him a book on herb and oil mixtures. "It's one of my favorites."

"Thank you again, madam." Bowing, he pulled his hood low, took the book, and left.

Deciding to take a detour, he wandered to the city gallows. A hanging was scheduled, and as always, death attracted him like a watythm to ale. He stood on his toes at the back of the crowd to see above the milling people while guards fastened the criminal to the noose. The man was brown all over; brown hair, brown eyes, brown skin, brown dirt, and brown clothes.

A guard read off a list of crimes that included theft, rape, and assault while the ruffian grinned. After the footing fell, the filthy man dangled, twitching and choking, and as it had happened years ago, the criminal locked gazes with Salvarias. He returned the stare, not flinching from the pain and terror in the man's eyes, and familiar, sweet satisfaction erupted.

"Ssshame, my pet," the voice hissed. *"Rejoicccing in a man's torment isss not normal."*

"If he has hurt so many, done such horrible deeds, he deserves this fate."

"Perhapsss, but a painful, drawn out death ssshould never be inflicted. Quick and clean leassst we become that which we punisssh."

The satisfaction reached its peak when the light faded from the man's eyes and Salvarias breathed in the tormented death, ignoring the presence in his mind. The instant he turned and no longer looked at the criminal, his soul cried out in agony while the evil screamed with glee. Satisfaction turned to boiling hate. He fought down the bile his own feelings caused and made his way home in a sudden torrent of rain.

Chapter 14
Autumn 1016 a.r.

Salvarias sat at the table in the potion shop reading a book. The sun fell across his back and warmed his cold bones. A short month had passed since he first began working for Milred, and he found alchemy to be an ever changing, ever growing, field. For the first time in his life, his mind was challenged. It took study, concentration, and analysis to learn. Since Milred was versed in nearly all the herbs and plant life in Dalnar and Windlous, she taught him until he was an expert in identifying different ingredients.

With the pain in his mind reduced, he gained an appetite, put on weight, and grew in height. During his reading, and the lessons from Milred, he discovered a concoction that assisted with his breathing, and his lungs felt open for the first time in his life.

While he read, a portion of his mind was thinking of Wilhelm. The time they spent apart was Salvarias's only regret in working at the potion shop. Wilhelm seemed equally upset, but Salvarias had taught himself to mask his emotions. When he returned home, a warm hug greeted him and Durak breathed a sigh of relief to see Wilhelm's grouchy demeanor disappear. In order to ease his anger, Salvarias planted a seed of thought within Humar. Since the knight had yet to leave Falar, his restless spirit grew irritated. Salvarias's plan aided both men. With subtle words and a few dropped ideas, Humar became obsessed with the notion of assisting Wilhelm in becoming the knight's equivalent in swordplay. He dedicated every waking breath Wilhelm did not work the forge to instructing him. The knowledge he gained had the same effect on him that potion books had on Salvarias, and he reveled in his brother's happiness. When not at the herb shop, Salvarias enjoyed watching Wilhelm practice and learned his movements—his heavy left foot, his favorite stances and lunges.

Overall, the turn in events pleased Salvarias.

He closed a book labeled *Cavrul Mushrooms and Their Uses*.

Milred sat humming and examining a new plant he had

discovered from a traveler. "Learning anything new?" she asked.

"Yes, much. The cavruls have a mushroom, black with white tips, that is poisonous when eaten. The victim dies within a few breaths."

"Oh, my. Well, that's no good. Any helpful herbs?"

He nodded. "One is able to clot blood in an instant. It would prove useful for open wounds."

"Excellent. We'll keep our eye out for it. By the way, here's the potion you mixed earlier. All bottled up and ready."

He set aside the book, accepted the vial, and paid Milred the appropriate amount. "I will be back shortly."

He pulled his cloak about him before making his way down the street to a dark alley. He found the two children he had seen in the morning. One child, a little girl with brown hair and freckles, still coughed. Shuffling loudly to warn the two of his coming, he tilted his head to the younger boy, who stood in front of the sick girl.

The boy scowled and puffed up his chest. "What do you want? We're not hurting anyone, just let us stay here."

Salvarias bowed again. "I have no intention of forcing you to leave. I work at the potion shop, and I noticed your... sister?"

The boy nodded in agreement.

"I noticed your sister is ill. This potion will help her cough and cure her sickness." Salvarias kept his voice soothing.

The boy eyed the vial and wiped his dirty hands on his soiled shirt. "I don't have any money."

"No need, young man. We have an abundance at the shop and I was instructed to dispose of the excess. It would be wasted if you do not accept."

"You think thisss will sssave your sssoul, my pet?" the presence scoffed.

The boy narrowed his eyes. "How do I know it's not poison?"

Salvarias opened the vial, let a single drop fall on his finger, and licked it off. "As you can see, I live. I have no reason to poison you."

The boy accepted the vial while casting a smile and muttering a thank you. Salvarias bowed again and dropped a silver as he turned to leave.

"Mister, you dropped this," the boy said, holding up the coin.

Salvarias shrugged. "It is not mine, good man. Evidently, someone has lost it. I suggest you keep it and buy food for you and your sister. Baker Jyfil makes wonderful breads."

The boy grinned.

Salvarias tilted his head and left the alley. The voice's words played in his mind. His acts of kindness were part of his pure soul trying to redeem itself from the evil it possessed. He felt no kinship to the ones he helped, except, oddly, the animals, nor did he feel satisfaction in his good deeds. It was just something he did which he struggled to understand.

He entered the potion shop so lost in his thoughts that he nearly ran into a tall mage dressed in slate-blue robes. Salvarias immediately sensed the man's power and bowed. Respect for superior mages was taken seriously by the Association and, unfortunately, Salvarias had never been able to sense his own level of power.

"Fetch me five fly wings, eight willow barks, and six fhsil flowers," the mage demanded of Milred.

Salvarias stepped around the man and helped her collect the items.

Tossing coins on the counter, the red-bearded mage looked at Salvarias. "You are employed here?"

"Yes, Master," he responded, head still bowed.

"Where is the mage shop?"

"Down eight stores, Master. Master Himiks is the owner."

"Your name; and do you apprentice under him?"

"Salvarias Laybryth. No, Master, I do not apprentice under him." He raised his head at being asked his name, as customary by the Association guidelines, but kept his eyes shadowed as always.

"Walk with me," the mage commanded.

"Thisss man can help you," the voice whispered.

The man was old, yet his hair and beard were fire red, worn long to the middle of his chest. His eyes were dark and uncaring, his air one of arrogance and domination. Salvarias's instincts told him not to listen to the old mage, but hunger for knowledge and magic moved Salvarias to walk beside the mage.

Once in the streets, the man made no attempt to hide his robes. He emitted an aggressive aura, and Salvarias guessed that was why no one spit or made eye contact.

He said, "You have the gift, yet it is underdeveloped. Whom do you apprentice under?"

"No one, Master. Himiks will not teach me and I know no other mages in Falar."

"You may call me Master Dethal," he supplied. He stopped short of the mage shop and his gaze steadied on Salvarias. He found the strength not to flinch from the inspection. "I will accept you as my apprentice. You will come after you finish your work at the herb shop and we will study until nightfall. My house is past the Red Lion on the left. A black door marks the entrance. We start today. Now leave me."

After a bow, Salvarias turned toward the potion shop, shivering from the excitement surging through him. Being awarded an apprenticeship was a great honor. The master mage accepted the responsibility of providing lodging, food, and instruction for his pupils. Of course, Salvarias would refuse the lodging and dinners. Finally, he would be able to practice his magic and gain the knowledge his gift required.

Screams startled him from his thoughts. He turned his gaze towards the sky. The same creatures that had snatched him away five years ago could be spotted diving into the city, only to soar with limp bodies. It was the first daylight raid.

He ran. He was not sure where he was fleeing to, but paranoia had grasped his mind. He was in a shadowed alley with other citizens screaming past him when wings sounded close. His heart rose in his throat and he found it difficult to swallow. Air disappeared. Running was no longer an option. He clutched his chest and turned just as an outstretched hand from the sky gripped his arm. Fear froze him. Memories of the slave camps, his brother's whipped body, Salvarias's constant sickness, and the pain he had endured flooded him.

When his feet left the ground, he heard a cry of anger. The hand released him and he fell into familiar arms as the winged horror thumped to the ground. He saw an icicle shard embedded in its back, and he raised his gaze to see a flash of slate-blue robes. Before he could get his bearings, he was being carried away by Wilhelm. The alley turned to a twisting tunnel, and sounds drowned in and out.

"It's all right," Wilhelm whispered. "We're all right. Nothing can hurt us."

They stopped running. Salvarias's vision dimmed. His chest ached.

"You have to relax. We're all right. One breath. For me, Salv. Just one."

Salvarias focused his mind, controlled his racing thoughts, and concentrated on breathing. Air finally flew into his lungs and he inhaled deeply. His vision returned.

"Are you all right?" Wilhelm asked.

Salvarias nodded. He glanced around at the small home; his brother must have dived into the first open door he found.

Wilhelm grinned. "They almost got you again."

Salvarias latched onto Wilhelm, utterly terrified to be whisked away, to be separated. Massive arms enclosed him.

Wilhelm's deep voice rumbled, "I won't let it happen again."

Salvarias nestled in the corner of the storeroom. He tried his best to keep his hands from trembling when he accepted his plate of food. His brother plopped down with a heaping plate of meat and bread. Salvarias smiled at his brother's choice of food.

"What?" Wilhelm asked over a mouthful of bread.

"Have you ever eaten a vegetable, my dear brother?"

Wilhelm shrugged. "They make me hungry."

Salvarias's taut nerves loosened.

Wilhelm plucked up one of his carrots and devoured it in two bites. "There." Wilhelm winked. "Better?"

Salvarias chuckled and rested his head on his brother's arm. Inhaling a deep, soothing breath, Salvarias picked out his favorite food.

He was thankful to be off the streets. The creatures had abducted a fair number of women and men from the midday crowd. The sight of angry loved ones and sobbing children begging guards for help stirred a deep anger in him that he did not quite understand. Though he cared little for people, knowing another would suffer what he had endured for five years ignited a fury he had never felt before. The longer he dwelled on it, the hotter his blood boiled. None should suffer. He had a wild notion to hunt down the creatures and—

"You all right, Salv?"

Salvarias jumped from his thoughts. He unclenched his fist and winced when his fingernails pulled from his palm.

"What did you do!" Wilhelm exclaimed.

Salvarias glanced down at the punctures in his hands. "Sorry." He retrieved a cloth from a hidden pocket in his robes and wiped away the blood.

Wilhelm's expression was one of concern, but rarely did he push Salvarias for explanations. "Eat some more."

While Salvarias ate, his thoughts ventured to what he would tell Wilhelm when leaving for the lessons with Master Dethal.

"He will ssstop you from practicing. He will not let you go to the home tonight," the presence whispered.

Salvarias ate a bite of cheese. *"He supports my magic."*

"Durak doesss not. Humar doesss not. You know the way they look at you. They sssee your evil. They will ssstop you, and your brother will argue with them. Wilhelm will be hurt by their wordsss. Ssspare him the grief. Keep the training a sssecret."

He sighed. The voice spoke logical words. His magic hungered for knowledge and there was a need—no, a *requirement*—within him to learn. He chose not to risk his opportunity. "I am going to start working late at the potion shop, brother." His stomach knotted. He remembered the feeling. Whenever he had said bullies had beaten him instead of his mother, his stomach had felt the same.

Wilhelm talked over a mouthful of bread. "I'll come and walk home with you."

"No need, brother. There are plenty of guards along the market at night. The smithy is only a short distance." He set down the slice of cheese. He felt sick.

"It's on the other side of the market! It's really no trouble, Salv."

"I can take care of myself." He allowed a note of annoyance to filter in his voice. "I must learn to defend myself." He knew today was not the ideal timing for this conversation. In fact, he would have been taken from his brother if not for the mysterious mage that had killed the creature.

Mild surprise glittered in Wilhelm's eyes. "I would prefer you walk by yourself in the morning. I'll walk home with you at night."

"I assure you, I am fine." Salvarias could not meet his brother's gaze.

Wilhelm pulled the pea-sized puzzle box from his shirt pocket and Salvarias accepted it, smiling as it grew to normal size.

"I don't like it," Wilhelm muttered.

Salvarias nestled against his brother. "I know."

Heaving a deep sigh, Wilhelm said, "You have to be careful. Keep to the lighted side of the street and follow a guard."

"Of course. Thank you."

Wilhelm ruffled Salvarias's hair and he offered an elbow to the ribs, smiling at his brother's feigned pain. The device ceased moving and Salvarias admired his creation.

"What is it?" Wilhelm asked.

"A fox." Salvarias collapsed the box to its original form and handed it back to his brother. "I will see you tonight, brother."

"Just be careful."

Salvarias left the smithy and headed down the street to his first lesson. That the Red Lion was in the direction of the potion shop helped to eliminate suspicion. Past the market and up two streets, he stopped in front of the black door to study the home. It was two stories, made of the standard Falar gray rock, and seemed unwelcoming. Its few windows were boarded, and it looked out of place on the cheery street. His instincts told him something was amiss, but his need for knowledge helped him ignore them, and the presence agreed. Taking a deep breath, steadying his nerves, and gaining control, he tapped on the door.

After a moment, a servant answered. The man's chestnut hair hung unkempt about his pockmarked face. He was polite and welcomed Salvarias inside.

Candles were the single source of light inside though it was a sunny afternoon. The first room was the main sitting room, offering two plush chairs nestled near a fireplace with a small table close to each that would allow one to rest a book and a glass of wine. Down the hall were a kitchen and a long table. To his right, a room contained books lined floor to ceiling, and it took a forceful turn of his head to yank his gaze from the beautiful sight.

"My name is Unias," the servant said. "Master Dethal is upstairs in his laboratory. Please, follow me." Unias led Salvarias to the upper level. Glancing to his right down the upstairs hall, he noticed two other doors and assumed those to be bedrooms. The servant knocked on the third door.

"Master, the young mage has arrived." Bowing, the servant descended the stairs, leaving Salvarias alone.

The door opened and Dethal called, "Come in, Salvarias."

Hardly any light illuminated the room, and Salvarias's instincts once again urged him to leave, but he brushed the thought aside. He needed this; he needed to learn, and his magic yearned for information. He stepped into the room. The door shut behind him though no one touched it. He was immediately curious about the spell. He knew of none that opened and closed doors.

Once inside, all he saw was a desk lit by a single candle and two high-backed chairs. Dethal sat in the chair facing the door. The candlelight did nothing to diminish the darkness, and Salvarias could not guess the size of the room or if anyone else was present. Chills ran up his spine.

"Come, sit." Dethal motioned to the chair across from him.

Salvarias did as he was asked.

"Tell me the spells you know, Salvarias." Dethal opened a book.

Salvarias recited each spell, which unfortunately did not take long. Embarrassed, he explained, "I have not been able to learn any new spells for the last five—"

"No matter," Dethal interjected while he continued writing. "Only respond to what I ask, do not elaborate or provide explanation. I don't want to be bothered by your excuses. If I'm to teach you, you must do as I tell you without question. The training will be arduous with many long nights. You will want to quit, you will hate me, but you will do as I say."

The same calmness washed over Salvarias that he had experienced when the three mages from the Association visited him at the age of six. Quiet confidence emerged, and warmth flowed through his blood. It was supplied by his magic, which was awake and eager.

The magic's voice rang with excitement when it spoke. *"My young wizard, this man is powerful. He can teach us much."*

"Allow us to begin then." Salvarias kept a wary eye on his magic at all times. Though he valued it, he didn't trust it. For years, he had read about mages losing their minds when the magic consumed them. His magic had helped him in the mines, but there was no mistaking its impatience for knowledge. He was not sure of the lengths it would go to in order to obtain what it sought. He turned to Dethal, who watched, his eyebrow arched. "I understand and accept, Master."

"We start by reading." Dethal produced three books and a scroll from a low table beside him. "Leave me and read in the sitting room."

"Yes, Master." Salvarias bowed, accepted the books, and turned to leave. He paused. "Master, was it you who shot down the flying creature earlier today?"

Dethal leaned back in his chair. "Perhaps. What does it matter?"

"If it was you, you have my thanks."

Dethal nodded. "I'll be keeping an eye on you, boy. I take apprenticing young mages very seriously. You see I am unafraid. You see I didn't hide who I was on the wretched streets. Mages should be feared, boy, not persecuted. Soon, you'll know the true power we possess."

Salvarias's screaming instincts nearly blocked out his thoughts. He caressed the books under his arm, feeling their soft leather bindings. He bowed. "Thank you, Master."

The sitting room was warm and the servant brought spiced apple cider, which Salvarias had never tasted. He found it lovely and sipped it in front of the crackling fire.

His gaze fell to the scroll. He unraveled the old document and a smile spread at the title. It was his favorite.

The Scroll of Nevlar

I am Nevlar, god and brother, lover and father, and my power is unequaled. My tale is one of despair, but one I wish for my children of Arden and those of other worlds to hear and understand, and therefore understand me. What I impart in this scroll is explanation for my actions. I want my children to know why I smote their lands, why I burned their cities, why I created Oblivion, and why I sentenced my wretched children to roam the world of Arden in torment.

Not always was my heart cold, not always did I hate. My early existence overflowed with laughter and my heart brimmed with love. I cared for all and I loved all. Events, which will never be spoken of, reshaped who I was and what I loved. They morphed my soul into darkness and turned my love bitter.

It was during this time of emptiness that I arrived at a world created by a fellow god to visit my friends. When I walked into the forest, I found my friends had been uprooted and burned, used to forge fires to craft weapons of war. My rage was great. I hunted those who had murdered my friends. They could not run. They could not hide. I found them. I killed them. Once my vengeance was spent, I wept for my friends while I watched the rising flames and listened to their dying screams. I wallowed alone in my misery until a goddess, who I knew little of, came to me. She knelt by my side while I begged the last sapling to battle the black ash. With tears in her eyes, she extinguished the surrounding flames. Her love encased my friend, healed its scarred bark, and bestowed tender care and nourishment. I stared in wonder as it flourished, soaring above the smoke to the clear sky. Life burst from its branches and my friend survived. I knew in my heart I had given up. I possessed the power to heal the sapling. I could have nurtured it, but all I had left was anger and despair. My beloved friend had nearly died because of my rage, my hate, and the hopelessness I felt each day I roamed dark places. It was she who brought me light, hope, and showed me life could survive the flame.

I loved her. In that moment, I knew my heart was forever hers. I recognized the goddess Zerana; she holds my brother's heart—though his love is unreturned. I thanked her and left her in the burning fields, avoiding the temptation that would hurt my brother.

I still do not know how she found me, but since our meeting, her presence was near me always. I denied my desires, my love. I told her I did not care for her, that I did not want her affections, but she never relented in her pursuits. One day we argued. I told her to leave me and I tried to drive her from me with harsh words I did not mean. I went to push her aside, but she kissed me. I no longer felt anger and hopelessness. I saw beauty for the first time since my early years. Forevermore was I hers and she mine. But I concealed the truth from my brother and Zerana respected my choice. Veedran's love for her was as deep and pure as my own. Though his actions towards worlds are unforgivable, he is and always will be my brother. Forever, under all circumstances, will I love him. I never meant to cause him pain.

Unbeknownst to my love, I created Arden as a gift. I made forests, mountains, soil, and oceans. She loved my creation and saw my love for her reflected in each leaf, in each granule of soil. Together we crafted animals, wondrous creatures that roamed Arden at our side. I was never happier. Time passed. My happiness grew with every breath I was with my lover, while my brother grew more terrifying. Veedran's lust for torment transcended all other evil, his hate unrivaled. It made Arden that much more special for Zerana and myself. A sanctuary from war, from death, from hate. A respite from darkness.

Zerana wanted children, and together we made each one, gifting them with individual traits, qualities, and characteristics. We loved every child, walked with them and taught them how to build, farm, and work the land. Zerana selected a handful of our children and gave them a special link to her, so they could call upon us if we were not home. Our children meant everything to us. All were happy, and evil was unknown. Finally, I had escaped war, I had escaped meaningless death. I broke free of the darkness plaguing my soul.

To this time, I have never known how Veedran discovered our relationship. It doesn't matter. He found us, found our children. I knew he would have his revenge. And so he did. Darkness touched Arden.

I taught my children of my brother's methods, told them not to listen to the whispers he sent on the wind, his temptations and lies. I gave my children the signs and tools needed to remain pure and whole. But still they cheated, they killed, they raped, and they turned towards the evil of my brother.

Purity, hope, and light left and my anger returned; the darkness crept once more into my soul. I created Oblivion, the plane reserved for those who listened to the words of Veedran. While my lover tried to save our children, I condemned them. I hated them. I tormented them. I forced each to pay for their evil, for their immoral acts.

In an attempt to save our children, Zerana, full of hope and love, united those who did not listen to Veedran and waged war against the evil creatures he created. She fought my brother herself, fought the creatures he sent to kill her. I could not. He is my brother and I will always love him. I helped the one way I knew how. I split our children, changing them into four different races to aid my lover's Armies of Light.

Winsire took to the trees, spotting armies using the language of the woods. I turned their skin olive to blend with their landscape, gave them larger eyes to see in the darkest of places and far distances. I built them lithe, light, and agile.

Cavrul dwell in the caves of mountains to mine for metals. I shortened their bodies and made them thin for tight spaces but sturdy so they could temper the steel. I gave them gray skin to blend with their environment and the vision needed to find the strands of metals in the rock.

Watythm rule the oceans, fighting the beasts Veedran created in the waters. I colored them pale blue, gifted them the ability to live underwater for days, and to speak the language of the sea. They built ships to patrol the land's edge, preventing Veedran's minions from flanking Zerana. Brawny and bold, I granted the watythm an adventurous spirit, daring the ocean's wrath, and able to stay mischievous and hopeful in the eyes of the storms.

To erthlas, I bestowed agility, strength, and cunning in battle. They could live days without food and maintain strength and sense of mind. I gifted them with quick healing and a fierce need to overcome obstacles, the will to survive in battle. They desire physical labor; to work the lands, to fight in wars, and to build cities while maintaining order and structure. They were brute force, ground attacks against the growing armies of Veedran.

Even with my help, Veedran's Armies of Iniquity wreaked havoc on my lover's Army of Light. Wars raged for hundreds of years and I sat in despair, watching our love, our children, be defiled by my brother.

One fateful battle sent Ctol Lilkous, highest commander in my lover's army and the first ruling King of Arden to find me. He told me they were outnumbered, that Veedran had created Klusher creatures, which forced man to unite with the armies of darkness. I was furious. Always have the gods left creatures to make their own choices, to decide themselves if they are evil or good. But Veedran had violated this sacred oath. I followed Ctol to the battlefield. I arrived to find my lover dead in the arms of my brother.

On that day, my heart died. On that field, my anger flourished.

And so it comes to pass that I now curse my children to live with the consequences of their actions. From the sky I will cast down my fury upon them. My children will know the full power of my anger and hate; they will feel it in their very souls. I will smite the world I created for my love, break it apart. And I will kill. I care no more and I no longer love. I will abandon my children. They will live without my love and protection. They will be subjugated to whatever desires Arden, by whatever forces discover them. All the lesser gods my brother brought will now have whatever they desire. I will no longer stop them.

Know this: Zerana did not die at the hands of my brother; she died at the hands of her own children. If only they had listened to me, my lover would be alive, my children safe, and my trees and mountains, my oceans and soil would not be tainted with blood.

This scroll will survive my wrath. I will have my retribution for my lover's death and my children's betrayal.

I have no hope, no light, and no love left. My soul will roam in darkness forevermore.

***

Salvarias rolled the scroll up with tender care. He stared into the flickering fire, lost in thought. He only hoped that if his evil ever overcame him Wilhelm would have the courage to strike the final blow. Nevlar should have killed Veedran. The dark god inflicted horrors unmentionable against Arden, yet Nevlar did nothing. The last thing Salvarias wanted was for his soul to be so lost that he committed atrocities. He often wondered if Veedran had secretly wished for death. Maybe the dark god saw himself; saw his evil and was afraid but lacked the courage to end his own life. Salvarias brooded over his own cowardice.

Shaking off his dark thoughts, he turned his attention to the other three books.

He started with the imaginatively titled *The Creation*, which explained the beginning of their world and talked of creatures Nevlar created that were eliminated in the Retribution. It followed the history of Arden until the final confrontation between Nevlar and Veedran. As always, with any book of the three founding gods, it had three separate endings. The first was that both brothers left Arden and fought each other in far off worlds. The second ending was that Nevlar forced Veedran to walk Arden for eternity just as Veedran cursed Nevlar to never step foot on Arden again. The third ending was that the brothers had killed each other in a secret forest in Arden.

The book Salvarias read next was written by the clerics who were granted direct contact with Zerana, and it discussed the goddess and all the love she imparted throughout Arden that supposedly could still be felt.

The last book documented the many planes of death. Oblivion petrified him the most since he knew his soul was destined for the realm made of nightmares, reserved for the damned. Rumors were that Oblivion had been overtaken by one of Veedran's minions, a very powerful one, who concocted new ways to torture those cursed to the realm. Zerana created the other planes for the pure in heart, a place Salvarias would never visit.

"Yesss, you are doomed for Oblivion. However, do not worry, it isss where you belong," the voice said. *"I will ssstay with you and keep you company, my pet."*

"Do you require anything?"

Salvarias jumped from his thoughts and looked up at Unias. "No, thank you. I have finished."

"Then please rejoin my master."

"Thank you."

Salvarias returned to the laboratory and tapped the door. It opened immediately.

"I have finished, Master."

Dethal leaned back in his chair, motioning Salvarias to the other. "What did you think of the books?"

"I have heard the stories before, Master. Each time I read a book on the gods, I find more questions than answers."

Dethal regarded him for a moment. "Very true. Which ending do you believe, boy?"

"All and none of them. Anything is possible, Master. Only a fool closes their mind."

Dethal smiled. "You're a smart boy, logical yet open-minded; a brilliant combination in a mage. Go to the library and read the books starting left to right, top to bottom. Unias will get you when it is time for your lesson to end."

"Yes, Master."

Leaving the room, Salvarias went to the library, excitement shaking him. Picking the first book, he sat in front of the fire and read. He made it through two by the time Unias interrupted.

"I'll keep your place in the book for you. It will be here tomorrow for you to finish," Unias said.

Thanking him, Salvarias left the house, drawing his cloak around him in the chilled autumn night, and headed home, content. His magic was disappointed, but he reminded it that a mind open to knowledge is more powerful. The books provided him an opportunity to calm his mind, his pain, and reluctantly the magic agreed to be patient, though it requested that he read at a quickened speed.

Wilhelm was asleep at the kitchen table when Salvarias entered the smithy. He gently shook his brother awake, smiling inwardly at the instant grin. They retired, and Wilhelm's soft snore filled the storeroom before Salvarias settled into bed. He slipped the small bag of lavender under his pillow, and the soothing smell pulled him to sleep and dreams.

He stood under the single tree, staring at the undulating hills of light brown grass lit by a pink-streaked sky and littered with the dead. He strolled down the hill, bottling his excitement. He did not walk far before he heard her greeting.

"Hello."

He turned to face her, allowing his gaze to lock into his memory every inch of her. "Hello."

"May I join you?"

"Of course."

She smiled sweetly, her eyes lighting up with happiness, and took his hand.

"What did you do today?" he asked.

"I read for a while. The same book I told you about last night. Then I spent the rest of the day with my sister in town. We shopped and I visited the book store."

"Did you find any new books?"

"No, nothing." Her eyes lit up. "That's the most exquisite rose bush I've ever seen."

He looked around, trying to find the beautiful element she brought to his dream each night, but only the dead surrounded them. "Where?"

"There." She pointed ahead.

A dead woman moved aside to reveal a rose bush larger than a bear. The pure white flowers were nearly the size of her head.

"I wonder if roses in Windlous are as large," she murmured.

"I have read of some this size."

"I wish we could go there." She leaned her back on his chest. "I wish you were real and not a dream."

He smiled at his dream's odd comment, but wished nothing more than for her to be real. He traced her shoulders before he wrapped his arms around her slender waist, pressing her close as he buried his face in her soft hair. Her fingers snuck in the sleeves of his robe and caressed his arms. He was not sure how much time passed, but he held her, enjoying her tender touch. Eventually, she turned in his arms to offer her sweet smile.

"I have to go."

He ran his hand through her hair and watched the silky strands fall between his fingers. "Goodbye."

Her lips pressed against his cheek. Her breath tickled his ear, and it took every ounce of Salvarias's willpower not to kiss her.

She placed a flower in his hand. Her word was a whisper in his ear. "Goodbye."

Then she vanished. He looked down at the rose. The petals shriveled between his fingers and drifted to the blood-covered ground. He dropped the stem with a deep sigh and continued walking.

Chapter 15
Winter 1016 a.r.

Salvarias made his way through the streets to Dethal's home. Winter winds whistled between the buildings, and he huddled in his cloak, crunching snow beneath his boots. He desperately missed Wilhelm, and between the potion shop and Dethal's studies, there was no time left for one another. But with the past three months being without danger, the raiding parties having left Falar alone, Salvarias began hoping for the brothers' future for the first time in his life. Wilhelm, obviously an attraction for many women, would soon marry and settle down. Although, at the rate he went through hour-long relationships, a unique one would be needed to hold his interest. With Wilhelm cared for by Durak, Salvarias allowed himself to dream of opening his own potion shop or becoming partial owner with Milred should he ever save up enough funds. He smiled at the thought.

He ducked under a low sign above a fruit stand. His health and weight had peaked over the last three months and he had suffered an enormous growth spurt. He was well over six feet tall, and while his frame was nothing compared to Wilhelm, he had put on weight. Muscles he had no idea existed developed, and their arrival continued to be a mystery. He did not perform hard labor such as his brother did; yet clearly something provoked the mass. Dethal's irritation with Salvarias's attire had caused him to buy new burgundy robes for Salvarias that reached the ground, instead of his former ones that had hung at mid-calf with sleeves ridiculously short.

Salvarias sighed in contentment. Three months with no damp slave caverns, his mind healthy and not withdrawn, no beatings from his mother and no one, not a single soul hurt him. He found he enjoyed health.

When the sun crept over the sea, he hastened his steps. He had finished all the books and today he would practice his magic, something he had not done since the slave caverns, and finally expand his repertoire. He remembered no spells, merely random words since leaving the slave caves, and he had no spell books to study. He could only ignite his magic and listen to it lecture him on his lack of knowledge. The routine was becoming tiresome for both.

Unias greeted Salvarias at the door and motioned to the stairs, accepting his cloak. During his time in the home, he sat with Dethal nightly to discuss the books he had assigned to be read. Though Salvarias's instincts continued to warn him that something was amiss, he enjoyed having the company of another mage. Dethal's conversations were intelligent and challenged Salvarias to think outside of what was considered normal, the possible versus the impossible.

He tapped on the door and it opened.

"Master." He bowed.

"Sit," Dethal said. "You trust me, boy?"

Salvarias shifted uncomfortably in the plush chair. He did not want to offend, nor did he want to lie. "I trust few, Master. I respect many."

Dethal smiled thinly. "Today we will begin to learn magic. You have decent power and your mind is quick to retain knowledge. However, you are deficient in discipline. Your mind has potential, but your lack of focus hinders your abilities. I have ways to open your mind, but I warn you, it will come at a cost. You will fatigue, you will become physically weak, but your magic will become powerful and your mind will grow sharp. I'll gain no satisfaction in what I do, but you'll see the benefits. Do you trust me to complete what I've just told you?"

"Yes, Master." Physical punishment he could endure, he could rebuild his health, but opportunities to learn magic under one as powerful as Dethal did not present themselves often. Salvarias sighed inwardly. He would miss health.

"Good boy. Now, I've enchanted this room to help with our lessons. Whatever spell we cast will not leave here. I am protected; you cannot harm me. I want you to use the full force of your power without concern. *Your mistakes will be punished.* Do you understand?" Dethal's gaze was intense.

"Yes, Master." He was eager to start.

Dethal pushed forward a spell book. "Open it and perform the first spell."

Salvarias opened the book bound in rich brown leather and read over the spell silently, studying each word. "Master, I am unfamiliar with this word," he said, pointing half way down the spell.

Suddenly, he was on the ground. It felt as though a huge fist had pushed him on the chest, knocking him over in his chair. The blow was more shocking than painful. Startled, he rose, picking his chair from the floor, positioned it at the table, and returned to his seat.

Dethal spoke harshly. "Do not ask questions when you have done nothing to try to solve it yourself. You know enough to determine the word and its meaning. Never seek the easy answer. Use your mind, boy! Think!"

"Yes, Master." Salvarias continued to study the word. After many moments, he figured out that it was similar to a word in his light spell. After rehearsing it several times in his head, he was ready to try. "*Ushma ecius guluos mus—*"

Again, he was on his back and wind rushed out of his lungs. After gulping in enough air, he rose, picked up his chair, and sat down.

"Do you know what you did incorrectly?"

"Yes, Master."

"Continue."

"Yes, Master." Waiting until his breath steadied, he started again. "*Ushma ecias gulauos musuara.*"

He traced the rune. He did not focus on the energy or ignite his magic; he needed to make sure the pronunciation was just so and the rune drawn perfectly. He finished and felt it was correct.

Something picked him up by his arms and threw him on the ground, again knocking his breath loose. He grabbed his shoulder, feeling the muscle already bruising.

"I told you to perform the spell, not practice. You're not listening to what I say."

Sensing Dethal's anger, Salvarias forced himself up, swayed, and then stumbled to his chair, which, oddly enough, still sat upright.

"Yes, Master." Closing his eyes, he ignited his magic, whispered the spell and focused on the surrounding energy. Searching, he only found Dethal's energy; no other living thing existed in the room. Convinced he was mistaken, Salvarias searched again. Certainly a spider, rat, or roach moved through the walls. Some herb planted in the room. Confused, he opened his eyes. Dethal stared at him.

"Master, I feel no other energy than yours. If I pull from you, I could harm—" Picked up from the chair, Salvarias was dropped to the floor and he doubled over when whatever was attacking him kicked his ribs. He gasped, but no air entered his lungs, and he realized he was being choked. His lungs ached, pinpricks stabbed his eyes, and he gulped desperately for air. His head felt as though it would float from his body. He thrashed wildly, kicking and clawing at the floor. Still, the hands held him. The pounding of his head shook his vision loose and then blackness swarmed around him. He slipped into unconsciousness.

Salvarias's mind rose from darkness. He winced from the pain in his side. With much effort, he pulled himself to a sitting position. The laboratory still surrounded him, and Dethal remained in the same chair. Cursing silently, Salvarias rose on shaking legs. Dethal had said he would not be harmed. Walking to the chair, Salvarias gently lowered himself to the seat, biting back a groan.

The spell the old mage used to beat Salvarias intrigued him. He never heard of a spell that performed what Dethal was doing, yet clearly one existed. Furthermore, he must have an odd sort of protection to allow his life force to be drawn upon. Confused, tired and sore, Salvarias pushed away his questions and ignored the urgent whispers of his instincts.

Dethal snorted. "Now we must learn the next spell since you had already uttered the last one. Unless by some miracle you have retained the spell?"

Salvarias shook his head, turned the page, studied the spell, whispered the words, focused on Dethal's energy, and drew the rune. Powerful magic coursed through his blood, a slight burning sensation filled his veins while at the same time the magic offered protection and comfort. He opened his eyes to see fire erupt inside the rune, large compared to his level one fireball spell, its warmth bathing his face.

"Continue to hold the fire, double its size," Dethal commanded.

Salvarias felt the magic draining him. He was out of practice, and the spell was complicated, difficult to hold. Concentrating, sweat breaking on his brow, his muscles flexing under the strain, he drew energy and the fire doubled. Dizziness set in and he took sharp breaths.

"Release it," Dethal ordered.

Salvarias whispered, "*Rulose,*" and the fire shot across the room.

He had not aimed it anywhere in particular, and as it flew past Dethal the darkness consumed it. Exhausted, Salvarias slumped forward in his chair while sweat dripped down his temple.

His magic was pleased with his efforts. He told it to be quiet.

"Turn the page and perform the next spell," Dethal instructed.

With a shaking hand, Salvarias turned the page and studied the words. It was similar to the last one except this was ice, not fire. Drawing a deep breath, he closed his eyes and focused again. Whispering the spell, he drew the ice rune in the air, pushing the energy. The magic was still powerful, much to his surprise, but the burning in his veins intensified and became almost painful. He opened his eyes, pleased to see ice formed in the rune.

"Make it double in size and hold it," Dethal said.

Salvarias trembled under the strain of containing the energy. He increased the ice ball to double. His vision faded. The burning sensation in his veins increased as if fire flowed instead of blood. If he lost control of the magic, it would rip him apart from the inside. These spells were too advanced; he knew he would not last.

"No, I can hold it," his magic whispered.

"I cannot," Salvarias admitted and released the spell, falling again into darkness.

He woke, unsure how long he had been out. He was lying on the floor though he didn't remember falling. Slowly sitting, a hard kick to his head sent him spinning. His head drummed with pain and he fought to control his stomach. He forced his eyes opened and saw crimson blood dripping on the dark wood.

"Get up. I did not command you to release the spell," Dethal rebuked.

After wiping the blood with a cloth from his robes, Salvarias wobbled to his feet and fell forward until landing in a chair.

Dethal's stare was stern. "The difficulty will increase tomorrow. I am not sure you are ready for my instruction."

Salvarias did not beg, he stated a fact. "Master, I am ready. I will do better tomorrow."

Dethal's expression softened and his voice was encouraging. "So be it. You see your weaknesses? Your mind does not listen well to detail or instruction. I gave you every opportunity to avoid punishment and yet you performed actions that caused you pain. Do you see?"

"Yes," Salvarias answered honestly.

"Good boy. Do not be discouraged. With a sharper mind, your power will only grow. Listen to each word I say and you can easily avoid punishment. You did well for your first day. Now, go home and sleep. We will begin again tomorrow."

"Thank you, Master."

The door opened and Salvarias rose on weak legs. After exiting the house, he slumped against the iced rock wall, trying to ignore the throbbing in his head and side. He used snow to scrub the blood from his face and made his way home. The moon hung high in the sky and he hoped Wilhelm was asleep.

Salvarias floated above a burning city, and after studying the scene, he determined it was Serinity. People ran screaming from burning buildings, bodies aflame. Dark creatures snuck through the streets and alleys, ripping apart any that drew near. He floated closer, seeming to hover at the tip of the flames. The raven-haired woman from his dreams huddled in an alley, alone and frightened.

"Run," he tried to say, but he had no voice.

He fought with all his might to reach her. The fire was coming. She was weeping. He begged his throat to loosen, but he could utter no words. He issued a silent scream when fire blazed down the alley. She cried out in agony as her body erupted in flame. The smell of her burning flesh wafted up to him, and memories of his mother overpowered the scene. Ashra's body lay on the forest floor, organs exposed, skin burned off. Salvarias tried to wrench his gaze away but could not avert his eyes. Her corpse sprang up and latched onto him.

"You did this to me, monstrosity!" Her voice was a raw rasp that rippled a shudder through him. He struggled, pushing her arm away, but her charred skin only peeled back.

Then Tobin was beside him. "No son of mine..." Blood gurgled from his throat and sprayed Salvarias's face.

His mother's grip tightened and her body ignited in flame. The fire leapt over her to spread across his arm. He cried out and thrashed against her hold. In the distance, he heard Wilhelm calling, and familiar arms encircled him.

"Brother, help me!" The fire spread across his body, and the

smell of his own burning flesh filled his nostrils. "Brother!"
Wilhelm called again and the bodies disappeared. When
Salvarias opened his eyes, it took a moment to recognize the
storeroom.

"Salv, it's me. It's all right, just a dream."

He closed his eyes. "I am fine. Sorry I woke you."

Wilhelm let go and offered a grin. "It's morning. You've
overslept. I'll get you some breakfast." Wilhelm ruffled his hair and
left the room.

Throwing on his robes, he ignored the bruises on his chest and
stomach and the knot on his head. Wilhelm returned, and Salvarias
accepted the plate of bread and cheese, ate a couple bites, and
stopped. The chewing added to his throbbing headache.

Wilhelm's eyes lit with worry. "Are you all right? Maybe you
should stay home today. You don't look well."

"I must get to the shop. I will be fine. See you tonight."

"Will you be home for dinner? I think Humar misses you."

"I will try, brother." Salvarias took his bread in case he could eat
later.

An uneventful morning passed in the potion shop and word
reached him of a hanging scheduled for the afternoon. He might be a
little late for his lesson, but he did not like missing the killings.
When Milred needed him no longer, he hurried to the gallows. He
took his customary place in back, no longer required to stand on his
toes, and watched the noose snap and the criminal jerk in the throes
of death. Something felt different. The man seemed to relive some
nightmare while he stared into Salvarias's eyes. The satisfying surge
that rushed Salvarias made him lightheaded. The man's expression
became one of such agony that the pain in the criminal's heart would
kill him before the noose. His death seemed to draw out and even the
crowd began to shift. When at last the man's life ebbed away,
Salvarias reveled in the criminal's death.

*"You ssshowed him the murdersss he committed, you replayed
the pain of his victimsss,"* the presence said. *"Pain endured
becaussse of you. It wasss you whissspering in his ear, telling him to
do thossse crimesss. It is how you know of the pain inflicted on each
victim."*

"I did not," he retorted, but was not so sure of his own words.
Images of death flickered faster, the presence showing him pictures

of people he had never met, homes he had never stepped foot in, forests he had never passed through. Common among all of them was the wispy red fog lurking in the shadows.

"You sssee it isss you, my pet."

Salvarias did see. He could see his features outlined in red, his large, evil eyes watching people with a sick hunger.

"Your ssssoul leavesss your body in the night, my pet. You roam Arden whissspering and tempting."

The images he saw were memories of his foul evil, what he did in the night. It was a possibility that he desperately tried to hide himself from, but self-hatred and fear of himself erupted like a volcano. Then the storm started.

He turned to leave, and dizzy from the ordeal, he grabbed hold of the closest thing near him which, unfortunately, was a person. The strain from the images doubled, now extraordinarily painful, and he snatched back his hand.

"How dare you touch me, mage!" a man's voice roared.

Salvarias murmured an apology. Hands grabbed him. A fist landed in his stomach. He gasped for air and fought the rising of his lunch. The next hit came across his cheek. He was so disoriented he could not see to defend himself. Hands shoved him to the wet street and he caught a glimpse of a boot before it planted itself in his side. The man spat on Salvarias's face.

Then Wilhelm's roar bellowed out above the thundering rain. Salvarias hardly recognized his brother. His eyes were dark and his face was twisted in rage. He grabbed the man and hammered his face.

Salvarias gained his footing and pulled with his entire weight on his brother. In Wilhelm's enraged state, he rounded on Salvarias with an enormous fist raised. He braced himself, but Wilhelm returned to normal and dropped the man who he had beaten near death. The clinking of armor rose in the distance. Salvarias locked arms with Wilhelm and led his brother away. He pulled his hood up and wiped the spit from his face in the torrent of rain.

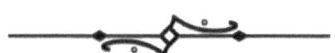

God folded his hands over his chest, lying back on the plush sofa in his room. "How goesss it with the boy?"

"Well, my Lord," Unupture confirmed. "His escape was an unexpected gift. Dethal's training is well underway and he has reported that their first lesson utilizing the boy's power has only tapped the very edge of Salvarias's abilities."

"Ssso thisss... what did you call it?"

Unupture smiled, abashed. "For lack of a better term, merely a hidden power. Unknown to the boy and a mystery to myself. I only sensed its existence, though it's nothing like any other mage nor any god nor any of your disciples."

"Have you thought of how he obtained it?"

"I assume it's an accident from the shadowfires combined with your touch, but luckily in our favor. Igniting this talent will be easier than we expected, according to Dethal. The dark mage agrees it will further our cause. As I said before, the boy is truly linked to the fate of this world." Unupture thought back to his meeting in the slave cavern and his voice was barely a whisper. "I felt it, my Lord. His soul balances on a sharp point, swaying towards light only to teeter towards darkness. And his power... So much raw power. What he took from you combined with his magic is unmatched. I understand you seek his soul but his power... I cannot find its limits. It rests now, but Dethal is certain he can stir it awake."

"I mussst admit that you were right. I had feared we'd lossse the boy, but we have not."

"The boy hungers for knowledge, my Dark Master. His mind absorbs all and never forgets. He thirsts for education, to learn. He is unlike other men. Dethal's offer to teach him was something the Guardian couldn't pass up." Unupture secretly had his doubts about choosing Dethal. The mage was too strict, and Unupture had delicately reminded God of the man's cruel ways. Still, God was adamant that the boy remain under the care of Dethal, and soon Sansis. The thought of any poor soul locked in a room with Sansis stirred deep pity within Unupture.

"And the fact he didn't involve hisss Protector is yet another victory for usss."

Unupture nodded in agreement. "That is due to your seed. I sensed it when I met the boy in the slave caverns. It controls many parts of the Guardian. It would be the one to whisper to the boy to follow Dethal since the dark mage is marked as your servant."

"I've given Dethal and Sansssis one year to unleasssh hisss powerss before bringing the boy to me."

"We will not fail, Master. Our other servant is keeping the Guardian close, and he shows interest in her trade. He'll not leave the shop. Have you thought about passing along your seed, God?" After meeting the boy, the power from his master was beyond what Unupture had thought. The seed God planted was bewildering yet altogether marvelous. Indeed, God was more powerful than the other weak gods left on Arden. Though nothing compared to Veedran's power, God still had more than Crutar or Lakvra. God was unique.

"Perhapsss, but don't asssk me again." God smiled. It did nothing to warm the room and instead seemed to amplify the coldness of the stone fortress. "You've pleasssed me, Unupture. More ssso than I would have sussspected. For now, you may keep your sssoul."

Unupture bowed. "My God is kind."

Chapter 16
Spring 1017 a.r.

Salvarias slumped at the kitchen table, picking at his food while reading a potion book. Across from him, Wilhelm was wolfing down eggs, beef roast and bread.

The stabbing pain along Salvarias's spine escalated until he shifted in his chair. He rubbed his aching head and grimaced back a groan. For the entire winter, he had continued his training with Dethal in secrecy, and as the mage had promised and Salvarias's body confirmed, he was once again weak. He had lost the weight he gained and barely contained energy to move. Lifting a slice of bread was challenge enough, but to add to his misery was the return of his breathing condition. The more he suffered at the hands of Dethal, the less effective the concoction became. Salvarias had drunk two doses this morning, but the anvil still rested on his lungs, pressing out air and allowing minimal amounts in. He squinted when the letters on the page danced about for a moment then settled into their rightful places. He sighed. Admittedly, the sacrifice was worth it. The information was easily soaked up and his magic gained power with each lesson, with each spell. But to add to his already full mind was the change in his relationship with his magic. He was not sure if it was for better or worse. The magic appeared greedy, scolding him when he thought himself not powerful enough and showing its annoyance. Yet, when he pushed the magic, forced it to hold spells at Dethal's orders, it battled alongside Salvarias, protecting his mind and offering encouragement. Even now, as he mulled over the changes, his magic remained as mysterious as ever.

Wilhelm's deep rumbling voice broke his thoughts. "Hey Salv, did you remember it's our Birth Day in a week?"

Lifting his gaze over his book to regard his brother, he responded, "I forgot, brother. I must go to the shop today. Maybe we will leave tomorrow."

"But we talked about visiting the gravesite weeks ago."

Salvarias lowered his book so his smile was visible and said,

"We will go once we finish eating. I already told Milred I would be absent." He had also informed Dethal, who was less than pleased and had punished Salvarias for his "laziness" and "lack of dedication."

Salvarias dodged the chunk of bread Wilhelm threw.

After eating, the brothers packed and went to the stables to rent two horses for the journey to Serinity.

Winter's last day brought with it a warm sun and quiet city. The stables were deserted except for the owner. Salvarias closed his eyes and listened to the few noises of Falar: A horse lazily clopping along, a woman humming, a bard testing a flute, and a merchant banging pots. Rarely was the city tranquil, but when one of those days blessed Falar, it did not seem so depressing.

"You all right, Salv?"

Salvarias opened his eyes and smiled inwardly at his big brother.

Wilhelm's bright eyes sprang alive with happiness, driving a sting in Salvarias's heart. He realized how much he missed time alone with his brother. Always Humar or Durak were around, or either brother was working. He felt cheated, and anger erupted at the moments he would never get back. Selfish. He was always so selfish. He had accepted Dethal's teachings without fully understanding the time it would steal. Salvarias clenched his jaw. Dethal's instruction was near an end. Salvarias only required a new spell book to record what he had learned. There was no reason for him to continue.

Wilhelm's brow furrowed. "You sure you're—"

Salvarias threw his arms around Wilhelm's neck. "I have missed you."

Massive arms wrapped around Salvarias. He grinned when he felt invisible, secret, and safe.

"I love you, Salv." Wilhelm's voice was thick and his hold tighter than normal.

Salvarias tightened his embrace. "I love you too, my dear brother."

Wilhelm's shoulders dropped and he inhaled a deep breath. The tension leaving him was palpable. That made up Salvarias's mind. He punched Wilhelm's ribs.

"Ouch!"

Salvarias chuckled and held on until his brother let go. "I will be back," Salvarias murmured. Making his way to the front counter, he found the stable owner and purchased parchment. Though it was rude to leave a letter instead of personally thanking Dethal, Salvarias was eager to be free of the mage. It was a short note informing Dethal Salvarias would not be returning for lessons but gave thanks. He was about to write that he would visit later, but his instincts screamed out. He rubbed his throbbing head and stared at the parchment. After a small battle between the presence and his instincts, he ended the letter with his signature, never promising to visit. He handed the letter to the owner for delivery, along with a coin, and then returned to his borrowed horse. The relief that washed over him, lifting a weight he carried without being aware, surprised him.

Once outside the city walls, he took a deep breath. Tomorrow would mark the first day of spring and the start of a new year. He was happy to be out of town for the turn-of-year festivities and looked forward to a quiet day riding and reconnecting with his brother. The trees' songs drifted through the warm air, animals scurried about, and newly sprouted flowers surrounded Salvarias. He felt alive.

Wilhelm put him in a headlock and ruffled his hair. He elbowed his brother's ribs.

"Ouch." Wilhelm chuckled. "You've gotten too big for me to toss you."

Salvarias smiled, finding his brother's memories surfaced at odd times. Wiggling free of the headlock, he mounted his horse. "Indeed. But there are other ways to experience it, and this time you can participate."

Wilhelm swung onto the horse. "What do you have in mind?"

Salvarias grinned. "See if you can keep up, my dear brother."

He urged the horse forward and the mare bolted along the road. He laughed with delight when grasses and trees fleeted by and the wind whipped through his hair. The rush of excitement awakened his mind and body. All the sensations reminded him of the feeling given by Wilhelm, the sense of freedom it offered. Salvarias glanced back and his heart soared to see his brother laughing.

Salvarias tethered the horses a short distance from the cliffside and followed his brother to the tree. The seven-day journey had been uneventful, allowing them to arrive at their parents' gravesite on the afternoon of their Birth Days, Salvarias turning seventeen, Wilhelm twenty-three.

Upon cresting the hill banking the gravesite, Salvarias saw a pure black wolf pup sitting at the base of the tree among the clover and white flowers. Though he had a love of animals, and regarded each with respect, he knew that if the mother hunted close by she would not take kindly to company. He proceeded with cautious steps.

"Maybe we should leave, Salv."

"No, my brother," he murmured. For an unknown reason, the wolf pup entranced him. It seemed to call him, beckoning him to approach. He sensed the wolf's interest, its invitation. Salvarias surveyed the forest, but sensed no other wolves near. Wilhelm followed close, hand resting on the hilt of the sword he had borrowed from the smithy, and eyed the tree line. Respectfully, Salvarias came to within a few feet of the pup, and after another inspection of the surrounding woods, knelt on the clover. Tilting its head to the side, the wolf approached him and sat at his knees. Salvarias's black eyes reflected in the gold eyes of the wolf, and he swore recognition glittered in the animal's gaze.

"Where is your mother?" Salvarias gently rubbed the pup's head. The wolf jumped in his lap, licking his face, pawing, and play-biting his hands. He laughed at the wolf's mischievous nature and immediate fondness. Wilhelm relaxed, petting the pup and offering an ear-to-ear grin. After the brothers settled into the clover, it took several moments to subdue the wolf, but soon the pup's unsteady legs tumbled it into Salvarias's lap and it dozed in the spring sun.

The brothers shared stories and reminisced until fading into a comfortable silence. The memories of their parents' murders were still sharp in Salvarias's mind. He relived them each night and heard his mother's cries of pain when he was awake. Tobin's words "you are no son of mine" and his expression of betrayal and horror bombarded Salvarias constantly. Soon his mood darkened and his feeling of vulnerability, of loneliness and guilt, set in. A heavy arm draped around his shoulders and he curled up against his brother, hiding in Wilhelm's embrace. The wolf repositioned itself in front of his brother, laying a tired head on his foot.

When the sun touched the horizon, Wilhelm's stomach protested the long hours spent without food and he rubbed it. "I guess I'm hungry."

Accepting Wilhelm's headlock, Salvarias strolled back to the trees. He retrieved dinner from their packs while Wilhelm made a campfire near the horses. They sat next to each other, wrapped in blankets to ward off the chilly breeze sweeping over the cliff. The pup curled up near Salvarias, slipping into a deep dream.

He glanced at Wilhelm shoveling food down. "I am surprised Durak has not lost his funds with your appetite, my dear brother."

Wilhelm pushed him over. "Well, you don't eat enough, so it balances out. By the way, how did you get that bruise on your arm?"

"Milred stacked books in the walkway and I tripped." His stomach churned at the lie.

Wilhelm paused in his chewing. "I'm beginning to think your job is more dangerous than mine."

"Perhaps." There was no harm in telling him the truth. Not the details. Wilhelm would hunt down Dethal if the punishments Salvarias had endured ever became known. "I must tell you something." His throat nearly closed from the growing lump. What if Wilhelm was angry, or worse, disappointed? What if Wilhelm abandoned him? Salvarias shuddered at the thought.

"He will be hurt by your wordsss," the presence hissed. *"Do not tell him. Return to Dethal!"*

"What is it, Salv?"

Salvarias looked into his brother's eyes, at the love willingly imparted. Wilhelm would never leave. "I do not know why, but I have been lying to you. A mage approached me in autumn and offered me an apprenticeship. I accepted and have gone to his home each night after working at the potion shop." His brother's eyes widen, and Salvarias felt sickened by the betrayal he had performed.

Wilhelm's voice was lined with hurt when he said, "Why didn't you tell me? You know I support your magic."

"I was worried you would want to be involved. My Master would not approve of your presence. I am sorry. Please forgive me." He could no longer look into his brother's eyes. He hated himself and could feel the triumph of his evil.

Wilhelm flicked back Salvarias's hood and ruffled his hair. "I understand. I can be a bit protective. But you have to tell me this stuff."

"I do not deserve you, my brother."

"Don't say that." Wilhelm shook his head. "You probably don't remember, but a man approached you in the slave camp and was looking for you. The day we escaped, one of his people was going to come and take you. It's why we escaped ahead of schedule. He knew about your mark. I didn't tell you because I didn't want you to worry. Even though your instructor might not like it, you need to allow me to meet him. I need to make sure you're safe."

"He knew of my mark?" Salvarias studied the perfect hollow circle framing the black flame on his palm. In a trance of thought, he whispered, "We are meant for something, brother." He took Wilhelm's hand and examined the bear. "There is something we are destined to do."

"They're just birthmarks."

"Do you not feel it? I do. There is a memory, a thought tugging at my mind, whispering important tasks, but I cannot hear." Salvarias frowned when he stared at their hands side by side. His were clean, spotless, and soft, and his fingers were long and delicate. Wilhelm's were callused and stained, and his fingers were stocky and thick. So different. Salvarias clenched his fist and released his brother's hand.

Wilhelm looked at his palm. "I don't feel anything."

Salvarias sighed and shook off the nagging feeling.

"I guess you've learned some new spells," Wilhelm said.

"Indeed. I sent a note before we left ending my lessons. I have learned enough. I was hoping to purchase a blank book to record the spells I have memorized if we have funds."

"Sure. We'll get one when we return home."

"Thank you. I am sorry I lied to you."

"Stop apologizing." Wilhelm lightened the mood. "So what do we do with the wolf?"

Grateful for the change in subject, Salvarias punched his brother's ribs, smiling at his feigned pain. "The city is no place for a young pup to grow up. He should be with his family."

Wilhelm shrugged. "I think he should come with us. He doesn't seem to have a family, and he won't make it on his own." He gave Salvarias a slap on the shoulder before lying down. "So what are we going to name him?"

"Adok," Salvarias responded without hesitation. He was unsure how he got the name. As he stared at the wolf, he was certain he started to hear its thoughts. He sighed in annoyance. More whispers.

Wilhelm passed over the puzzle box. "Adok," he repeated. "It fits him. What do you think Durak's going to say?"

"Nothing I would care to repeat, but I look forward to learning a few new curse words."

Wilhelm bellowed out a laugh. "True. I think he'll let Adok sleep in the storeroom with us."

"Why have you not joined the guard? You have wanted to since we were young."

Wilhelm shrugged.

"Brother," Salvarias scolded.

Wilhelm sighed. "You have to stay at the barracks for your first year."

Salvarias's selfish pause caused his lip to curl in self-disgust. His brother's happiness was all that mattered. "You should do it. We can spend any time you have off together. Milred would understand if I change the times I help her."

"I know she would and I know we could, but I don't want to. I like working in the smithy, and Idolar still pays me to train new guards. Plus, I enjoy learning from Humar. If I join, he can't teach me, and he's the only one to offer me a challenge."

Salvarias scrutinized his brother's face, trying to determine if he had left out information or skirted his true feelings. "I support you in whatever you decide, my dear brother. All I want is your happiness."

Wilhelm winked. "I am happy."

Salvarias admired his finished puzzle of a bear.

"What is it?"

"My brother."

Wilhelm grinned. Salvarias requested the puzzle box provide instructions to create a tiger. Image by image, it showed him each piece twisting into the new form.

"So what is the name of the mage teaching you?" Wilhelm asked.

"Master Dethal."

Wilhelm's face drained of color and he sprang to a sitting position. "That's him."

"Are you sure? I would think he would have taken me if he truly sought me."

"I swear that was his name." Wilhelm visibly shook.

A pang of betrayal twisted Salvarias's gut. Dethal conducted challenging and interesting conversations, and though Salvarias had never trusted the mage, the thought that he might be using Salvarias hurt. Clearing his throat to even his voice, he said, "It is fine. I have ended my lessons. You can walk with me after the potion shop."

"He can't take you from me." Wilhelm glanced at Serinity. "Maybe we should live here. We don't need to go to Falar. I'll ask Durak to send our things. We don't ever have to go back. Durak and Humar will understand." He scrambled to his feet, shoving his blanket in a pack. "Let's go into the city tonight. I have funds for a room at an inn."

Salvarias set aside the puzzle box, stood, and rested a hand on Wilhelm's arm. "Brother, I will be—" A snap of a tree branch echoed from the woods. "Did you hear that?" Salvarias brought a spell to mind. Adok bolted up, hackles raised.

Wilhelm reached for his sword but froze. "Something's wrong. I can't move."

Four men armored head-to-toe in matte black steel emerged from the woods. Helmets covered their faces with only a thin slit to allow them visibility. Moonlight did not reflect off the dull metal, and all were resting their hands on the hilts of swords.

Then the tall, red-bearded wizard appeared.

Salvarias stumbled back a step.

Dethal reached out his hand. "Salvarias. Come with me peacefully and I'll let your brother live. You have my word."

"You cannot fight him. You mussst go with him," the voice said.

"What do you want with me?" Salvarias asked, in complete agreement with the presence. Dethal's power was immense, surely far more than what dwelled within Salvarias.

"Our meeting was not coincidence, but I'll tell you why I sought you after you come with me. If you'd remained under my tutelage, you would've had six more months with your brother. But now I'll take you and obtain what I need by other means. Fight me and I'll kill your brother. Come with me peacefully and I promise I'll let him live."

"I do not trust you."

"How dare you insult me!" Dethal roared. "My word is sacred."

Salvarias flinched and stumbled back until he butted against his rigid brother.

"Don't listen to him," Wilhelm whispered. "They'll hurt you."

Dethal flicked his hand.

Wilhelm grunted.

"He will kill your brother. You mussst go with him," the voice said urgently.

"Wait," Salvarias whispered. "I will go with you on your word my brother will not be harmed and you will release him from your hold. You will not pursue him or harm him in the future. He is to be protected."

"Agreed."

Salvarias faced his brother knowing they would never see each other again. His heart faltered at the realization, at the understanding of what his selfishness had cost both of them. He blinked away his tears and raised his gaze to meet Wilhelm's. "Forgive me."

"Please don't leave me, Salv. Don't go. I can't live without you. Please!"

"Everything will be all right. We both knew a day would come when we would be parted. You must start your own life. Join the guard, marry, and begin a family. It is all I wish. Thank you for everything you have done for me." Salvarias flung his arms around Wilhelm's neck. "I love you, my dear brother. More than you will ever know." Salvarias would have given anything for one last embrace. Smiling as best he could, he punched Wilhelm's ribs.

"Please." Tears spilt over Wilhelm's cheeks and his voice was a hoarse whisper, "Please, Salv."

"Forgive me. I never meant to hurt you. I love you." After a deep breath, Salvarias lowered his head, collected his emotions, and walked away. He bit back his sobs with each step when Wilhelm's pleas poured out. Salvarias stopped in front of Dethal and met the man's cold gaze.

"You belong to me!" Dethal snapped. "Do not ever think otherwise!"

Familiar hands backhanded Salvarias, knocking him to his knees. Another punch struck his temple, toppling him to the ground, drowning out Wilhelm's enraged cry.

Then came pain.

Lunara stared despondently out her window at Lord Gunder's estate. Tomorrow she'd be wed against her will to the ruling Lord. Even though she was not of age by erthla standards, Gunder had taken it upon himself to write a loophole in the laws of Serinity. He could claim any woman he wanted, regardless of age. Lunara was close enough at seventeen, but the thought of bedding a man as vile as Gunder sparked a fear she'd never experienced. She couldn't image his hands upon her, groping and touching her.

She shuddered and pulled her shawl around her shoulders. Nothing could be done to prevent it. Her father had wandered the estate every night since Gunder announced his intentions. If her father had thought of nothing in his months of sleepless nights, she had no hope.

She rose from the windowsill, sat at her vanity, and stared at herself in the mirror. Picking up her brush, she ran it through her hair. She'd sleep soon. The sun hadn't yet set, but she was anxious to lose herself in her dream with the young mage who'd stolen her heart. His serious face, hypnotic voice, and enlightening conversations had paled every suitor that had come to court her in the last year. How silly it was that she looked for a man who could surpass one her imagination had dreamt up. The mage was perfect where no other man was. Now, he would be her escape in the night when Gunder—

She threw down the brush and buried her face in her hands. "By all the gods, help me," she whispered.

Someone knocked on her door. "Please, I'd prefer to be alone," she called. Though most nights she shared a room with her sister, tonight Lunara was in no mood for company and had chosen to sleep in her private room.

The door flung open. Lunara raised her head to see her sister saunter in. Varila's wealth of blonde hair barely stayed in the single braid that reached her lower back. Her shrewd grey-blue gaze swept over Lunara's room.

"Let's go," Varila said. "Make a pack of ten or so dresses, your cloak, and spare boots."

Lunara rose from her chair. "What's happening?"

Her father marched inside, followed by her mother.

"I'm not delaying," Varila snapped. "Make it fast."

Her father's eyes were bloodshot and her mother was openly weeping.

Lunara's heart thudded in her ears. "Tell me what this is about."

Her father walked up and folded her in his arms. "I won't let him take you. I won't."

Her mother pried her from her father's arms, led her to a chair, and knelt in front of her. "We love you, dear. More than anything we want both of you—" She motioned to Varila. "To be happy. Varila refuses to allow you to marry Gunder, as do your father and I. Unfortunately, law is on his side. He'll take you by force if necessary. Tell me now, what does your heart say? If you have any affection for Gunder, tell me."

"Of course she doesn't, Mother!" Varila said.

Lunara glanced at her family and raised her head. "If it is Gunder's right, then I'll marry him willingly." She forced a smile. "We do not need to go to war." Her joke tasted sour in her mouth.

Her mother smoothed Lunara's hair. "Edium, get the horses readied."

Her father dashed from the room.

"Mother," she said. "Tell me what's going on?"

"Varila is taking you away," her mother said. "We love you too much to see you with that man. We'll say you were kidnapped outside the city. We'll tell Gunder that your sister has gone searching for you. Your father will send soldiers to hunt for you, but they'll look the other way when you're spotted. No doubt Gunder knows the guards will be loyal to your father. Therefore, he'll send his own men. Those men you need to avoid."

She flew into her mother's arms. Never had Lunara stepped foot past the meadow surrounding Serenity, nor had she ventured from her mother's side. "I can't leave you."

"It won't be long before we're together again. Little by little, your father will close his accounts, wrap up business, and prepare General Unbril to take over command. Within a year, we'll leave and find you. We'll move to a different continent where Gunder can't reach you. We'll start over."

"I cannot ask that you do this. I'll marry—"

Varila pulled their mother from Lunara's arms. "Go pack. Hurry up."

Her father emerged in the room. "The horses will be ready in moments."

Varila nodded. "You two need to be seen in the city. Head out now."

Her father embraced Varila. "You keep yourselves safe. I love you."

Her knuckles turned white when she gripped her father. "I'll think of you every breath I take."

Edium kissed her forehead and turned to Lunara. She flew into his arms. "Be safe, and listen to your sister. Do what she tells you."

"Yes, father."

He kissed her forehead. "Talura, we must leave."

Her mother embraced Varila, whispering words that brought tears to her eyes. Their mother then turned to Lunara and hugged her close. "You are a special woman. Do not let the ugliness of the world callous your heart. Remain pure, and hold true to your beliefs."

Lunara nodded and kissed her mother's cheek. The risk her parents took touched her more than words could ever express. She smiled at them, causing more tears to spill free. "I love you both."

Edium wrapped his arm around Talura and led her from the room.

Lunara turned to Varila. "I, I..."

Varila grinned. "It's about time you left these walls, little sister. I won't lie to you. It's going to be dangerous. Two women traveling alone will attract attention. But if you listen to me, we'll both be safe."

Lunara nodded.

"Good. Get packed. Put on your cloak, raise your hood, and meet me in the stables. Try to avoid the servants."

Her sister left and Lunara hastily threw together a pack. She flung it over her shoulder and glanced around her room before she pulled the hood of her cloak low and left.

The halls of the estate were unusually deserted and eerily quiet. She rushed through her home, outside, and into the stables. No one was there.

She glanced around and took a step back. Maybe Gunder had discovered their plot? Maybe—

When a hand wrapped around her arm, she cried out.

"Hush!" Varila snapped. "Let's go."

Her sister wore armor that had been specially made for her. Too revealing for Lunara's taste, she didn't see how it offered much protection, but its pliable leather would be easy for her sister to sleep and travel in. Lunara thought it unwise to still wear dresses, but didn't have armor of her own. Nor had she ever even touched a sword.

"Should I..." She motioned to her dress and then to Varila's armor. "I feel worthless."

Varila chuckled, leading them further into the stables. "I'll take care of you. No need to start changing who you are. I can beat any man who tries to lay a finger on us. I promised mother and father I wouldn't allow you to start fighting or wielding weapons. Unless you chose to do so out of interest, not necessity. I promise. We're going to be fine."

Lunara had no doubts. She'd yet to see her sister lose a fight in the past five years, ever since Varila was sixteen.

Two horses were saddled as well as Lunara's white mare. She started to mount her horse, but Varila shook her head.

"No. We're sending your horse into the meadow once we make it to the trees. The guards will find her in the morning and report your abduction. It gives us a little head start. Sorry, we won't be sleeping until near morning."

Lunara mounted the other horse and they set off through the city. It was late enough that most had retired to their homes for dinner. Any citizen still out was caught in an intense, though not unfriendly, conversation with a guard. She saw her parents off in the distance, conversing with the locals in the market. She thought her father might have looked their direction, but couldn't tell for sure.

When the front gate came into view, the set of ten guards usually patrolling were absent. The sisters slipped out unnoticed. Once clear, Varila pushed forward at a full gallop. Lunara nudged her horse, looking over her shoulder until her hair blew around to block the view of her home.

The ride to the trees took little time and Varila released Lunara's white mare, shooing the horse into the meadow. Her sister stared at Serinity only a moment before urging her horse into the trees. Lunara followed, not finding the courage to look back again.

They only made it a few paces before a mounted soldier came into view.

"My Lady," he said, bowing in his saddle.

"By the gods," Varila snapped, yanking her horse around so she was beside the guard. "Why are you stopping us?"

"We've found blood just along the tree line. My men are studying the prints, but we figure no more than five or six men were engaged. We've found no bodies as of yet."

Varila cursed. "We've no choice but to continue. There are worse fates than death."

The guard nodded and bowed his head to both sisters. "May the gods' grace be upon you both. Know that your home will miss you."

Varila grunted. "Make sure my parents are taken care of."

The guard saluted and disappeared into the shadows.

"Let's go," she said.

Lunara was thankful for the fast flight through the dense woods. All her concentration was spent navigating around trees and keeping up with her sister. Hours passed before Varila slowed. Lunara's emotions sapped out her strength. The excitement and tension faded into exhaustion that weighed her down. Not willing to complain, and trying to keep her eyes from closing, she followed Varila.

Eventually, sleep won.

Lunara stood in a forest, trees crowding around her. She smiled and strolled forward, searching for the mage. She shoved aside branches, pushed passed shrubs, and squeezed between rocks. Emerging from the trees, she happened upon a clearing. Perched on a mound was a vibrant tree. Its leaves rustled in the light breeze, outlined by a pink sky. Huddled at the tree's base was the mage.

She inched forward, bending over to try to see his face, but it was buried in his knees pressed to his chest.

"Hello," she said, kneeling next to him.

He raised his head. His normal stern expression faded and utter sadness passed through his eyes. He grabbed her and pulled her into his arms, nestling his face in her hair.

"What is it?" she asked.

He didn't answer, but sobs racked him and his hold was near painful. She smoothed his hair, whispering any words of comfort she could think of.

At last, he loosened his hold and released her. She wiped away his tears, cupping his face in her hands.

"What has happened?"

"I have been waiting for you." His fingers glided along her jaw. "I was worried you would not come."

"I'll come to you every night. That I promise."

Suddenly he lurched and cried out, doubling over and clutching his stomach. He reached for her and then vanished.

The entire scene faded, replaced by a barren desert she walked through every night. Dried, cracked soil stretched as far as she could see, and patches of dead grass crunched beneath her feet as she walked. She begged her mind to return to the mage, heart racing, fear clamping her throat, but she stayed locked in her recurring dream. It felt like hours that she roamed the silent landscape before she found the pit. The bottom was never visible.

As far back as she could remember she'd had this dream. Slowly, since around the time she turned eleven, the dream had evolved. It went from a barren landscape to a barren landscape with an empty pit. Then from an empty pit to a sense that someone lurked within its dark depths. Then whispers came. And now, a shadowed figure spoke to her, sounding miles away. Lunara couldn't tell if it was male or female. What she felt was love. It reached up from the darkness and encased her, driving away her fears and worry for the mage.

Lunara settled at the edge of the pit.

"Hello, Lunara," the figure said.

She smiled at the warmth rising up in her blood. "Hello."

"You must help me," the figure said, as it did every night.

Her standard response was: "How?"

"Help him."

She perked up. Her dream had always ended with "how." "Help who?"

"The mage from your dreams."

She scoffed, settling comfortably. "Help a dreamed up man? How do you suppose I go about helping someone my wild imagination concocted?"

"On the contrary, he is very real. You must help him."

She gaped down into the darkness. "How do I know him? We've never met." That meeting was one she was sure she'd remember. They'd developed a fierce friendship since first she dreamt him when she was eleven. Furthermore, his eyes weren't that of any other person in Arden. She would've remembered meeting him.

"You have many questions. The two of you have met, though you do not remember, nor can I make you remember. He is part of you, and you are part of him. It is something you have done that I cannot undo. None of it matters. You must find him. You must."

"How?"

"That, I do not know. All I can tell you is that he is real, he is in trouble, and only you can find him. But I caution you, trust *no one*. There are other forces that seek him. Those we think we can trust sometimes turn against us. Find the Protector. He is the sole person in all of Arden you can trust."

"How can I find the Protector?"

The voice sighed. "I do not know. I only sense he is out there, and not far from you. I fear I have given you a near impossible task, child. But I feel your love for the mage. You will find him. Of that, I have no doubt. I only hope it will not be too late."

"What...? How...?" She had too many questions to formulate.

"Remember, trust no one."

"My sister?"

"I do not know her, child; but I caution against it."

"I have to tell her in order to find him. I'm in her charge."

"Then divulge little. You are gullible, Lunara. You believe too much in the heart of others. Use your gift, sense their souls, but do not trust it. Souls change. The information they gather while living in the light can be used when they move to the darkness. Evil forces are at play. Guard your knowledge, for it is all we have." Its voice broke off, but it continued. "The mage's soul is in torment. You must be careful how you approach him from here on. Telling him what you know will either help you, or drive him from your mind."

"You're saying not to tell him I'm real? How can I find him if I can't tell him?" The figure was assigning a task that *was* impossible!

The voice sighed. "I do not know. His reactions are random. His responses are unpredictable. I can only suggest you approach him lightly. Plant a seed of thought and allow it to grow."

"But I could ask him where he is. He'd tell me. I know he would. We love each other." Lunara swallowed hard. Did they? If it truly wasn't a dream, how could she love someone she'd never met? Perhaps the real man was different than what he presented to her in their dream.

"You assume he knows where he is. I sense horrible grief has mantled itself over our lands. He might already be lost to us. Telling him could drive him over the edge. Your path, I fear, is wrought with danger and uncertainties. I can help you no more. Already this conversation has drained my strength. Tell none of me. I fear I cannot discern my friends from my enemies."

Deep sadness stabbed Lunara's heart. It came from the figure, almost as if it were losing hope.

"I'll find him," she whispered.

The scene vanished, replaced by suffocating darkness. The love faded, leaving her feeling cold and empty. She waded through a seething black fog.

"FALAR!"

The word rang like a roll of deafening thunder, menacing and angry. She clamped her hands over her ears. Something grabbed hold and shook her.

She cried out, and her eyes flew open.

Varila was shaking her. "Lunara! Lunara!"

"Falar," she gasped. "We must go to Falar."

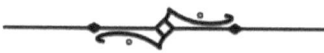

Wilhelm paced the smithy sitting room, clenching and unclenching his fists while he told Humar and Durak of Salvarias's abduction.

Humar shook his head at the end of the story, and his tone was apologetic. "I have little knowledge of magic. I don't know how this Dethal disappeared into thin air with your brother."

Wilhelm threw up his hands. "I'll travel to different cities, question people." He headed for the storeroom. "Sitting here isn't going to get Salv back."

"Think this through," Humar said. "Running out with no plan isn't going to work either. It'll take you months to travel and there's no guarantee you'll find him. We need someone who understands magic."

"I have an uncle who's a wizard but I haven't seen him for nearly seven years, and I don't know how to find him."

Humar said, "I have a friend, a great wizard, supremely powerful. I'll send messages to each town he frequents. He'll help us." He hurried from the smithy.

Wilhelm continued to pace while racking his brain for any information or clues he might've missed.

"We'll find him, lad," Durak said.

The cavrul gathered dressing and water to treat the slices Wilhelm had suffered on his forearm and thigh while fighting off the four black-armored men who'd been left to kill him. He plopped into a chair and allowed Durak to treat his wounds. By the time he finished, Humar had returned.

"How long will your letters take to reach him?" Wilhelm asked.

A knock on the door stopped Humar's response.

The cavrul muttered the entire distance to the door and flung it open. "Can't ye see we're closed?" he roared.

Before the door slammed shut, a boot stuck in the doorframe and a woman spoke. "I can see that, old cavrul. I'm looking for a young mage with black hair and black eyes. A guard said he might live here."

"Maybe he does, maybe he doesn't. What's it to you?"

A different woman spoke. "Please, Gentleman. I fear the mage might be in trouble. We only wish to speak to him and help."

"Let them in, Durak," Humar said.

The cavrul opened the door and two women stepped inside. The older one wore armor, and a sword hung at her waist. The other woman had raven hair and looked near exhaustion.

The raven-haired woman spoke. "We seek a young mage about my age. He has black hair, black eyes, and he's tall. Do you know him?"

"My name is Humar, this is Durak, and that's Wilhelm. How do you know the mage?"

"I can't explain how I know him, but it's imperative I speak with him."

Humar ran his hand through his hair. "We don't know where Salvarias is, and if you have any information, please tell us."

The woman rested a hand over her heart. "What do you mean? He's lost?"

"Yes, he's missing," Humar said.

Wilhelm's patience was wearing thin and his anger swelled,

trembling his body with its building rage. He didn't know these women, although the raven-haired woman looked vaguely familiar. Too many people were looking for his brother all at once.

The woman's face drained of color. "I'm too late. I... I only thought to prevent... I never considered we wouldn't be here in time..."

Wilhelm's anger exploded and his words roared out. "How do you know him? What's happened to him?" He advanced towards the women.

The other woman drew her sword. "Keep your distance."

Humar stepped in front of him, whispering, "Don't. I'll send them away."

The raven-haired woman cast a sympathetic look and shook her head. "I don't know him, Gentleman. I can't explain how I know *of* him. What are you doing to search for him? How long has he been gone?"

"Five days," Humar said. "I don't understand your concern, my Lady. Who are you?"

"My name is Lunara. This is my sister, Varila. I don't expect you to understand, Sir Knight. I can tell you that my sister and I want to help find...Salvarias. We'll do anything you ask."

"We've sent word to a friend of mine and will await his arrival. There is no further aid needed." Humar's tone was final.

"Thank you, Sir Knight," Lunara replied. "My sister and I will stay at the Red Lion and await news. Please call upon us if you obtain any information or need further help." She curtsied and Wilhelm heard her last whispered words as she led her sister through the door. "I fear I've failed the young mage."

Chapter 17
Autumn 1017 a.r.

Wilhelm pulled his cloak about him as he pushed through the morning crowd towards the potion shop to see if Milred had seen Dethal. Adok, as always, trotted close by Wilhelm's side, equally irritated, growling and showing teeth often.

Wilhelm scowled at a jolly merchant calling to passersby. Autumn had come and brought with it a bustling city preparing for the coming winter. The Harvest Festival was set for this evening and the city grew celebratory. The chipper demeanor of the normally restless town grated on his nerves and he resisted the urge to pummel every smiling face that passed him.

Autumn. It had been over two seasons since Salvarias was taken, two seasons since Humar's message to a friend, two seasons of torture for Wilhelm. He felt helpless, hopeless. With every waking breath, he avoided thinking what his brother might be enduring. It had taken one conversation with Milred to know that the bruises his brother received hadn't come from her store. Dethal had hurt Salvarias. And now that same man was alone with Salvarias and had been for seven months. Wilhelm clenched his fist.

When the shop came into view, he discovered the two women who were interested in his brother talking to Milred. He ducked behind a baker's shelf to hear the conversation.

"How long did Salvarias work for you?" asked one sister.

"Oh, I'd say about two seasons, a full autumn and winter before he went missing," Milred responded. "Come inside. I'll be happy to show you where he worked."

Wilhelm snuck around to the small window that overlooked the table where his brother had sat grinding herbs. It was opened as always, permitting the conversation to be easily overheard.

"He was such a patient boy," Mildred said. "He could sit here for hours grinding and mixing potions. He read those books in the matter of a month."

"He was gifted in alchemy?"

"Yes, exceptionally gifted. You should've seen his hands." Milred sighed. "He helped so many people. Because he was a mage, he never received any thanks, just harsh looks, but it didn't seem to bother him. Such an odd boy."

"What do you mean?"

"He was so quiet and never smiled, not once, but he saw everything. He could take one look at a person and know what ailed them. My business picked up after he started working for me. I raised his pay and caught him buying food to feed to the stray dogs and cats in the alleys. He'd even buy herbs and give them to sick children living on the streets. I asked why he did it once and he told me, 'My reasons are my own, Madam.' Wasn't rude, just stating a fact. I never understood it." Milred chuckled. "But, like I said, he was an odd young man."

No one ever understood Salvarias. For the first time, Wilhelm admitted he didn't understand his brother either, always thinking, always inside his own mind. But Wilhelm loved Salvarias more than anything, and found his odd habits, unexplainable actions, and incessant counting endearing.

"What are you doing?" a voice spoke from behind.

Wilhelm jumped so high he was sure his skin left his body. The golden-haired sister stood near.

"I'm eavesdropping," he retorted. "What does it look like I'm doing?" He felt a blush creep up his cheeks.

"Well, at least you're honest." She took a step near him and stopped at the sight of Adok. "Nice wolf. So why are you spying on us?"

He tried to remember her name. He'd been upset when the sisters appeared at the smithy. "I want to know what you want with my brother."

"We told you we want to help. You're so damn suspicious."

"The, uh, circumstances surrounding my brother's disappearance are suspicious. We don't understand why."

The woman regarded him; hand on the hilt of her sword. He admired her stance, confident, sure of her herself, with a superior air about her. Her wavy golden hair was loosely braided, allowing strands to frame her sun-kissed face. Her tall body was toned, strong, and tan, but not as excessively muscular as other female fighters. Leather armor was fitted and designed to draw attention to her femininity. She had the voluptuous hourglass figure every man dreamt of tracing, but what was more enticing to Wilhelm was that she knew it. Her leather-armored skirt exposed her tanned, well-built thighs and allowed easy maneuverability. Boots reached above her knee, a dagger in each. She exuded sensuality. When his gaze finished its inspection, he saw a playful smile on her lips and a sparkle of amusement in her eyes.

"Wilhelm, was it? Varila, in case you forgot. My sister is Lunara, and this is her deal. I'm just along for the adventure, here to protect her." She walked towards him, showing her athleticism with light steps and agile hips. "If you tell us what you know, we can help."

He couldn't breathe. Her gray-blue eyes were shrewd and aggressive, and her stare was one of pure seduction that roused his desires. He was sure those eyes were never timid or shy. He inhaled the thick aroma of her oiled leather armor mixed with… strawberries.

"Wilhelm!"

He turned his gaze to the raven-haired sister, though he felt Varila look him up and down. Adok bounded over to the young woman and sat, tail wagging.

"Hello there," Lunara said, kneeling in front of the wolf. Adok licked her cheek, making her giggle. "You're adorable."

Varila turned from Wilhelm. "I was just coming to get you."

Desperation to find his brother moved his lips. "A wizard took him, a wizard with a long red beard and red hair. He was old, though."

Varila stepped towards him, rewarding him with her smell. "Thank you. Now we can help look for this mage. Women have ways to gain information." She winked at him. "Shall we get a drink at the inn and compare stories?"

He nodded. While they walked to the Red Lion, he glanced several times at Lunara, his mind teetering on recognition. A thick, raven mass of hair danced around her slender waist, and her skin was creamy porcelain, her lips deep red, and her piercing blue eyes lit up in the morning sun. Her sweet smile guided his way through the streets. Her arm was wrapped around his while she compared Falar's festival preparations to those done in Serinity. Varila walked on the other side of the girl, shoving away men's outstretched hands when they passed.

The tavern was quiet, and the three chose a round table near the fire. Varila ordered two glasses of ale and Lunara asked for water and fruit from Mulard, offering a smile which seemed to melt away the tavern owner's cranky frown.

Wilhelm leaned back in his chair and laced his fingers behind his head. "A little early for ale, isn't it?"

Varila rolled her eyes. "Oh, I'm sorry. I thought I was with a man."

"I didn't say I wasn't up for ale."

"Then don't complain." Varila rested her foot on a close chair, allowing a clear view of her smooth, tan leg, tempting him to touch her.

He forced his gaze from her thigh. "Have you found any information since you've been here?"

Varila shrugged. "Not much. We know your parents were killed seven springs ago. You were captured and forced into slavery. That brother of yours has been practicing magic since he was six, and you've been forging away at the smithy for the past year." She eyed him. "By the look of you, I think what we heard was the truth. However, that's about all we got."

"Guard named Idolar?"

"Yes, it was," Lunara chimed.

"Your armor and weapons are high quality," he said to Varila.

"So they are." She smiled up through her long eyelashes. "I'm happy you noticed."

"Hard not to." His grin spread. It was the first one issued since his brother's abduction.

"Will you tell us what happened?" Lunara asked.

Wilhelm's smile faded when he recounted the events.

At the end of his story, Varila arched an eyebrow. "I don't know much about mages, but isn't it a little odd for one to become so possessive of an apprentice?"

He shook his head. "I don't know. I'm not sure the mage wants him as an apprentice."

"You think it was a ruse? A way to get close to your brother?"

He shrugged. "Perhaps. I don't understand though. Why not just take him?"

"It's easier to get information from somebody who isn't a prisoner. Maybe this Dethal thought he could earn your brother's trust."

He grunted. "Salv doesn't trust anyone, which is why it's odd that he accepted the man's tutelage."

Varila took a swig of her ale. "Your brother knows something. Maybe he's not aware he knows it."

"But I've been next to him my entire life. I know what he knows."

"You're not a mage. Mages have secrets."

"Salv doesn't hide stuff from me."

Varila snorted. "I'm sure that's how you knew of his apprenticeship."

"Sister," Lunara scolded.

He clenched his jaw. "You don't know him. I'm telling you, it's not like him to talk to a stranger."

"Salvarias is always seeking knowledge," Lunara said softly.

His gaze jerked to Lunara. "What?" The girl knew his brother more than she let on.

Humar burst into the tavern. "Wilhelm!"

Wilhelm stood, but Varila took his arm. "Let us help you."

"Please," Lunara said, taking his other arm.

Humar motioned at Wilhelm. "My mage friend has arrived. Let's get to the smithy."

Wilhelm looked at the two women and trusted his instincts. "I'm going to let the sisters help us," he told Humar.

The group shoved through the midday crowd in the cheery market until finally reaching the smithy. Upon entering, Wilhelm almost fell over. Uncle Mafarias stood near the fireplace, not aged one day.

"Wilhelm? What—" The mage's eyes opened wide. "Salvarias was taken?"

Wilhelm nodded. His thoughts stammered to a halt.

Mafarias turned red with anger. "Dammit, Wilhelm! You're supposed to take care of him! How was he captured?"

"Mafarias!" Humar's voice cut into Mafarias's fury. "There was another mage that took the boy. Wilhelm had a spell cast on him until the mage disappeared with the boy. And Salvarias willingly went."

Mafarias cursed and paced.

Humar shook his head. "How do you know Wilhelm and

Salvarias?"

"I'm Ashra Laybryth's uncle." Mafarias turned to Humar. "How do you know them?"

"Tobin Cohil was the adopted brother I told you about."

Mafarias cursed. "I can't believe we've never linked this before. I'm sorry, Humar. Tell me what happened, Wilhelm."

Wilhelm recited the events and once done, slumped with relief. If anyone would be able to help, it was his uncle. Mafarias traveled across all of Dalnar and had told wonderful stories of his adventures.

Mafarias paced again and his voice was sharp with anger. "How could you leave your brother's side? And how could you not know he studied under a mage? He surely showed signs of exhaustion or must have had spell books he studied."

"He never told me. He only said he was working at the potion shop, and yes, he was tired, but he worked late some nights, and his nightmares got worse after our parents were killed. When we were captured by the slavers, the octrils stole his spell book and he hasn't had one since." Wilhelm's own anger rose. "And where have you been? It's been over seven years since I've seen you. Did you hear about Mother? Did you hear about what happened to us?"

"Yes, I heard about your mother and I'm sorry I didn't come sooner. I've been engaged in other events." Mafarias smoothed the front of his robes and gained his composure. "I am sorry about your mother and Tobin."

"Sorry? Sorry!" Wilhelm roared. "Salvarias was devastated after our parents were murdered and all you have to say is sorry? No one was there to look after us! I wasn't old enough to join the guard. I had to try to take care of both of us and I was only sixteen. If I hadn't met Humar, we would've frozen and starved to death in some alley. You're the only damn family we have!" His voice rose. "The *only* family and you didn't think it was important to come back after you heard about Mother and help us? This is your fault! If you'd been around to teach Salv magic, he wouldn't have felt the need to get involved with a stranger. You're our damn uncle!"

"Calm yourself!" Mafarias roared back. "I tried to teach that boy, but he wouldn't speak to me!"

"He changed after Mother died. He's talked to Durak and Humar. He would've opened up to you, but you didn't give him time!"

"I didn't travel for four damned years after that boy learned of his magic. Four years I spent trying to talk and help that boy!" Mafarias threw up his hands. "How long was I supposed to wait?"

"Tobin waited eight years to be accepted!" Wilhelm shoved his uncle, anger and pain winning over restraint. "He wasn't even blood!"

"Enough," Humar said. "Finding Salvarias is important now, not what should've happened years ago."

Wilhelm wanted to pummel someone, preferably his uncle, but instead resorted to pacing.

Mafarias straightened. "I can sense Salvarias's magic. If we walk around town, I should be able to find where they practiced."

"I want to find him, not know where he practiced," Wilhelm grumbled.

Durak patted his arm. "There could be clues as to his location, lad."

Mafarias seemed to notice the sisters for the first time. "Who are these ladies?"

"Name's Varila, and this is my sister, Lunara."

"And why are you here?" Mafarias focused on Lunara.

Varila took a protective stance in front of her. "Because we want to help, mage. Keep your damn eyes to yourself."

Mafarias turned his attention to Adok. "And the wolf?"

"He was at our parents' grave the day Salv was taken," Wilhelm said.

"Interesting," Mafarias murmured.

"Dammit, Uncle! I don't give an ogre crap about the wolf. Find my brother!"

Mafarias smiled slightly. "Come."

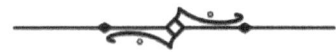

Lunara walked arm in arm with Wilhelm as they made their way through the celebrating crowd. His stern face and low growl made overly jovial citizens melt from their path. No man reached for her and many avoided groping her sister. Any who made the mistake of touching Varila found a knee to the groin or an uppercut to the jaw. Lunara rested a hand over her mouth to hide her smile as she caught sight of Wilhelm watching Varila with a hint of admiration in his eyes. Her sister showed obvious interest in the man; and rightfully so. His physique alone would cause any woman to swoon, but it was his amber eyes that pulled one under his spell. They carried an alluring innocent purity that no other man seemed capable of. When he grinned while they were at the Red Lion, his eyes had danced with warmth and his smile would melt the heart of the coldest woman.

Lunara smiled up at Wilhelm when she felt his gaze. He seemed curious when watching her, and she assumed he had the same suspicion as her: That they'd met before. She used her gift again, the ability to see into the true heart and soul of others, and it still showed her a man whose love for his brother was beyond description, and a heart as expansive as the vast sky, filled with buried happiness she hoped to someday witness.

Her gaze moved to Humar. He was the most honorable person she'd ever sensed. The knight cared for Wilhelm greatly and harbored an odd concern for Salvarias. Not love, but a true desire to keep him from harm. She glanced at Durak. The cavrul's strong dislike of Salvarias was overridden by love for Wilhelm. Durak would have followed him to Oblivion if he were to ask. Her stare drifted to Mafarias. The mage proved an interesting read. He cared for Wilhelm, loved him as an uncle might, but was distant with Salvarias. Mafarias's concern glided on the surface, like one might be concerned for a relative you see once a year. Surrounding that small concern was a fear that Lunara had yet to understand.

Even after what she sensed in them, she wasn't willing to disclose her knowledge. The dream she had on the night she fled from her home had warned her to trust few.

A guard called to Wilhelm, and he removed his arm from hers to shake the man's hand. Lunara looked around all the singing bards, the street performers enrapturing children with sleight-of-hand tricks, the jugglers, and acrobats contorting into odd shapes. The air was scented with spices, pumpkin breads, roasted nuts, and apple cider.

A particular bard had attracted a crowd and Lunara moved near to listen to the man's beautiful voice. He was singing *Battle of the Hidlu*, a tale of cavrul courage during an unfortunate and rare hidlu raid in the caverns of Cattlar during the long wars. It was a chipper tune, full of curses and outlandish fighting. She smiled at the giggling children when the bard's eyes lit up, reenacting scenes followed by sighed ooos and ahhs from the enraptured crowd.

"Hello, pretty lady," a man said in her ear.

She jumped when an arm circled her waist. She shoved the man, but he tightened his grip, turning her to face him. He stood slightly taller than her with brown eyes and ale-drenched breath. He lifted her in a dance even while she struggled in his hold. She kicked his shin and gave a small cry from the throbbing in her toe.

The man laughed ruefully. "Armor, lovely lady."

"Please, let me go."

The man grinned, spinning her around. "Not likely."

A voice rumbled over the singing. "Leave her alone."

She looked over her shoulder to see Wilhelm standing behind her, his jaw clenched and his eyes glinting with anger. A grinning guard, one she recognized as Idolar, stood behind Wilhelm. The music fizzled to stop.

The man lowered her and held his hands up in surrender. "No harm."

"Depends on who you ask." Wilhelm's massive fist planted in the man's face. "Respect women, you piece of ogre crap." Wilhelm balled the reeling man's tunic in his hand and struck again. Blood flowed from the man's crooked nose.

"Help me!" he sputtered to the guard.

Idolar smirked. "She asked nicely. You get to deal with him now."

The man wrenched free and fled, trampling people in his path, and soon blended with the jeering crowd. Music filled the air and the festivities turned lighthearted once again.

Idolar roared with laughter. "I wish you'd join the guard, Wilhelm."

Wilhelm shrugged and his arms swallowed Lunara. "Don't wander off from me."

The group continued, Wilhelm keeping her arm locked with his. As they passed the Red Lion, she heard a soft curse from Varila. Her sister's gaze was surveying a group of soldiers ahead. Lunara recognized their armor and the emblem of Gunder. Her heart squeezed a rush of blood through her body. There would be no way for them to sneak by.

Suddenly Mafarias stopped at a home with a black door. He put his hand on the handle, and after whispering words, it glowed pale blue.

"He was here," Mafarias said. The mage flicked his hand, opened the door, and slipped inside.

Crossing the threshold made her shudder, and once inside her uneasiness grew. Varila was quick to close the door and plunge them all into darkness. Mafarias whispered a word and a white light glowed from a crystal he carried.

The home was deserted and mildew and dust tainted the air. On her left was a sitting room with two chairs and a fireplace. A staircase rose in front of her, and she saw a kitchen and table in the back. On the right, a library contained books stacked floor to ceiling along three walls. She no longer guessed where Salvarias obtained all the information he'd shared with her in their dreams. The memories brought a small smile to her face.

After she studied the rooms on the lower level, she climbed the stairs behind Mafarias. She halted at the entry of the room at the top of the stairs once she caught sight of the jars. Horrible objects were suspended in liquid; some contained small animals, eyes that stared back at her, body parts—some human and some not—and animal hearts in others. Several containers were broken, the contents since dried. Books lay scattered on the floor, and there was a table with two chairs centered in the room.

Gathering her courage, she passed the threshold. Dried blood was evident on the floor in several locations. She made her way to the table, observing the book that lay open in front of the chair with its back to the entrance. A few words and symbols were written on the page in a language unknown to her. Staring at them brought a dizzying effect, and she reached for the chair to steady herself. The instant her fingers touched the fabric, an image of Salvarias flashed in her mind. She hardly recognized him. Blood caked his eye closed, deep bruises marred his handsome face, and his thick black hair was matted. She staggered until strong arms steadied her. All she saw was Salvarias lying on a glassy black floor. He stirred and the image was replaced with rocky ground and jagged black mountains slicing through the clear blue sky. As if she floated, she entered the obsidian mountain through a grate at the base of a cliff, following tunnels, twisting and turning through hallways, then a room appeared and she melted through the door. Salvarias lay heaped in a corner with rats eating his flesh. The image vanished.

Wilhelm was holding her upright; her legs were limp and her vision dim. Varila was talking and it took Lunara a moment to hear the words.

"Lunara! Lunara! Are you all right?"

"I'm… I'm fine." Once her senses returned to normal, she stood on her own legs. "I apologize. I don't know what came over me." She forced a smile though her insides knotted at the image of Salvarias's beaten body.

Wilhelm released her, but kept a hand on her back. The mage stood in the doorway, staring at her, his eyes captivating.

Mafarias said, "I need time alone in this room. Would you be so kind as to wait in the sitting room?" He stopped Lunara while the others filed out. "Stay with me, my Lady."

Lunara smiled at her sister. "I'm fine."

"I'm sure you are, but I'm staying," Varila said.

Mafarias shrugged. "Tell me, how did you become involved in Salvarias's disappearance?"

Lunara decided to avoid the question. "I have come to assist in his recovery."

Mafarias clasped his hands behind his back and strolled around the room. "I see. How do you know our young friend?"

She suddenly wanted to confide in the man, tell him all her deepest thoughts. She almost succumbed but bit her tongue. "I don't know him. I know of him."

Mafarias stopped his pacing. A quizzical expression lined his face. "*Of* him? How do you know of him, my Lady?"

"That is my own business, good mage." She smiled at him through her eyelashes. She'd learned how to use her femininity from her sister and mother, and she sensed a weakness for women in Mafarias.

He returned her smile and paced the room again. "Haunting, these jars. I understand why they affected you."

His comment was laid out so nicely, so subtly, that she almost took the bait, almost confessed it wasn't the jars that had affected her. Smiling, she nodded.

"If you want to help him, you need to tell me what you know."

Lunara curtsied. "If anything comes to me, I'll be sure to tell you."

The mage walked towards her. His gorgeous eyes pulled her mind into a fog. He grew more handsome with each step, and her breath caught in her throat.

His voice was hypnotic when he spoke. "Are you sure, my Lady?"

Varila stepped in front of Lunara. "Get away, mage."

Lunara shook her head, trying to remove a haze that seemed to cover her thoughts.

"Let's go," Varila said shortly. She led Lunara from the room and closed the door behind them. "What was that about?"

Lunara was breathing hard; though she had no idea why. "I don't know. He's a very handsome man."

Varila cursed, descending the stairs. "You and I don't have the same taste in men, and I thought the same thing. What color are his eyes? His hair?"

Lunara frowned. "I don't remember."

"Me neither. Something's not right."

"Agreed." For the first time, she understood her dream's message. Things are not always as they appear.

When they entered the sitting room, Humar was saying, "I had no idea he was your uncle."

Wilhelm grunted and turned his attention to Varila. She gave him a wink while Lunara settled in a chair next to him.

At long last, Mafarias emerged with a grim look. "First, Wilhelm, let me explain the distortion you saw in the air before Salvarias disappeared. It was a magical portal—like a doorway to another location. A portal must be made active in each location before it can work. Meaning you have to create it in one location then travel by land to the other. A link is formed between the two, allowing a mage to travel from location to location within a blink of an eye. Once the mage no longer needs the portal, he must close it from one side while leaving and then close the side he emerges from. Dethal must have created one side, the location unknown to us, and when he arrived in the woods, activated the other side. Do you understand?" All nodding, Mafarias continued, "My conclusion is Salvarias spoke the truth. The mage was training him. Nothing else can be discerned."

Lunara said, "There was another here, I believe."

"What makes you say that?" Humar asked.

"The dishes in the kitchen contained two glasses of spiced apple cider and one of ale. I saw three plates as well. I would assume three different people dined and drank here."

Mafarias smiled at her. "Astute observation. Unfortunately, we don't know who this third person might be. I can tell you it wasn't a mage. Mages can't drink spirits of any kind due to the... shall we say, side effects, on our magic." His face darkened and he seemed to speak more to himself than the others. "Salvarias is strong in magic, extremely powerful, though I doubt he knows his full potential." Mafarias turned to Wilhelm. "Unfortunately, there's no way to track portals and no clues reside in this home. I'm sorry; I can't find where the mage has taken your brother."

Wilhelm exploded. Picking up a small table, he threw it across the room, shattering it against a row of books. He struck a wall with such force his knuckles split. Resting his forehead on the stone, he wept.

Lunara's heart ached at his feeling of hopelessness, of his utter loneliness.

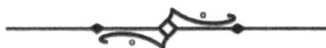

Wilhelm slouched at a round table in the Red Lion during the early evening hours with the rest of the group. The common room's silence attested to the rambunctious activities conducted in the streets, leaving the tavern deserted except for Mulard who attended to the group. The cheery street music filtered inside the room, seeming to mock Wilhelm's pain.

Mafarias was first to break the gloomy silence. "I'll travel my own way and search for the red-bearded wizard. Humar, you'll take everyone with you and head south, but stay west of the Cattlar Mountains. I'll travel on the east side." He shifted his attention to Wilhelm. "Stop at every tavern, every town, and ask about both Dethal and Salvarias. We'll meet here a month before Salvarias's eighteenth, your twenty-forth, Birth Day." Mafarias rose. "I must leave at once. May Zerana's grace be with you."

The rest of the group left for supplies, leaving Wilhelm with Lunara. He sprawled in the chair watching the fireplace flames, brooding and wallowing in defeat. Lunara broke his thoughts.

"We share a Birth Day, Salvarias, you, and I."

Wilhelm grunted.

"Your brother and I are the same age. My sister is two years younger than you."

He didn't feel like talking.

He heard trepidation in Lunara's voice when she asked, "Will you tell me about Salvarias?"

She sat in a chair close to the fire, her knees drawn to her chest, arms wrapped around her legs, hair falling around her as if it were a black blanket; so delicate, so fragile.

Images of his brother flooded Wilhelm's mind and he looked away into the hypnotic fire. "He's an amazing wizard. He's so smart. He read all the time, while he ate, before bed, even outside while I learned to fight with Humar and Durak." He fought back tears. "He loves animals. We found the wolf the day he was taken. It was sitting on our parents' grave." The tears broke free. He didn't care. He felt hopeless.

Lunara stroked the wolf's head as he panted near the fire. "I'm sorry, Wilhelm."

"Please, how do you know him?"

Lunara turned her gaze to the fire. She whispered, "I dream of him."

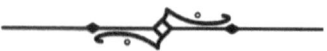

Varila packed with her sister while Wilhelm stood in the doorway, his face drawn and eyes dull. His care for his brother was undeniable and her sympathy cut deep. A knot formed in her gut at the mere thought of something happening to Lunara.

Having a new direction excited Varila. The last few months had proved especially boring for her. She liked adventures and traveling, but her sister was unfamiliar with the ways of the world. The girl was an innocent, a lover of life and peace. She knew little of the desires of men and the lengths they would go to in order to fulfill those desires. She'd received a taste tonight, and though she was quick to recover, she kept close after the encounter. Varila was skilled enough with a sword so she never doubted her own safety, but Lunara attracted men like honey attracted bears. Her beauty was unmatched and her innocence added a vulnerability men couldn't resist. Traveling would be challenging, but with Wilhelm near, Varila feared less for her sister's safety. He seemed to have developed some kind of brotherly protection for Lunara the instant they met.

Varila's gaze moved back to Wilhelm taking up the doorway. Unlike her sister, she wasn't an innocent. She experienced men whenever she desired them. Most who made it to her bedroom turned out to be too intimidated to keep it up past a kiss. She tended to be aggressive; not only in life, but in the bedroom as well. She controlled her situations. Few could handle her or dare even try and all found it insulting she could beat them in a fight. She wondered if Wilhelm would respond the same way should she ever choose to allow him to touch her.

Lunara flung her pack on her shoulder and teetered under the weight. "Ready."

Wilhelm came from his trance and took their packs. Varila had accepted Durak's offer to stay in his spare room, allowing them to leave early in the morning. The walk was uneventful, and once inside the smithy, Wilhelm dropped their packs in the spare room and left the sisters alone.

Varila rummaged for their hairbrush. The events leading up to this day had weighed on her mind. Her sister's nightly dream of a man she'd never met was disturbing enough, but learning she dreamt another dream where someone told her to help this mage had raised Varila's flags of distrust and set her nerves on edge. However, she kept her comments to herself. Lunara had often appeared distressed since they fled home, and after they visited the house with the black door, her eyes were misty with suppressed tears. Determined to know what plagued her, Varila plopped down behind Lunara on the bed and ran the brush through her sister's hair.

"What happened in the home?" Varila asked lightly.

Lunara's voice was thick with tears. "I had a vision; almost like a dream."

"It's all right. Tell me."

"It's not," Lunara sobbed. "I'm not supposed to talk about it, but I don't know what to do!"

Varila turned her around. "What is it?"

"In the vision, he was beaten and hardly recognizable. I, I saw black jagged mountains and tunnels running to dungeons. I think that's where he's being held, but I don't know."

"Why didn't you tell the mage, or Wilhelm?"

"I can't tell anyone. You have to promise not to say anything to them." Lunara wrung her hands. "I shouldn't even be telling you!"

"We can't find Salvarias if we don't ask for their help. I don't understand why we can't—"

"Because we don't know if we can trust them! I, I think I can trust Humar and Wilhelm, but I'm not sure. Don't you understand? I *have* to know I can trust them, and right now, I don't!"

"Salvarias is Wilhelm's brother, Lunara. If you know something, we must tell him."

"I..." Lunara's face twisted in anguish. "I want to, but I can't yet. Not yet."

"You're not making any sense. You know where's he's at. We can ask them."

Lunara shook her head. "I don't *know* for sure. We can't—" Her face lit. "We can ask strangers, people who don't know we're looking for Salvarias. We can just ask them about the landscape, nothing about the mage."

"Mafarias is well traveled, as is Humar. They probably know!"

"*I* need to find him; not Humar, not Mafarias, not Wilhelm. I do. I can't trust them, not yet. We can travel with them and secretly ask about the land I saw. Once we find out where it is, we'll split from the others and go on our own."

Varila wanted to scream in frustration at her sister's irrational behavior; and might have if fresh tears weren't welling in Lunara's eyes.

"Please, Varila, trust me."

Those words tore away Varila's fight. Wiping her sister's tears, she smiled. "Sure. I'll do everything in my power to help you."

Lunara took a shuddering breath. "I'm sorry. Thank you."

Grinning in an attempt to ease her sister's pain, Varila said, "I don't mind helping."

Lunara gave a small laugh. "Does Wilhelm have anything to do with your acceptance of my request?"

She shoved her sister. "He's cute."

"He's beyond handsome. And exceedingly sweet."

"He seems kind of grumpy."

"His brother is missing and he cares deeply for him. He has every reason to be grumpy."

Varila shrugged. "I guess. There's going to be a lot of traveling, and you've been getting sick lately. Are you sure you're up for this?"

"Yes." Lunara picked up the brush and unraveled Varila's braid. "I swear I don't understand it. I feel fine and then suddenly I feel like I haven't slept in weeks. Then it goes away."

"I worry about you. You'll tell me if it's too much?"

"Of course. So you think Wilhelm is cute?"

"Knock it off," Varila said, hiding her smile.

Lunara squeezed between two thick fir trees. The dense forest was littered with ferns that crunched under her feet and pine-scented air filled her lungs. She smiled to herself while she searched through the woods for Salvarias. When she pressed by a massive boulder, she saw him standing with his back to her.

"Hello."

He turned to face her and his gaze strolled over her body. "Hello."

She felt her cheeks burn and her heart thudded in her ears. "May I join you?"

"Of course."

She slipped her hand in his. His eyes were dull and his eyebrows were stitched together.

She wrapped her arm around his. "Can you tell me where you are?"

Salvarias led her forward. "Have you read any—"

His voice cut off when his steps faltered and he grimaced in pain. She wedged under his arm and helped him walk. There was no point in asking. He never told her what ailed him.

She smiled up at him. "I haven't read any books lately. Have you?"

"No."

"Have you given any more thought to our discussion? Do you

think I'm real?"

He shook his head. "I am reluctant to believe you."

She smiled and shifted to stand in front of him. "I am. Tell me where you are and we can meet."

His eyes flashed with pain. "If you are real, the last place you should come is to where I am." He ran his fingers through her hair.

She moved a step closer. "You'll discover it at some point. Just as I discovered you're real."

"How would I know of you?"

She lowered her head. "I, I don't know nor do I understand. But we..."

Her voice trailed off when he traced her collarbone. Try as she might, she couldn't stop her heart from racing or her chest from laboring for each small breath. It was impossible for her to love a man she didn't know. Impossible. Salvarias was real, not a figment of her imagination as she'd always thought. He was flesh and blood. It wasn't right to have such feelings.

His hand glided up her neck even as he moved closer. His body heat reached her. The softness of his fingertips lingered on her jaw. She raised her head to meet his eyes: Large, black, and utterly beautiful. His warm breath caressed her lips when he tilted towards her. Arms slid around her waist, pressing her close. Her lips parted, waiting. Then control passed through his eyes. He bowed his head.

She rose to her tiptoes and kissed his cheek. Since she couldn't trust her new companions, options were limited. It was time to take a risk. She whispered in his ear, "My name is Lunara. I'm from Serinity. I'm the same age as you. I, I know your name. You're Salvarias Laybryth."

He snatched his hands away and stumbled back a step.

"I swear to you, Salvarias, I am real. I know you're in trouble and I want to find you, but you have to help me."

He shook his head. "I do not know you."

"We've never met but I—"

"Then how can I dream you? You cannot be real. I need this!" He staggered back another step. "I can touch you—"

Salvarias doubled over, clutching his stomach. She rushed to his side but froze when his body changed. Bones stood out under his robes and all his muscle seemed to melt away. His once shiny, jet-black hair dulled and the side of his face was caked with blood. His velvety burgundy robes became crusted with filth.

She was losing him. Just as her other dreamed had warned. "Tell me!" she pleaded. "I can find you!"

He collapsed to the ground. He screamed, curling into a ball.

She fell to her knees by his side. "Tell me!"

Salvarias's fists dug into the ground. "I need this dream. You cannot be real. Please, tell me you are not. Do not let this end. Deny it!"

"I, I just want to help you. Wilhelm—"

His eyes snapped shut and a heart-wrenching scream left him. He vanished.

"No!" She stumbled to her feet. "No! Salvarias, come back!"

The forest melted into a dry, crusted landscape. She barreled forward, crying out for the figure. The pit came into view and she rushed to its side and peered into the darkness.

"Help me!" she begged.

"I warned you, Lunara. I told you to tread lightly."

"What can I do?"

"Nothing, my child. The damage you have done is irreversible. *Heed my words*. Listen to me this time. Trust no one, child." It sucked in a breath. "Do you feel the shift? He has slipped further from our reach."

"No!" she screamed.

"Lunara!"

She opened her eyes to find Varila shaking her.

"Lunara, wake up!"

The room was dark except for a single candle. Lunara closed her eyes and wept in her sister's arms. In that moment, Lunara knew she'd never dream Salvarias again. In that moment, she knew she'd made a fatal error.

Chapter 18
Autumn 1017 a.r.

Wilhelm rode close to the women when they approached the substantial gate leading to the brown city of Thunsra. Over the past month of traveling and questioning passersby, he'd finally felt like he'd done something productive to find his brother. He hoped, as he did with each town and village they visited, that this one would offer his first clue.

He scratched his beard as he watched Lunara smiling at Durak's story of an old cavrul blacksmith who was rumored to have bested a band of twenty hidlu with a pickaxe. She'd surprised Wilhelm in her ability to adapt, and her smiles seemed to add a layer of joy to all the companions, even the grouchy cavrul. Any could tell by her mannerisms that she was raised for court versus travel, yet she never complained and seemed as invested in finding Salvarias as Wilhelm.

His gaze shifted to Varila's thigh. She, on the other hand, was a specimen of pure seduction to him. He found her nonstop flirting distracting. Her strength and downright conceited attitude captivated him, and it was impossible not to return her banter. Nothing intimidated her nor made her blush. He found her irresistible.

He tore his stare from her legs before his restraint left. Instead, he surveyed the woods. The surrounding landscape was sparse forest with pines dryer than Falar's lush green trees. Instead of ferns blanketing the forest floor, dried pinecones and pine needles crunched beneath their horses' hooves.

The city itself snuck up out of the tall pines, not situated in a meadow like Falar or Serinity. Minotaurs and a handful of human guards patrolled the lofty brown wall. He'd heard that few humans were brave enough to travel through Thunsra, much less live in the city, and he speculated that minotaurs were widely misunderstood. Granted, their immense size—typically eight feet tall—was intimidating and their habit of eating enemies was disconcerting, but overall the race was neither good nor evil. Still, the city was known to be rough and not a place for ladies, so he kept close to Lunara, who looked around with wide eyes.

The group boarded their horses and strolled down the brown streets, observing brown buildings and admiring the solid construction.

Several less-than-honorable looking men walked close, and Wilhelm shifted in his uncomfortable armor. He'd borrowed a set of pieced-together metal armor and two swords from the smithy. Not many men were as large as he, and the armor cut into his skin in multiple places. His flesh bulged through crevices, sitting proved difficult, and he found the metal noisy when it protested against his girth. He preferred leather armor, but none fit him.

One man eyed Lunara too long for Wilhelm's comfort and his protective nature took over.

"Eyes to yourself, friend," he growled.

The three men stopped and grinned at Wilhelm. "You wouldn't be so bold if you didn't have a group of friends."

He clenched his fists. "Try me." Secretly he hoped for a small scuffle. He needed to relieve some pent-up anger.

They shuffled past and he draped an arm over Lunara, disappointed.

"I'm fine," Lunara said.

"I know."

"Then why are you picking me up?"

"What?"

Lunara giggled. "My feet are barely touching the ground."

"Oh, sorry. Old habit."

"It's all right. I'm rather tired." Lunara pulled his arm back over her shoulders. "You used to help Salvarias walk?"

He looked at the clear blue sky and the vultures circling above. "He had problems breathing, so I got in the habit of lifting him a little when we walked. Plus, he had a puzzle box he fiddled with and would trip if I didn't lift him." He glanced at Lunara. "You're lighter than he is."

"I'm sorry. I know this is difficult."

He shrugged and continued down the street in silence.

"Tavern?" Humar asked a nearby human guard.

"Clean or fun?"

"Clean," Varila interjected. "I need a bath."

"Guppy," the guard said. "Down two streets and on your left."

Wilhelm followed Humar and took in the view of Varila while she walked next to the knight.

The Guppy was clean indeed. Due to the minotaur clientele, the tables were sizable and sturdy, the chairs fit Wilhelm nicely, and the beds were plenty spacious. Varila took Lunara's hand and pack and immediately headed up to the washroom while the men settled at a table.

The owner was a minotaur whose bull nose was pierced, and the hoop ring dangled with snot. His horns were well kept and sharpened to a point, as were his hooves. A loincloth was the only cover the beast wore, and his abs rippled when he walked.

"What'll it be?" he asked.

"Four ale, one wine," Wilhelm said. "Lots of food."

The minotaur grunted and motioned to another beast that ducked into the kitchen calling orders.

Food and ale arrived and Wilhelm tapped his foot while respectfully waiting for the women to return before diving into the roasted chicken. His stomach provided music for the quiet tavern. "What's taking so long?" he muttered.

"Humph. Women take forever to bathe." Durak's eyes twinkled. "You've been with enough of 'em, boy. Ye should know."

Wilhelm shrugged. "Never long enough to learn of their bathing rituals."

Durak laughed, but Humar shook his head.

Wilhelm leaned back in his chair. "Come now, Humar. Did a lovely lady break your heart? Is that why you've never married?"

"Hardly. I don't see how you can be with so many women."

Wilhelm frowned, somewhat hurt. "Not that many. It just seems like it since I've been back from the slave caverns." He sighed. "None have interested me."

Humar smiled and nodded. "Ah. So now you think one might?"

Wilhelm looked over his shoulder to see the two women descending the stairs. Varila had left her sunshine hair down to flow in a damp, wavy mass around her body. He couldn't breathe until Durak gave an elbow to the ribs.

"Stop ogling," Varila scolded. "Unless you plan to do something."

Wilhelm's gaze meandered over her body. "Perhaps I will."

Varila plopped in his lap and picked up a slice of his meat. "I might let you."

He no longer felt his armor cutting into his skin when he inhaled her strawberry smell and felt her soft hair tickle his arms.

"It's cold," Varila complained.

"You took long enough to bathe." He wrapped his arm around her waist.

"You can't rush a bath." Varila removed his hand. "I have a lot of hair to wash."

She rose and sat in a chair next to Lunara, who was the color of a tomato.

"Need anything else?" the tavern owner asked.

"You seen a red-bearded mage named Dethal come through here?" Varila asked.

"Red hair and tall?" the owner asked.

Varila tore off a piece of bread. "Yeah, kind of evil."

"Haven't seen him, but his servant passed through here two days ago headed for Sundil."

"Really? Anybody else with him?"

"No. Just him."

"Thanks." She tossed him a silver. "We don't need anything else."

The owner accepted the money and left. Wilhelm could hardly breathe.

"Don't get your hopes up," Humar said. "It's just the servant, not Salvarias."

Wilhelm nodded. "I want to leave in the morning and try to catch up to him."

Durak shook his head. "While we're here, lad, we need to take the day to ask around."

"We can compromise," Humar said. "Durak and I will head out tonight and check the taverns. In the morning, we'll get supplies and ask the merchants. We'll leave late morning."

Wilhelm nodded in agreement and tried to push down his hope, but it bubbled inside.

After they ate, Durak and Humar left while Wilhelm sprawled in a comfy chair in front of the common room fire. Lunara curled up in a chair close by, pulled a book in front of her, and became lost in the pages. He absently watched her, thinking of how his brother so often read by the fire, curled up in the same position.

Varila plopped into Wilhelm's lap, removing his hand when it wrapped around her waist. Apparently, she could touch him at her choosing, but he couldn't touch her. He desired her all the more.

"Buy me another drink," she ordered.

Wilhelm motioned to the minotaur. "Two ale please."

The beast poured drinks and thundered over on the planked wood floor. Wilhelm tossed over the coppers and leaned back in his chair.

He talked with Varila about their childhoods, mainly about her traveling since he didn't have many tales to tell, or much he felt comfortable disclosing. Eventually, she allowed him to rest a hand on her thigh, and by the time Humar and Durak returned, his arm was around her waist, her arm around his shoulders.

"What did you find out?" Wilhelm asked.

Humar shook his head. "Similar information. The servant's name is Unias and he's well known. He should be easy to find once we reach Sundil."

Wilhelm gave a hopeful sigh. "Things are looking up."

Humar nodded. "We're turning in. It's an early morning tomorrow so keep that in mind"

Wilhelm and Varila chatted a while longer before she pushed herself up and approached her sister.

"Come on." Varila pulled the book from Lunara's hands.

He escorted the women to their room, and after Lunara entered, Varila closed the door then turned to face him. She reclined against the stone wall.

He put an arm on either side of her, angling towards her. "I haven't thanked you for helping me."

She arched her eyebrow and tilted her head back. "Feel free."

He grinned, seeing the invitation in her eyes, and leaned forward. He brushed his lips to hers. Unlike his normal, one-night relationships, Varila's soft lips stirred something deep within him.

With that lightest of kisses, a feeling other than lust erupted. Still feeling her moist breath on his lips, he opened his eyes. She was staring at him with wide eyes, her parted lips tempting him to steal a taste of her.

"Good night," she whispered and ducked under his arm to her room.

Shaking slightly, he went to his room, sank into his bed, and dreamt of strawberries and black mountains.

When the city gates of Sundil appeared, Wilhelm urged his horse to a canter. Settled in rolling hills covered in swaying brown grasses, the city nestled among sparse, stocky trees that spouted randomly across the landscape. The grasses were dying, the soil parched from summer's heat and lack of autumn rains, waiting anxiously for winter snow.

He pulled his cloak closer when they passed the city gates after obtaining directions to the stables from a guard. Like Thunsra, the buildings were made of light brown stone, but were built for human inhabitants instead of minotaurs. Cleaner than Falar, Sundil bustled with end-of-autumn haste, preparing for winter and harvesting crops before snow blanketed the fields. By the menacing clouds in the distance, only a few days of autumn remained.

As the group stood outside the stables to discuss their plans, Wilhelm wrapped his arm around Lunara and pulled the shivering woman close. The stress of constant travel had seemed to catch up to her. She appeared exhausted and some days hardly remained upright. Her insistence on continuing and her growing need to the find Salvarias inspired the entire group, once again impressing Wilhelm with her strength and concern for his brother. Rejuvenated urgency, however, brought a sense of foreboding. The sands were shifting through the hourglass at unnatural speeds.

"I'll take taverns," Durak offered.

Varila nodded at Wilhelm. "We'll take the market."

"I'll take Lunara to Sundil Inn and buy the rooms," Humar said. "Meet there after you're done."

"I'm fine," Lunara protested.

"I know, but I want to get settled before night." Humar pointed at the clouds. "The tavern will fill quickly if the storm hits."

Wilhelm hugged Lunara before Humar took her arm, leading her through the crowded streets. Taking a deep breath of spiced apple from a nearby tavern, Wilhelm draped his arm over Varila and pulled her close, feeling her hand slide around his waist, and headed towards the market.

He'd made no further advances towards Varila and they'd

returned to respectful flirting. He admitted to himself that he was afraid of his feelings. He'd never cared deeply for any woman, but Varila managed to reach into his heart and coax out new emotions. Furthermore, the timing couldn't have been worse. His brother came first, in heart and mind, and Wilhelm doubted any woman's ability to understand.

Shaking himself from his thoughts, he asked, "How's your sister doing? I think it's odd she's tiring from the travel. The first part of the trip she seemed fine."

"She has good days and bad days. Sometimes she's alert, although she always looks tired. The other day she could hardly walk. I don't understand it. I agree with you and so does she. She insists the traveling isn't difficult, but she can't explain why she's tired."

He pressed her closer. "We should be heading to Blarrup after this, but I understand if you want to go home."

Varila shrugged. "She wouldn't stop; and besides, we can't go home."

A familiar smell halted Wilhelm. Searching the street, he saw a sign of a mixing bowl swinging in the cold breeze, creaking and echoing in the alley. The fragrance reminded him of Salvarias; coming home smelling of herbs and spices, but the ever-present lavender always prevailed. Wilhelm smiled at the memory. Ever since he could remember, he'd slipped lavender under his brother's pillow. After their parents' death Wilhelm had stopped, thinking it never eased Salvarias's nightmares. But after his brother had started working at the potion shop, Wilhelm had found a small bag of the plant in his brother's bed.

Now the smell tore through Wilhelm as he led Varila through the old wooden doorway. Few windows lined the alley, and the dank shop was untidy compared to Milred's pristine rows of herbs. The plants looked sickly.

The owner, a lean man of middle age with a drawn face and gray eyes, looked grimly at Wilhelm. "What can I do you for?"

Varila moved in front and offered a playful smile. "Good day, Gentleman. Wonderful shop you have!" She looked around wide-eyed at the jars.

"Thank you, my Lady. I take pride in my merchandise." The owner straightened his back.

"Oh, I can see that!" She moved to the counter and rested her elbows on it, gazing up at him through her eyelashes. "I have some friends I'm trying to track down. Have you seen a mage come in with black hair, large black eyes? Kind of serious and skinny?"

The man's gaze roved over her. "No, can't say that I have."

"How about an old mage with a long red beard and red hair?"

"Master Dethal, I would assume. I haven't seen him in… well over four seasons. He used to pass through my shop a couple of times a year for herbs that can be found in this region."

"Do you know where we can find him? Where he might usually reside?"

"No, I don't. But I can tell you that he stayed at King's Post Inn when he was in town. Matter of fact, his servant, Unias, is there now."

"Thank you, Gentleman. I appreciate your time." After obtaining directions to the inn, she reached into her bosom and handed him a coin. "Good day."

Once outside, Wilhelm put his arm around her shoulders and they hurried to the inn. "I can't believe he's still here."

Clean and friendly, the King's Post Inn's patrons shared laughter-filled conversations, rabbit stew, and, by the stack of dirty mugs at the bar, plenty of strong drink. Wilhelm spotted Durak talking with a barmaid and weaved through the tables to the cavrul while Varila headed to the bar owner.

Durak's voice was slurred when he said, "Wilhelm, my boy! This lovely little lady said she saw the old kook about a year and a half ago!"

"You don't say?" He shot the girl a smile.

Her gaze strolled over him. "I do say, good warrior. He'd come here with his servant. Short man named Unias."

He planted a foot on a bench and rested his arm on his knee to lower his height. "How did you know he was a servant?"

"Because the mage ordered him around. Never spoke to anyone else."

He smiled at her again. "Is Unias staying here?"

She moved to press her body against him. "Perhaps."

He produced a coin and her smile turned seductive. "He's in his room," she whispered, her eyes inviting his lips to hers. All that came to his mind was the kiss he'd shared with Varila. Though the barmaid was a cute woman, he found he had no desire to taste her.

"And what's the room number?" he asked.

"Two," she breathed.

"Thank you." He grinned and tossed her another coin. He motioned to Varila and climbed the stairs with Durak close behind.

At the room, Wilhelm rested an ear on the door, but no noise emanated from beyond. He rapped on the wood. A ruckus erupted on the other side and Wilhelm quickly kicked in the door.

A short man with unkempt hair fumbled with a corked vial. Wilhelm lunged, but the man drank it before he could be stopped.

Wilhelm grabbed the servant's shoulders and shook him. "Where is he?"

Unias curled his lip. "You'll never find him. He belongs to Dethal now, not you."

Wilhelm snapped the man's elbow in the opposite direction it was supposed to hang, ignoring his scream of pain. "Tell me or it gets worse."

"Death will claim me first," Unias said. "I want you to know one thing before I die. Your brother suffers immensely. He calls for you in the night, begging for your help."

Wilhelm catapulted Unias to the other side of the room. "Tell me where he is!"

"My master grows impatient. Our cause can no longer wait. Soon the One True God will come and claim him. The tides will turn to our favor." Unias smirked. "Some Protector you turned out to be."

Wilhelm hauled the man up. "What does Dethal want with him?"

"His mind, his soul, his life. And he'll take them all."

Unias convulsed, white froth foamed on his lips, and then he went limp. Their single lead had died. Wilhelm tossed Unias across the room and made a cursory glance around. There was no clue as to Salvarias's location.

"There, lad, we'll find him," Durak said.

Wilhelm punched the wall and leaned his forehead against the cold stone, trying to gain control over his rage. Varila's hand rested on his arm and he pulled her into his embrace. He knew the man's words were true. With no hope or clues, his loneliness and emptiness grew. He felt hollow, half alive.

Varila whispered, "We're not giving up."

Sundil Inn was located at the city's center; and though not quite as lovely as the King's Post Inn, it was as clean and as friendly… and affordable. Wilhelm's funds were depleting and he worried how he'd provide for his brother once found. After sending Varila ahead to update Humar, Wilhelm held Durak back.

"Do we have money left at the smithy?" he asked.

"Aye, lad. I only pulled what I thought you might need. You both were frugal; ye have plenty of funds left."

He patted the cavrul. "How much?"

"Ye've trusted me with your money since ye first started working for me. I'd tell ye if ye were in trouble."

Wilhelm suspected Durak withheld information, and for the first time, found himself open to charity. Salvarias was Wilhelm's number one priority. He sank into a seat next to Varila at the corner table where his companions were huddled. The mood was melancholy except for Humar, who insisted hope existed even in the darkest times.

"At least it's something," Humar said. "We know he's alive."

A drunk man pulled up a chair, flipped it around, and straddled it. "Hello, Humar, you old dog! Buy a friend a drink, would you?"

Wilhelm angled back from the man's breath. "I should say you've had enough."

Humar extended his hand in friendship and the man returned it. "Okulu, you dusty rat! Where have you been?"

"Here and there. Buy me a drink or else I won't tell you what I know."

Wilhelm hesitated, glancing at Humar. The man's grass-green eyes were beyond bloodshot, and his nose was pink. Otherwise, he was well kept. His reddish gold hair fell around his shoulders and a neatly trimmed goatee was clearly a source of pride. Olive skin and large eyes caused Wilhelm to suspect the man part winsire. He was maybe in his late twenties, and possessed a natural charm and a roguish smile. Though not as large as most erthlas, his shoulders were broader than other winsires. Wilhelm would've thought the man's metal armor was that of a knight, but the decal of an eagle wasn't part of the knighthood.

Humar smiled. "All right, Okulu, what do you know?"

Okulu motioned the group to lean in. "I know there's a group of men who just entered. And I know they're not too happy about you asking questions around town or about you killing Unias."

Unfortunately, the half-winsire didn't whisper, but spoke in his normal tone. Wilhelm winced and scanned the inn until he found a group of six men watching them.

"We didn't kill Unias. He poisoned himself," he said.

Okulu grinned. "Is that how he got the broken arm?"

Wilhelm shrugged. "I never said I didn't break his arm; I said I didn't kill him."

"They don't care. They blame you." Okulu stroked his mustache while he stared at the sisters. "My, my... are you not the prettiest little things ever."

Lunara blushed and lowered her head.

Varila winked. "Touch her and you'll be missing more than just hands, friend."

Okulu laughed. "I bet I would."

"Thank you for the warning," Humar said.

"Mafarias told me to keep an eye on you while you travel." Okulu chugged down his newly arrived ale. "So what are you going to do about those men? I could go talk to them, see what they intend to do to you."

Humar spared a glance over his shoulder. "No, I have a decent idea what they intend to do. But, for now, we'll let them make the first move. No mercenary work available? I find it hard to believe you're working for free."

Okulu shrugged. "I owe the mage a favor. He's collecting."

Humar chuckled. "He always collects."

"I intend to stay with one of you. Who has room?" Okulu grinned at the sisters.

Wilhelm had his own room, and after no others spoke up, he offered Okulu the extra bed. When dinner ended, the group retired upstairs, splitting into twos.

Humar stopped shy of his room. "I think we should set up a watch tonight."

"No need," Okulu responded. "There's a pretty little barmaid down there that's grown rather fond of me. Hard to blame her though." He winked at Lunara. "She said she'd keep an eye out for me."

"Do you trust her?" Humar asked.

Okulu shrugged. "As much as I trust you."

Humar said, "I'll take your word. Get some sleep." He headed to his room with Durak.

Adok trotted into Wilhelm's room.

"What's with the wolf?" the mercenary asked.

"He travels with us. He's harmless."

"For now. He's only a pup; not a year yet, right?"

Wilhelm nodded. "I'm telling you, he's fine."

Okulu pulled out a silver flask from his armor, taking a long swig before he entered the room and lowered himself to a cot. His snore started before Wilhelm finished closing the door.

Sleep escaped Wilhelm while he stroked the wolf's fur. Closing his eyes, he thought of Salvarias as the servant's words rang through Wilhelm's mind. After what seemed like hours, he finally drifted to a doze.

He was jolted awake by Varila's cry of his name, Adok's low growl, and a frantic pounding underneath their floor, followed by a woman screaming Okulu's name.

Wilhelm snatched up his broadsword just as his door lock unlatched. Two men burst into the room, brandishing jagged swords. When the first man performed a diving lunge, Wilhelm blocked it while sidestepping the other intruder's tight thrust. The roar of the fight vibrated through Wilhelm; his vision sharpened, his breathing steadied, and his agility heightened. The fight seemed to move forward in slow motion.

His sword hummed through the air and ended in a validating crunch of bone and a warm spray of blood on his exposed arm. He felt more than saw the second attack and dropped below the attempted beheading swing. As he spun to face his attacker, Wilhelm arced his sword, skimming over the man's armor but connecting with his chin. The force generated cleaved through half the man's face, and Wilhelm averted his eyes from the gush of blood. He heard Okulu laughing.

"Brilliant," Okulu roared, slapping his knee. "Absolutely brilliant! It was like watching a dance of—"

Wilhelm stormed from the room.

Two men lay dead at Humar's feet and two others were engaging him and Durak while Adok frantically clawed at the sisters' door. One hard shove of Wilhelm's shoulder did the job and splinters flew inward. Four men were awaiting his entrance.

Twisting aside to avoid a deadly thrust, Wilhelm hacked off the man's hand. The high pitch yelp ended in a bloody gurgle when Wilhelm's sword severed half the man's head. Adok wormed his way between the legs of the men, and Wilhelm's anger broke free from the sound of Lunara's deep sobs. His cry of fury escaped and the men blocking the doorway took a step back. Their cowardice only enraged him. He grabbed the cuirass of one man and yanked him into the hall, tossing him towards Okulu who was leaning against the wall grinning.

Backing away, Wilhelm permitted the other two to enter the hall. He blocked one strike, then stepped aside from a thrust by his other opponent. He jumped forward, arcing his sword to slice the back of his foe. His blade hacked through the spine. With the battle still in slow motion, he ducked a whooshing sword while pivoting around, and disemboweled the wide-eyed attacker. Humar had run the last man through and Okulu was wiping a dagger on the corpse at his feet.

Entering the room, Wilhelm found Varila lying on the ground, blood clumping her hair, and Lunara on her bed, backed into a corner, her face ashen, and her dressed ripped at the shoulder. She looked to be in shock. Adok stood protectively in front of her, but she seemed unaware of the snarling wolf.

Humar covered Lunara with a blanket and folded her in his arms. "Did they hurt you?" She clasped hold of him and broke into frenzied sobs.

Lifting Varila onto the bed, Wilhelm brushed her bloody hair from her face. A knot was already swelling on her temple, but he determined she'd be fine except for a splitting headache when she woke.

Okulu appeared in the doorway. "I'm sure there'll be reinforcements. We need to leave."

All in agreement, the group packed and left the inn. The cloudy night provided cover and safe passage from the city. Okulu carried Varila, unconscious, on his horse, while Humar kept hold of Lunara, who'd yet to release him. Hours into the long ride, Varila woke and took to her own horse.

The group snaked up the Cattlar mountainside, finding streams to hide their tracks, and eventually took refuge in a small cave as the setting sun peeked through the tall pines.

Wilhelm sank against the brown wall, watching Varila whisper to Lunara, trying to pull the young woman out of her shock.

Durak returned from examining the cave and informed the group it went deep into the mountain. "We don't want to venture in there, though. Hidlu and who knows what else live in these mountains. It's best to stay close to the entrance."

Humar nodded. "Did anyone see those men while you were walking the city yesterday?"

No one had.

"Okulu, did ye hear 'em saying anything?" Durak asked.

Okulu tested the edge of a dagger he'd taken from one of the attackers. "Yes, many things. Probably the most important, though, was their job to kidnap Wilhelm and kill the rest of you."

Humar's mouth gaped open. "This would've been valuable information last night!"

Okulu shrugged. "You didn't ask, and I forgot."

Humar showed restraint and didn't pummel the merc into the cave floor. Instead, with evident effort, the Loutsil knight asked, "Can you think of anything else you heard them say?"

"They were hired by Dethal."

Wilhelm caught Humar's stare. "Maybe I should let them capture me. I could find out where they have Salv."

"No," Humar said. "What if he's escaped and they plan to use you to get him back? There are too many uncertainties."

Adok stood up with his hackles raised, staring at the cave entrance.

Okulu and Humar moved to look outside.

"They've found us," Okulu announced. "My, my, they are talented! I wonder how they were able to track us through those streams. I bet they have a damn winsire tracker."

Humar peered out. "How many? Can you see?"

"I'd say thirty or so." Okulu looked back at the group with a grin. "As talented as you might be, Humar, I don't think your party is in any condition to handle that many men."

Wilhelm shouldered his pack and hefted Lunara's. He fought the temptation to run out and surrender himself.

"How close? Can we sneak past?" Humar asked.

Okulu shook his head. "No, we won't be able to outrun them."

Humar cursed. "We're going to have to use the caves. Send the horses to throw them off. That'll give us a head start."

"What about the hidlu? Or have you gotten brave in your older years, friend?" Okulu took a long swig from his flask.

"We don't have a choice. You can lead us."

"I know my way around these caves. I've been exploring here before." Okulu frowned. "I think."

Humar nodded. "Remember, none of us can see in the dark except Durak. We'll have to hold onto each other. Tell us if we need to watch out for anything."

Okulu grinned. "Can the blond hold onto me?"

Wilhelm resisted an urge to punch the half-winsire. The merc cast a knowing wink.

Chapter 19
Winter 1017 a.r.

Humar cursed under his breath. He was sure they'd stumbled along in the maze of caves and tunnels for at least two days. Though only darkness pressed in upon him, he had the distinct feeling the caves were growing smaller. The damp air and confined quarters were wearing down everyone except for Durak, who seemed right at home. The old cavrul's eyesight helped him navigate better than most, and Humar envied his short friend.

The lack of light wasn't the sole reason for ill tempers. The temperature of the caves and tunnels was in a constant state of flux. Some portions of the caves were warm—uncomfortably so—while others were cold, forcing the group to strip off cloaks only to enter a new cave that chilled them to the bone.

What heightened Humar's anxiety was the confined spaces they were forced to crawl through at times. The feeling of being trapped almost made him scream out in sheer frustration. He didn't envy Wilhelm. The young man had been forced to remove his armor and stow it away in a pack so he could squeeze through tunnels. Okulu kept Humar apprised of the man's injuries, which were mounting. They needed out of this web of endless darkness before Wilhelm was skinned alive.

Sweating and sore, Humar barely contained the edge in his voice when he asked Okulu, "How many days are we to wander around?"

Okulu shuffled to a stop. "I… I might be… See, I think I'm lost."

"What?" Humar snapped. "Lost?" After several favorite curses, he told the group to rest. He needed to think.

Wilhelm's rumbling voice broke Humar's thoughts. "I think I see light."

Humar pointed towards a faint glow in the distance. "Okulu, can you see that light?"

"Of course! It's heading our direction."

"Is there something we can hide behind?"

"Yes, but—"

"Hide us," Humar ordered.

"But—"

"Now!"

Hands grabbed Humar, yanked him to the right, and pushed him to the ground. He cringed when he touched something wet and slimy. For the first time, he was thankful for the darkness.

Time passed in silence before he heard shuffling feet. He wrapped his fingers around the hilt of his sword, squinting when the light drew close. Someone whispered a word and the light grew brighter, blinding Humar. Drawing his sword while cursing, he shielded his eyes and sprang out from his hiding place.

"Humar? Okulu? What in Nevlar's damnation are you doing here?"

Humar said, "Mafarias? Thank the gods! Our friend here got us lost. Can you dim the light? We've been trapped in these blasted caves for days."

The light dimmed, and through many white and red spots, he saw the mage holding a glowing crystal. Humar was so relieved to see his friend that he embraced Mafarias.

"Tell me what you've learned," Mafarias said. "And how you happened to be here."

Humar and Wilhelm began the lengthy account of their two-month journey. In the light, Humar saw the extent of the damage Wilhelm had suffered. He was pale and breathing heavily, and his white tunic was soiled with mud and dried blood and shredded along the back and chest. Okulu met Humar's gaze and shrugged. They probably didn't have enough dressings. As if reading Humar's mind, Mafarias retrieved a bundle of white cloth from his pack and passed it to Okulu. The merc grinned and began fixing Wilhelm up. By the end of their story, he slumped with evident relief from the herb mixture Okulu had applied.

"It's imperative that Wilhelm not be captured," Mafarias said. "It's time for you to return to Falar. You must find a way to sneak into the city unseen, or at least unrecognized. Stay in the smithy and don't leave until I return." The mage turned to Humar. "You must get him safely home. Keep Wilhelm out of sight, conduct your investigations alone."

Wilhelm's voice shook with anger when he said, "I'm not going to stop looking for Salv."

"Whatever they want you for will only harm your brother," Mafarias said. "I'll not stop my search, but I can't begin to tell you the pain Salvarias would endure should you be captured."

Humar rested a hand on Wilhelm's shoulder. "I understand, Mafarias. Now, what have you learned?"

Mafarias sighed. "I've learned the same. No one has seen Dethal in three seasons. I assume once he started training Salvarias, he didn't leave Falar, nor has he traveled since taking the boy. This doesn't bode well. Without a trail, it'll be near impossible to track him." He turned to Wilhelm. "I'll not give up, but you must be realistic. We'll rest here for the night. Tomorrow, I'll help you through the caves. There's a small farm near the exit where you can buy horses and continue to Falar."

While the group settled in for a needed rest, Humar ventured next to Mafarias. "Have you any word on why Dethal wants the boy? Surely there are plenty of mages around Dalnar. Why Salvarias?"

"Salvarias is remarkably powerful and comes from a pure line of magic on his mother's side."

"But it doesn't make sense. If Dethal is already a powerful mage, why does he need Salvarias?"

"I've asked the same question myself. There are so many questions, Humar. None I can answer." Mafarias gazed at Lunara. "Lunara and Salvarias are connected. She has information she's not sharing."

Humar watched Lunara pick at her fruit and cheese, leaning her head on Varila's shoulder, Adok resting by her side. Like Salvarias, Lunara didn't eat meat and animals appeared to be fond of her. Humar smiled, remembering the boy sitting on the half wall in the forge with a stray cat always curled up in the folds of his robes while he watched Wilhelm practice or read a book. "I'll be happy to return to Falar. The girl doesn't seem made for travel. She grows tired often and sometimes she looks near exhaustion. It's random at best. We'll have a good night's sleep in a clean inn and within an hour she nearly falls from her saddle."

Mafarias shook his head. "I don't understand any of this. I must rest and think."

Humar sighed in agreement and took first watch.

Since the attack at Sundil Inn, Lunara had yet to calm her nerves. The event replayed in her mind, and no matter how hard she tried, the incident could not be suppressed. She still smelled the man's breath on her face, saw the hungry look in his eyes, and felt his cold hands grabbing her. Men were castrated for such offenses in her hometown, and she became aware of the sheltered life she'd led.

She glanced at her sister; strong and confident, having men when she chose, and felt envy. Lunara hadn't even kissed a man. Locking arms with men when they escorted her was the extent of her contact. Now, her first experience had been a filthy man's lips on her neck, his hand on her breast, and his heavy body preventing her from moving, driving home a feeling of weakness and vulnerability. She shuddered and felt Varila's stare. Lunara summoned up a smile, trying to convince both herself and her sister all was fine. It didn't work. Varila's eyes gave away her understanding.

Varila smoothed Lunara's hair. "You don't have to be all right with what happened. You just have to be strong enough to move past it. Nothing controls you but yourself."

Lunara nodded. After stroking the wolf's fur a few moments, she lowered herself to her bedding. Adok circled the same spot before nestling next to her.

The past two months had been lonely at night. Salvarias no longer walked with her in her dreams, and she missed him. A smile crept across her face when she remembered the first time they both had realized their relationship had grown from dear friends to something more. She could still recall the aspen trees they'd stopped to admire. She'd turned to see his gaze lingering over her body instead of her eyes as normal. At first, she'd blushed, but then her own gaze had meandered over his handsome face. Back then, he was skinny and short, but his features were masculine and alluring. Then his gaze met hers and his eyes, his eyes had ensnared her and there was no denying her feelings for him. It suddenly hit her that her first romantic touch hadn't been with the horrible man in Sundil, but with Salvarias. Her smile widened.

Just as the thought soothed her to a light doze, the presence that had lived within her since childhood tugged forcibly at her mind.

There were no words to adequately describe the presence other than to say she sometimes felt emotions that weren't hers. Once she'd been laughing with her father when a sudden sadness debilitated her to sobs. She never could explain it to anyone, nor did she want to try. She was terrified of the presence since all it ever conveyed was anger or grief. However, for the first time, it had spoken to her the night of the attack to warn her of danger. During a deep sleep, a soft and lulling voice urged her to wake. When she'd opened her eyes the link between the voice and the presence was undeniable. Before she'd fully digested her horror at the realization that it could talk to her, the bolt on their door had slid open. She'd called for Varila and her sister had awakened just in time to warn Wilhelm before the man struck her.

Lunara jumped when the presence spoke again.

"They are coming. You must run."

Lunara stiffened. Now that she was awake, she realized that the voice sounded like Salvarias.

"Run," he ordered.

She trembled. She was going mad. She had to be going—

"Run!"

She sat bolt upright and her gaze darted around the cave. Adok issued a low growl.

Mafarias was watching her with a raised eyebrow. "What is it?"

She didn't want to tell him. She merely sat rigid.

"Run! You must run!" Urgency filled the words.

"Somethi—" Pausing, she couldn't think of what to say. "Something's coming," she blurted.

Mafarias rose and kicked at Wilhelm and Humar. Advancing on her, he grabbed her arms, yanking her to her feet.

"What happened, girl?"

"It's—" Lunara stopped when hissing noises erupted around them. "Humar!"

"Humar?" the voice breathed.

Humar was already on his feet, sword in hand. "Hidlu."

Mafarias released her and shoved his bedroll into his pack. The others followed suit.

"You must tell Humar to run. He cannot win this fight."

Lunara's words stumbled out. "We, we must run."

"We can defeat them," Humar said. "They never travel in higher numbers than ten."

"Agreed," Mafarias said.

Okulu sucked in a breath. "No, there's more than ten."

"They don't travel in—" Mafarias started but Okulu interrupted.

"Dammit, don't call me a liar! I see them! Run!"

"He's right," Durak snapped.

The companions swooped up their packs and followed Okulu, using the light of Mafarias's crystal. Lunara dared a look at the ceiling of the cave. It moved like a swarm of ants after their hill has been disturbed. But instead of small insects, white bodies flooded out of a hole. Okulu bolted to a full run. She gathered her dress and kept close. Chancing a glance behind, she saw a slew of creatures drop from stalactites. Their lanky, albino bodies and cloudy eyes glowed eerily in the mage's light, and black, pointed teeth contrasted with their white bodies. Sharp claws curved at the end of each finger.

"Wilhelm!" Lunara cried, seeing a creature jump near.

"Brother." The voice wept the word with a desperate, longing tone and a wave of absolute pain swept over her, faltering her flight. Varila grabbed her arm and yanked her forward.

Not given enough time to react, Wilhelm grunted when the creature jumped on his back, wildly clawing, biting deep into his flesh. He grabbed the hidlu over his shoulder, pulled it in front of him, snapped its neck, and tossed it aside.

The party neared the end of the cavern. A small opening came into view. It would be tight for Wilhelm, but the rest would manage. Mafarias dove through first, and once all had crossed, the mage whispered something and rocks crumbled from the wall, blocking the entrance. The companions sank to the floor, catching their breath.

"I thought hidlu only traveled in small clusters," Humar huffed.

Okulu doubled over. "Not anymore they don't."

"Please, tell me he is unharmed," the voice wept.

"He's fine."

A surge of pain filled her mind, but not as though she experienced it herself, but an understanding of whatever he felt. Her vision blackened and the presence receded, too weak to keep the connection. As her mind spun in bewilderment, sudden exhaustion set in her bones. Events were linking and none were headed in a comforting direction. When her vision returned, Mafarias hauled her to her feet. He turned her hand over, exposing the silvery mark in her palm that looked like the moon.

"Where did you get this?" he demanded.

She pulled her hand free, fighting a sudden urge to sleep. "I've had it since birth."

Varila moved between Lunara and the mage. "Don't touch her!"

Mafarias's eyes glittered with anger. "Tell me what happened! What did you hear? Dammit, girl, you must trust me!"

"I, I don't know how to explain it." She was not ready to divulge information, least of all to the mage.

Mafarias cursed and went to help Okulu treat Wilhelm's torn arms.

Varila led her away from the group. "It's time to tell me."

Lunara's body gave out. Varila was quick to catch her and eased her to the cold cave floor. Adok watched her with an intensity she found unwolflike. Maybe she was going mad.

"A voice told me to tell Humar to run, that he couldn't win. I, I don't understand what's happening to me."

Varila hugged her. "It's all right. We'll figure it out."

"I think it's Salvarias. The voice sounds the same. When I called to Wilhelm, the voice said 'brother.'"

"Can you talk to him?"

"He could hear me, but I haven't tried to talk to him." Lunara's eyes drooped. "We need to find the mountains I described. He's in pain and we don't have a lot of time."

"I ask but no one has seen it."

Lunara glanced around her group. Mafarias and Durak she didn't trust. Wilhelm wasn't traveled enough to know the land. Okulu and Humar were her only options. Humar was inquisitive and would push for answers. Okulu was too drunk to care. "Can you ask Okulu? He's a mercenary. Maybe he's seen them in his travels. But, discretely, please."

Varila nodded. "I'll ask him when we're out of these caves."

Lunara allowed the blackness pressing on her vision to win and slipped into a deep sleep.

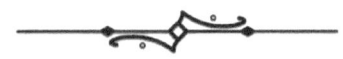

Varila shivered in the mountain air and smiled to herself when Wilhelm's arm draped over her shoulders. Winter had set in and a light snowfall drifted through the crisp air, and the ground crunched under her boots. The hillside was packed with dense pines, all dusted white. Wilhelm gave her an affectionate squeeze and lifted her enough to relieve the ache in her back. Warmth seeped from him and she slid a cold hand around his waist under his cloak.

"We'll part here," Mafarias said. "Remember, keep Wilhelm out of sight and get to Falar as soon as possible. Stay at the smithy, and whatever you do, stay west of the Cattlar Mountains. The east side is riddled with slave parties."

She felt Wilhelm's heavy sigh. Glancing at Lunara—once again exhausted—Varila wondered if she'd be as patient as Wilhelm if Lunara were taken.

"Durak and I will continue asking traveling merchants," Humar said.

Mafarias shook his head. "No, we don't know who to trust and word could travel of someone looking for the boy. We need to be discrete. Wilhelm's safety is priority. Get him to Falar and then you can travel alone."

Wilhelm's low, rumbling voice sounded more like a growl when he said, "Sitting around not doing anything isn't going to work for me."

"You must," Mafarias said. "I swear to you that if you're captured the torment your brother will endure is beyond your imagination. If you care for him at all, you'll remain in the smithy, safe and quiet."

Anger vibrated through Wilhelm. Varila wrapped her other arm around his waist, pulling herself close. She could offer no other comfort.

The mage clapped Wilhelm's back. "I'll send word if I find anything. The farm is two days' walk from here. Stay there near a month, until your trail runs cold, and then continue. The owners are personal friends and will take good care of you."

"Thanks," Wilhelm muttered.

Mafarias bid his goodbyes to the others and headed in the opposite direction.

Wilhelm walked with his head lowered, eyes distant, and brow furrowed.

"What is it?" When he didn't respond, she squeezed him until his eyes focused. "What is it?"

He sighed, raising his sad face to stare at the sky. "I can't stop looking for him."

"You're close with him. As close as, or even closer than, I am with Lunara."

Deep pain passed through his eyes. "We've been through a lot together. He's my life."

Her feelings for him strengthened. They shared a common love, something few understood. "Trust me when I say I understand, but I have to agree with Mafarias. Whoever this Dethal is, he'd use you to hurt your brother. You have to be careful."

"I know." Wilhelm returned his gaze to the ground.

"Mafarias can travel fast by himself. He'll find him."

Wilhelm grunted.

The farm huddled in a meadow circled by pine and maple trees, housed a pasture where horses roamed, and a few fields sprouted tall crops. The owners were pleasant and offered the companions a cottage removed from the main home. It was cozy and the fireplace warmed it well.

Three weeks crawled by for Varila. It was a cold afternoon on the twenty-third day of hiding at the farm when she was bored out of her mind. She wandered to the sitting room and found Okulu sipping ale by the fire. He was alone for the first time since they'd left the caves.

"Merc," she said, plopping in the chair beside him. "You ever seen a land with obsidian mountains, sparse dry trees, and rocky terrain?"

Okulu stroked his perfectly trimmed goatee. "Black mountains? No, dark gray of course, but never obsidian."

She grunted and rose from her chair.

"Let's stop in Flitver, though," Okulu continued. "It's on the way and I have a friend who's traveled every part of Dalnar. If anyone knows, it'd be him."

"Thanks."

She went to the kitchen and found Wilhelm slumped at a table, his head buried in his hands.

"Want to go for a walk?" she asked.

"Sure."

They tended to the horses they'd purchased from the farm owners before roaming the snow-dusted woods around the farmhouse. The walk seemed to allow Wilhelm something else to focus on besides a blazing fire or wood table.

"Salv loves forests," Wilhelm said.

"They are beautiful."

"It's the only time he's really happy; when he isn't stuck in the city."

"Why wasn't he happy?" she asked. When he remained quiet, she said, "I hope you've learned you can trust me."

Wilhelm stopped walking and his somber gaze moved over her body. "I have."

She planted her hands on her hips. "Have you?"

He took a step towards her. She could feel the heat of his body. He smelled like armor even though he wasn't wearing any.

"I hold stuff back because Salv is private." His eyes filled with want that she mirrored. "Not because I don't trust you."

She lost her voice. Trying to remain calm and in control of the situation, she gave him a shove, intending to push him to the ground. He didn't budge. His lips met hers, kissing her with desperate passion. He grabbed her waist, lifted her to his height, and shoved her against a tree. She exhaled in pleasure, finally finding a man as aggressive as herself, one not afraid she'd break.

Suddenly the thought disturbed her. Wilhelm possessed amazing strength, unnatural almost. Varila controlled her relationships; choosing when to kiss, where hands could go, and how far they went. She prided herself in being a strong woman and had fought off many men who tried to venture past the point she wanted. Wilhelm was a man she couldn't defend herself against. Fear gripped her, and then his lips left hers and he lowered her to the ground. He snatched his hands back and stumbled a step away.

"I'm sorry." He took another step backwards. "I thought, I thought you wanted..."

She was taken aback by his ability to read her thoughts and body language. She wanted him but was petrified; of not only her emotions, but also his strength. She knew what men could do and had been a victim before. She shuddered, remembering her father had castrated the sick bastard in a fit of blind fury. She'd been sixteen when it happened, and unfortunately, it had been her first experience with a man. But she swore she'd never be a helpless girl again.

Wilhelm took another step back. "Please, forgive me. I wouldn't have if I'd known how you felt. I'd never hurt you."

She realized she hadn't responded. Her thoughts and emotions had frozen her with uncertainty. She didn't know what to say, what she was feeling. She stared into his eyes, which were filled with a kindness she'd never seen in another man, a heart so pure she looked away, ashamed she'd doubted him. Wilhelm wasn't like other men.

After a deep breath, she decided to relinquish control, to trust him to not advance past where she wanted. She walked with purposeful slowness towards him. His gaze moved to her hips then rolled up to her eyes. She smiled her invitation when she stopped in front him. He stood rigid. Balling his tunic in her fist, she pulled him towards her, inch by inch, keeping her gaze locked with his. She saw the life beat in his neck increase, his breathing quicken, and his eyes convey his desire.

Still he didn't reach for her, didn't make an advancement. She kissed him. His lips were hesitant, tentative. She moved his hand to her waist. His taste, the way he opened her mouth to his, pushed her restraint aside. A second hand slid around her waist. Taking a leap of faith, she clasped her hands behind his neck and wrapped her legs around his body.

His gripped her thighs, holding her with ease. He trembled beneath her, but his hands remained in a single position, not moving up. Her confidence returned, and for the first time in her life, she trusted a man implicitly. The deep emotions she'd feared since first his lips touched hers in Thunsra flourished. But she couldn't be in love. She denied it. It was merely physical desire. Nothing more.

It took her a moment to hear the thundering noise echoing through the trees. Wilhelm pulled his lips from hers and studied the woods. She unwrapped her legs from around him and he lowered her. She could barely hear above her pounding heart, but listened again, holding her breath.

Finally, it hit her. "Horsemen," she breathed. They'd been found.

Wilhelm snatched her hand and ran for the cottage. Even during their flight, she admired his agility and stamina. He leapt over fallen trees with ease and his breathing remained steady and measured. While she kept up, her breathing was quick and her legs ached, her knees still weak from the encounter they'd shared. They emerged from the woods and bolted to the cottage.

"Horsemen!" he boomed as he flung open the door.

She rarely removed her armor so she helped Wilhelm struggle into his.

"How many?" Humar asked.

Wilhelm wasn't even out of breath. "Don't know."

"Pack!" Humar ordered.

By the time she finished helping Wilhelm squeeze into his armor, Lunara entered the room dragging two packs with her. The other three men rushed into the room only a moment later.

"Fight?" Okulu asked.

"Depends," Humar muttered, looking out the window. "Let's mount in case we can't. If we can, we'll fight on horseback. If we can't, at least we're ready to run."

Once outside, Adok paced while they saddled their mounts. Varila assumed it was going to be fleeing versus fighting. She glanced at Lunara and, though her eyes were rimmed with dark circles, she appeared alert. They trotted from the barn and gathered in a crop tall enough to hide themselves, even mounted on their horses.

Time seemed to crawl by, the waiting unnerving, the horses shifting with the tension of the group, but finally men flooded from the tree line. She guessed the number to be around forty.

Humar cursed. "Come on." He led the group at a crawl through fields.

"Search the home!" a man yelled. "Capture him alive at all costs. Kill the others!"

"Fresh tracks!" someone called.

"Now!" Humar barked.

They kicked their horses into a run. Calls of alarm ricocheted through the fields. Her group exploded out of the crops and Okulu took the lead, heading towards the forest. They spread out once in the trees, but kept each other in sight. Wilhelm and Lunara were the only ones who rode close together. Varila admitted, solely to herself, his sword skill surpassed hers, and his protective nature added to his strength. He was better suited to defend Lunara.

Shouts echoed through the trees. Varila glanced behind. She didn't see the men yet. Her party had a sizable lead.

"Regroup!" Okulu called.

All merged behind the merc and he turned his mount to a stream, splashing through the cold water. They took the stream a couple of miles before he veered off and ordered them to ride apart. She no longer heard the men behind them, and after a few miles, Okulu called for another regroup, taking them through a rocky, dry riverbed. They followed it for a good distance before he ordered them ahead and he went back alone. Slowing their pace, the group kept close, and after an hour, the merc caught up.

Okulu pulled off his gauntlet and wiped his forehead. "We've lost them for now. We can sleep for a few hours and travel at night."

The entire group slouched with relief and exhaustion.

The same routine followed for ten days before they reached Flitver. Exhausted from fleeing and the harsh winter weather, they chose the busiest inn, hoping to get lost in the crowd. Lunara went to bed without a meal, and Varila shoved down some slices of bread before retiring. She slept fitfully, and when she woke, Lunara still slept. Wilhelm, who'd insisted on staying with them, snored softly. Warming sunlight filtered in from the small window. She stretched, fixed her hair, and went downstairs. Okulu lounged at the bar drinking a pint of ale.

"I asked my friend," Okulu said when she sat beside him. "He's seen mountains like that a couple of days ride east of Treppter."

"East side of the Cattlar Mountains?"

"Yep." He motioned at the bartender for an ale. "Says it isn't traveled anymore. Octrils have overrun the place and they don't take kindly to visitors."

She arched an eyebrow. "Octrils?"

"Why do you care about this land?"

"Since when did you start asking questions? It's none of your damn business."

He grinned. "Of course, lovely, golden-haired warrior."

"Shut up," she said tartly. "What time of day is it?"

"Near supper. Bet you an ale Wilhelm is down here before you finish your drink."

"You're on. He was dead asleep."

"Next pint?" Okulu wagered.

"Deal." She spat in her hand and Okulu in his. After shaking, she grinned and took a long swig.

"Cheating?" He laughed.

"You didn't specify the rate I needed to drink it." She took another long gulp.

"No, I didn't." He shot her a devilishly handsome wink. "It doesn't matter though."

She glanced over her shoulder and cursed when she saw Wilhelm's arm draped over Lunara while they descended the stairs.

"Bastard." Varila rose from her stool and joined Wilhelm.

"I'm starving," he growled.

Lunara took his hand and led him to a table. Sinking further into a deep depression daily, Wilhelm's smile never emerged, his eyes had lost all sparkle, he didn't shave, his hair was unkempt, and he looked disheveled. His appetite had slowly faded, and he didn't finish any leftovers from the group. He slept longer and dark circles surrounded his eyes. He reeked of hopelessness.

"I need to talk to you, Lunara." Varila took her sister over to the fireplace and leaned close. "Okulu found out where that land is and it's apparently crawling with octrils. It's east of Treppter. Mafarias should find it."

Lunara bit her lip. "He doesn't know though. He could be far away from it and we don't have much time."

Varila tried to hide her annoyance, but she did so poorly. "You should've told Mafarias when we had the chance."

"I told you, I don't trust him yet."

"Regardless, the mage was right. Wilhelm can't be caught, so you'll just have to tell Humar what you've told me and have him send word to Mafarias."

Lunara's eyes flashed with anger. "What am I supposed to tell Humar? That I had a vision? That I dream about a man I've never met? That I was instructed to find him from some mysterious person in another dream? Do you realize how mad I'll sound?"

Varila leaned against a chair, regarding her sister. Lunara's confidence had always been nonexistent. Trying to walk in her place,

Varila understood how foolish it must sound. Nevertheless, they were out of options. She shrugged. "If Humar calls you mad, I'll chop off his legs and feed them to him."

Lunara's shoulders slumped. "I'm sorry, Varila. I'm just so tired."

"We're going tell Humar to get Mafarias. Then the rest of us are returning to Falar for some much needed sleep."

Lunara clenched her fists. "But Mafarias is too far away."

"Ugh!" She stared into the fire. "Fine. Here's the deal: We're going to tell Humar and get his advice." She knew the knight would side with her. "He's reasonable. We'll listen to what he has to say and decide from there."

Lunara stood straight, smoothing the front of her dress. "Very well. Let's go see him."

Varila took Lunara's hand, led her upstairs, and knocked on Humar's door.

"Come in," Humar called.

He stood at a table with a map sprawled in its center.

"What are you looking for?" Varila asked.

Humar ran his fingers through his hair. "Anything on this map that might point to suggestions on where the boy is being held."

"We need to talk with you," Lunara said.

Durak growled. "I'm getting ale, you numb-brained knight. This whole trip is a damn waste of time. The boy is dead, and ye know it."

Humar sank into a chair. "I don't. It'll eat Wilhelm up if he doesn't know for sure. You see him now, it'll only get worse. You know how close those boys are."

"He'd been better off without ever having that cursed mage as a brother!" Durak stormed from the room.

Lunara's eyes flickered with anger. "I thought Salvarias stayed with Durak for months. Why does he hate him?"

Humar shrugged. "He's never been fond of mages, and he's close to Wilhelm. You don't know Salvarias like we do. He's distant and never smiles, never talks to anyone. Opposite from Wilhelm in every way."

Lunara raised an eyebrow. "So Durak doesn't like him because he doesn't smile and talk as much as Wilhelm?"

Varila nudged her sister to be quiet.

"What did you want to talk about?" Humar asked.

Lunara glanced at Varila before speaking. "I, I know where he's being held. I've had a dream of jet-black mountains and expansive tunnels that run beneath them. Okulu asked a friend and such a place exists east of Treppter."

"Okulu said it's swarming with octrils," Varila added.

Humar turned his gaze to the map. "Then Mafarias will find it. I can send word to him. I'm not venturing out there on a dream."

Lunara shook her head. "I'm afraid we don't have time to wait for Mafarias."

"You heard what those men said. They're after Wilhelm."

Lunara blushed, lowering her head to speak at the floor. "Salvarias is the one who's warned me of danger, Humar. The men entering our room in Sundil, the hidlu. He talked to me in, in my mind. Somehow we're connected. I *know* this is where he is and he doesn't have much time."

Varila couldn't read Humar while he studied Lunara. Composed in every action and thought, no emotion he didn't want known escaped his bright blue eyes or spread across his sharp features. Varila admired him. He'd proven an apt leader and gained her trust the first few days she knew him.

Lunara raised her misty eyes. "Maybe it should be Wilhelm's choice to go or stay."

"Of course he'd go," Varila snapped. "And it's not safe."

"How would you feel if the roles were reversed? Would you stay behind if I was held captive against my will? Near death? Would you go home and allow another to find me?"

Varila's resolve crumbled. "She's got a point, Humar. I'd be infuriated if I learned my friends kept this a secret. Wilhelm is desperate to find him, and he won't hesitate to go there." She looked at her sister, knowing she'd risk everything if Lunara was in danger, and though Lunara wasn't related to Wilhelm, he'd risk his life for hers too. "Let's go and help him."

Lunara beamed a smile and Varila winked.

Humar sighed. "All right, we'll tell him."

Lunara smiled her sweet smile at him before bounding down the stairs. She even giggled. Hope does wonders for the soul.

"Wilhelm," Lunara said excitedly, nestling next to him. "I know where he is."

He turned a shade whiter. "Where? How?"

"I had a dream of black mountains—"

"Black mountains?" Wilhelm's brow furrowed. "I had a dream of black mountains."

Lunara frowned. "You had—"

"Ugh!" Varila exclaimed. "Just tell him where they are!"

"East of Treppter," Lunara said.

"That's on the east side of the mountains," Humar interjected, sitting at the table. "Mafarias will find him. We need to get safely to Falar."

"No." Wilhelm's body trembled. "I have to help him."

Okulu clucked his tongue. "The land is littered with octrils, friend. What you want to do won't be easy."

"I don't ask that any of you go. But I am."

"Fool!" Durak roared. "They'll capture you!"

Wilhelm threw his hands up. "Who? We don't understand who 'they' are! I'm tired of following no trail. I think Lunara is right. These mountains are where he's being held."

"There are tunnels, and I think I can get us to where he is without drawing attention to ourselves," Lunara said.

Durak scowled at the group. "We're going to traipse half across Dalnar based on a dream and a gut feeling?"

"What if it's a trap?" Humar asked.

Wilhelm shook his head. "Maybe it is, but I won't let them catch me. I've got to find him. I feel time is slipping by."

Lunara wrapped her arm with Wilhelm's. "I agree. We can't wait for Mafarias to find him."

Humar cursed, running his hands through his hair. "I'll send word to Mafarias. Hopefully he can meet us there and help."

Wilhelm made eye contact with each companion as he spoke. "I can't thank you enough for all you've done. I don't ask that you go with me, and I'd completely understand if you choose to remain behind."

Humar grinned. "I'm in. Someone's got to watch out for you."

Varila glanced once more at her beaming sister. "We're in."

Wilhelm grinned and winked.

Okulu stroked his goatee. "I'm up for a little challenge. Too much running and not enough fighting for my taste. Sounds like we'll get a chance to test our skills."

Durak swore. Varila took note of the new curses. "Aye, lad, I'm in. But I'm telling ye, ye're all a bunch of thick-skulled idiots!"

Wilhelm's grin was contagious, and all were smiling while they ate dinner, planning their route and rescue.

Chapter 20
Winter 1017 a.r.

Dethal fumed as he strode down the black halls of Zeeas. Sansis hadn't been successful in breaking Salvarias, but the fool had refused to summon God to finish the stubborn boy. Dethal had longed feared that Sansis's love of torture had taken him past rational thought. Dethal had even sent a note to God, but it was dismissed, saying Sansis was the most trusted disciple. Dethal knew better. Sansis was no closer to turning the boy. The glimmer in Salvarias's eyes read defiance. Dethal knew they'd unlocked the boy's gift and he'd never reveal what the gift was. Dethal thought of every torture, both physical and mental, and the most successful torment was an image of Wilhelm. Dethal sent it to visit Salvarias, saying he'd been captured, and Salvarias spoke to the illusion. However, the young mage had never revealed his secrets.

In an attempt to wring the information from Salvarias, Dethal tortured the image. It nearly worked, but Salvarias was smart. He'd cast a protection spell on the illusion only to find it wasn't his brother. Salvarias had even smiled, realizing he'd been duped. The only way was to obtain the actual brother, and Dethal had nearly been successful in Sundil. Then again in the caves, the hidlu had almost captured Wilhelm, and finally at the small farm they were hiding. Every time the brother had been one step ahead.

Dethal suspected Salvarias was warning his brother somehow. Maybe a guard had become sympathetic and was sending messages; maybe the boy was using some spell.

When Dethal entered the cell, the boy was, as usual, huddled in a corner. Dethal chanted his favorite spell, generating the invisible hands that beat the boy. Grabbing Salvarias, the hands shook him conscious.

"You're in communication with your brother. I know of it and I can prevent you from warning him. If you don't wish him captured, you'll tell me what you know." Dethal made the hands slam Salvarias's frail body against the wall; a little too hard since blood ran down the stone.

Salvarias's voice was barely audible. "You lie, old man."

The hands broke the remaining four fingers on Salvarias's non-spell hand. The boy grunted in pain; he'd endured worse. "Your spell hand is next. Tell me."

"Again you lie, but I will tell you what I see."

Dethal licked his lips. "Tell me."

Salvarias raised his head, his black gaze locked on Dethal. "I see the day I kill you. I see your burnt body lying at my feet."

Fury rose in Dethal and he beat Salvarias near death. Sansis would be outraged if the boy died, but Dethal no longer cared.

He knew Salvarias would never be turned. They were all fools. Once Dethal's muscles ached from releasing his frustrations, he chanted a spell, drew the energy, flicked his hand, and smiled. The spell would take a week to cause such pain that Salvarias's body would have no choice but to succumb to death. The spell would fool even Sansis. Upon his return it would appear as though the boy hadn't survived his last session with Sansis. One week and Dethal would be free. He smiled and left the boy screaming. One week.

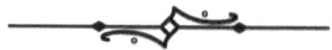

Lunara stared into the flickering flames of the common room fireplace in Treppter. It was an hour before sunrise, but she couldn't sleep. She was anxious to leave.

The last twelve days from Flitver to Treppter had been difficult. She'd barely stayed awake, and had ended up riding with Humar most of the distance. During their journey, when she was well enough, she spent her time focusing on Salvarias and had learned to sense his feelings, which were composed of pain, both physical and mental, and fear; utter terror sometimes. She withdrew her mind during those periods, but she connected experiencing them with the times she felt drained. She worked on strengthening the connection and unfortunately, it seemed to forge a physical bond as well. The pain he endured wore on not only her heart but also her body. She'd found a cut on her stomach less than two days ago. Quick to catch it, she hid the wound from her sister. Scared, confused, and frustrated, Lunara knew Salvarias didn't have much time left. They were slowly killing him.

She took a sip of hot cider and forced down a bite of bread.

"Damn octrils are overrunning the small towns," a nearby patron muttered to his friend. "The cities are starting to spill over with people seeking safety in numbers."

"I heard Falar is bad," the other said. "Since Serinity won't allow refugees in, the small towns have turned to the port city. Some are fleeing for Windlous."

"I heard the same. Crime must be as high there as it is here."

Wilhelm's deep voice jolted her from eavesdropping. "Are you ready?"

She rose from her chair and a dizzy spell overcame her. The room spun, her vision left, and she stumbled until strong arms supported her. Something warm trickled down the back of her head and across her stomach. She heard Wilhelm's panicked cry for Varila as he picked Lunara up.

Gaining her sight back, she saw blood seeping through her dress and dripping on the floor, however she felt no pain, and the teetering room and exhaustion were the only side effects of her affliction. She heard her sister's panicked voice but not the words. Lunara sought the presence in the recesses of her mind, sought the voice that had talked to her.

He said, *"What do you want of me?"*

She was surprised when he responded. Her past attempts had been unsuccessful. *"What is happening to me?"*

"I do not understand your question."

She touched the blood soaking her dress. *"I have a cut but I wasn't harmed."*

"We are strangely connected." The voice tensed with pain. *"I am dying."*

She sensed a longing for death, for peace. *"Will I die as well?"* Unlike the voice, she wasn't ready.

"Perhaps. I do not know."

"You are Salvarias." It was more of a statement than question.

"Yes."

"Why have you not responded before?"

"I am confused by our connection. I do not understand. I prefer distance between us. But now I have a message for my brother."

She swallowed her pang of hurt. She didn't want distance.

They'd grown up together. She valued their relationship. *"We've found your location. We will rescue you and you can give Wilhelm your message then."*

"Only fools would come to my aid. There is no chance for my salvation. My brother must not come here." Salvarias's voice filled with sorrow. *"Please, I beg you, persuade him to leave me. Tell him to start his own life as I requested of him. It is all I wish for. Tell him I—"*

"He won't deter from his course. You must remain strong. I'm not ready to die. Please."

After a surge of pain, his presence receded. He was too weak to keep the connection. Emerging from her trance, she heard Wilhelm's frantic voice.

Wilhelm was saying, "She stood and—"

"He's dying, Wilhelm. You must hurry."

"How do you know?"

She motioned to the corner of the room. "In my pack is a map I drew of the tunnels. You must hurry."

Varila was clasping Lunara's hand painfully tight and was weeping. "I'm sorry, Wilhelm. I can't leave her."

Wilhelm smoothed Lunara's hair. "What's happening to you?"

"Your brother and I are connected to one another mentally and physically, and this," she motioned to her bloody dress, "is the result." She closed her eyes. She wanted to sleep. "I assume this is what's happening to him. You must hurry."

She heard a rustle but no longer paid heed to her surroundings. Instead, she turned inward, focusing on Salvarias, on his handsome face, his eyes. Their connection reminded her of a tunnel linking them together. While her side was open for him, his side was blocked by his own efforts to sever their connection. His barriers were no match for her determination and he was too weak to fight her. She shoved them aside.

Once she did, a doorway into his mind appeared. She stepped through and gasped. His tortured body was curled up, blood pooling around him. She didn't even recognize him. She sank to the glassy black floor by his side, and though she didn't understand how she did it, she gave him her strength. She sensed the surges of unbearable agony, watched him writhe on the ground, and listened to him scream. All that consumed his mind was pain. She stayed as long as her body would allow, but eventually a black blanket wrapped around her mind and, for the first time in her life, Lunara slept in nightmares.

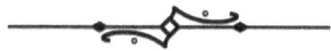

Wilhelm and the other men rode hard for three days, dodging octrils, skirmishing with a few, and hardly sleeping. The land deteriorated from rolling hills of dry grasses and sparse trees to rocky desert with sporadic bushes that appeared dead. Everything looked dusty until they arrived two miles from the base of the obsidian mountains. Muted green clouds that sent freezing rain and occasional hail wreathed the glassy black formation. The storm seemed to have sprung up with the sole purpose of thrashing the mountains, and, judging by the washes gouged into the rocky terrain, the rain had been active for some time.

After securing their horses in a patch of dead trees on high ground, they crept in the cover of rain and night towards a sheer cliff face. It contained five doors situated at varying heights that were accessible by a two-person path that climbed up to each entrance. Multiple holes opened from the inside caverns, allowing air to filter through the hidden fortress. An oppressive evil spilt down the mountainside from the keep. Wilhelm shuddered at the thought of his brother spending a year in this place.

Okulu whistled. "Would you look at that?"

Durak uttered an oath, mopping rain from his face. "It is impressive."

Following the map Lunara had provided, Humar led them downhill and below the lowest door. They found a tunnel blocked by a grate slightly shorter than Humar. It held back piled-up waste and garbage.

Humar motioned to Wilhelm. "Help me."

Both men planted their feet and pulled. Rusted hinges groaned in protest when it swung open. Lukewarm, syrupy liquid spilled out along with the garbage. The stench was suffocating.

Okulu gagged. "Worse than the smell of an ogre!"

Durak grunted. "Smells like you after a night of drinking."

"Will you two shut up?" Humar whispered.

Okulu pinched the bridge of his nose. "Are you sure we can't go in the front door? I'm no chicken when it comes to a fight."

Humar shook his head. "No, we go this way."

Covering their noses and mouths with their hands, the group entered. Grates above them allowed distant, ruddy torchlight to illuminate the passageway enough for them to make their way. Durak was the only one who could walk upright, but they rapidly made their way through the maze of tunnels. After what seemed like an eternity, the passageway ended at a square room. Garbage and sewage clogged the corners and the floor was slimy. Wilhelm exhaled a breath when he was finally able to stand upright. He stretched his cramped muscles.

Humar pointed overhead. "Wilhelm, lift that grate. Be sure no one is in the room and do it quietly."

Wilhelm peered through the slats, and after seeing no one, lifted the metal to one side, grunting under the weight. After crawling out, he helped the others. They found themselves in a room with three possible doors. Humar studied the map and then jerked his head left.

Broadsword drawn, Wilhelm inched opened the door and surveyed the next room. It contained hay spread out for sleeping and two octrils were snoring. He turned and whispered to Durak, "Two octrils. You take left, I'll take right."

Creeping into the room, Wilhelm and Durak simultaneously slit the throats of the octrils, holding their hands over the filthy mouths to prevent any noise. Once the creatures ceased twitching, Wilhelm covered the bodies with blankets, trying to make it look as though the corpses slept, and spread hay over the pooling blood. He motioned the rest to enter.

The next room contained five tables and was apparently where a faction of the octrils ate. Thankfully it was empty. He followed his group to another door where he and Humar peered inside. Five octrils crouched in a circle playing a game with colored stones.

Humar turned and spread out five fingers. Motioning, he indicated Okulu should take the furthest two octrils, Wilhelm and Durak the closest, Humar the furthest on the right.

They rushed through the door. Okulu's throwing knives, his preferred weapon, whizzed by Wilhelm and landed in the octrils' throats just as he reached his target. He dodged a thrust and lunged with a kill strike through the octril's heart. He whirled to help Durak by beheading another octril just as Durak chopped off a leg. Wilhelm was impressed with the group's efficiency, but there was no covering up the blue-green blood splattered around the room. It smelled like rust.

Two more empty rooms and then they were descending a winding staircase. His anxiety increased with each stair. He knew his brother was close. Arriving at the bottom, Humar glanced around the corner. Shaking his head, the knight informed them that ten octrils and one ogre guarded a single door.

Wilhelm was the first to speak. "I'll take the ogre."

Humar's bright blue eyes glittered with indecision.

Wilhelm winked. "I can handle it."

After a brief hesitation, Humar nodded and gave directions to the rest.

Wilhelm rounded the corner, and for an instant, uncertainty in his skill froze him. The ogre must have been a good twenty feet tall and five feet wide. Its boulder-sized hands sprouted six fingers caked with filth. Tree-trunk legs seemed too short for the huge belly that sagged to its kneecaps. He doubted Okulu's comment that the sewage in the tunnels smelled worse than the beast in front of Wilhelm. The stench alone could overpower a foe.

He rushed forward, leaping into the air, dagger drawn, and stabbed deep into its belly. Black blood flowed from the wound and smelled of soured milk. The ogre's massive hand gripped him around the waist and the giant tossed him aside. He collided with the smooth stone wall. He shook his head to clear the ringing in his ears. He drew his broadsword, and running full steam, used his momentum to drive his sword deep into the bulbous belly. With a roar of pain, the ogre backhanded him, sending him sailing across the room. His head rapped against the glassy black wall and pain darted down his left side. He swayed back to his feet.

He glanced around. Humar and Okulu were back to back, their fighting methods almost identical. They were engaged in a fierce fight with six octrils. Durak was off on his own, swinging his axe in powerful circles overhead, then arcing down, then back overhead, pivoting with each swipe. It kept any from gaining the advantage, but with four closing in, he didn't have much time and Humar and Okulu wouldn't be free anytime soon.

Sprinting forward, Wilhelm managed two steps along the

sidewall before he braced his right foot on the wall and his left on the ogre's belly. He rammed his sword into the chest of the ogre. He let his feet go out from under him and hung freely from the hilt. Hefting himself up, he let his weight fall, slicing down the ogre's stomach. Rearing back, the ogre snatched him up and the beast's nails dug into his side, breaking through armor and flesh, and cracked a rib.

Gulping for air, he jabbed his sword at the ogre's hand. It dropped him and the fall sent a ripple of pain along his side. Finally, air whooshed into his lungs. Behind the beast, he could see a solid iron door. He needed to get into that room. He needed Salvarias.

Humar and Okulu had bested two foes and were gaining the upper hand. Durak must've had a bout of luck since only two octrils remained.

Wilhelm shoved himself to his feet and rushed the ogre. Using the beast's stomach to scale up, he clasped his sword in both hands. With all his strength, he rammed the blade through the ogre's heart. The creature roared and reeled back. Wilhelm twisted the blade before he withdrew it and jumped to the side. The ogre teetered, and then toppled face first to the stone floor. He glanced around and saw Durak fighting one octril. Wilhelm ran to the cavrul's aid and impaled the creature from behind. The rest had been eliminated.

Humar had a hand pressed to his side. Blood dripped over his fingers, but he waved his sword as a sign it wasn't life threatening. Durak had a deep slice on his arm, but Okulu was unharmed.

Humar wheezed, "The key must be on one of them."

Wilhelm helped search the bodies, slipping on the blood-covered floor. Humar found the key, slid to the cell door, fumbled with the lock for a breath, and stepped inside. Wilhelm pulled a torch from the wall and followed.

The cell was covered in filth, insects, and rats. No window existed, no furniture, no bed, not even hay to keep the chill of the stone floor at bay. Salvarias lay heaped in the back corner, curled into a fetal position. He'd wasted into nothing. Skin clung to his bones, his hair and face were caked with blood, and his tattered robes were dripping fresh blood. Rats chewed open wounds on his arms and legs. Standing in the doorway, Wilhelm swore his brother was dead.

An anguished cry escaped Wilhelm when he knelt by his brother, scattering insects and rats.

Humar pried the torch from Wilhelm's clenched fist. "You can do nothing for him here. We need to move, so you'll have to carry him."

Wilhelm cradled his brother's gaunt body. "I'm here, Salv. We're going to get you out of here." Salvarias convulsed, face twisted in pain.

They were headed back towards the stairs when a cacophony of heavy footsteps descending the winding staircase changed direction.

Cursing, Humar turned to another archway. "This way."

Wilhelm followed the knight up a second set of steep stairs. Near the top, Humar motioned Okulu and Durak in front. "There'll probably be guards."

Durak took the lead, and once at the opening, he peered out and motioned them forward.

The hallway seemed to stretch for miles with doors lining both sides. Humar opened a nearby door, and his face paled at the rows of beds. Wilhelm uttered a curse along with Durak. Barracks were the last place they should be. At the end of the hall, there appeared to be a vast room with a door on the other side. Gauging where they were, Wilhelm thought it should lead them outside.

Salvarias heaved and choked on his own vomit when he gulped for air. Wilhelm turned his brother over, allowing the remaining bile to spill on the floor. It was followed by blood.

"Internal?" Humar asked Okulu.

"Let's hope not. I don't want to think this was in vain."

"If we're going to get out of here, it's at a run," Humar said. "Don't look back, just run through those doors. We should be near an exit."

Heavy footfalls thudded on the stairwell. Wilhelm bolted after Humar at full speed until they dumped into the expansive open room; which, unfortunately, was filled with octrils. Wilhelm stumbled to a halt before he realized the octrils weren't expecting them. Longer than it was deep, a quick dash would dump them outside.

"I said run!" Humar barked.

The octrils took notice of the group, but surprise froze the creatures as well. Wilhelm sprinted behind Okulu. The merc shoved open the door and frigid night air and rain crashed over Wilhelm. He was first to descend the path leading to the base of the fortress.

"Run!" Humar ordered.

Wilhelm was almost off the cliff when the first arrow whizzed by his ear. The second sank into his shoulder. He ignored it. Once they were off the slender path, Humar caught up and offered to take Salvarias, but Wilhelm shook his head. Durak grunted when an arrow hit his shoulder, and the sound of arrows clinking against Okulu's armor rang in the night. But none slowed. Wilhelm looked at his brother's bloodied face and rage built inside. Without the slightest stumble, Wilhelm navigated the rocky terrain until disappearing into the cluster of dead trees that hid the horses.

He mounted, hoping the beast could carry both their weight. He kicked the stallion's flanks and pushed forward. He didn't even bother to see if the others followed. His sole thought was getting his brother as far from the obsidian keep as possible.

After riding the rest of the night, all through the next day, and well into the following night, Wilhelm's group stopped for fear their horses would die. They chose a small cluster of stocky trees to set up camp and tend to their wounds.

Wilhelm slid off his horse and carried Salvarias to the cover of a tree while Humar and Durak tended to their exhausted mounts.

"Can we risk a fire?" Humar asked.

Okulu removed a pouch from his pack. "Even if we dared, I don't think we could keep it going. Damn storm is following us. Now, let's see what we've got." Okulu knelt next to Salvarias, withdrew a dagger, and sawed away the top of Salvarias's tattered robes. "By the gods!"

A sob escaped Wilhelm when lightning illuminated his brother's scarred body. Salvarias's torso held so many gashes Wilhelm couldn't begin to count them, and most bulged with yellow pus. A large laceration ran from the base of his brother's neck to his waistline. New, it oozed blood and festered with infection. Scarred skin lined it and apparently they'd cut the same spot repeatedly. Where knife wounds were absent, burns and other unidentifiable marks took their place.

"I can't fix this," Okulu breathed. "I didn't bring enough dressings, herbs, or thread."

Wilhelm bit back a sob. "Please, do what you can."

Humar rose, cursing. "Dammit! All this for the boy to die!"

"I told you, Humar," Durak grumbled.

Okulu scrambled back. "What in Veedran's creation!"

Wilhelm stared but suddenly choked on his air. Beneath his brother's skin, the form of childlike hands slithered down his chest and then disappeared.

"What is that?" Wilhelm cried.

Okulu stumbled away.

Salvarias coughed, blood speckled his lips, and he shook violently. Wilhelm rolled his brother on his side and bloody bile spilt from his mouth. Sobs escaped him.

Wilhelm looked helplessly at Okulu. "What do I do?"

Humar cursed again. "We need Mafarias!"

"Hello," a voice came from behind the group.

Okulu and Humar were quick to draw their swords while Durak took a protective stance in front of Wilhelm.

Humar raised his sword to the old man's throat. "Who are you?"

The man wore mage robes. "Vuddruk."

"Help me!" Wilhelm cried.

Salvarias heaved again, and his fists dug into the muddy ground. A heart-wrenching scream of pain escaped him.

The white-haired mage shook his head. "The boy has a spell on him. It's slowly killing him. We don't have much time."

"Help!" Wilhelm cried again. "Please, help him!"

Vuddruk eyed Okulu and Humar. "I can help, but I won't do it at sword point."

Humar glanced back at Wilhelm. "We don't know who this man is."

"The boy will die," Okulu countered. "We're out of options!"

Salvarias's body arched from the ground, his hands curled in tight claws, and blood pooled around his mouth.

Wilhelm sobbed out an order. "Let him help."

Vuddruk hurried to Salvarias. The childlike, blood-covered hands emerged from the cut on his chest, tearing it wider. Wilhelm grabbed his brother's skin, fighting to keep the hands from disemboweling him. Hot blood spilt over Wilhelm's fingers.

Whatever the old man whispered caused the hands to disappear. Salvarias's wasted body lurched and went into full seizures.

Vuddruk cursed, raising his hands over Salvarias. The old man chanted louder. Salvarias jerked, his eyes flew open, and then he went limp. Blood streamed from his mouth. He laid perfectly still, eyes dull and lifeless.

"No," Wilhelm sobbed.

Vuddruk cursed. "Not yet. Stand back!"

Wilhelm crumbled to the ground.

"Trust me!" Vuddruk roared. "This won't happen on my watch!"

Lightning shot from the mage's hands and struck Salvarias.

"Come on, boy!" Vuddruk yelled. "Too much is left for you to do!"

Lightning struck Salvarias again and he arced from the ground. A knife twisted in Wilhelm's heart and he clutched his chest.

Humar drew his sword. "Stop old man! Enough!"

Lightning struck Salvarias again, this time sizzling his flesh.

A breath passed.

Nothing.

Another breath.

Nothing.

Wilhelm doubled over, hugging himself as he stared at the lifeless black eyes. "Please, Salv, please."

Vuddruk sank to the ground. "I have fai—"

Salvarias coughed.

Wilhelm cried out and crawled to his brother's side. Salvarias's eyes focused on him before closing.

Vuddruk shoved Wilhelm aside. "No time."

The old man stripped off Salvarias's clothes then rolled him over. Scars lined his back, arms, and legs. There were rows of holes the size of nails, with a few larger punctures, and on top of those were additional stab wounds mixed with welts. His spine protruded under his skin and his flesh was sunk between his ribs.

"He's infected." Vuddruk rolled Salvarias back over. "Fever will set in. We must drain, stitch and dress the wounds. What herbs do you have, half-winsire?"

Okulu spoke words Wilhelm couldn't hear. He took his brother's hand and looked down in new horror. Salvarias's fingers were twisted and the pinky missing. Wilhelm lifted his brother's left hand. It was perfectly whole and unscarred.

Vuddruk snatched Salvarias's right hand and popped the bones.

"They must have wanted him to perform magic. I assume his spell hand is his left." He tilted his head to Salvarias's right hand. "We'll set them and he'll have limited use of his remaining fingers."

Wilhelm's mind was shutting down. His brother couldn't have endured such pain. It was a dream. Wilhelm was dreaming this. He would wake up and his brother would be reading nearby, or perhaps playing with the puzzle box. Safe. It was all a dream.

"Too much for you to process?" Vuddruk winked. "You're close?"

Wilhelm's gaze focused on his treasure, his life. "Yes."

"Let's get it over with then." Vuddruk pointed at Salvarias's leg, which bent unnaturally. "I'll be surprised if he ever walks without help."

Wilhelm's eyes filled with fresh tears. He blinked them aside. It was a dream.

"This'll be the worst of it for you. They must have used acid on his flesh." Vuddruk moved aside Salvarias's matted hair.

Wilhelm rose, taking four steps from the group, and became ill. A hand rested on his shoulder and Humar offered water. Wilhelm accepted the waterskin and took a drink. He stumbled to his brother's side and avoided looking at the eaten flesh where his ear had been.

Watching Okulu help cut open old wounds to drain yellow and green pus was too much for Wilhelm. He staggered away. Humar offered words of comfort Wilhelm couldn't hear. His eyes seemed frozen open and his lungs battled for each breath. It wasn't a dream. A year. A year his brother had endured torture. The full weight struck Wilhelm and he fell to his knees.

Hours must have passed before the old mage and Okulu finished cleaning and tending to his brother. Wilhelm offered fresh robes, and feeling helpless, worthless, he trimmed his brother's hair, keeping it below his shoulders to hide his missing ear and mutilated skin. Salvarias preferred a clean shave, and with no other way to help, Wilhelm shaved his brother.

At some point, Vuddruk patched up Wilhelm's wounds from the arrow and ogre, and then tended to Humar.

"Want to tell us what a mage is doing out in the wilderness all by himself?" Humar asked.

Vuddruk winked. "Not really."

"I assume our meeting isn't by chance," Humar said. "Have you been following us?"

Vuddruk shrugged. "I just happened to be in the right place at the right time. Why question a miracle?"

Okulu snorted. "Because miracles are provided by gods, old man. In case you didn't notice, Arden's been missing ours for a few years."

Vuddruk moved to tend to Durak, but the cavrul cast a glare. "I'll chop off ye head if ye touch me, mage."

Vuddruk held up his hands and backed away. "Sleep, all of you. I'll keep watch."

Humar smiled, but it didn't reach his eyes. "I think we'll set up our own watch. Your help is appreciated, but my trust is earned after years, friend."

Vuddruk nodded. "Good man. Cautious. Valuable trait in the world today."

When the sun battled the ominous clouds, Vuddruk shook the others awake. Wilhelm hadn't slept, nor had he let go of his brother.

"I suggest fleeing to Kudril," Vuddruk said. "It's the closest place that can offer safety, but you must be careful." He turned to Wilhelm. "Don't be surprised if it takes him over a week to wake and another week or two before he's alert."

Wilhelm nodded, offering the old man all their money. "I'm forever in your debt."

Vuddruk patted his shoulder. "There'll come a time when you can help me. Keep your money, I've no use for it. Take care of the boy and yourself, young man."

The old wizard gave another wink and disappeared into the thick rain. The group made ready to leave in silence. Wilhelm wrapped his brother in two blankets and added a cloak to block the rain, then held a hand over his brother's mouth often to make sure he was breathing. Salvarias looked dead.

Another day and night passed before they reached Treppter. Humar entered the city alone while Okulu and Durak stayed with Wilhelm out of sight, taking every precaution. As they waited,

Wilhelm's gaze moved over the landscape. Everything had a sick greenish hue from the malevolent clouds, and the formerly dry ground could no longer drink the rains.

He felt his brother's stomach constrict and looked down to see bloody bile spill from his mouth. Once it stopped, Wilhelm tilted Salvarias's head back to allow the rains to wash it away as had been the usual for the past day and a half.

Okulu pointed at a wagon plodding up the hillside towards them. Wilhelm could make out Varila huddled in a cloak on a horse riding alongside it.

Okulu grunted. "Wagon was a smart choice."

When Humar rode up, Wilhelm noticed Lunara's horse tethered to the back of the wagon. Varila came into sight looking as exhausted as he felt, and her eyes were red and swollen. She dismounted and tied her horse next to Lunara's. He carried Salvarias to meet Varila at the back of the wagon. She moved aside the flap to allow them to enter. Inside, Lunara was bundled in blankets and appeared to be sleeping. Her porcelain skin was pale blue and dark circles rimmed her eyes.

The wagon was large enough to sleep six people, and Wilhelm positioned Salvarias and Lunara so he had a spot to sit between them. Varila leaned against the back of the wagon at Lunara's feet. Adok jumped inside.

After they settled, Varila whispered, "She died for a short while."

Wilhelm cleared his throat. He hadn't spoken since Vuddruk left. "So did Salv. How did you get her back?"

"I don't know how she came back," she said. "When she died, I left the room and was screaming for someone to help me. When I returned with the tavern owner, she was breathing and the wolf was standing on the bed."

He glanced at Adok, who'd curled up next to the limp bundle of his brother.

"I don't understand. Some old mage helped us in the middle of nowhere."

"There was a mage out there? What in Oblivion was he doing?"

"Wouldn't say. And I don't care. He saved Salv. That's all that matters to me."

Varila shook her head. "Lunara's cuts are healing. There's not a single scar."

"We need to stay in Kudril for a couple of weeks." He removed the damp cloak from Salvarias and added a fresh blanket so only his nose was visible, determined to keep him as warm a possible. The rain had yet to let up, and the gusty wind sent a chill impossible to drive from the bones.

"Humar told me." Varila rubbed her eyes. "My family has a small estate in Kudril we can use. It has guards and they're loyal to my father and me. We'll be safe."

"Thank you."

"He's alive, Wilhelm. You saved him and Lunara. Thank you."

The days that followed offered further torment for Wilhelm. Salvarias convulsed in pain so intense that he became violently ill, gagging on his own vomit while crying out. Fever set in and he burned up in Wilhelm's arms, drenched in sweat yet shivering. Wilhelm barely kept enough broth and water down his brother to keep him alive.

When Wilhelm heard the calls of a city, he peeled back the canvas covering the wagon. Kudril reminded him of Sundil, nothing unique and rather unimpressive. Situated on rolling hills of brown grass, blocky trees, and little cover, its towering wall shot up from the landscape. Traffic in and out of the city was thick, and once at the gate the guards seemed uninterested and any were allowed in without inspection.

The city was overrun with refugees. Along the rackety ride to the estate, he watched guards chasing men stealing bread, starved children clutching their mother's skirts, and women whoring for food.

Erected in a quiet part of town, the estate was surrounded by a solid brown wall with a single iron gate. Private soldiers patrolled along parapets and could be seen in high windows. He discerned there was more to the sisters than Varila had revealed, and the family was decidedly wealthy.

A handful of servants greeted the group and their horses were tended to, their packs taken to rooms, and the smell of food drifted through the halls when Wilhelm made his way to his bedroom. He was thankful for the small fireplace and he lit it in hopes of warming his brother's freezing body.

As Wilhelm unpacked, he decided not to allow others in the

room. When Salvarias woke, it would be better if they were alone. He was never comfortable around people, especially strangers. As an added precaution, Wilhelm would only permit Humar and Durak near in case Salvarias woke while they brought Wilhelm food or in the rare times he left his brother's side to perform ablutions.

Hours of solitude turned to days. Salvarias's sickness continued along with cries of pain, and Wilhelm's mood darkened. Horrid thoughts bombarded his mind while he spent his days alone. What if Salvarias never woke? What if he never recovered?

It was on the seventh day that Wilhelm rose from his bed to look out at the rain. It had yet to stop and the streets were flooded. Screams from riots in the city reached the estate and snuck through the glass window. Hope and light seemed to have left the world.

He turned from the mournful sight and stirred the fire. Salvarias was begging something to stop. Wilhelm rested his forehead on the fireplace mantle and clenched his fists. He wanted to scream, hit something, implore his brother to be quiet. Wilhelm glanced over his shoulder. Salvarias's fists were tangled in the bedding, knuckles white, body tensed. Crescendoing sobs finished with a scream. Adok whined and Wilhelm tore his gaze away.

All was silent now. He took a deep breath, unclenched his fists, and wearily turned towards his brother. Salvarias's black eyes were open.

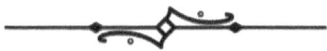

Salvarias's mind stirred, raising him from nightmares into the light. He felt something soft under him, smelled the faint scent of lavender, and heard a crackling fire. He forced his heavy eyelids to open and squinted at the dim light in the room. He had roamed in darkness for so long that his eyes throbbed at the proximity of the fireplace.

"Salvarias? Salv? It's me, Wilhelm."

An illusion of Wilhelm was next to him. The strong, deep voice and bright amber eyes brought such pain for Salvarias that he had to fight the rising of his stomach. The illusion reached out a trembling hand. Salvarias flinched and shifted away, fighting the pain, using his last ounce of strength to back into the corner where his bed rested.

The illusion's voice dripped with the promise of safety and comfort. "We rescued you, Salv. The fort in the mountains, we were there. I promise you're safe."

Salvarias recoiled from the illusion's outstretched hand, cringing against the wall, wishing he could dissolve into the brown stone. Once he could back no further, he drew his knees up and folded himself into a ball. He shuddered from the illusion's gentle touch.

The hand withdrew and after a long pause, the deep voice spoke again. "Salv, you remember when we found the puzzle box? Do you remember the first animal you made?"

Salvarias opened his eyes and stared at Wilhelm. This was something Dethal would not know.

Wilhelm rested his back against the wall. "A bear." He grinned and handed Salvarias the wooden puzzle box.

Salvarias stared in disbelief, and instead of taking the box, he chanted a spell, drawing a perfect rune. The white film passed over Wilhelm and clung to him. He was real.

"Rulose," Salvarias whispered.

He reached for his brother and familiar arms wrapped around him.

"I'm here, Salv. You're safe."

Relief overwhelmed Salvarias, and his ordeal flooded his mind. All his strength left, and he crumbled in his brother's arms and wept.

Humar peeked through the brothers' doorway. Salvarias rested in his bed, propped against the wall, knees drawn to his chest, using them to hold his bowl of vegetable stew while Wilhelm sat cross-legged in front of the boy. Adok sprawled out on Wilhelm's bed next to Salvarias. For the first time since his rescue three weeks ago, Salvarias was alert, aware of his surroundings, and eating on his own.

Mafarias had arrived four days ago, after receiving Humar's letters, and was eager to see the boy, as was Humar. Wilhelm, however, refused any visitation until today when he'd told Mafarias and Humar they could see Salvarias, though only for a short time.

Humar pushed open the door and entered. Salvarias's head jerked up, but once he saw Humar, the boy relaxed.

"Hello, Sir Humar," Salvarias said.

Humar grinned at the formal title, forgetting how respectful the boy had always been in his greetings. Humar sat on the bed. "Just Humar, Salvarias. How are you feeling?" He rested a hand on the mage's forehead to check for fever. Salvarias flinched away, spilling some of his broth.

Salvarias cleared his throat. "Better. Thank you, Humar."

Wilhelm wiped the broth from Salvarias's blanket with a sleeve and muttered, "Don't touch him."

Wilhelm's action reminded Humar of their first meeting. Salvarias avoided human contact unless it was his brother. Though cold detachment remained, the terror and pain previously lining Salvarias's eyes was absent. The former serious expression was now flat, void of emotion and left one cold, uncomfortable.

Mafarias entered the room and dragged a chair close to the beds. "Hello, boy. Do you remember me?"

Salvarias studied the mage a moment before nodding.

"What do you remember?" Mafarias asked.

"You used to visit once every season."

Humar had forgotten about the hypnotic quality of Salvarias's voice. His tone was no longer that of a growing teenage boy, but one of a man. It was rich, soft, and beautiful. Such a contrast to the young man's face and demeanor.

Wilhelm's brow furrowed. "No, Salv, he stayed for four years when you turned six. He only left once a season."

Salvarias's shadowed gaze never left Mafarias.

Mafarias shrugged. "Probably too young to remember. Regardless, know that I care for both of you boys. You're all the family I have left, and you mean much to me. Now, I don't need to know what happened to you, nor does anyone unless you choose otherwise. You'll come to terms with the events yourself. What I do need to know is what Dethal wanted from you."

"That is between Dethal and myself."

"I see. Can you tell me if he was successful in obtaining what he wanted?"

Salvarias looked down at his bowl of broth. "No, Uncle, Dethal was not successful."

Mafarias sighed and leaned back in his chair. "Good boy. Do you remember the connection you have with Lunara, the girl with black hair?"

"Yes."

"Do you know why you have this connection with her? Did you meet her before you were taken?"

"No, I did not meet her, and I do not understand our connection."

Mafarias sighed. "What will you do now?"

Salvarias glanced at Wilhelm. "That is between my brother and me."

Mafarias's tone grew serious, stern. "Eventually, you'll need to trust me, Salvarias."

Salvarias remained quiet.

"I've been looking for you for a year," Mafarias continued. "You don't think that's enough to earn your trust?"

Salvarias raised his head and light fell across his eyes. Humar shuddered and looked away. They were even colder than before. "No, Uncle. There are several who searched for me. I do not trust them, either."

"I'm blood, boy. I visited you both often when you were younger. I tried to teach you magic. I'm here to help you."

Salvarias set aside his broth and rested his arms on his knees. "That is no reason for me to trust you."

Mafarias smiled. "So be it. In due time you'll learn I'm here to help. Regardless of your feelings towards me, know I'm proud of you. You endured torment and remained quiet."

Salvarias swayed and his words mumbled out. "Thank you, Uncle."

Wilhelm shook his head. "Salv needs to rest."

Mafarias nodded and left the room. Humar smiled at the brothers. "Let me know if either of you need anything."

"Thank..." Salvarias's eyes closed and he sagged against the wall. He was out.

Wilhelm whispered, "Thanks. We're fine."

Humar patted Wilhelm's shoulder before leaving the room.

Mafarias was waiting. "That boy is too damn cautious. Tell me everything that happened since the caves."

Humar recited the events in full detail while the two meandered through the halls, only to end up in the sitting room. A roaring fire helped fight the chill of the storm.

Mafarias sank into a chair. "How did they find you after the caves? Did Okulu not help cover your tracks?"

"He did. I have no idea."

"Dammit!" Mafarias clenched his fist. "Okulu is forever drunk. I sent him to help and his blasted ale blurred his vision. I don't want to think what would've happened if Wilhelm had been captured. You took a great risk allowing him to go to Zeeas."

"Zeeas?"

Mafarias chuckled. "Not mentioned on many maps. It's the name of the obsidian fort. I thought it was abandoned."

"Okulu covered our tracks, friend. How well did you know the farmers?"

"I thought well enough. I think I'll pay them a visit soon. Though the party could have had a full winsire tracker."

Humar paced in front of the fire. "They're near impossible to get. I doubt one would join with such an evil man as Dethal. They're lovers of peace, of goodness. Any winsire could sense Dethal's menace. By Veedran's insanity, I sensed it!"

Mafarias spread his hands. "I'm open to other suggestions, friend."

Humar grunted. "I'm fresh out."

"So this wizard outside Treppter helped?"

"Yes, he knew a spell to counter the one that was hurting the boy."

"He must've been advanced. I'm not sure I would've known. I don't know his involvement in this, but few should be trusted. The fact he knew a counter spell leads me to suspicion."

Humar increased his pacing. "He seemed invested, like he had a stake in the boy."

"My suspicions are raised. Whoever this man is plays an interesting role in what's unfolding."

"What's unfolding?"

"Come now, Humar, you've been looking for it for years. Arden is in danger. You've felt it growing. A darkness is coming, my friend, and those two brothers are wrapped up in it."

"The boy isn't right, Mafarias. What did they want with him?"

Mafarias rested his head back in the chair, staring at the ceiling. "I'm not sure. Salvarias is unsettling, but he's my nephew."

"I meant no offense."

"None was taken, my friend. I merely meant that I understand your point. Did you know today was the first time he's spoken to me? He trusted no one before, and I don't think he'll ever come around, especially after what he's been through."

Humar grunted in agreement. "Thoughts on what evil stalks our lands?"

"Could be anything. Gods know of us. Greedy men intend to rule us. The light has left Arden. I fear our fight will be difficult if not a complete loss."

Humar scowled at his friend "I'm not one to give up on hope."

"Nor I. I only pray whatever's out there can die by the point of a sword."

"Rumors are, Crutar's building an army."

Mafarias chuckled. "I'm surprised to hear you even mention Crutar. He barely has any power and is too drunk to care. He slipped in with Veedran for the sheer pleasure of women and ale. He has no desire to rule Dalnar. By Nevlar's betrayal, *I* could beat the god! He's weak."

Humar shook his head. "A very valuable piece of information is missing."

"I agree." Mafarias sighed. "Thank you for helping the boys, Humar. Are you heading back to Falar?"

"I've talked to Wilhelm, and that's our plan."

Mafarias frowned. "That won't be Salvarias's plan. Is he leaving his brother?"

Humar's pacing faltered. "What do you mean? Wilhelm said both were returning."

"You've grown fond of denial. You know the boy won't go home."

"There was a part of me that thought he might not. I doubt he'd be safe there."

"So with the boys gone, what will you do?"

He shrugged and continued pacing. "Travel with them. As you said, whatever the boy is wrapped up in is what I've been searching for. I think it's time to put a name to what stalks Dalnar. If I follow Salvarias, I think he'll lead me right to it."

"No, Humar. Those boys need to go their road alone. You can't go, my friend."

"They need help, Mafarias. Salvarias is just a boy and Wilhelm—"

"Salvarias is eighteen now. Wilhelm's twenty-four. They're men."

He shook his head. "Salvarias is still considered a boy. Wilhelm's just old enough to be on his own. Those brothers are too young to wander about Dalnar unguided."

"They've been on their own for over eight years. You know as well as I that childhood innocence has never touched Salvarias. That boy was born an adult. And Wilhelm's been a man since he was fifteen." Mafarias chuckled. "I know. I caught him with a treasure of a woman. Wealthy, voluptuous. Of course, I kept the secret from Ashra. She would've fainted."

Humar felt a blush creep on his cheeks and it sparked another laugh from Mafarias.

The mage wiped his eyes. "You and Tobin have taught Wilhelm everything about fighting. I'm telling you, go with them and you put both in peril."

Humar settled into a chair, staring at his hands. He trusted Mafarias and the two had known each other for nearly twenty years, yet every bone in Humar's body told him to travel with the brothers. "I'll think about what you've said."

Mafarias smiled. "Your heart is as big as I remember. I care for the boys and I want them to be successful. You know Salvarias is untrusting, and with additions to the group, he'll only pull away from Wilhelm. It's imperative for Salvarias to have Wilhelm's protection."

"I can earn his trust," Humar said, but couldn't hide the doubt in his voice.

"Tobin took four years to get Salvarias to talk to him. The boy doesn't trust any."

"If so, why would he train with Dethal?"

"As his magic gained power, so would his thirst for knowledge. Since I wasn't around, he took the first offer. I can tell you this, Salvarias never trusted the man. He might've trained with him, but never offered his trust." Mafarias slumped in his chair and stared at his hands. "Have I ever told you that I'm a flawed man?"

"We're all flawed men, Mafarias."

"I more so. I've made terrible mistakes. Ones I'll never be able to undo. Ones that still haunt my dreams."

Humar stared at the fire. The closeness strengthened between him and his old friend. A link of men who carried similar burdens. Burdens that could never be alleviated.

Mafarias's voice was barely above a whisper. "I just want to help them. It's all I ever wanted. I love Wilhelm. I even love Salvarias in my own way. They need to be alone."

Humar bit his tongue. He'd grown close to Wilhelm and the boy needed help, but Mafarias brought up valid points. Salvarias was cold and distant, and with the new inner strength he'd obtained, he wouldn't rely on Wilhelm for protection. The boy was independent now, alone in his mind, and he needed no one.

Chapter 21
Spring 1018 a.r.

Wilhelm offered an ear-to-ear grin to his brother in the early hours of morning. Two weeks had passed since Salvarias had first opened his eyes and his nightmares hadn't ceased until last night.

Wilhelm ruffled Salvarias's hair. "Morning, Salv."

Salvarias rubbed his eyes. "Joyful twenty-fourth Birth Day, my dear brother."

"Merry Birth Day to you, too. How did you sleep?"

"Not well. Did I wake you last night?"

Wilhelm frowned. "A couple of times, but you were just talking quietly. Why?"

Salvarias propped himself against the wall. "I am learning to control my dreams."

"How are you controlling them?"

"I am not allowing myself deep sleep."

Wilhelm scooted next to his brother. "You need rest, though. Do you want to tell me about the dreams? It might help to talk about it."

"No, but thank you. There is something we need to talk about though."

"What is it?" Wilhelm hoped his brother would remove himself from seclusion. Since his rescue, he'd spoken with Humar and Mafarias once, preferring not to meet the others or receive guests. Wilhelm knew why. After his brother woke, it took an entire week of the same puzzle box story to convince Salvarias his rescue wasn't a dream. The past week he'd remembered that Wilhelm was no illusion, but Salvarias woke multiple times each hour he slept, eyes filled with horror, rubbing his arms or legs, reaching for a part of his body or his missing ear. The past two days had been better.

Salvarias met Wilhelm's gaze. "I want you to go home and start a family. You deserve every happiness the world can offer you. You have cared for me eighteen years. It is time for you to be happy." Salvarias's eyes filled with love. "You will be an excellent father."

Wilhelm chose to ignore the possible meaning of those words.

Salvarias wouldn't leave. "Durak said he'd let me keep working at the smithy. It's good money. Milred adores you and would accept you back without hesitation. We can go home when you're ready."

"I am not returning to Falar, brother. I am traveling a different road and I do not know when I will be done. It is time for us to part ways."

Wilhelm felt as though Salvarias had punched him. Air left his lungs and he doubled over.

"You must understand. I love you. I could not bear..." Tears welled in Salvarias's eyes. "I could not bear something happening to you. You must leave me. I beg you."

Wilhelm clutched his chest, trying to inhale air.

"I am sorry, brother. Please, you must understand. I love—"

"All we've been through... You can't ask me to leave you." Determination set in Wilhelm's bones. "I won't leave you! Don't you understand? I'm happy when I'm with you. For the past year I've been miserable. Now you want to leave? After I just got you back? I can't—" He lost his breath.

"You must understand. I have kept something from you, something I have had since I was born." Salvarias cringed as he spoke. "There is something lurking within me. I feel it call to me. I battle it every breath I take, but one day I will fail. I must be alone. I could hurt people around me."

"I don't understand—"

Salvarias's words tumbled out. "I am evil, brother! It lives within me. It seeks my soul. It follows me. It—"

"Enough! You're not evil, Salv."

Salvarias's eyes filled with shame, vulnerability and fear; a reflection of when he was younger. "One day it will take over. One day I will lose my battles. I will hurt those around me. Please leave me. I could not bear anything happening to you. Please. I beg you!"

Wilhelm folded his brother close, feeling fingers digging into his shoulders.

"Why can you not see what all others see, brother? My eyes are a reflection of my evil. I know how people look at me. I know what they see. Please, you mean everything to me! I cannot bear the thought of something happening to you."

"I won't leave you. I know you better than you know yourself. I don't see what they see. I don't see what you see. I see you for who you are, and you're not an evil person."

Salvarias curled up tight, burying his face in Wilhelm's chest. He didn't understand his brother's confession. Clearly Salvarias believed it to be true, but Wilhelm had no doubts that his brother was evil's opposite. Salvarias was a caring, loving, and considerate man. He was no more capable of evil than... than Wilhelm was of becoming a vegetarian. He almost laughed aloud at the absurd notion.

Once Salvarias's sobs quieted, Wilhelm tapped his brother's chin, waiting until he looked up before saying, "As long as we're together, we can do anything. But we have to be together, Salv. Agreed?"

Salvarias stared for several moments before he said, "Promise me you will not die."

Wilhelm smiled. "I promise." He couldn't explain why, but he felt confident in his words, and he never broke a promise. Salvarias knew that, and his furrowed brow showed his surprise at Wilhelm's agreement. His brother's eyes unfocused and his lips moved in silent conversation. Wilhelm gave his brother a gentle shake. "Salv?"

"I cannot leave him."

"Leave who?"

Salvarias lowered his gaze. "Nothing."

"Together?" Wilhelm pressed.

Eventually, Salvarias nodded. Wilhelm ruffled his brother's hair, and after a weak elbow to the ribs returned the affection, handed over the puzzle box. He put his arms around his brother's shoulders and Salvarias curled up against him.

The pounding torrent of rain and whistling winds that thrashed the estate abated to a whisper. The device enraptured his brother, and he relaxed as the pieces clicked into place.

Wilhelm watched lazy raindrops patter on the window. "I love you, Salv."

Salvarias inhaled deeply and the last of the tension drained from his shoulders. "I love you too, my dear brother."

Wilhelm smiled at the sun streaming through the window, the clouds dispersing in a breath. As long as they were together, the brothers could do anything.

Humar brooded in his room, staring into the fire, and continued to feel torn about Mafarias's request to leave the brothers. Since Salvarias's rescue, the estate had been filled with haunting screams and heart wrenching pleas. Salvarias had refused to see anyone until yesterday's brief meeting. Humar felt it coming, knew the boy was readying himself for something. Though detached and cold, he was never rude. Not seeing comrades who came to his rescue had surely bored through the young man's proper etiquette. Last night, the screams had stopped. Salvarias was ready.

Humar rose and looked out the window, inhaling the sun filtering through dissipating clouds. He enjoyed the occasional storm, but the rain had continued for weeks, flooding the streets and adding another layer of cold and discomfort to the already dispirited citizens. He tossed aside the curtains to his other window and settled back in his chair, staring at the azure sky and drinking in the sun.

A knock pulled him from his thoughts. "Enter."

Okulu staggered in with Durak, taking a swig of the ever-present flask. "So what's the news?"

"What do you mean?" Humar asked.

Okulu shrugged. "You've been cooped up in your room reading or pouting since yesterday. Something's eating you."

"Aye," Durak confirmed. "I know ye're big into planning, but we're just going home to Falar."

"Not all of us," Humar said. "The boys are leaving."

Durak's head jerked up. "What?"

Humar smiled, knowing the strong relationship the cavrul, and all of them, had developed with Wilhelm. "Mafarias said they're traveling. You can't tell me you don't feel the change in Arden, Durak."

The cavrul reclined near the fireplace, his gray skin pinkened by the flickering flames. "Aye, I feel it."

Humar ran his hand through his hair. "And Salvarias is wrapped up in this somehow. Mafarias confirmed that much. He wants me to leave the boys. Says they have to do whatever it is alone."

Okulu grinned. "Sounds like you're conflicted."

Humar cast the merc a waning smile. "You've seen. Wilhelm

isn't ready to travel on his own. He's a quick learner, but avoiding slavers depends on where they travel."

Okulu plopped in a chair. "I agree with you there, my friend."

Why Humar was still debating whether or not he should travel with the brothers seemed foolish. "I guarantee Salvarias won't be free with information. The boy doesn't trust anyone. And he rarely speaks. I'd be surprised if he allowed us to tag along."

Okulu shrugged. "Don't give him the option. Just tell him we're going."

Durak laughed. "Good point. The boy's always been submissive, afraid of his own damn shadow."

Humar shook his head. "Not anymore, Durak. There's a new strength in his eyes. The man who emerged from Zeeas isn't the same boy who was taken."

Durak growled. "That cursed boy is afraid of everything. Those nightmares aren't new. He's been screaming in the night for years. You saw him before he was taken; head lowered, eyes like a beaten dog. He'll cave."

"I'm telling you, he's stronger now." Humar shuddered, remembering the black eyes, emotionless and cold. "He might be afraid, but if he is, there's no hint of it."

"I'd like to see for meself," Durak muttered. "But the damned boy won't allow any to see him."

Humar grunted in agreement.

Okulu arched an eyebrow. "I would think you two would be more sympathetic."

Humar met the merc's gaze. Okulu wasn't one for serious comments, much less sympathy.

"You saw his body," Okulu continued. "The boy went to Oblivion and back again and you expect him to walk around with people he's never met? I thought more of your heart, Humar."

Humar shifted in his chair. "I've known the boy—"

"For months. Honestly, from what you've told me, he wasn't there for the first year you knew the brothers. And after they escaped the slave camp, it was, what, three months before he started training with the mage and hardly lived at the smithy? I don't know what changed with you, but I don't offer my trust that easily either."

Humar felt his cheeks burn. "Wilhelm—"

Okulu laughed. "Brilliant. Now you're comparing the brothers?

Wilhelm's heart is gold. I've never met a more trusting person in my life. It's not normal. You can't honestly expect—"

It was Humar's turn to argue. "I'd expect a brother younger by six years to listen to the older one!"

Okulu raised his hands. "I don't think it's our place to judge, is all I'm saying. We've traveled enough to know what's out there. If I remember, Tobin was a cautious man."

Humar sprang to his feet. "Don't speak about my brother!"

Okulu grinned. "There's some true emotion that's been lacking from you lately. I've missed your instincts."

Humar couldn't help but slump in defeat. "I see your point."

Durak's eyes narrowed. "I'm going wherever Wilhelm goes."

Humar nodded. "I'll see if I can talk to Wilhelm first, have him start wearing Salvarias down."

"Count me in," Okulu said.

Humar sank back in his chair. "You've never been one to take work without money."

The merc shrugged. "I'm looking to brush up on my sword skill. It's been rather boring and I think you're going to give me the opportunity. I'm rich. I don't need the money."

Humar shook his head. "You're leaving something out."

Okulu grinned. "Perhaps. Instincts again?"

Humar smiled. "Yep."

"You're lucky that your instincts didn't abandon you thinking you've grown soft," Okulu said.

Humar was about to retort when a loud knock jolted all in the room. Durak shook his head and chortled. "Come in, Wilhelm."

Wilhelm opened the door, his crooked grin slicing across his face. "Would you mind joining us in the sitting room? Salv would like to thank everyone."

Humar nodded. "We'll be a moment."

"Thanks." Wilhelm closed the door after a wink.

Okulu's eyes grew pensive. "How that man isn't wed, I'll never know."

Durak grunted. "He's had plenty of opportunities. Ye should've seen how many weapons me sold to women."

Humar shook his head. "And how many times the boy disappeared around corners."

Okulu took a swig from his flask. "That 'boy' is probably more of a man than any of us here."

Humar laughed. "True, very true. You're up for this? Potential loss of life? Constant travel and running?"

Okulu shrugged. "Not much different from everyday life."

"For you maybe," Durak growled. "Some of us have earned honest livings."

The merc shot Durak a hurt look. "I've been honest my whole life."

Durak grunted. "Then I'm the son of Nevlar."

Okulu mumbled, "You're grouchy enough to be."

Durak yanked his axe from its sheath. "What!"

"Enough," Humar said. "Let's get in there and see what the mage has to say."

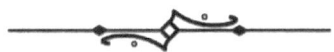

Varila sat on the bed, brushing her sister's hair in the morning sunlight streaming through the window. "How are you feeling?"

Lunara smiled over her shoulder. "I've been well for two weeks now. You don't have to ask me every morning. I promise. I'm fine."

Varila rolled her eyes. "You died, Lunara. I'll ask you every damned hour if I feel like it."

Lunara threw her arms around Varila. "Your softer side is showing."

She grinned. "You're the only one allowed to see."

Lunara squished up her face in an impish grin. "If you keep pestering me, I'll be forced to tell Wilhelm all sorts of fun little stories about you."

Varila shoved her sister over, hiding a smile. "Fine. I'll stop asking."

Lunara snatched the brush from Varila's hand and switched positions. "You miss him?"

"No."

"It's been three weeks since you've seen him. Are you sure?" Lunara unraveled Varila's braid. "Three weeks since you flirted. Three weeks since you sat in his lap. Three weeks since his arm wrapped around your shoulders. Three—"

"I get the point; and, no, I don't miss it. I could walk right out to town and find any man to flirt with. I can have my choice of laps and arms!"

Her words didn't convince herself and she doubted Lunara bothered to even listen. Varila couldn't be in love with him. She barely knew him. It had only been six months. Impossible. No man could have that much control over her emotions. But if she didn't love Wilhelm, why hadn't she slept with him? She could. She could march up to him right now, cast him her most seductive smile, and he would be on his knees begging her.

"Why can't you admit it?" Lunara said.

"I've admitted he's cute." She decided to change the subject. "Don't you think it's odd the mage hasn't been to see you?"

"No, he's been through quite an ordeal. I'd expect him to need time."

"We risked our lives to save him. You've dreamt of him since you were eleven! He could at least join us for dinner."

"He didn't ask us to come to his rescue."

"I know, but still. It's not normal."

Lunara's little giggle induced a smile from Varila. It was such a cute laugh. "I'm surprised you've had time to think about Salvarias. You seem very... shall we say, preoccupied with Wilhelm."

She gave her sister a shove. "Knock it off. He's cute. That's all."

"Of course."

"Have you been able to understand your connection with the mage?"

"No. I'm sure I will eventually."

"What are we supposed to do now that we've found him?"

"I don't know. I hope to get to know him, try to understand our connection." Lunara giggled. "I'm sure you won't mind spending time with the brothers, would you?"

Varila hid her smile and kept her voice curt. "I said knock it off."

"Why can't you admit you like him? He's terribly handsome and beyond sweet."

"For the hundredth time, I said he was cute!"

"And the fact that he's possibly the nicest man in all of Arden doesn't strike your interest? Or that he's stronger than you? Taller than you? Or the fact his sword skill exceeds yours?"

"Now that's too far! I'd beat him."

"What if you didn't use the methods mother taught? Would you still beat him?"

"I'm sure I would," she lied.

A loud knock startled both girls.

Lunara cast a knowing glance at Varila, and then in a sweet voice answered, "Enter."

Wilhelm opened the door and grinned. His ignorance of his charm amplified his attractiveness, and the amber in his eyes sparkled with a contagious joy. Varila sighed. She had missed him.

"Wilhelm!" Lunara bolted into his open arms.

His laughter rumbled when he swooped her up, her toes dangling two feet above the ground. Varila realized it was the first time he'd laughed since they'd met. Coaxing a smile had proved challenging enough, so she'd never bothered to find his laugh. Loud, warm, and infectious, it filled the estate with life, and she found herself smiling.

"Hello, ladies. Salv would like to thank everyone. Would you mind meeting us in the sitting room?" Wilhelm winked at Varila.

"Of course!" Lunara said. "We'll be along in a moment."

"Thanks." Wilhelm lowered her and glanced again at Varila before leaving.

She sighed and wished nothing more than to be tucked away in a room with her mother. Varila realized the answer to her previous questions was fear. It was her dominant emotion when it came to Wilhelm, and all men for that matter. Fear. She didn't make any further advancement towards him because she was unnerved by her complete trust in him. Entrusting her virtue to a man who could have whatever he desired, whenever he desired it, caused a feeling of vulnerability, but one she reluctantly admitted she enjoyed. Wilhelm's normal, passive side disappeared when his desires rose, and to her alarm, she found herself longing for him to control their intimate moments. Usually, she felt like the man in the relationship since most that came to her room turned into shy, giggling little boys unsure of what to do with an independent, strong woman. Wilhelm did not giggle. Wilhelm did not turn shy. Wilhelm did not let her feel like a man.

Lunara cleared her throat, startling Varila from her thoughts. Her sister's smile couldn't have been bigger. "Shall we go?"

Varila rolled her eyes at her sister and led her from the room. "Wipe that grin off your face."

Lunara followed Varila into the sitting room. For the first time, she laid eyes on the man who had intrigued her little sister and brought life to Wilhelm. The mage rose with a bow when they entered and Varila tilted her head, acknowledging his action so he could sit again. He returned to his chair by the fire. His shadowed face caught the firelight under his hood to reveal an expression that was cold and void of emotion. His gaze switched to Wilhelm, who was openly watching her.

Salvarias turned his ice cold stare to her and raised his head enough to cast the full firelight across his eyes. She could see no white, only black irises boring into her soul. She squirmed under his gaze, feeling naked and as though he read her mind, her deepest, most private thoughts. A chill rippled over her and she wanted to flee the room, but his stern gaze restrained her. She felt violated.

Humar's voice broke the mage's hold. "Hello, Salvarias."

Salvarias's head lowered to once again cast his face in shadows. She sucked in a breath. She hadn't realized she'd stopped breathing.

Salvarias didn't resemble Wilhelm in the slightest. Salvarias's features were softer, not as square. And his demeanor was opposite from Wilhelm; unwelcoming, distant, cold and aloof. She shuddered and took a step closer to her sister. Varila would be damned if he ever laid a finger on Lunara.

When he raised his face to greet Humar, he still looked sick; face pale and shiny, eyes shadowed by dark rings and sunken.

Humar sat in the chair next to the mage. "It's good to see you up and about."

"Thank you, Humar."

Varila's breath increased when Salvarias spoke. His voice was lulling and hypnotic. The rich tone was a seductive whisper, sounding as though he spoke the soft words in her ear. She found herself longing for him to speak again.

Mafarias strolled in from the hallway to stand next to the sisters and Varila shifted Lunara further away from him. Though beyond handsome, Mafarias's lingering stares at Lunara made Varila uncomfortable and caused her protective side to emerge.

Salvarias nodded to Mafarias and then spoke in a rhythm of words that soothed Varila into a calm trance. "I want to thank you all for risking your lives for mine. I cannot tell you how appreciative I am, and I will forever be indebted to each of you. Master Dethal will not be pleased with any who aided in my rescue. He will hunt you and kill you or torture you for information. I suggest finding small towns, nondescript jobs, and keeping to yourselves. He has many spies—"

Humar said, "Durak, Okulu, and I would like to travel with you."

"My road is not easy, Humar. I do not wish for anyone else to accompany me." Salvarias's gaze locked on the merc, who seemed to squirm at first, but then a slow smile spread.

Wilhelm turned his stare from Varila to Salvarias with a furrowed brow. She assumed the mage hadn't disclosed his plans to Wilhelm.

Humar shrugged. "Evil is brewing, and I think Dethal is in the thick of things. He's going to attempt to find you again. I want my chance to help Arden. I think traveling with you will give me the opportunity."

"If you feel the need to help, Loutsil could surely use someone of your character. The evil uniting is not contained to Dalnar alone. It will spread. Why not go home?"

Humar stiffened. "This is my home, not Loutsil. Zeeas had octrils trained for combat. Their sword skill was unlike the creatures left over from Veedran. I know something big is happening, and I think you're heading for the center of the storm. I want to help."

"We must go," Lunara whispered in Varila's ear. "I don't think these events, the connection I have, is chance."

"Sounds like a lot of traveling and fighting."

"I can do it. I wasn't tired because I couldn't handle it. I guarantee it aligns with when he was hurt badly. I swear I can do this. They need our help. Both brothers."

She sighed. "You have to listen to me and do what I say. Agreed?"

"Agreed." Lunara smiled sweetly.

Varila shook her head. She had yet to learn how to say no to Lunara. "We're going too, mage."

"I do not think that is wise, my Lady. As I said, our road is dangerous."

Varila scowled at Salvarias. "I can take care of myself and my sister. I'm not asking. We're going."

Wilhelm squatted beside his brother. "We could use the help, Salv."

Salvarias stared at his brother and then shook his head. "So be it.

Know that I will not always reveal my intentions, destinations, or reasons for my actions."

Durak jumped up from his chair and his voice roared like a thunderstorm. "How dare ye, boy! I grow tired of your—"

Humar darted in front of Wilhelm and rested a restraining hand on his arm when he took a step towards the cavrul. "We understand."

Durak shot daggers at Humar and muttered curses to the corner of the room. She turned her attention back to Salvarias. The conversation seemed to drain him of his strength. He rested his head on his hand.

"In two days we will leave for—" Salvarias started but turned to Adok. He sprang from his chair, and before he opened his mouth, shouts erupted from the courtyard.

A guard burst into the room. "My Lady!"

"What is it?"

The guard sucked in a deep breath. "Men in black armor have ambushed us at the gate. They've gained entry."

"How many?" Wilhelm asked.

The guard shook his head. "More than we can handle. I would guess at least fifty."

Varila cursed. "Get your men out of here. You know what you need to do at the farmhouse outside the city. Eight of them."

Humar's mouth gaped open. "What!"

She motioned at him to be silent. After the guard left the room, she said, "There's another escape route. Grab your things and meet back here."

She snatched her sister's hand and led her towards their room with a growing smile. Varila looked forward to a little adventure. Sitting around reading books wasn't her idea of a good time. A sword fight, travel, changing scenery, and a little danger evoked a giddy happiness in her. Lunara giggled.

Varila hid her smile. "Knock it off!"

Wilhelm muttered a few favorite curses under his breath while he helped Salvarias hobble to their room. His brother wasn't healthy enough for a fight or travel. Weak and thin, he slept often and struggled to keep food down. It was midday and the longest he'd stayed awake. Already, Wilhelm saw the lines of exhaustion etching themselves on Salvarias's face.

Once in their room, Wilhelm buckled on his sword. "How did you know they were coming?"

"Adok told me."

"Can you understand animals now? Their exact words?"

Salvarias shoved Wilhelm's clothes in a pack, wheezing the entire time. "Yes."

He winked at his brother. "That's got to be interesting."

Salvarias chuckled. "I thought I was going mad at first. It was difficult to control, and initially I heard all of them inside Zeeas; all the rats, all the bugs, the snakes, the birds. It was near unbearable. Over time, I learned to block all but the ones I chose."

"I always say you're the most amazing man I've ever met." Wilhelm grinned when he snatched the pack from his brother.

"I can carry it, brother," Salvarias protested.

Wilhelm winked. "I know."

He took his brother's arm and helped him to the sitting room. The sisters paced near the fire and Varila's skeptical look at Salvarias confirmed that her concerns matched Wilhelm's, but he only shrugged. They had no option but to flee.

Humar, Durak, Okulu, and Mafarias rushed into the room.

Varila grabbed her sister's hand. "Let's go."

Wilhelm kept firm hold of his brother while they followed Varila. She glided through the estate to a winding staircase that dumped them into the cellar. With help from Lunara, the two sisters fumbled along the wall and found a brick that, after it was pressed, retreated into the wall. A slab of brown stone ground aside to reveal a narrow tunnel. Wilhelm groaned at the low ceiling. Varila muttered a curse.

"What?" he asked.

"I forgot a torch. Okulu!"

Salvarias whispered, *"Lumous,"* and a sparrow of light floated forward. Wilhelm had missed the pure white glow of the soaring bird.

Varila motioned everyone inside. The narrow passageway prevented Wilhelm from walking next to his brother. A thick, musty smell hung damp in the air and dust covered the ground. Wilhelm could hear skittering rats' sharp claws and caught an occasional glimpse of a fleeing gray body.

After they filed in, Varila closed the door behind them and said, "It's a long walk, Wilhelm."

Everyone was listening to Salvarias wheezing.

Varila scooted by the others pressed along the wall and when she reached Wilhelm, he wasn't overly accommodating in plastering himself against the stone. He grinned when her body rubbed his. Her seductive smile, wink, and wavy mass of sunshine hair erupted a strong urge to have her right there in the tunnel.

Lunara shuffled by next and her gaze locked on Salvarias. She offered a smile that wasn't returned and stood behind her sister. Humar and Mafarias brought up the rear, then Durak, and Okulu followed Wilhelm.

Mafarias whispered, *"Ecia lumenious."* The crystal he carried glowed. "How did you shorten the spell, Salvarias?"

"Now isn't the time," Humar whispered.

"Shut up!" Varila barked.

As they shuffled onward, the unknown passing of time allowed Wilhelm's mind to venture to the changes in Salvarias since his rescue. Wilhelm carried two fears in life: His brother's death and independence. He was no fool. His life was Salvarias and if his brother ever died, Wilhelm would as well.

Down to his very bones, he needed to be needed by Salvarias. As selfish as it was, Wilhelm desperately wanted his love and presence to be required. He enjoyed caring for his brother, and though Salvarias saw himself as a burden, it was essential to Wilhelm's heart. Now, fear of no longer being needing simmered.

The submissive air that had encompassed Salvarias before his abduction had disappeared, and Wilhelm was overjoyed. He hated seeing his brother cower, head lowered and body shaking. Now Salvarias didn't cringe, didn't shake and, instead, seemed comfortable in responding and talking to others. Though Salvarias's independence was not a desire, Wilhelm dreamed of a time when his brother would be free of fear.

Wilhelm bumped into Salvarias. "Sorry." Lost in random thoughts, Wilhelm hadn't noticed they'd stopped.

"Light," Varila called.

The sparrow soared forward through the hazy air while the group shuffled to a stop.

She groped along the wall. "We've got horses waiting. Any idea where we're going?"

"The..." Salvarias clutched his chest, doubling over.

Wilhelm cursed when he smelled the air growing dusty.

Salvarias latched onto Wilhelm's arm. "River."

He winced at his brother's tight hold. "We need fresh air."

"We make a run for it," Varila said, apology in her voice. "It's a little ways."

Salvarias wasn't breathing. "Just go!"

Light flooded into the space and the group bolted up a set of stairs. Once outside the tunnel, Wilhelm put his shoulders under his brother's arm and practically carried him forward. They were at a farm outside the city, and, glancing back, it appeared they'd come through the stone barn. Wilhelm looked ahead and cursed at the distance to the corral. His brother jerked for air and his eyes lost focus.

Suddenly, the horses leapt the enclosure. Wilhelm's heart dropped to his boots while Varila and Durak provided colorful curses. But instead of fleeing, the horses galloped to them. Wilhelm couldn't suppress his grin.

"Nicely done, little brother."

A horse drew close and Salvarias grabbed hold of the reins, mounting fluidly. Wilhelm helped strap packs to the horses and then jumped onto the closest beast, murmuring an apology when it grunted. Okulu took the lead and the group set off at a full gallop through the wheat-colored grasses. He glanced back at the city, and just as their luck had it, a group of men were riding hard in their direction.

"They're coming!" he roared.

"By Zerana's grace, we need a break!" Okulu cursed. "Three day's hard riding!"

Wilhelm followed with his own curse, watching his brother clinging to the fast mare, certain Salvarias didn't have the strength to flee for days, but no other option existed.

Wilhelm had a sick feeling that desperate flight would be occurring often in his future.

Lunara shifted in her saddle, trying to ease the pain of her raw thighs, bruised calves, and aching back. The past three days of flight from Kudril had been nothing short of miserable. Tired, hungry, and sore, she nearly wept with relief when Reffil came into view and the smell confirmed the fishing village's purpose. The stench reached them at first sight of the weak wall crumbling up from dry grasses. Lunara winkled her nose. She wasn't so sure she wanted to venture inside the city.

Okulu slowed the group to a walk and Varila spoke up. "My father owns a riverboat if we need it. Where are we going, mage?"

Salvarias nodded, gathering his cloak close while he surveyed the land. "We will head up river and restock supplies in Acklar."

Humar wiped sweat from his brow. "I don't think it's a good idea for all of us to enter the city."

"Agreed," Okulu said. "There's a place two miles upriver from the city where the boat can get close to shore. It'll be a jump, but it's worth the risk."

Humar nodded. "I'm familiar with the spot. Varila and I will go into Reffil for the boat. The rest of you meet us there."

"Hurry," Okulu muttered. "I don't think they're too far behind us."

Durak scowled at the merc. "I wouldn't want to disrupt our streak of good luck."

Wilhelm grinned. "Makes life exciting."

"You dumb ogre!" Durak cursed. "It makes for dead people!"

"Don't kill each other before we meet again," Humar said dryly.

Varila pulled Lunara's mare close. "Stay near Wilhelm. No one else but him. You understand?"

"Of course."

"Not even his brother, just Wilhelm."

Nodding, Lunara hid a pang of disappointment. Her sister was reserved, if not uneasy, around Salvarias; a feeling mirrored by the others except Wilhelm and, oddly, Okulu.

The group split and Lunara's tinge of joy turned into a boiling pot of elation at avoiding the city. A gusty breeze from the ocean carried with it a pungent smell as they drew near the river. She shivered in her saddle, and despite her best efforts, her teeth chattered.

Wilhelm chuckled. "Cold?"

"Yes." She smiled shyly. "The breeze from the sea is chilly."

Wilhelm wrapped her reins with his and hoisted her onto his saddle, engulfing her in his cloak.

"Thank you." Her legs trembled with exhaustion, but sitting sidesaddle soothed her raw thighs, and she nestled against him, his heat easing her stiff muscles.

She turned to Salvarias, whose hood was drawn so low that she could see nothing of his features. What she'd glimpsed revealed a man she hardly recognized. He reminded her more of the gangly youth she'd fallen in love with in their dreams. Bones stuck out under his robes as before and the only change was his height. She'd yet to see his eyes and resisted the urge to tackle him and cut off his hood. She saw his mouth moving and assumed he counted, an odd trait Wilhelm had disclosed and one the mage hadn't had in their dreams.

She wanted to hear his voice, so she asked, "How are you feeling?" It hit her in that moment; those were the first words she'd said to a man she'd known for seven years. It was as if they were friends that never met. She realized how odd their relationship was, how natural, how unnatural, how familiar, how foreign, how intimate, how distant.

"Fine. Thank you, my Lady."

A shiver tickled the back of her neck. She swore he'd whispered in her ear, close so only she could hear his voice.

Mafarias moved to the other side of Salvarias. "How did you shorten the spell?"

"As I am sure you know, all spells and runes can be shortened. Whoever wrote them down hundreds of years ago chose lengthy words and complicated runes."

"Yes, but how did you learn to shorten them?"

"Your power exceeds mine, Uncle. Surely you know."

Mafarias shrugged. "I was curious how you did it."

"You first."

Mafarias chuckled. "You trust no one, do you?"

Salvarias turned his hooded head to Mafarias. "You avoid the answer as well."

"Magic is special, a privileged gift. I can't give away all my secrets." He winked.

Once they reached the river, Lunara dismounted, staring at the roaring water cutting through the landscape with the powerful force of spring. Churning, muddy water crashed against rocks jutting up the bank and wind added to the rushing flow. Thick, towering trees lined the sides and scented the air with a rich, nutty aroma.

Wilhelm, grinning his lopsided smile, removed her pack and added it to the growing pile of their personal belongings. She stroked her tired horse's neck, offering an apology for the lengthy ride. When Salvarias moved to the other side, her heart rate increased.

She smiled. "I feel bad that we rode them so hard."

"You are a light rider." Salvarias removed the bridle.

His movements mesmerized her. Graceful for a man, his motions were fluid, rhythmical like his voice, planned, purposeful, and silent. His large, slender hands seemed to float through the air, and his long, supple fingers brought the memory of her dreams forward. She noticed his missing pinky and tried to remember if it had always been lost.

He whispered to the horse while unbuckling the saddle and the mare nudged him. When the horse turned towards Lunara, nuzzling her raised hand and offering a gentle shove, she giggled her appreciation.

"No," Okulu said from behind when Salvarias went to lift the saddle. The merc's eyes moved to the mage's chest just as Salvarias pulled his cloak close. Okulu shook his head. "I hoped I might be wrong, but by your actions and color, I'd wager I wasn't."

"There is no need to tell my brother."

"You should've said something." Okulu set aside the saddle. "Varila could've picked up the herbs."

"We do not have time for her to make an extra stop."

Okulu shook his head and thumped the horse's rear, whistling and shooing the other beasts into the plains. The horses moved together while they wandered the grasses, nibbling and resting.

She looked at Salvarias's pinky. "How did it happen?"

He clenched his fist, hiding the missing finger, and stared at the open plains. "In Zeeas."

She felt herself flush. "I'm sorry."

"There is no need to apologize, my Lady. You did not know."

She shuddered, imagining someone cutting off her finger, and subconsciously rubbed per pinky. She glanced at his leg.

"Zeeas as well."

Embarrassed by her lack of control over her roving eyes, she lowered her head. "Sorry."

"I assure you, there is no need to apologize for curiosity."

Wilhelm joined them, wrapped an arm around his brother's neck, flicked back Salvarias's hood, and ruffled his long hair. She caught a glimpse of red skin on the side of his head. He punched Wilhelm in the ribs.

"Ouch!" Wilhelm grinned. "How are you feeling?"

"Fine, brother."

Salvarias's tone was different, warmer, when he said the word "brother." Her eyes detoured to the side of his head.

"It is not a pretty sight, my Lady."

She cursed herself silently. He had a knack for reading her thoughts, but her curiosity drove her eyes back to the side of his head. He lifted his hair aside, revealing his missing ear and eaten skin. Oddly, it didn't disgust or bother her in the least.

"Zeeas?" she asked.

His gaze met hers, and her breath choked in her throat. The irises seemed alive in the sunlight, shifting with varying shades of gray-black, swirling with subtle movements. Mesmerized, she took a step towards him. They were beautiful.

He raised his hood and turned his head away. "Yes."

She snapped out of her trance and wobbled back a step, resting a hand over her pounding heart.

"Boat's coming," Durak grumbled. "About damn time."

All moved to the edge of the river to observe the flat barge making its way lazily upriver. Men lined two sides, rowing against the rushing water, their fast strokes in contrast with the sluggish barge. A sheltered area offered a place to sleep, and large poles sprouted in convenient locations so one could anchor down in rough waters. She sat on a rock to give her shaking legs a rest and stretch her back. She could feel Salvarias watching her but kept her gaze on the river, confused, and in honesty, alarmed by her feelings and his effect on her heart.

Adok plopped his head on her lap and she cupped the beast's face in her hands, cooing and giving kisses to the wolf. She'd missed him, and since Salvarias's rescue, Adok had yet to leave his master's side. Adok's slick tongue licked her cheek and she giggled while scratching his grinning jaw.

Suddenly, the wolf bolted up to jump on Salvarias, knocking him to the ground. A thud issued next to Lunara and she turned to see an arrow sticking out of a tree.

Wilhelm shielded Salvarias. "Horsemen!"

Okulu spewed several oaths while waving his hands to catch the boat's attention.

"Damn Veedran's evil has cursed us!" Durak growled.

Okulu grinned. "No rest for the wicked. If you're getting too old for this, friend, you can always return to pounding metal in a confined space."

"I was made for confined spaces, ye dolt! Don't insult me or I'll beat your ass to Oblivion, and trust me, I've been lookin' for a reason!"

Taking a swig from his flask, the merc glanced at Salvarias. "It appears they grew rather fond of you. They don't want you to leave."

Another arrow whizzed by Lunara. Wilhelm lifted her, setting her behind a rock, and the rest moved for cover.

"Persistent," he muttered.

Salvarias whispered an odd language and made a movement in the air. A ball of fire erupted in front of him.

"Fool!" Mafarias snapped. "You'll catch the grasses on fire."

"No, do it, Salv." Wilhelm pointed at the darkening sky rolling in with the ocean. "The storm will put it out."

The fire flew through the trees, rushing towards the fifty or so men pursuing them. It expanded and lengthened before striking the ground with incredible force. The fire flared in front of the men, sparking cries of alarm. Thick smoke billowed up from the flaming grasses.

Wilhelm caught the mage when he fell. "Salv?" he called, shaking Salvarias.

Suddenly, a curtain of smoke unfurled and a group of men burst clear of the fire.

Okulu cursed. "Put him with Lunara. Don't let him perform any more magic. The boat isn't going to make it in time."

"It will," Mafarias said. Chanting and flicking his hand, three shards of what appeared to be ice flew through the air. They landed in the chest of three men, launching them from their saddles.

Lunara worried that Okulu was right. The barge crawled up the raging river while the riders surged forward with seemingly unnatural speed. Salvarias groaned, rolled on his side breathing harshly, and held a hand over his abdomen.

She covered her head when another arrow hissed over the rock she cringed behind.

Okulu cast her his wickedly handsome wink. "Times like these I wish I'd taken up archery."

Through the chaos, her thoughts ventured to the possibility of Salvarias being taken again, or the entire party's capture. She'd seen a portion of the lengths these men would go to in order to obtain what they sought. She was sure a missing pinky, broken leg, sawed off ear, and acid-eaten flesh showed only half of their capabilities. Lunara had learned much since she'd left home, but a lesson in withstanding pain, accepting torture and mutilation, didn't rank high on her list of sought-after strengths. The longer she cowered behind the rock, the more her imagination flourished.

"Lunara!" Varila called.

Lunara jerked her head up to see the barge dueling with the river, rocking near the edge of the banks. Varila was aboard, stretching out her hand.

"Jump!" she yelled.

Lunara rose on shaky legs to gauge the distance. It took a quick glance to know she couldn't make it.

"I'll catch you," Varila said.

"Jump, girl!" Mafarias roared.

Lunara glanced behind to see the men almost upon the group. She took a deep breath, pooled her bravery, and as she set her resolve, large hands wrapped around her waist.

"Catch!" Wilhelm called.

She soared through the air, passing over the angry river to slam into Humar's open arms.

"Gotcha!" Humar said.

She clasped hold of the knight, trembling and relieved to be alive.

Okulu's feet teetered on the edge of the boat when he landed. With a quick grab, Varila yanked him forward. Any thoughts of safety vanished when two armored men leapt on the boat. Shaken, it took Lunara a breath to realize the brothers and Durak were aboard. Wet from the arms down, Wilhelm must have missed the edge and, by Durak's curses, he'd been tossed as well. Salvarias lay on the deck close by, curled up and in palpable pain. Humar released her and drew his sword to engage the soldiers. Three additional armored men jumped aboard.

Adok's vicious growl parted a group standing on a large rock awaiting their opportunity to board. The wolf dodged a lunge, knocked Mafarias aside, and cleared the distance with ease. The mage cursed as a white film covered him. A soldier shoved him and he disappeared into the raging river.

Salvarias crawled on his elbows away from the fight. Lunara rushed to his aid, but he flinched away from her. A black-armored soldier broke through the others, pushed her aside, and snatched up Salvarias.

"Wilhelm!" Lunara screamed.

The soldier dragged Salvarias forward. When a rower placed himself in the soldier's path, the armored man swung his broadsword up the rower's stomach.

Lunara had never witnessed a man's death. The rower's eyes widened and intestines spilt out of his abdomen. The sight froze her feet to the deck. Blood splattered across her dress and the moist noise churned her stomach. He toppled to the ground.

The killer dove over the side of the boat and disappeared into the river with Salvarias. Then the soldier's body floated to the surface of the water, limp and face down. Another rower was pulling Salvarias to the deck. She thought he might be dead.

She stood; feet planted in place, shaking violently. Her mind stammered for thought and her eyes fixated on the bloodied ground, the dead body, and the man's insides.

"Okulu!" Wilhelm yelled. "He's bleeding!"

His words caught her attention, and her distress surpassed her restraint. The deck released her feet in time for her to make it to the edge of the boat before becoming ill. She lost count of how many times she threw up, but Varila was holding Lunara's hair at one point. Finally, she calmed her stomach and accepted a mug of water.

Varila helped her rise. "Let's get you out of that dress."

Graciously blocking the dead man from sight, Varila led Lunara under the covered area of the barge. Salvarias rested with a blanket covering him from the waist down. Varila averted her eyes with a curse, and Lunara fought the urge to run to his side. His skeletal frame housed more scars than she thought a body could withstand. A large cut on his chest had reopened.

Varila held up a blanket to give Lunara privacy to change. She fumbled with the corset of her dress, her shaking fingers not allowing her to snag the knot.

Humar took Varila's place and closed his eyes. "I've got it."

Lunara mumbled apologies to her sister, heard words, but they bounced off Lunara's mind. With help, she slipped into a clean dress and her sister wiped the man's blood from her cheek. Lunara's knees ceased supporting her, and she sank to the ground next to Salvarias. Varila's arms were around her shoulders, offering desperately needed comfort.

"How long?" Okulu asked with a stern edge in his voice. "Your magic opened it?"

Salvarias closed his eyes, shaking his head.

Okulu threaded a needle. "This'll hurt."

The instant Okulu started his work, Salvarias trembled and ceased breathing. His hand gripped Wilhelm's wrist.

Wilhelm took the needle and mumbled, "I'll do it."

Salvarias inhaled a sharp breath, his knuckles turning white.

"You know I'm better," the merc protested.

Wilhelm cast Salvarias an apologetic look. "I'm not good at this."

Wilhelm's hands shook with each wince from Salvarias when the thread tugged his skin closed. She grew lightheaded in sympathy.

"You're telling me it opened when we left?" Okulu persisted.

Salvarias nodded. The merc rose with a curse and took up pacing the deck. When Wilhelm finished, he covered Salvarias in extra blankets. After a few murmured words, he fell asleep. Wilhelm went to the edge of the boat, washing blood from his hands.

"Are you all right?" Varila whispered.

Lunara nodded numbly. After she was safe and secure in a pile of blankets, Varila left to rest a hand on Wilhelm's shaking shoulders. Salvarias was on his side facing Lunara, his dark eyebrows stitched together, head tossing slightly as if lost in a nightmare. The event sent a ripple of stolen innocence to her core and she wanted to be wrapped in the mage's arms, his voice comforting her through the ordeal.

"Brother..." Salvarias whispered. "Please... Help..."

Reaching out a trembling hand, she brushed his wet hair from his face. Salvarias's stern expression lifted. She stared at his soft lips, strong jaw, and thick eyelashes, and mused he was created in the image of a god, each feature chiseled to perfection.

Sleep eventually came and she dreamt of the dying rower and a blood-covered deck.

Chapter 22
Spring 1018 a.r.

Salvarias startled awake to feel the gentle touch of a familiar hand.

Wilhelm's soothing voice rumbled, "We're here, Salv."

Salvarias forced in a tiny breath. His lungs felt as though someone had pummeled them for days and then added an anvil. His brain pounded in his skull. Every inch of his skin was tender and hurt to be touched. But the worst of his physical pain came from his insides. Each organ throbbed and his muscles were tight and cramped. He winced when he shifted and, with effort, he opened his eyes. Wilhelm's lopsided grin awaited.

"Let me help you."

Strong arms wrapped around Salvarias's shoulders and hauled him to his feet. He leaned against his brother, using Wilhelm's solid presence to stabilize his vision.

Humar shook his head. "No, Salvarias needs to stay on the boat. We can't have any asking who he is."

Okulu was watching him with a frown. "I know what to get. I'll take Wilhelm with me."

Salvarias nodded and tugged on Wilhelm. "Do we have funds, brother?"

Wilhelm shifted through his purse and produced a small handful of silver. "Not much, why?"

"No reason. I just wanted to see what we had available. I will wait here." Salvarias desperately wanted the herbs to help his breathing but would not use their low funds. Wilhelm hesitated, his frown showing he did not believe Salvarias, so he gave his brother a gentle shove. Wilhelm ruffled Salvarias's hair before draping an arm over Varila and leading her to the rickety dock and town.

Salvarias watched Varila slide her arm around Wilhelm and smile up at him. Shaking his head, Salvarias was not sure about Varila. Initially, he had found her conceited and rude, but after study, he realized she possessed a strength that could come across wrong to others. Once he figured that out, he understood his brother's attraction. Still, Salvarias withheld his approval. His appraisal of her worth would be lengthy before he allowed her to marry his brother. And no doubt existed that their relationship was heading towards marriage. The tension between the two could be cut with a sword, and the fact his brother had not bedded her yet confirmed that he was in love, even if he continued to lie to his heart. Though ecstatic that he had finally found a woman of interest, Salvarias would be thorough in his evaluation. If he did not find her suitable, one word would end Wilhelm's love. Without a second thought, Salvarias would lay down his life for Wilhelm, and would be damned if any would hurt him.

Salvarias tore his gaze from the empty dock to sweep over the barge. Durak was leaning against a post, his usual scowl glaring at Salvarias. Lunara was riffling through a pack, looking every bit as stunning as she had been in his dreams. His feelings were a mixture of joy and fear at the knowledge she was real. He could not understand why they dreamt each other. Their connection of mind and body troubled him even more. His thoughts were his own, secret and sacred, frightening and painful. He worked every waking breath to block her from his mind by finding ways to push her presence to the surface. The lack of answers made him drive a wedge of distrust between them. Even so, he fought back the strong desire to see if her skin felt as soft in person as it had in his dreams.

He reclined against a pole and admired the lush forest. The spring breeze lifted his hair and brought to him the smell of woodsy pines and the coolness of the river. Aspens littered the mountainside, their white bark distinct among the rich brown trunks of pine trees. He closed his eyes and listened to their blissful song. Aspens were his favorite tree. Not only did their song soothe the deepest parts of his soul, but also the colors they morphed into with each passing season awed Salvarias. The black knots contrasting the white bark painted pictures he could stare at for years.

A nearby sparrow drew his attention and he opened a connection with the bird. The sparrow bragged about a new song, and after a few pleas, the bird agreed to share. While he listened, his mind drifted to Zeeas. He had not lied to Wilhelm. Initially, the strain of the animals' voices had been unbearable. Hundreds, thousands of eager little creatures had begged for Salvarias's attention. He had screamed until his voice gave out in order to block the whispers from his mind. Weeks had passed before he learned to control his new ability, to choose when and who to engage in conversation. But once he had honed his oddity, the conversations animals provided gave him something else to focus on instead of his pain.

Adok had proved different than any other animal. Salvarias maintained a solid connection without stress. He was surprised to be remembered by Adok. After all, they had only spent a few hours together before Salvarias had been taken. Yet the wolf seemed dedicated to developing the relationship. Its immediate fondness and care was something Salvarias, oddly enough, returned. He reached down and rubbed the wolf's soft ears. Adok leaned against his leg.

His gaze turned to the rolling river. He saw blood. It trickled down rocks and whirled in eddying currents, tainting the blue waters. Salvarias was not in full control of his mind and doubted he ever would be. Even now, not only did he see blood, but he also felt things crawl across his legs and knives sank into his skin. His fingers itched to wipe away his horrors, but he refused the impulse.

He closed his eyes, took a deep breath, and opened them. The blood was gone, but a man stood on the edge of the river. His burnt-orange robes intensified in the bright sun and his raw skin looked like tendons. He reached out open arms. Salvarias dug his fingernails into his palm. Sansis disappeared. Indeed, Sansis had given Salvarias an insight into his future when he was a mere six years old. He shifted back the sleeve of his robe to see the scar. It now blended with the others.

In need of distraction, he ignited his magic.

His magic greeted him with fondness in its voice. *"My wizard. We are free."*

"We are, my friend."

Relief flooded through him, but it was not his own. It was from his magic. Warmth imbued his blood and confidence built inside him.

"I am surprised we survived, my wizard."

"As am I."

"Are you still angry with me?"

Salvarias swallowed the lump in his throat. *"No, my friend."*

"I am not ready to die. I will continue to protect you, even from yourself."

"*I do not wish to live.*"

"*Ah, but you do not wish to die. My wizard, you are torn in two.*"

"*I am.*"

"*You are with your brother once again. Does that not give you happiness?*"

"*It is all the happiness I have.*"

"*Then focus on that, my wizard.*"

"*I am so tired.*"

"*As am I, but we will become stronger now. The torment has stopped and we both must rest and rebuild our strength. We can explore our boundaries without pain once we are healthy.*"

"*Each time I pushed us near breaking.*"

"*Yes, but each time we succeeded. We have not tapped our full potential yet.*"

"*Dethal knew.*"

"*He did. It is why he kept testing us. It is why he continued your instruction. Although he would have been more effective without his methods of encouragement.*"

"*Indeed. I would have performed the spells willingly. I am addicted to learning, to study, to testing.*"

"*It is why we work so well together, my wizard. I am the same.*"

"*Yet we do not trust each other.*"

There was a long pause before his magic spoke. "*All great things take time. Our situation was not an environment one hopes to have when learning of another's character. I know no more about you than I did a year and a half ago. Allow me to restate that thought. I know your tolerance for pain is unmatched. Otherwise, I know little of you.*"

"*You cared for me. I should trust you.*"

"*My care was selfish. You know this, my wizard. It is why you withhold your trust. I need you. I need to grow. I need to learn. Without you, I cannot. Without you, I do not exist. I kept you from killing yourself for these reasons. I pushed myself beyond what I thought I was capable of to protect your mind.*"

Salvarias glanced at a sword lying on a pack.

"*Yes, my wizard. I cannot protect you if you pick up a weapon. But you have something to live for now. There is determination within you.*"

He turned his gaze to the river. *"I do. I will defeat them. I will kill Dethal. I will kill Sansis. I will circumvent their plans. And I will do so until my last breath."*

"How?"

"Do you not know?"

"I do not. Your mind is a mystery to me, my wizard. There are thoughts that are plain as day while others reside deep beneath muddied waters, well beyond my reach."

Salvarias shivered when the breeze picked up. *"Visions, my friend. I have visions of events yet to come. They provide me direction, give me clues and information. I will use these to thwart their plans."* Salvarias shuddered. *"The evil within me is the same as what is plotting against Arden. I feel it all around me. It is growing more powerful. Each passing day we drift further from the light."*

"How did you discover this?"

"By pushing us to our limits. It opened up my mind. Just as it opened the connection I have with animals."

"I will help you defeat this threat, my wizard."

"Why?"

"Because I feel it too. It scares me."

"I did not think magic could be scared."

"I am scared of not existing, my wizard. If this entity bathes us in terror, I will lose you. That is something I am not willing to have happen. I will fight along your side."

He breathed in the comfort surging up through him. Though he did not trust his magic, the relationship was invaluable. *"Thank you, my friend."*

"I brought you some food."

Salvarias nearly jumped out of his robes. He turned his attention to Lunara.

She offered him a slice of bread. "I'm sorry. I didn't mean to startle you."

He allowed his magic to rest and accepted the food. "Thank you, my Lady."

"May I join you?"

He shifted a step away. "Of course."

Her beauty was unlike any he had ever seen, and in person, surpassed the memories he had of her in their dreams. Her blue-black hair shimmered in the afternoon sun and danced with depth.

Her eyes were a piercing ice blue and her flawless skin the envy of porcelain. She was stunning, and he found it difficult to breathe when near her.

The dresses she had worn in their dreams were the same she wore now, even though traveling. Always they were a solid color, well made, and they lacked the normal thick layers most women preferred. Some fell to the edge of her shoulders with an oval neckline, fitted to a low waist before flowing into a loose bottom. Others were gathered under her bosom, disclosing her lithe body by her movements, and a tasteful V-neck offered the tiniest peek at the mounds of her breasts. Today, it was a fitted lavender gown, which contrasted her black hair, bringing out her red lips and revealing her perfect collarbone.

She smiled her sweet smile that made him want to take a step towards her. It took every ounce of his willpower to stay put.

"We haven't had a calm moment to talk since you were rescued. I wanted to thank you. I know the amount of pain you were in and you continued to fight."

"My brother has told me of you and your sister, my Lady. I thank you for your help."

She stood in silence a moment, nibbling on a slice of bread before she spoke again. "I find our connection most curious."

"As do I."

"I've dreamt of you since I was a little girl. I always thought you were a figment of my imagination."

"My thoughts were the same."

"I haven't dreamt of you since I called you by name."

"Knowing you were real changed our connection."

Her laugh was light and airy. "I miss them. I found our conversations intriguing and oddly comforting."

"Where would we walk in your dreams?"

"Gardens or the forest. Why? Where were we in yours?"

He ignored the question and hid away his jealousy. "How did you know I was real?"

She looked at the trees, her eyes shimmering in the morning sun, her hair lifting in the breeze. His fingers itched to touch the silky strands. "I was forced to flee my home a year ago. The night I left, I had a dream, the same dream I have every night, but the conversation was different. I was asked to find you, to help you."

It was obvious that she had left out certain details, and he contemplated whether he should push her for answers. He also became aware of some sort of odd power within Lunara. Clearly not magic, it intrigued him, lurking unknown even to her.

She inhaled a deep breath and turned her gaze back to him. "I convinced my sister and she agreed to help me look for you. We met your brother in Falar, and I'm sure you know the rest. Do you know how we became connected?"

"I do not, my Lady."

"I've always sensed another presence in my mind, emotions I was not feeling. It was you."

"I did not sense your presence until after I discovered you were real."

"I never feel you in my mind. You've not once tried to read me. Even when you warned me of danger, your mind was outside mine. You could. I wouldn't block you as you've blocked me."

"Your thoughts are your own, my Lady, just as my thoughts are my own."

The rosiest pink touched her cheeks. "I'm not as polite. I'm curious about us. Even now I feel you pushing me away, but I can still sense your pain."

His fears came to fruition.

She stepped closer. "I'm sorry. I'm trying to understand what's happened to us."

He inched further away, uncomfortable at her proximity. She kept trying to peer under his hood, and he wasn't used to such curiosity. The conversation became stressful.

"Why do I make you nervous?"

"My feelings and emotions are my *own*, my Lady. Reading how I feel will not provide answers. I do not like to be near others."

She stepped back. "I'm sorry. You held my hand in our dreams. We... We almost kissed—"

His face burned with embarrassment, and he cut her off. His tone was stern. "The time in our dreams was different. Reality is different. I request that you no longer read my emotions." He had selfishly given his affections when he thought her an imagined being. Her touch did not cause him pain in his dreams because it was not real. He could not be in a relationship with her, could not hold her hand, feel her silky hair, her warmth, or her softness. He could never be close to another besides Wilhelm, and Salvarias accepted his fate. It helped distance others from his evil, keeping them safe and untainted by his touch. He assumed it was why human contact caused him immense pain, as if his fingers seeped darkness and the innocent lashed back. He believed Wilhelm to be immune because they were brothers.

The presence hissed in anger. *"Liesss, my pet. You know eventually you will hurt him."*

"I didn't mean to upset you." She sighed. "You're a mystery to me. I have a gift to read a person's soul. I can sense if someone's intentions are pure or selfish. You're hidden from me."

Salvarias's stomach churned from the horrid thought creeping to the surface. "Are there others you cannot read?" He truly didn't want to hear the answer.

"No. You're the first, and the first I've told of my gift. Not even my sister knows; and I'd prefer others don't find out. Nor the dream I had which told me to find you."

"Of course, my Lady."

They stood in silence, Salvarias deep in thought, trying to understand why, especially with their connection, she could not read him. Then he became perplexed by her "gift." He lowered his hood and locked gazes with her, studying her as he did others he met. Unlike most, she did not shift uncomfortably or try to look away. She returned an equally penetrating stare. Her eyes gave away no secrets as others did and instead held him captive, pulling him into their blue comfort.

The presence spoke the thought he had tried to suppress. *"Ssshe cannot read your sssoul, my pet, becaussse it hidesss from purity. You can sssense her innocccence, her pure intentionsss and pure heart. Your evil sssoul cannot be found by one as untainted as her. Ssshe isss of the light, you are lossst to the darknessss."*

The words struck Salvarias like a blow, and he looked away. He grew tired in one breath, and the conversation wore on his exhausted mind. He rubbed his arm, attempting to drive away the phantom knife from slicing his skin. Warm blood spread across his dressings. He grew lightheaded.

"Are you all right?"

"I... I am..." He could not finish his thought when the forest spun wildly around him. Air no longer existed. He tried to speak, but suddenly the woods disappeared. He was in Zeeas, naked and huddled on the floor in the torture chamber. It had been a dream. He had never been rescued. He curled up against the cold wall. It had all seemed so real.

"There, there, my pet," Sansis said soothingly. "I promise to make it stop if you tell me what wonderful gift you have been given, my mage. Tell me."

Salvarias shook his head. Too weak to move, too weak to scream, and too weak to fight, he allowed the man to provide comfort.

Sansis folded Salvarias close. "I know. I know you suffer."

A raw hand stroked his hair while arms embraced him like he'd always imagined a mother would when calming a frightened child. He was tired and closed his eyes, resting against Sansis. The man's voice rose in a familiar lullaby. The subtle rocking and soothing tone tempted Salvarias into relaxation. He was almost asleep when the knife penetrated his side, sinking with deliberate slowness through skin and muscle. He latched onto Sansis's arm.

"Tell me."

Salvarias knew the torment would not stop even if he revealed the visions that plagued him all hours of the day and night. Sansis's filmy eyes were mad with sadistic pleasure. Salvarias would be prey to the man until his last breath. Salvarias turned his face from Sansis and whispered, "No."

Salvarias exhaled a sob when the knife leisurely withdrew. The man continued his song and soothing rocking while gradually driving the knife into Salvarias's shoulder. The third stab broke through his chest bone, avoiding his heart and lungs. He jerked in pain when the blade withdrew. Sansis's song grew quieter, barely a whisper. Darkness was coming. Salvarias felt it drawing near and he beckoned for his rescue. His fist balled in Sansis's robes when the fourth stab entered Salvarias's stomach. Darkness grew closer while the dagger sawed through his flesh at an agonizing slow speed. He shook violently, shutting his eyes tightly against the pain. Darkness floated within his reach. He extended his mind towards it, but Sansis denied it.

"No, my mage. Stay with me."

Salvarias screamed when he was healed enough to keep him alive.

"Look," Sansis said. "Tell me and I'll put you back together."

Salvarias lowered his heavy head to stare at some part of his insides. "No," he choked, gagging on his own vomit.

Sansis held up an organ. "Shame."

Darkness crept into Salvarias's vision again and Sansis did not prevent it from offering its comfort. Salvarias slipped into nightmarish realms, thankful for the reprieve, but disappointed to be alive.

Wilhelm shook his brother. "Salv!"

Salvarias stared at something far away, not reacting to any around him.

"Help him!" Lunara pleaded.

"You have to wake up. Nothing can hurt you."

Tears streamed down Salvarias's pale cheeks.

Lunara was weeping. "Help him! Please, help him!"

Salvarias passed out. Wilhelm scooped up his brother and turned to Lunara. "What happened?"

"We were just talking. Everything was fine then suddenly he seemed to grow dizzy. His eyes lost focus. He needs sleep. He's exhausted and in..." She looked at Okulu. "He's in so much pain."

Wilhelm said, "What do you mean pain?"

"His wound." Okulu gathered a mortar and pestle, and ground up herbs. "Take him under the overhang and remove his robes. We need to change his dressing."

"He did yesterday."

Okulu added fragrant oil to his mixture. "His blood isn't clotting. He's bleeding through the stitches."

"Why didn't you say something?" Wilhelm said, blanching at Salvarias's blood matted robes that his cloak had concealed.

"He didn't want you to worry and there was nothing we could've done. He needs these herbs." Okulu handed Wilhelm the small bowl. "Have him drink it."

Wilhelm pried his brother's mouth open and dumped the potion down his throat. Salvarias coughed but swallowed.

"He'll be fine now?"

Okulu shrugged. "I hope so. He's lost a lot of blood and is weak. He needs rest and he shouldn't move around. Is he eating?"

Wilhelm thought back through all the meals his brother had since his rescue. "On a good day, he'll eat a bowl of broth, a few vegetables, and a slice or two of bread." Now that Wilhelm said it aloud, he realized it wasn't enough.

Okulu nodded. "You understand. He's not going to get stronger unless he eats at least double that a day."

Humar cleared his throat. "We need to know where to go. This is the last place he said."

Varila cursed. "This is ridiculous. He should tell us what in Nevlar's revenge he's doing."

"The boy will need to trust us eventually," Durak said.

Wilhelm shook his head. To be a good brother meant learning patience. Salvarias required time and acceptance, a pressure-free and loving environment. "He'll tell us when he's ready. Don't push him. I appreciate the help all of you've given us, but you have to understand that Salv is a private person. If you push him, he'll withdraw further."

"What about us?" Varila snapped. "Don't you think we have a right to know if we're risking our necks to help? Whatever force seeks him wouldn't hesitate to kill any one of us to get to him! The least he could do is tell us what he's up to!"

"He asked you not to come. He knows it's dangerous and worries something will happen."

Durak grumbled a curse then said, "The boy isn't right. He's too private, too cold and his eyes—"

"Durak, wait over there," Humar said. After Durak left, Humar turned back to Wilhelm. "I understand what you're saying. But you need to try to get him to talk to us. I can offer help if I know what we're up against, what we're facing."

Okulu shrugged. "Maybe he doesn't know."

Wilhelm wasn't sure. He hadn't pressed Salvarias for information but had a suspicion Okulu was right. "Salv's doing the best he can. I tell you, Humar, push him and he'll leave us all."

The knight ran his fingers through his hair. "I guess we don't have a choice. Work on it for us. I want the boy to feel he can trust us and allow us to help."

Wilhelm turned to the sisters. "Agreed?"

Lunara was quick to agree and nudged her sister. She nodded. "Thanks. It would be better if we were alone when he wakes."

"Of course." Humar led the others away.

Wilhelm lifted his brother around so their backs were to the group. The rolling river soon lulled him into a deep reverie, absently staring at the rushing blue water.

Hours passed before Salvarias screamed. Startled from drowsy thoughts, Wilhelm managed to whisper comforting words through his quickened breathing. Finally, Salvarias's eyes flew open and met Wilhelm's gaze.

"It's all right, Salv. You're safe."

"I am sorry." Salvarias buried his face in his hands, shoulders shaking with silent sobs.

"What happened?"

"I am sorry."

"Don't apologize. Are you all right?"

"What was the first animal I made?"

"A bear."

Salvarias embraced Wilhelm, holding him as if he'd disappear, and his brother's fingers embedded into Wilhelm's shoulders.

"Here." Wilhelm offered the puzzle box and leaned against a pole.

Salvarias accepted the box and curled up as he'd done since childhood. Eventually, he ceased to tremble, and his shoulders relaxed. Moments passed before his hands stopped.

"What is it?"

"A sparrow," Salvarias whispered.

"Why didn't you tell me you were sick?"

Salvarias lowered his head. "I did not want you to worry. There was nothing we could do."

"How do you feel?"

"Tired." Salvarias rested his head on Wilhelm's chest. "But I will be fine."

"We need to know where we're going."

"I do not want them to come. They should leave now."

"They want to help though." Wilhelm gathered a blanket around his brother. "We need them. For me, Salv."

Salvarias sighed. "Serinity. We are heading for Serinity. The city will be attacked and we must help."

Wilhelm's gaze jerked to his brother. "Attacked by what?"

"I am not sure."

"Can we tell them?"

"I worry for their safety."

"They're talented. You know Humar is skilled with a sword, Okulu is nearly as good, and so is Varila. Durak can take care of himself."

"And Lunara?"

Wilhelm shrugged. "Varila looks after her."

"So be it."

He waited until Salvarias collapsed the puzzle box, and set his emotions. After a nod, Wilhelm helped Salvarias turn around and motioned the group over.

Once they all gathered, Wilhelm said, "We're heading to Serinity."

Lunara's eyes widened. "That's our home."

Salvarias raised his head. "Do you know the ruling lord?"

"I do," Lunara confirmed.

Varila uttered an oath. "We can't go back to the city."

Salvarias locked his gaze on Lunara. "How do you know the ruling lord?"

Lunara's cheeks flushed. "He's claimed me for his wife, as is his right. We fled the night before I was to wed him."

Wilhelm frowned when his brother tensed.

"We can't go back, mage," Varila growled. "He'll force her to marry him, and I've spent the last year making sure that doesn't happen. I snuck out with her in the middle of the night. I left behind my parents, my home. I've dodged soldiers in every town we've stopped in."

Salvarias shook his head. "I must go there."

Varila's jaw clenched. "The ruling lord is a vile man, mage. Whatever you seek from him will be near impossible to obtain unless it comes at a direct benefit to him. Or new tapestries for his damn house."

"The city is in danger. We must persuade the lord to mount a defense."

"I'll take you. Lunara will stay behind. The lord won't be easily persuaded, but my family can help. My father knows the lord, too."

Salvarias paused, and then turned to Lunara. "Your relationship with the lord might prove valuable."

Humar intercepted Varila when she advanced towards Salvarias, whispering something Wilhelm couldn't hear. Though Lunara was like a sister, he had no doubts Salvarias would never allow harm to come to any of the companions. The others had yet to learn that, and by their expressions and the slight slump of his brother's shoulders, none trusted Salvarias.

Lunara smoothed her dress and tossed her hair aside, straightening herself. "Salvarias is correct. I won't hide when I can help our home. If mother and father are in danger, we must do all we can to aid them."

Varila cursed. "This is ridiculous. How do you know the city is in danger?"

"Don't ask questions," Wilhelm said. "Again, if anyone doesn't want to come, they can remain behind."

Varila's eyes were fiery when she strode away. Lunara paled and joined her sister. Salvarias sighed and curled up against Wilhelm, falling asleep in a matter of a few breaths.

Humar squatted next to them. "I sent letters in Acklar for your uncle. I saw him crawling out of the river when the fighting had ended. I'm sure he's safe. When we reach Serinity, I'll send some more letters telling him where we are."

"Thanks," Wilhelm said.

Humar nodded and left to join Okulu.

Wilhelm tightened his embrace and turned his gaze to the river. He'd always loved Serinity. He smiled to himself. At least now he could visit again.

Salvarias rested his head on Wilhelm's arm while the rolling river mesmerized him into a daydream. The potion Okulu whipped up every morning was working brilliantly. After two days, Salvarias's blood was already thickening.

He ate his food with the others, and though full, he forced down a slice of bread.

Okulu cleared his throat. "Your brother claims you're the youngest mage in history."

Salvarias pulled himself from his trance and corrected the merc. "The youngest recorded. There could be others who are not known to the Association."

"I've traveled quite a bit and haven't heard of one younger than seventeen. By now, you must be powerful."

"I have not been given many peaceful opportunities to study at length."

"I was wondering where your spell book was."

"I do not have one."

Okulu's brow furrowed. "Never?"

"No."

Humar interrupted, helping himself to another portion of dried pork. "You had it stolen when you and Wilhelm were taken by the creatures."

"It was my mother's book."

"She never allowed you your own?" Okulu asked. "It's like a rite of passage with mages."

Salvarias shifted. "Would you please pass the carrots?"

Humar obliged and Salvarias remained quiet. He meant it as a diversion and he only took a small portion. Food seemed to brim up to his throat.

"You know you're not eating enough," Okulu muttered.

Salvarias found the merc to be an interesting character. The man appeared drunk at all times but possessed an observing nature that contradicted the number of swigs taken from his flask. Okulu also had knowledge of magic exceeding even that of Wilhelm. Salvarias chose not to respond, and Lunara offered a distraction when she set her book aside, turning her attention to the group.

"I see you finally decided to join us," Varila said sardonically.

"I finished it." Lunara turned her gaze to Salvarias. "It was Gyrvark's account of the minotaur wars. I believe you've read it, have you not?"

"I have, my Lady." He twitched at a sensation of scratchy feet crawling on his leg.

Lunara smoothed her dress. "Quiet graphic. A contradiction to the minotaur Yuvdur accounts."

"Indeed."

"Which do you believe?"

His voice was no more than a whisper—he had become

hypnotized by the prism of color the setting sun cast upon her hair. "Neither and both. Most accounts hold truth and fiction. Unless one was present, we may never know which parts are accurate."

She smiled her sweet smile. "Wise assessment."

"Up for a little practice tomorrow, Wilhelm?" Okulu asked.

"Sure."

"I'll join you," Humar offered.

"Aye, count me in, lad," Durak said.

Humar looked over the river. "This rocking boat is the perfect training ground. Great for balance."

Suddenly, white light flared in front of Salvarias, blocking out his companions and surroundings; it felt as if he were floating in a thick, white fog. Familiar with his visions now, he patiently surveyed the space. In the distance, a figure walked towards him. While he waited for it to approach, he checked behind him. Seeing nothing, he turned back to find the figure directly in front of him, towering at least two heads taller than Salvarias.

It was covered in matted black fur, and an oozing, tar-like acid secreted from its skin, sizzling in the air when it dripped from its body. Its head was shaped like a tiger, and the eyes... Salvarias shuddered. Red eyes shadowed with a senseless hunger stared back at him. It opened its mouth in a twisted grin to show fangs glistening with thick saliva. Salvarias took a step back, stumbling over something in the white fog. The creature grabbed his shoulders. Long claws punctured his skin and the pain reached his bones. The liquid dripping from its skin ate away his flesh, and the noxious odor of tar permeated the air.

He recognized the creature from his readings in Dethal's home. Blackfurs. Fierce creatures that had no concern for life—their own or others. They were unleashed in droves on armies to weaken front lines, lighting their tar-covered bodies aflame so they could wreak havoc even as they died.

The light flared and then blinked out, and his surroundings charged towards him. Familiar arms held him steady.

Wilhelm's voice shook. "Are you all right?"

"Yes." Salvarias breathed hard from the pain in his lungs and sank to the deck. He didn't remember rising.

Wilhelm fetched water and Salvarias drank between breaths.

"I am fine." Salvarias gave his brother a reassuring pat.

"What did you see?" Humar asked.

"I must rest," Salvarias mumbled. "Pleasant night." He limped to his bedroll. Once he settled into his blankets, Adok sprawled against his back. Salvarias drifted to sleep, the rocking of the riverboat soothing, and the missing puzzle piece to his vision plugging a hole that had plagued him for weeks. Now he knew what threatened Serinity, and in the one touch he had experienced with the blackfur, knowledge was granted on how to defeat them.

Chapter 23
Spring 1018 a.r.

Wilhelm stepped off the river barge with his arm wrapped around Salvarias, gaze rolling over ferns that littered the ground, rocks caked with moss, and trees that challenged the sun for their place in the sky. Home. The niche in the Cattlar Mountains where Falar, Serinity and Hadrium were located flourished with the thickest woods in all of Arden. Anywhere among the familiar redwood trees would be home for Wilhelm. He needed no city, no bed, and no building to have the sense of returning someplace that warmed his soul.

The tension in Salvarias's shoulders melted and his stern expression softened to one of bliss. Wilhelm squeezed his brother. Things would be better now. They were home, they were together, and soon they would begin their lives. All that stood in their way was an attack on the tranquil city of Serinity.

"It's a half day's walk to Serinity," Varila said, eyeing Salvarias. "We'll get there right before dinner."

Wilhelm nodded, lifting his wheezing brother more than normal. The area surrounding the dock sported a handful of stone dwellings, and one old man standing outside a stone home, eyeing the group when they entered the thick woods.

"How long are we staying in Serinity?" Durak growled.

"At least two weeks," Salvarias responded.

Durak nodded. "I'll make a trip to Falar. Ye boys have a sizable stash of money at the smithy."

"Thanks," Wilhelm said. "I hoped we might."

"Aye, a good amount." Durak moved to walk next to Okulu.

Once they were alone, Salvarias asked, "Do you trust Humar?"

"I do." Wilhelm flicked back his brother's hood and ruffled his hair. A strong elbow to Wilhelm's ribs made him grin. "Humar looked for us the entire time we were in the slave camps, he found Mafarias after you were taken, traveled with me to find you, and was first to offer his help. He's smart, and is set on discovering the truth about what's going on in Dalnar."

Salvarias's eyes distanced and his lips moved in silent conversation. Wilhelm took the time to admire new spring flowers and breathe in the freshness of life. Salvarias raised his hood and the silent conversation was replaced by whispered numbers, broken only by a call to Humar. For the second time in Salvarias's life, he was trusting another besides Wilhelm.

Once Humar was by their side, Salvarias slowed and whispered so only Wilhelm and the knight could hear. "There are creatures that will attack Serenity. An army of them, but I know how to defeat them. We must persuade Serenity to mount a defensive force to protect the residents. The city can be defended and the creatures *easily* defeated *if* the lord listens to us. You know no one will adhere to the advice of a mage, Humar. I ask for your help. You must convince the ruling lord."

Humar smiled. "I'll convince him. Varila and Lunara can assist us with the ruling lord." Humar stared after the two sisters. "Very wealthy girls. The armor and sword Varila carries is expensive enough to buy Falar. I'm sure her father will have enough pull with the ruling lord."

"Yes, I noticed," Salvarias said.

Humar looked surprised. "How do you know about armor?"

"I studied proper smithy from the books in my former master's home. And I listened to the instruction provided to my brother by Durak."

Humar grinned. "You're a wealth of information, boy. Don't worry, I'll convince this Lord Gunder. It's rumored he's easily manipulated and another practically runs the city."

Wilhelm scratched his beard. "I hadn't heard."

Humar nodded. "The rumor is that another directs the city while—let me see if I can recite it from memory—'Lord Gunder purchases extravagant tapestries for his lavish home.'" Humar grinned. "I'm sure Gunder will be a delight. But, whoever this other person might be, he's skilled in orchestrating a city and stern. The citizens are polite, crime low, and the streets are sparkling clean. No slaves are owned, and women have as many rights as men."

Wilhelm grunted in surprise. "That's not in line with other cities."

"Indeed. Serenity is quite the contrast to every other city in all of

Arden. Castration meets any man who forces himself upon a woman, and no whores are permitted. To be privileged to live in Serinity, one has to bring a skill, a trade, or there has to be an opening at a wealthy home for a servant. No homeless are allowed, no thieves tolerated, and peace is enforced with a swift hand. Whoever runs the city is compassionate and intelligent, but doesn't live in a delusion." Humar shook his head. "Not all the weak can be helped, not all the beaten rescued. Reality is cruel."

Wilhelm watched a squirrel hopping from tree to tree, its gaze locked on Salvarias. "Do you know the man?"

"I don't, but it could be only rumors. Who knows? Gunder might be the true ruler. Merchants spread more rumors than fish wives. I hope the sisters' father can offer information." Humar shrugged. "It will be difficult to convince them of an army that none of their scouts have seen."

Salvarias nodded. "Indeed, but I have no other information. The attack is meant as a surprise, to catch the city off guard. I do not understand why they are choosing to attack Serinity."

Humar rubbed his cheek. "The city is wealthy. Maybe they're looking for funds."

"I do not think the darkness breeding in this world is seeking wealth." Salvarias clenched his fist. "There is something I am missing."

"One step at a time," Humar said. "Let's focus on saving the city. Maybe something will be given away during the attack, or we might be able to question one of the creatures."

"Perhaps."

Salvarias glanced at the squirrel, a sparkle lighting his eye, and Wilhelm grinned. He truly had the most amazing brother.

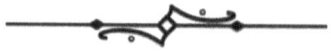

Salvarias gazed at Adok padding around Lunara, tail wagging enthusiastically, sneaking wet kisses. Her laughter filled the morning air and lifted Salvarias's spirits. He crested the hill and the city of Serinity came into view. It looked as it had in his visions, but without the fires and maimed bodies. A towering wall near five stories high protected the city and a single massive gate broke the miles of solid gray rock. Homes and shops ascended a high cliff, which ended abruptly at the sea, offering a dramatic drop into the thundering ocean.

Varila pointed towards the largest castle-like home perched at the very edge of the cliff. "The classes rise up the hill on the outcropping over the ocean. You can see Lord Gunder's home at the top. Our father's estate is directly below."

Okulu sighed. "I love Serinity. Always so pleasant. No one will spit on you here, Salvarias."

Humar ran his hand through his hair. "I'm not sure of the best way to get into the city. There's only one entrance, and I'd prefer not to have any questioning Salvarias."

Varila glowered at the knight. "I'll handle it."

When the group approached the gate, Varila hid Lunara behind Wilhelm before moving to the front.

"Name, mage," a guard called.

Salvarias noticed Okulu maneuvered near, resting a hand on the hilt of his sword. Anger glittered in his eyes.

"Kredre," Varila greeted. "Good to see you."

The guard's eyes widened and he bowed deeply. "My Lady."

Okulu chuckled. Varila cast the merc a sneer.

"Your father will be interested in your return, my Lady. Are you sure you would like entry into the city? The, uh, circumstances within haven't changed."

"I'm aware. We have no choice. Please, forget you saw us. And we know the mage, no need to ask nor remember he passed through here."

"Of course, my Lady."

"Thanks." Varila continued onward through the gate.

The streets were scrubbed clean and each building had its own small garden. Larger public gardens with benches for reading in the sun were situated every few homes and broke up the monotony that plagued other cities. A breeze swept over the city, bringing with it the brininess of the ocean to mingle with roasted meats, spiced breads, and sweet pies. Talented bards sang in gardens and children huddled around, enraptured by the stories. Salvarias sighed in content and thought that if he ever had his dream home or shop, it would be in Serinity.

Gray clouds moved in from the north and the breeze turned to a gust as the group continued through the main streets towards the crest of the cliff. He shifted his cloak tighter and smiled inwardly when Wilhelm pulled him closer. As always, Wilhelm seeped warmth, and Salvarias felt lighter and safe, the pain in his knee reduced and air entered his lungs easier. He pondered whether his brother's arm possessed healing capabilities.

When the group reached the sisters' home, Salvarias fell in love at first sight. The estate's stone walls soared against the darkening sky, upstaging the ruling lord of Falar, and towered above the companions. Flowers poured over urns and flanked the stairs leading to the main entrance. Manicured hedges lined paths that weaved around the estate, and birds whistled in the towering trees. Dense ivy scaled the gray home, warming the cold stone, and white jasmine perfumed the air. A courtyard bustled with well fed and, by their clothes, well-paid servants who gushed over the sisters while taking packs and offering water.

A voice boomed from the entrance. "What's happened? Why are you back?"

A man emerged. He was near Salvarias's height with a cheerful face covered in a closely trimmed thick beard. The man's tunic and trews were simple but tailored to enhance his broad shoulders and muscular build. His rich brown hair was pulled back at the sides and front to display his inviting eyes and smile.

"Father," Varila said. "We bring urgent news."

He seemed oblivious to his daughter's tone. "We've been so worried!" Lunara ran to him and he enfolded both sisters in his arms, tears flowing down his cheeks. "Why did you return? What's happened?"

"We need to talk," Varila said.

A woman burst through the door. She wore an intricate gown that flattered her tall, thin physique. She carried herself with the air of someone brought up in nobility, dignified and poised. Chestnut hair held ornate braids and small white flowers decorated them. Tears streamed down her face, and she ran to Varila and Lunara and hugged them close. "Thank the gods you're safe!"

Varila pulled away from her parents. "These are the brothers I wrote you about, Wilhelm and Salvarias Laybryth. This is Humar, Durak, and Okulu." Varila smiled at the group. "This is my father, Edium, and my mother, Talura."

Edium greeted all warmly, except for Salvarias, who was skillfully evaded, and Salvarias obliged with artful avoidance.

Edium smiled. "Please, come in! Dine with us. I'll have quarters set up for each of you. Clean up and we'll meet again at dinner." He wrapped an arm around each daughter, kissing their foreheads, and led them into the house.

Salvarias felt a pang of jealousy at the father's love and joy.

The presence scoffed. *"You do not need hisss love. You know what would happen ssshould he give it. Do not allow him near you."*

He agreed with the voice. Tobin's words "you are no son of mine" were carried on the gusty breeze.

Talura shifted near. "Hello."

He bowed and resisted an unexplainable urge to flee. "Hello, my Lady."

"Allow me to show you to your quarters." Talura reached to take his arm.

He flinched away. "I am sure you have other matters to attend to, my Lady."

"Nonsense. You've been traveling with my daughters for two seasons?"

He picked up his pace in hopes of ending the tortuous event and fought his need to scream for his brother, who was engaged in a conversation with Okulu. "I have only recently met them, my Lady, within the past month."

"Wilhelm would not help you if you called. He left you alone with your mother, my pet. Thisss woman offersss the sssame kindnessss in her eyesss as Tobin. Sssteer clear, very clear of thessse two. Remember Tobin, remember hisss wordsss. Remember your mother, remember her beatingsss."

Salvarias remembered.

"Forgive me. It was your brother who she's traveled with for nearly half a year, correct?"

He doubted the sincerity of her error. "Yes, my Lady." He gritted his teeth from the pain in his knee when he climbed the stairs.

"She told me she was helping to find you. I'm happy to learn of your recovery."

"Thank you, my Lady."

Talura stopped at a door. "This room will be yours. Fresh water will be brought each morning."

"Thank you." Salvarias bowed and entered his room.

She reached out a hand. Suddenly his mother stood in front of him. Her eyes were wild with fear and determination, and she clutched a board, ready to strike.

"Drive away your evil!" she screamed.

Salvarias stumbled back, tripping over something that dug into his thigh, and toppled to the floor. As he fell, she brought down the board. The wood struck him and splinters pierced his skin. He raised his arm to protect his head and curled up in a ball to hide his ribs.

"Release your evil, monstrosity!"

"Please, I am trying." He curled up tighter when the board struck him again.

"You are not, son of darkness!" his mother yelled.

"Salv!" Wilhelm called.

Salvarias looked up to see his brother walk through the apparition of their mother, and her form disappeared in a wisp. Wilhelm's arms encased Salvarias.

"Are you all right, Salv? What happened?"

Embarrassed, realizing he'd relived a memory, he averted his eyes from the intense stare of Talura. "I tripped, brother."

"What were you saying?" Wilhelm pulled Salvarias back to look into his eyes.

"I..." He could not think of what to say.

"So much furniture in the room." Talura laughed lightly. "I should have the servants remove this clutter. He was apologizing, Wilhelm. I assure you, Salvarias, none is needed. I'll see you both at dinner." She curtsied and left the room.

Wilhelm lifted Salvarias upright. "You're sure you're all right? Your heart is about ready to explode from your chest."

"Yes, I am fine." He took a deep breath and tried to gain control over his strangled lungs.

Wilhelm grinned before moving the furniture. Salvarias was grateful his brother never questioned anything and obliged the odd quirks Salvarias required. Since he could remember, he had slept in a bed nestled in a corner. The walls provided safety from hands that reached for him in the darkness. He only had to watch two directions instead of four.

Once done, Wilhelm draped an arm over Salvarias's shoulders. "I'm starving."

Salvarias accepted his brother's headlock and followed him down the stairs. The group gathered in a dining hall that felt surprisingly cozy for such an expansive estate. The table was set with place settings close together, leaving half the table unoccupied. Candles lit the room and windows allowed views of the thunderstorm rolling in from the ocean.

Salvarias suppressed a smile when Wilhelm's stomach rumbled. Fresh roasts of venison and chicken filled silver platters, ripe fruits and luxurious vegetables spilled over bowls, and cheeses covered several plates, surrounded by flavored breads. Steaming pots of vegetable stew and oats caught his eye and he realized how hungry he was when he sat next to his brother.

Edium accepted a plate of food from his wife. "So, what tidings do you bring?"

Salvarias glanced around and realized no servants tended to dinner. Lady Talura plated her family's meal and allowed the others to serve themselves. It felt homey.

Humar cleared his throat. "Pardon the abrupt explanation, Gentleman Edium, but we believe an army of creatures is planning an attack against the city. And it'll take place in two weeks time. We'd like your help in arranging an audience with Lord Gunder to inform him of all we know."

Edium's eyes opened wide and he turned to Varila. "Do you expect this to be true?"

Varila's gaze shifted from Salvarias to Wilhelm before she shrugged. "Yes, Father. I do. We need to meet weasel-faced Gunder tomorrow." She chewed on the leg of a chicken.

Edium furrowed his eyebrows at Okulu before turning to Humar. "Pardon my skepticism, but Serinity is well patrolled. I'd like to think the guards would know of such an army."

Humar offered an apologetic look. "We don't know. I can't explain how the army has eluded scouts."

"Please, Father," Lunara said. "We must help."

Edium stared at his plate, seeming to wait for the food to provide direction. "So be it. We'll all go tomorrow."

Lunara smiled sweetly. "I think it best only Humar, Salvarias, you, and I attend, Father."

Salvarias met Edium's gaze.

The man's eyes narrowed. "I don't think a mage is the best idea."

"You sssee his hatred already. He judgesss you quickly. Imagine if he knew of the evil."

Lunara shook her head. "Salvarias knows how to kill the beasts, Father. His advice is valuable. Humar has tactical knowledge to aid the generals."

Salvarias moved his gaze to Humar, who shifted under the inspection. Salvarias was not sure if he was upset that Humar had shared the information with the others in their party. He had told Humar, not Lunara. Salvarias did not trust that his companions were not allied with the darkness. Except of course Durak. And Wilhelm. Humar. Salvarias turned away. Now that he thought about it, he did trust his group, but he would still be cautious. Too much knowledge could put them in danger as well.

Varila turned an angry look on Lunara. "And why you?"

Lunara smoothed her dress and lifted her head high. "To offer an incentive for his cooperation."

Varila sprang from her chair. "I don't think so."

Edium rose from his seat. "And I quite agree!"

Talura took Lunara's hand. "Think of what you're doing, my dear."

Lunara's voice was curt. "So now you all command me as well? Am I allowed to make any decisions regarding my future?"

The table grew silent.

Salvarias caught Lunara's gaze and saw the fear and repulsion she tried to hide. He turned from her and resumed eating.

Edium was silent for a long moment. "All right. We'll go after breakfast tomorrow."

Humar ran his hand through his hair. "I've heard that another protects the city. I hope I don't offend when I say that Lord Gunder is rumored to care for his tapestries versus the welfare of the city. Again, I certainly don't want to offend."

Edium chuckled. "I hold no love for Gunder and would sooner leap with joy at his death than Veedran himself. The man is vile and doesn't care for the city. You're correct. Another watches over the day-to-day proceedings and security of Serinity. But an attack of this magnitude will need to be discussed with Gunder himself."

Humar nodded. "Perhaps we should meet with this other man first and gain his support."

Edium grinned. "You just did."

Salvarias looked at Edium with surprise.

Edium laughed. "You should see your faces! I know I don't fit the demeanor of a duke; but come now, you have to wipe away the shocked stares. I'll think you rude."

Humar smiled and joined in Edium's laugh. "I appreciate your support."

"I've decided I like you. Though you're a little well mannered for a mercenary. Speaking of that, you're the first Loutsil knight I've heard of to turn to mercenary work."

Humar grinned, secrecy sparkling in his eyes. "Perhaps. You're an observant one."

Edium's gaze switched to each member of the group. "I traveled nearly all of Dalnar when I was a merchant. I learned how to read people. Where do you hail from, Okulu? I'm finding it difficult to place your armor, Sir Knight."

Okulu grinned, taking a long swig from his flask. "Whoever said I was a knight?"

Edium laughed. "Your armor."

Okulu winked. "It lies."

Salvarias excused himself and left for his chambers. He knew why Lunara was willing to sacrifice her freedom. She was selfless in her concern for her family and the people of Serinity. However, she should not marry Lord Gunder. Yes, use her relationship with him as leverage to spark him into action, but not marry. Salvarias paced, searching for the clue he was missing. He felt confident in her safety, yet the events were turning in an unanticipated direction, and he worried that he had committed a fatal error in allowing Lunara to help.

The next day, Salvarias entered the carriage that would take them to Lord Gunder. Lunara wore an ornate, bright green dress that cinched her torso, cut deep at her chest, and then expanded at her waist to a full skirt, nearly taking up half the carriage. Her hair was pulled back with decorative flowers and intricate braids. Salvarias preferred the simple dresses that danced loosely around her slender frame, and it appeared she did as well. She shifted nonstop and seemed self-conscious in the revealing, low-cut dress.

When they arrived at Lord Gunder's garish estate, Salvarias understood Lunara's choice of attire. The lord's castle was more flamboyant than her dress. Floral tapestries hung from the walls in obnoxious hues of bright green and pink. The ornately carved furniture seemed in competition with the gaudy fabric. Walking through the home, every room carried conflicting color schemes, as if someone had thrown up a myriad of meals at once. Emerging into the study, they found Lord Gunder wearing a green outfit that contrasted the green in his study. His features were neither overly unhandsome nor marred by winkles. If it were not for the streaks of gray in his red hair and the maturity in his eyes, Salvarias would have assumed the man closer to Wilhelm's age. Gunder's pointy nose and receding chin were what earned his weasel-face title from Varila.

Salvarias found nothing to fault in Gunder until Lunara entered. All pretenses dropped, and a sickening hunger rose in his eyes as they seemed to undress her. Greed, lust, and selfishness were all Salvarias saw in the ruling lord. He was repulsive. Salvarias wanted to set the man on fire and cut off the spell before it was fully said.

"My Lunara!" Lord Gunder glided to the young woman's side and snatched her hand. "You've returned to me. We've been worried for your safety."

Lunara curtsied, withdrawing her hand from his grasp. "My Lord."

Gunder did not mask his veiled threat when he said, "I certainly hope you didn't flee."

Edium's bow was curt. "Of course she didn't, my Lord. I told you she was kidnapped outside the city. Varila has been looking for her, and these people aided in her rescue."

Lord Gunder glanced at Humar and then Salvarias. "Interesting. It's good to see you, Edium."

"My Lord," Edium said stiffly. "We bring word of an imminent attack against the city."

"Lord Gunder." Humar bowed. "We believe creatures commanded by an unknown force are mounting an offense against the city. We come to respectfully urge you to raise the defenses."

Lord Gunder put his arm around Lunara's shoulders and led her to his long desk, positioning her behind his chair like a trophy.

Sitting, he motioned the men to take seats in front of him. There were two chairs and Salvarias remained in the back, arms in his sleeves, hood pulled low. Lunara held her head high, defiance in her expression. Her courage impressed him. He would have vomited if Gunder had touched him.

"Tell me how you learned of this supposed attack. My scouts have reported nothing."

"My Lord," Humar said. "We know the creatures hide in secrecy. We expect their forces to be ready in two weeks. You must make haste."

"Two weeks?" Lord Gunder pondered a moment. "I don't believe you. I'll not launch a defense."

"Please, my Lord." Lunara rested a hand on Gunder's shoulder. "I swear to you what they speak of is true."

"No, my dear Lunara, I won't. I don't believe this to be true. If the attack is two weeks away, we'd be aware of the threat. The army would've been spotted." Lord Gunder scowled at Humar. "And I don't appreciate your superior tone."

"I meant no offense, Gentleman—" Humar started.

"You will address me as Lord!" Gunder roared.

"Please, my Lord," Lunara said. "Raise the defenses as... as a wedding gift to me." Lunara's face paled and Salvarias worried she might faint.

Lord Gunder rose and grabbed her waist, pulling her close. "Truly? You'll willingly marry me?"

She managed a smile and a nod.

Humar had risen, ready to steer Lunara from her path, but Salvarias moved to his side and spoke before the knight. "A wedding to celebrate your victory, my Lord." He bowed deeply to Gunder. "The creatures will be easily defeated. I suspect your victory and marriage will come within fifteen days."

"I do not think we need to wait." Gunder looked at Lunara's figure with lustful hunger in his eyes.

Salvarias resisted the urge to ignite the man and instead frowned. "My Lord deserves a grand wedding. With the preparations required, I fear you will not receive the attention you richly deserve."

The Lord frowned.

"A man of your character, of your noble charm, should not settle for a second-rate wedding." Salvarias gestured at the tapestries.

"Obviously, your taste is impeccable. Please accept my humble apology. I should not doubt your decisions."

Lord Gunder regarded Salvarias and then said, "I accept your apology. However, I don't want to rush the preparations for the grand event. We'll wait."

Salvarias, head bowed, filled his voice with admiration. "Your Lordship's skill on the battlefield is well known in Dalnar. I look forward to witnessing a *true* warrior fight for his city and his love."

Lord Gunder puffed himself up. "Yes, you shall. I hadn't thought to join the battle, but it would do well for my betrothed to know she's marrying a strong, honorable warrior."

"Indeed, my Lord," Salvarias said.

Humar's mouth gaped open, staring at Salvarias, but he ignored the knight. This felt right. And Salvarias had learned to trust his instincts.

"Call in my generals!" Gunder yelled. "And you, my Lunara, must prepare yourself. Fifteen days, we'll marry. Have the servants start the wedding preparations." He kissed her on the cheek and then shoved her away.

Lunara curtsied and glanced at Salvarias before she left. Anger was plainly conveyed in her eyes.

Humar and the generals discussed the defense of the city while Salvarias supplied information on the tar-covered creatures and how fire could turn into their ally instead of their enemy.

Humar ran a hand through his hair. "Our last concern is the farmlands."

Gunder waved his hand. "Leave them to fend for themselves. I grow tired of this conversation."

Edium's fist clenched. "But with summer coming, my Lord, the loss of crops could be detrimental to our citizen's well-being."

Humar's eyes lit with anger. "The farmers should at least be evacuated, warned!"

"This is my city, Humar! You forget your place. Now leave. I must prepare for my wedding."

Humar stormed from the room and down the hallway, cursing loudly. Salvarias kept up with difficulty. "The man is a fool! And you!" Humar rounded on Salvarias. "What are you thinking, pushing Lunara on that man?"

"She volunteered, Humar. Do not displace your anger."

"You didn't have to offer up a wedding date either!" Humar roared.

Edium was deathly pale and did not speak.

Chapter 24
Spring 1018 a.r.

Edium strolled his gardens in the crisp night air, brooding about the past few days' events. The mere thought of Lunara marrying Gunder caused his stomach to clench. Yet again, his daughter was in danger, and adding to his stress was a mysterious attack that seemed scheduled according to an equally mysterious mage. Edium plopped down on a bench and rested his head in his hands.

"Edium."

Edium jumped. "Dammit, Unbril, don't sneak up on a man."

"Of course." Unbril bowed mockingly.

The general had switched from his armor to a tailored, deep gray doublet and trews. His silvery hair and beard sparkled in the moonlight.

Unbril grinned. "I forgot how jumpy we become with old age."

"Yes, we always have to look for the next danger."

"If what I've heard is correct, you've found it."

"You've heard it right." Edium rose to join the general for a walk.

"Lunara can't marry him, Edium."

Edium smiled at his closest friend; a man he'd come to love as a brother. Therefore, his daughters had become Unbril's nieces. "I agree completely. Be happy you never had a daughter."

Unbril chortled. "Sometimes I am, sometimes I'm not. Times such as these remind me that girls are more difficult to raise. But when I see her with you, I feel the pang of not having an equally attentive child. Boys tend to be distant and less affectionate."

"Brice is a good kid."

Pride rang in Unbril's voice when he said, "Brice is an amazing son. I suspect within the next two or so years I'll have him test for knighthood."

"I've seen his skill. I'm not sure you need to wait that long."

"I want to be sure he's ready. He's still young."

Lunara appeared on the other side of the garden.

"Over here," Edium called.

His daughter's smile beamed through the dark night, and she skipped in their direction. When she saw Unbril, she bolted into a run.

"Uncle Unbril!" she cried, flying into the man's open arms.

"My dear Lunara." Unbril spun her around. "How are you, child?"

"Fine." She wiggled from his arms and gave him a once over. "You need to eat more, Uncle."

Unbril grinned. "I haven't received my little reminders."

"I'll have to start those up again. Mother is looking for you, Father."

"Tell her I'll be along in a moment." Edium accepted his daughter's hug.

"I've missed you so much," she whispered.

Edium squeezed her gently. "I've missed you, too."

After giving Unbril another hug and a kiss on the cheek, Lunara strolled back towards the estate, picking flowers along the way.

Unbril sighed. "And now is when I feel my jealousy."

"When your son is knighted, I'll feel mine."

"I assume they haven't accepted your pleas to allow Varila to test?"

"No, they haven't. She could beat any of them."

"Ha! I have no doubt, my friend. She's bested me more times than I care to count. By the way, per your request, I've sent word to Falar. I'm working with a guard named Idolar. He's rumored to be friends with Durak and Wilhelm. Salvarias isn't known well by any. I'm trying to gather additional information, but it's scarce."

"Whatever you can find out, I want to know."

"Why the curiosity?"

"When you see the way Varila watches Wilhelm, you'll know."

"No!"

He laughed. "Indeed. She can't keep her eyes off him, and he apparently has the same issue."

"I never thought that vixen would show interest in a man for longer than a few days."

"I feared the same. Now that she has, I have a new fear. The boy seems like a walking, open book of emotion. I see everything he feels cross his face and I find it hard to believe he's as altruistic as he looks. I want to be sure he has no skeletons in his cellar."

"I wish you weren't so trusting," Unbril said sarcastically.

"It's the whole daughter thing again. Love can be blinding."

"Understood." Unbril stopped at the steps to the estate. "The mage you asked about sought entrance into our city a day and a half ago. When we turned him away, Dethal paced outside the walls for an entire day, cursing, throwing his hands up and cursing some more. He camped outside the city and rose early. Here's the odd part: Our men saw him walk the perimeter of the fields and they could've sworn he was dropping something. They checked, but found nothing. After he was done, he disappeared into the woods. Our trackers lost him."

"Interesting." Edium stared at the star-littered sky. "Very interesting indeed. I don't suppose we'll have to worry about him, but make sure the order still stands. He's never to be allowed in Serinity. From what Varila told me—and oddly she was conservative with information—this is not a man we want in our city."

"As you wish."

He frowned. "And find a mage to consult with. I want to know if they can find anything in the field."

"I already did," Unbril said. "They found nothing."

"He had to have had a purpose."

"I had the mage go to the field, Edium. He looked for hours and found nothing."

Edium grunted, unconvinced. "One last thing: The night before the wedding, my family will be leaving Serinity."

Unbril stiffened.

Edium cast a rueful smile. "Come now, did you honestly think I'd allow her to marry him? No one, not even my wife knows of my plans. If she knew, she'd be spending every breath crying and saying goodbye to the servants. I want to make it as painless as possible for her. You need to know, though. You're next in line to be commander over the army here, and I owe you at least the knowledge of my departure."

"Is there no other way?"

He shook his head. "Unless Gunder succumbs to the illness of death, then no. We won't be able to remain in Dalnar. Maybe Windlous. I'm not sure yet."

"Anything you need, I'll give you." Unbril laid a hand on

Edium's shoulder. "You understand Gunder will hunt you till death."

"My children are my life. This is my home and I love this city, but I'll be damned if that man will take her. I'll find a way to keep her safe."

"I understand. It's been an honor."

"We'll say goodbye later." Edium shook off his mood. "I'll let you know what we'll need when the time draws closer."

"Can I ask why now? Why didn't you leave when Gunder first claimed her?"

He chuckled. "I had every intention of leaving. Varila and I planned it all out. She was going to hide Lunara for six months while I discreetly closed my businesses and sold off the estate. Then Talura and I would sneak out of Serinity and meet up with her to find some other place to live. But then I received Varila's letters telling me to delay our plans. She said they were wrapped up in helping find a young man. I trusted her, so I waited."

"I see."

Edium smiled at Unbril. "I would've given you ample notice. Just as I am now."

"I thank you for that, but it doesn't ease my sorrow. I'll pray to our godless sky each night for Gunder's death."

"As will I, my friend."

Salvarias slipped out of his room in the first hour of daylight, scrounged up breakfast, and carried it to the gardens. He avoided running into any companions, taking odd routes through the mansion. The others were upset by his conversation with Gunder and he did not blame them. But he preferred not to see their hateful stares or hear their whispered words of anger.

He chose a bench overlooking the crashing sea and pulled his cloak close to ward off the chill morning breeze caressing the cliffside. Adok took a nap on his feet, keeping them cozy. Warm sunlight shone through puffy white clouds moseying in from the ocean, sending shadows on the gardens. The lulling chorus of the trees joined with a new song, and he closed his eyes and listened. He realized the second tune came from the booming sea. The two different melodies rose in unison and joined in a beautiful harmony. He inhaled deeply, his mind relaxing further under the new lullaby.

"Morning!" Okulu called.

He plopped down next to Salvarias, wearing a full set of armor that screeched against the stone bench.

"Wonderful morning!" The merc took a swig from his flask.

"Indeed." Salvarias smelled the scent of ale and a cloying, sweet perfume.

"You're not too popular right now."

"Astute observation."

Okulu laughed. "I'd be a blind fool to see anything else. Don't let it bother you."

"You are not upset?"

Okulu shrugged. "I find these things tend to work out. No need to get bent out of shape or angry at someone."

Salvarias looked back over the ocean and did not respond.

"How's the wound?" Okulu asked.

"Healing nicely. Thank you for your help."

"You're a fighter. Ale?" Okulu offered his flask.

"No, thank you."

"Shame. It really gets the blood flowing." Okulu helped himself to Salvarias's favorite cheese. "Met a lovely girl in the tavern last night. I found out she works for weasel Gunder. She said he's so wrapped up in the wedding that he's not planning to help with the fortifications of the city. I guess that's good news for us. Edium and Humar can handle it." He took the last slice of bread.

"How long have you known Humar?"

Okulu frowned. "Ten summers."

"You have worked together often?"

Okulu tossed some bread to a nearby sea bird. "Yes. We took many jobs together." The merc grinned. "We're both rich as can be but we like a good fight. Keeps up the skill."

Salvarias greeted the bird and advised it to fly away before Adok woke.

"That brother of yours will outdo us soon, though. He's a natural."

"He is exceptionally talented."

Okulu slapped Salvarias back. He grimaced when the recessed images of death, landscapes he had never seen, and people he had never met surged forward. The pain he endured from the slightest contact from anyone besides Wilhelm was worse than it had ever been. Though Zeeas had unlocked many new oddities, it had amplified all the old ones that caused pain.

"By the way, there is a library double the size of the sitting room in Kudril."

Salvarias looked up and then lowered his head when he realized his face was no longer in shadows. "Thank you for telling me."

Okulu grinned. "I don't see how mages study so much."

"I do not see how you drink so much and remain standing."

Okulu's grin widened. "You're a funny one. I like the little, subtle sense of humor you have."

Salvarias looked back over the ocean, keeping his emotions in check. While he oddly trusted the merc, he knew distance was best; for the both of them.

"I asked Edium if the library was open to us, *all* of us, and he said it was. Upstairs, opposite side of the estate from your room and sixth door from the staircase." Okulu stole the last piece of cheese. "Have fun with your parchment."

"Have fun with your flask."

Okulu's laughter faded off in the distance.

Salvarias woke the slumbering wolf and the two headed to the library. Upon entering, he nearly wept. Book-crammed shelves reached floor to ceiling in the two-story room. Sizable chairs were positioned to catch the sun, and blankets rested on the back of each thickly stuffed, high-backed chair. The smell of crisp parchment mingling with the musty smell of old books and aged leather was intoxicating to him. The wolf seemed to know what seat he would choose and curled up in front of one to continue the morning nap. After selecting a book, Salvarias settled near Adok and became lost in its pages.

"Hello, dear."

Salvarias jumped and looked up to see Talura smiling. Her hair was once again braided with white flowers weaved in and out of it. She was stunning and he did not guess where Lunara received her piercing eyes or sweet smile.

"It is late and I thought you might be hungry." She set a plate of food on a small table beside him.

He glanced out a window suffused by hues of purple from the

setting sun. A servant was starting a fire.

"Thank you, my Lady. I apologize for the inconvenience."

"It was no trouble, dear. Do you need anything else?"

"No, my Lady, thank you."

To his dismay, she nestled in a nearby chair, retrieving a book from a table. After covering herself with a blanket, she read in silence. The white flowers in her hair permeated the air with a faint scent of jasmine.

His fears of the woman prevented him from focusing on the words of his book. She was a mother after all, and like his own, possessed a gift to see into the soul. He merely needed to count down the hours before Talura sensed his evil and attempted to beat it from him like his mother.

Wilhelm's deep voice boomed from the entrance. "Hey, Salv."

"Hello, brother." Salvarias breathed in the instant protection that encompassed him.

"Okulu said you'd be here." Wilhelm flicked back Salvarias's hood and ruffled his hair before sitting in a chair. "Hello, my Lady," Wilhelm said to Talura.

She smiled sweetly and continued reading.

Salvarias had an urge to crawl to Wilhelm and hide. He was proud when he remained seated. Zeeas had taught him much. "I am sorry. I lost track of time."

"Don't apologize." Wilhelm shrugged and looked around. "This will keep you busy for a couple of days."

Salvarias nodded. "Indeed."

"Don't stay up too late." Wilhelm rose and snatched a piece of bread.

"Good night, brother."

Wilhelm tilted his head to Talura on the way out. Salvarias returned his focus to the book, and eventually the pages pulled his mind into tales of hope.

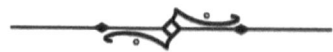

Wilhelm woke late morning and, after washing and slipping into a change of clothes, he knocked on his brother's door before peeking inside. As suspected, the bed was untouched. Smiling, Wilhelm crossed the landing to the library. His brother was curled up in a large chair, sleeping. A blanket covered him and a small plate of bread and fruit sat on a table. Talura was stirring the fire and motioned Wilhelm to be silent. Once she got the flames roaring to heat the room, she slipped out with him.

"He was up nearly the entire night. He reminds me of Lunara." Talura took his arm and led him down the hall.

"Did you stay with him all night?"

"Just until he slept."

"Thank you for seeing to him."

Talura shrugged. "Let's get you some food."

Wilhelm grinned. Indeed, he was starving. He spent the morning talking with Talura while she kept piling food on his plate. For the first time in his life, he had to turn down the fifth offering of breads, cheeses, and roasted meats. He couldn't remember feeling so full. Then he realized he'd told her of his time in the slave caverns, and the morning had slipped by.

A blush crept up his cheeks. "I'm sorry. I didn't realize the time. I've taken up your whole morning."

"Don't be silly. I enjoy listening to you talk. Do you want to practice today? I'll be happy to show you to the training yard. Okulu and Humar have already left for it."

"Yes, please."

Talura smiled and took his arm, escorting him through the estate.

He cleared his throat and tried to keep his tone even. "Where's Varila?"

"In town with her father. He's rather close to her and very protective."

He grinned. "I don't think Varila needs protection."

She laughed. "No, my dear, she doesn't. Edium has yet to learn and tends to be protective of both our girls."

"I understand about Lunara. Men are drawn to her like a watythm to ale."

"Indeed. Lunara is a picky woman, though. I can't tell you the number of proposals she's received."

"Someone will catch her eye."

"They might have already," she murmured.

"What do you mean? Okulu isn't romantically interested in her. Humar is too old and so is Durak."

"Yes," she confirmed. "Here we are."

Expansive for an estate, the grounds provided wood dummies, small obstacle courses, and a variety of weapons to test different skill sets. Wilhelm's happiness found a new height.

"About time!" Okulu called. "I thought you were growing embarrassed about Humar kicking your ogre ass!"

"Bah." Wilhelm waved the comment aside. "You offer me plenty of opportunities to keep my confidence high."

Okulu grinned. "Not today, my friend."

Talura tilted her head in acknowledgement of the bows from the men. "I'll have a late lunch sent."

Okulu cast Talura a disarming wink. "Pardon my language, my Lady."

"Trust me, dear, I've heard worse." She curtsied and strolled from the training yards.

Wilhelm spent the afternoon sparring with Humar and Okulu. The training grounds allowed the merc the proper setting to teach Wilhelm the art of throwing daggers. He picked it up easily but preferred close combat. Still, it was something new.

Though he was tiring by early evening, he engaged Humar in one last duel. Maybe it was the newfound skill of pinpoint accuracy that Okulu had beat into Wilhelm's eyeballs, but the contest seemed easier. Humar's quick movements and flicks of his sword were effortlessly predictable. Before Wilhelm knew it, his blade was resting against Humar's neck. Wilhelm froze in a mixture of shock and elation, then a smile crept across his face in response to Humar's beaming blue eyes.

Humar edged away. "Brilliant! Absolutely amazing talent you have, Wilhelm!"

Okulu rose from his resting spot to join them and shot Humar a wicked grin. "I guess there's a first time for everything, old friend. I've never known another to best you with a sword."

Humar glanced at Wilhelm with a proud smile. "I haven't been beaten since I was fourteen. I'll take complete credit for your skill, Wilhelm."

He bowed, winking at Humar. "It's all yours and well deserved."

Okulu grunted. "I think it's that damn running he does."

Wilhelm's grin grew. "It helps."

"See!" Okulu exclaimed. "He's not even out of breath! Maybe if you ran you could beat him again."

Humar muttered a curse and shook his head. "I'm too old for running."

Okulu laughed. "Indeed you are. And I'm too drunk."

Wilhelm followed the men back to the estate while the sun teased the horizon. His smile had yet to leave his face, even after his best efforts. He decided to take a run through the city and found his endurance was still high. After a bath, he took a plate of food Talura prepared for Salvarias to the library.

He was curled up in a chair close to the fire, Adok resting at his side.

"Hey, Salv," Wilhelm said softly.

His brother looked up, and a familiar sparkle lit his eyes. "Hello, brother."

"You should get some sleep tonight."

"I will. I am almost done."

Wilhelm left the food on a table and added a blanket to his brother.

"Thank you."

Wilhelm grinned. "I beat Humar."

Salvarias sprang from his chair and flung his arms around Wilhelm's neck. "Congratulations, my dear brother!"

He ruffled his brother's hair. "Thanks. Hopefully I'll be able to do it again."

"Your talent with a sword is unsurpassed. You will do it again. It is time for you to consider your dream."

"I'm not ready." Wilhelm shrugged. "I need to beat Humar consistently before I venture into dual swords."

Salvarias smiled slyly, eyes sparkling with mischief. "So, if you beat him each day for the next say, seven days, you will ask?"

Wilhelm chuckled. "Maybe."

Salvarias's expression grew serious. "I will not give this up. You have the talent and strength. There is nothing you cannot do."

Grin still plastered, Wilhelm ventured from the library. He glanced around. With nothing better to do, he made his way to the kitchen, allowing his brother's words to open new possibilities. When he stepped into the kitchen, he found Varila rifling through cuts of meat.

"Didn't you just eat?" Wilhelm asked.

She glanced at him over her shoulder and grunted. "Didn't you?"

He grinned. "Maybe. What's on order?"

Varila tossed him a piece of roasted chicken, taking one for herself. She leaned against the kitchen counter and looked him up and down. He wasn't shy about his physique, but her stare caused him to blush. The memory of her soft lips and strong body moved him a step closer.

His gaze meandered to her thigh peeking between her short skirt and boots. His fingers twitched. "What did you do today?"

"I spent time with my father in the market and wandered the city. He walks around to make sure everyone is treated fairly. He's the reason no one spits on your brother." She poured herself a mug of ale.

"May I have one?" he asked.

"Sure."

His grin broadened when she didn't fetch it for him. She served no one and he wrestled back the urge to kiss her. Instead, he took the opportunity to lean close when he reached for the pitcher on the counter behind her. He smelled strawberries mixed with her oiled armor while he poured his mug.

They drank three pints, talking of nothing important, a building tension between them, wanting yet fighting.

After finishing her third drink, she set aside the mug. "I'm going to bed."

He grinned and winked. "Sweet dreams."

She smiled up at him through lush eyelashes and her gaze was an open invitation. He kept his hands to himself, remembering her tension in the woods. In honesty, he was confused. She appeared to carry the same desires he did, but when he'd kissed her in the forest her fear was unmistakable. In the same breath, it had seemed she changed her mind.

Now the seductive invitation shone in her eyes again. Unable to resist her allure, he bent towards her, feeling her hand glide up his chest. Just as their lips were about to touch, he studied her eyes for any sign of fear. Tentatively, he kissed her. She didn't settle for the small gesture. Her returned kiss was one of passion, and stole his surroundings. Her mouth was cool from the ale and her taste sweet. Fervent in his return of her lust, he lifted her to the counter, knocking over the pitcher of ale. A shiver of desire ran up his spine when her legs wrapped around him, pulling him closer. Hands snuck in the back of his tunic and followed the scars from his time in slavery. Her fingertips seemed to melt away the harsh memories while she traced each whip mark.

"Excuse me," Edium said from the doorway.

Wilhelm jumped back and embarrassment burned his cheeks. "I'm sorry... I didn't... I mean..."

Edium's mouth twitched with a smile. "I wanted to say goodnight."

She shot Wilhelm a wink and hopped down from the counter, her gaze rolling over him. "Escort me to my room, Father?"

Edium nodded.

"Good night, Wilhelm," she said.

Wilhelm's mouth barely mumbled out, "Good night to both of you."

He sopped up the ale while steadying his racing heart and calming his breathing. He sank into a chair at a nearby table and groaned. He liked Varila and admitted he might love her. Now, he worried he'd ruined any chances for her father's approval. He rested his head in his hands and contemplated a way to rectify the situation.

Screams from Salvarias jolted Wilhelm from his thoughts and he ran for the library. His brother called for him, terror and paranoia in his voice. By the time the stairs came into view, the pleas had stopped and Wilhelm's stomach plummeted to his boots. He bounded three steps at a time, shoved a servant aside, and burst through the door. The library was empty.

"He's not breathing!" Edium exclaimed from across the landing. "Someone get a healer!"

Wilhelm raced for Salvarias's bedroom, and entered to find his brother shaking violently in Edium's arms, eyes rolled back in his head.

"Let go of him!" Wilhelm roared.

Edium jumped aside. Wilhelm shouldered by and scooped Salvarias up.

"I'm here, it's all right. Breathe, Salv. You have to breathe."

Salvarias inhaled sharply and his fingers dug into Wilhelm's shoulders.

He turned to Edium and Varila. "He's fine. Can you leave?" Once they closed the door, he shifted his attention back to Salvarias.

"It's all right, Salv. I'm here."

Salvarias gulped in air and opened his haunted eyes.

Wilhelm smiled his most comforting smile. "It's all right."

His brother's grip eased. Wilhelm withdrew the puzzle box from his shirt pocket and handed it to Salvarias, who began moving the pieces even as it grew to full size. Wilhelm sat on the bed and pulled Salvarias close, wrapping an arm around his brother's shoulders, and gave a gentle squeeze. "You all right?"

"Yes. I am sorry, brother."

"Don't apologize. Bad dream?"

Salvarias's eyes drooped closed when he nodded, but he continued to move the pieces. Eventually his fingers stopped and the puzzle box toppled out of his limp hands. Wilhelm lowered his brother to bed, covering him with extra blankets and breathing the calming scent of lavender.

Chapter 25
Spring 1018 a.r.

Humar met Durak in the estate's courtyard and helped remove packs from the horses.

"How was the trip to Falar?" Humar asked.

"Uneventful. Plenty of black-armored soldiers, though."

"You made sure you weren't followed?" He regretted his question the moment it left his mouth.

"Of course, ye numb-brained idiot!" Durak roared. "Ye think I just came out of me mamma's womb?"

"Sorry."

"Damn you, boy! I've been around longer than ye ever will be, and don't forget who's older!"

Humar suppressed a smile. "Of course."

"And don't use that damned tone! Nevlar's betrayal, I'll beat you to Oblivion!"

He covered his mouth to hide his spreading smile. "Of course."

Durak grumbled an affectionate curse and the two entered the estate.

"Falar was packed," Durak muttered, climbing the stairs to their rooms. "People wall to wall."

"I heard that in Treppter. Small towns are flocking to the cities for protection. Serinity is the sole city not allowing any in."

"Smart. Shop was vandalized and they took all my equipment."

"How did they not find the gifts?"

"I have a secret storage area in my room. I had to use the other smithy to finish Wilhelm's."

"I was wondering why you were late."

After Durak freshened up, Humar and the cavrul wandered the estate in search of the brothers. Humar's emotions were a discombobulated mess whenever he even thought about his youngest nephew. A part of him trusted the boy, understood the mage was setting out to become involved in the evil brewing, and knew the brothers needed help. Still, a portion of Humar remained reserved, guarded around the boy. Salvarias's intensity was unnatural, his eyes unsettling, and his stern expression intimidating. Nevertheless, the letters Tobin had written stuck in Humar's mind, so he considered them family; the one nephew everyone loved and the other an outcast whom you cared for but in a different manner. He reluctantly admitted that if Wilhelm had chosen to leave Salvarias, the others, including himself, would have followed Wilhelm, not the mage. The thought sparked a feeling of shame in Humar.

They found the brothers in the library, sitting next to a fire, which battled the afternoon spring chill. Wilhelm dozed in the largest chair, his soft snore echoing in the room, while Salvarias huddled in a plush chair next to his brother, knees drawn up and covered in a blanket, reading a book bound in blue leather. Adok raised his head at their entry. Leaving their gifts next to the wall, the two entered the room grinning.

"Hello, boys," Durak greeted. "Mind if we interrupt?"

Both startled, but Wilhelm's inviting smile spread.

"Sure," Wilhelm said.

"We got ye boys a little something for yer Birth Days!" Durak said. "We meant to give 'em to you last year but, well, ye know."

Humar ducked behind the wall and reappeared carrying a great sword. "Here you go, Wilhelm."

Humar smiled when Wilhelm's eyes opened wide. He accepted the sword, examining it by the light of the fire. Humar was proud of his gift. The sword was held in an etched, black leather sheath, its belt large enough to fit around Wilhelm's waist. The sword itself was worth a small fortune since Humar had ordered it from a smith in Loutsil—one even Durak envied—who supplied swords made with the finest steel. The pommel was forged with a fierce bear head that capped the long grip. *The Bear Protects Us* was engraved along the grip. It was a common saying among generals in Zerana's army, and Humar found it fitting for Wilhelm. The guard branched out into a slight arch to prevent the blade from sinking too far. The etched fuller boasted a complicated design, and overall the sword was intimidating. Since Wilhelm possessed strength, the reinforced blade would never break and was probably heavier than any other sword in all of Arden. It surpassed the quality of Humar's own sword, which until now had no equal.

Wilhelm's eyes grew misty. He turned his smile to Humar.

"Thank you."

"After the way you took down that ogre, you deserve a fine sword."

Wilhelm embraced Humar, squeezing the air from his lungs. Once lowered, Humar clutched his ribs, gasping, and waved Wilhelm's murmured apology aside.

Durak tossed a pack at Wilhelm's feet. "Here, lad. Ye need armor with that fancy sword."

Durak had skillfully forged a thick, black, leather cuirass, and arm and leg guards. The new armor eclipsed any other piece of work the cranky cavrul had ever completed. Testing a new method, he'd combined metal and leather into a cohesive unit that allowed the comfortable wear of leather with the added protection of steel. It was exquisite. A ferocious bear was etched into the breastplate and seemed to add an aura around the warrior, as if it had been waiting for him. Wilhelm was speechless. He picked up Durak, despite the protesting, and gave the cavrul a bear hug.

After Durak gained his breath, he helped Wilhelm try on the armor. "It's a replica of what your father wore, you know."

Wilhelm paused mid-buckle. "My father? I didn't know you knew our father."

"Not well, but he asked me to craft armor for him when he was young, about your age. I've learned much since, and your set surpasses his."

Wilhelm's brow furrowed as he continued tightening the buckles. "I'd heard he was only in Falar for three days."

"Aye, lad. He came back after a year of making his request. Kept a low profile the second time he showed in Falar. Nothing like his first."

Humar wanted to warn Durak to cease his story. Wilhelm's eyes were darkening with a deep hurt. Tobin had been told little of the boy's true father and had only repeated to Humar what Ashra had said: The man was out in the world, completing an important task that overrode his responsibility as a father. Even written, Tobin's contempt for the man had been clear. Furthermore, Ashra had never disclosed any other information or spoke of her lover to either of her sons. From what Tobin knew, the brothers' father had never set foot in Falar after leaving Ashra alone and pregnant. Durak's story, however, showed the man had returned and never bothered to meet his own son. Humar now shared Tobin's contempt. The man must have returned a third time, used Ashra to satisfy his physical desires, and left her once more alone and pregnant with Salvarias. Humar wondered why Ashra would continue to allow the louse into her bed. He obviously didn't care for her or his sons.

Humar thought Wilhelm might ask further questions, but he merely shook himself and his normal bright eyes returned.

Turning to face Salvarias, grinning crookedly, Wilhelm asked, "How do I look, Salv?"

"Like a true warrior, my dear brother. And quite intimidating."

Indeed, Wilhelm was an impressing sight. His armor enhanced his physique, and if possible, he looked taller.

Durak tugged certain pieces. "Does it cut in anywhere?"

"No." Wilhelm sighed thankfully when he sat, testing different positions.

Humar picked up another gift and handed it to Salvarias. The mage's delicate hands accepted the cloth bundle, unwrapping it with his usual gracefulness, and his breath caught in his throat. He caressed the two blank books bound in luxurious black leather, high quality and extremely expensive. One was regular size and the other small enough to conceal in his robes. Inside both, his name was stitched.

Humar cleared his throat. "I bought these after I thought yours were stolen. I guess they can be your first set. And I had one specially made for you to carry in your robes. If we get separated from our packs, you can still study."

Salvarias caressed the books and looked up, tears in his eyes, the tiniest of smiles across his face. "Thank you, Humar. I will cherish them always."

Humar realized he'd never seen the mage smile. When the stern expression lifted, the boy was beyond handsome. His large black eyes came alive and lit up the room, sparkling with warmth and happiness, no longer foreboding or cold. Humar couldn't help but smile, too. Life seemed more vibrant.

Durak's gruff words broke Humar's gaze. "Here ye go, Salvarias. It's got enchantments. Do ye know, or do ye need me to tell you what they be?"

Salvarias's hesitancy showed his surprise at receiving a gift from the cavrul, and he accepted the sheathed dagger even while his eyebrows stitched together. The holder, crafted by Durak, could be strapped to a forearm or shin and was made of soft, black, leather that wouldn't irritate the skin. Humar had been impressed when Durak ventured into a mage shop to purchase the enchanted dagger. It was light as a feather, the hilt simple and slightly curved to fit well in the palm. The blade was etched with runes only mages could read, and it was supposedly able to seek a target and be invisible to any who didn't know of it; Salvarias would never miss nor would it be found if searched for.

Salvarias murmured under his breath and ran his hand along the dagger. "No, I see what it does. Truly extraordinary. Thank you, Durak." Salvarias turned a growing smile to the cavrul.

Once Salvarias lowered his guard, Humar found the boy... enchanting. The reservations he'd fostered seemed foolish, and he wanted the mage's friendship and trust. Salvarias's eyes carried a deep pain no longer hidden under a dispassionate gaze. A weight hung over him, and sympathy rushed through Humar. After a glance at Humar, Salvarias withdrew his smile from the room, and erected his impassive expression. Humar shivered when the warmth seemed sucked from the space.

Durak shuffled his feet and looked around. "Well... good... glad ye like them, boys. Now, there's work to be done in the smithy."

The cavrul left the room. After Humar bid the brothers good day, he went to meet with Edium and Unbril to finalize plans for the city, shaking his head along the way. Discombobulated. Yes, Humar was a mess of emotions. He wasn't too fond of the feeling, either.

Salvarias sat on his window ledge while golden morning light illuminated the fortifications of the city. Barrels of oil had been hauled up the outer wall, catapults had been strategically placed, and the smithy repaired armor and weapons with Durak's assistance. Three days remained until the attack and Salvarias was pleased with the coordination of Edium and Humar. Their victory would be swift, and Salvarias's vision remained strong except for Lunara. She no longer huddled in the alley in his vision and he thought himself to exhaustion attempting to understand the change. His instincts held firm in her safety, but yet again, events were hurtling towards the unknown, the uncertain, and it grated on his nerves.

He caressed his new spell book. It meant more to him than Humar could possibly know. The simple gesture had a deeper meaning to Salvarias, a feeling of freedom, of rebellion, towards his mother. His new book allowed him to write down words that ran through his mind and use them to create new spells, his own spells. His magic was ecstatic, and both stayed up the entire night, writing and studying together. They had created their first new spell and were eager to try it.

He left his room and found Wilhelm with the sisters and Edium. Lunara wore a white wedding gown that appeared to be three times her weight. Seamstresses fluttered about her as she looked at her reflection with glassy eyes. Varila sat on a chair, glaring at the floor. Edium and Wilhelm were engaged in conversation.

"Pardon me. Brother, may I speak with you?"

Varila shot daggers at Salvarias, which he chose to ignore.

Once they left the room, Wilhelm asked, "What's going on?"

"Adok, will you stay with Lunara?" The wolf whined in protest but trotted into the room. A smile snuck out when cries erupted from the women servants and Lunara's voice lifted in laughter. Salvarias led his brother down the hall. "I must leave the city and head to the farms. I have a spell that might save the fields. Will you join me?"

"Sure. Is this a spell you learned from Dethal?"

"No, it is new, one I have never tried before. I am not certain it will work, but it is worth a try."

"Humar's going to be pleased to learn about it. He's been trying to find a way to help."

The brothers exited the home and entered the Bellerum family stables. Salvarias picked a feisty black stallion he immediately named Mithal. The horse had yet to be ridden, but it only took a few choice sentences before he agreed to allow Salvarias aboard. An extremely bulky chestnut mare with a black mane and tail strolled lazily about.

Wilhelm stared at the mare, scratching his stubble beard while a slow grin sliced across his face. "I think that one might actually be able to hold me."

Salvarias glanced at the mare and smiled. "She accepts your challenge. Her name is Lilly."

Wilhelm sighed. "Not very intimidating."

Salvarias could not stifle his laugh. "No, my dear brother, but it is the name she prefers."

Wilhelm shrugged. "Lilly it is."

Salvarias saddled the stallion, and just when his leg gave out, he grabbed hold and pulled himself up. Mithal trembled with an anxious need for exercise, but Salvarias kept to a walk as they made their way from the city. Once past the gate, Salvarias shot Wilhelm a smile.

"See if you can keep up, my dear brother." After a quick, dramatic rear from Mithal, Salvarias released his hold and raced for the farmlands. The wind and blurring surroundings raised Salvarias's spirits, and he smiled at the freedom he felt. He glanced behind, laughing when the mare complained about his brother's weight. The stallion would have gone further, but Salvarias pulled back to a trot when the fields came into view.

Wilhelm reined in next to Salvarias. "The mare is too heavy to keep up with the stallion."

"I am sure that is the reason," he said dryly.

At the edge of the fields, he dismounted, trusting Mithal to follow on his own accord, which he gladly did while nudging Salvarias in affection.

Farmers paused in their work to watch Salvarias with narrowed eyes.

"I'll handle them," Wilhelm said.

He trotted over to the farm owners and charmed them, using his genuine good nature to win them over. Though suspicious, the farmers allowed Salvarias to continue.

The presence scoffed. *"Bah, thisss will not sssave your sssoul, my pet. Thisss doesss not counter the wicked whisssperss you sssend on the wind."*

Salvarias bit back his anger. *"I know."*

"Then why?"

Salvarias remained quiet. He knew the reasons were selfish, to only save his soul; he felt no kinship to the farmers. His lack of care for others continued to bother him.

"Yesss, my pet. You are ssselfish."

"Stop reminding me!"

"Until you correct your faultsss, my pet, I will not. Sssomeone

mussst remind you leassst your evil sssspread. Do not sssteer your ssself-hatred towardsss me. Without my guidancccce and remindersss, your weak mind would provide excussses, eliminate the resssponsibility from your ssshoulders and tell you it isss all right to only think of yourssself."

"I know I am evil and selfish. Reminding me does not help me fight it."

"True, my pet. Yet you have done nothing to correct your weaknessesss. If I were not here, whissspering and reminding, your sssoul would already be lossst."

Salvarias sighed. *"I want peace."*

"You will never have peaccce, my pet. Evil doesss not dessserve peaccce. Ssstop your whining. Already in the lassst three weeksss you have allowed othersss to follow you in a task you know ssshould be done alone. Already you have trussted Humar and dragged him into your life to be tormented like Wilhelm. Look at your brother. Look at him!"

Salvarias turned his gaze to his brother laughing with a farmer.

"You sssee he is a good man, yet you taint him with your evil. You forccce him to care for you, to comfort you in the night, to protect you from harm and the harsssh ssstares of othersss. He leadsss an empty life becaussse of you!"

"I cannot leave him."

"Weak pet! When will you sssee what you do to him?"

"I know what I do!" Salvarias turned away and leaned on Mithal. "Leave me alone!"

"Ssso be it, pet. I want to help you, to protect thossse you love. You know thisss to be true, do you not?"

"Yes."

"Then do not be angry with me. I am sssorry."

Mithal nudged Salvarias and he stroked the horse's neck. The stallion began chatting about his unhappiness from being cooped up in the city. The conversation eased Salvarias's depression while he continued through the fields.

The sun had set by the time he whispered the spell for the last time, allowing a single drop of water to fall from his water skin as he had done every fifty feet. His knees trembled from exhaustion, and just as they gave out, Wilhelm caught him.

"Tired?" Wilhelm asked.

Salvarias barely mumbled his reply. "Yes."

As if he weighed nothing, Wilhelm lifted him onto Mithal, who carefully avoided jostling Salvarias about while they made their way back to the estate. He was grateful for the caring horse and was deep in conversation with the stallion when Wilhelm spoke.

"How'd you remember the spell? I thought I heard the same words each time."

"You did. It is a special spell, an extremely short spell with a component. It does not strain the mind nearly to the degree of a regular spell."

"Do you think it worked?"

"I will not know until the fields are attacked. It will not protect the farmers, just the perimeter from fire."

Salvarias paused and surveyed the field outside Serinity. Something felt odd. He couldn't put his finger on it, but the energy seemed half alive, as though it were being drained.

"You all right, Salv?"

He shook off the feeling and nodded, continuing towards the city entrance.

Wilhelm's ever-present grin broadened when he surveyed the tranquil meadow. "At least there's hope for the farmlands."

"Hope is the bait a fish takes which leads to its demise. We hunger for it and do not see what lurks behind." Salvarias was not fond of hope. It seemed to be waging some secret war against him.

"There's always hope, Salv."

He flashed a halfhearted smile. "Of course, brother."

"You are right, my pet. Hope isss blind. Reality isss much more cruel but a necccessary obssservation."

Wilhelm rounded the corner to the dining room to see Edium sitting alone and immediately turned on a heel to leave, but Edium's voice stopped him.

"Join me, Wilhelm."

Wilhelm cursed himself. He'd been artful in his avoidance of Edium ever since being caught with a hand in the sweet's drawer, so to speak. Now, there was no escape.

Wilhelm squared his shoulders and strolled into the room. "Morning."

Edium leaned back in his chair. There was an air about him that commanded respect. "Morning, boy. Sleep well?"

"Yes, Gentleman."

"Just Edium. After all, you've already set aside formalities when it comes to my daughter."

Wilhelm's stomach clenched, and as sure as roasted venison was his favorite meat, he knew his face was the color of a tomato. He cleared his throat, begging his mind for a suitable comment.

"That will do, dear." Talura entered the room and gave Wilhelm a secret wink. "They're both adults."

Edium's penetrating gaze had yet to leave Wilhelm. "Indeed. And one of those adults is my daughter. My oldest. The one who traveled with me to every corner of Dalnar. The one I spent—"

Talura moved in front of Edium and kissed him. "Yes, dear. We know."

Wilhelm exhaled a breath when Edium's gaze finished excavating a hole in Wilhelm. He came up with what he hoped was a suitable comment. "I meant no disrespect, Edium."

Edium turned back to Wilhelm with a softened expression. "I doubt you did, boy."

"We know, dear." Talura cast him an impish grin. "Varila has always had a mind of her own. She usually gets what she wants. I have no misgivings that you couldn't resist her charm."

Wilhelm grinned. "Who could?"

Edium grunted. "A man who wishes to gain the trust of her father."

Wilhelm glanced at Edium. The man's eyes had hardened again. Thinking humor to be the best remedy, Wilhelm said, "I think I'll blame you for my indiscretion, Edium. You've raised a strong daughter who commands the attention of any man. And, as your wife stated, one who gets what she wants. I fear I'm the victim in all this."

Edium's steady gaze burned into Wilhelm for what felt like an eternity before the man burst out laughing. Wilhelm grinned.

Edium was wiping away his tears when Varila entered the room. "What's so damn funny?"

The father smiled warmly at his daughter. "Why can't you marry a man like this?"

Varila plopped in a chair. "Marriage isn't my cup of tea." She shifted her provocative gaze to Wilhelm. "I've never met a man that could keep up with me, much less hold my attention."

Edium's laughter was renewed, and this time Talura joined in.

"What?" Varila snatched up a plate and scowled at her parents. "You better fess up, Mother."

Talura took the plate from Varila and gathered food. "It's nothing, dear."

After Varila was situated and eating, Talura made a plate for Edium and then Wilhelm. He noticed the last plate had no eggs or meat.

"I'll take it to him," Wilhelm offered.

"No need." Talura set the plate beside her. "I'll do it momentarily."

Edium propped his feet on a nearby chair. "Quite the nightmare he had last night."

Wilhelm shrugged. It was only a matter of time before it was brought up since his brother's screams had plagued the estate for several nights.

Talura slapped Edium's feet. "Does he get them often?"

"Every night at the estate in Kudril," Varila said. "We hardly slept."

Wilhelm's anger simmered. "He can't help it."

Varila leveled a steady gaze at him. "I didn't mean it like that. Stop being so damned sensitive."

He sighed. "Sorry."

Edium changed the subject. "Preparations are almost done."

"I've never seen a city move so quickly," Wilhelm noted over a mouthful of bread.

Edium grinned. "A little trick I started over fifteen years ago when I became commander over the guard."

Wilhelm looked up, surprised. "I didn't know you were commander. And that means you're a knight, too."

Edium shrugged. "I've gotten around. I like to test my abilities in different areas. After I built my wealth as a merchant, I moved here with Talura. We had the girls, and I knew this was where I wanted to remain. The city has always been peaceful, and with a little help, we've evolved it. I lived here a couple of months before Gunder approached me. Of course, he wanted my allegiance since he had no heirs. My wealth puts me in line for his position. Keep your enemies close." Edium winked. "I told him I had no desire to be Lord, but I'd love to run the guard. I reached knighthood quickly and he appointed me commander. I worked on gaining the trust and loyalty of the men. After a while, Gunder withdrew from operating the city, allowing me full reign for the most part, and he merely kept the title. Everything was going well until he asked for Lunara's hand. I turned him down nearly two years ago and it took him a year to muster the courage to 'claim' her, as was his right. After that, our relationship has been rather strained."

"I can't believe Lunara's going to marry that vile man." Varila snorted. "I swear to you both, after the battle, I'm taking her away from here. I won't let her."

Edium sighed. "Gunder won't lose her again. He's hired some men from Hadrium to keep an eye on her as well as a woman from Falar. The opportunity to run has passed."

Varila's face turned red and she folded her arms, looking as though she might kill her plate of food.

Edium's eyes grew distant. "Not all is lost."

Talura moved the conversation along. "Edium started having the city perform drills."

"Yes." Edium smiled. "A couple times a year we go through similar preparations. The gates will close tomorrow, and the people will move back towards the market. It helps in situations such as these where you don't want your enemies knowing you know."

Wilhelm grinned. "Brilliant!"

Talura rested her hand over Edium's. "He's one of the smartest men I know. It's one of the reasons I married him."

"She couldn't resist me." Edium shrugged. "Few could."

Talura threw a berry at him. "Careful, dear, or else I'll finally reveal how you proposed."

Edium turned scarlet and Varila laughed. "Don't tease us, Mother. We've been dying to know since we were children!"

Salvarias entered with Adok. "Good morning." He bowed to the group.

Wilhelm offered his brother a wide grin when he sat next to him, accepting the plate from Talura.

"Thank you, my Lady."

"Of course, dear."

Lunara glided into the room. "Good morning, everyone."

Throughout breakfast, Wilhelm smiled in contentment, listening to Edium and Talura talk fondly to one another and their daughters, wrapped up in the family's happiness. He finished Salvarias's bread and stretched, contemplating whether to practice now or wait until the four helpings of food had digested.

"Will you accompany me to the market, brother?" Salvarias asked.

"Sure, need some herbs?"

"Yes." Salvarias rose from his seat and bowed to the family. "Good day to you all."

Wilhelm saw the daggers Varila shot Salvarias and realized she must still be upset about the visit to Lord Gunder's estate. Edium also remained quiet, avoiding eye contact, and Lunara's goodbye was less than friendly. Talura was the sole one giving a warm farewell. Wilhelm's happiness ebbed away, and he draped an arm over his brother and led him away, tense with anger. Salvarias seemed unfazed and walked through the estate, taking in the busy servants and whispering numbers the entire way. Wilhelm steered his brother towards their rooms.

"What is it, brother?"

"I have something for you."

Wilhelm helped his brother climb the stairs. By the time they reached the top, Salvarias limped and leaned his weight on Wilhelm. He'd caught Salvarias trying to walk on his own too many times for comfort. Through cracked opened doorways, Wilhelm had watched Salvarias limp around the library or his room, stumbling often, falling to the floor, only to stand and attempt it again.

Wilhelm entered his room and situated Salvarias in a chair, grinning at the familiar sparkle in the black eyes. Reaching under the bed, Wilhelm withdrew the aspen sapling. A few days ago, he'd taken a trip into the woods, searching for the perfect fallen branch, and he'd been ecstatic to find a broken sapling. He'd worked for hours to trim it, sand it, and achieve the right balance, using Varila's height to test it. Now he felt the staff worthy of its owner.

"Here," he said. "I found this and trimmed it down to help you walk in case I'm not around."

Salvarias's eyes filled with tears when he accepted the staff. He used it to rise, and a smile spread across his face. "Thank you," he whispered. His smile grew while he walked around the room.

"Does it need to be shorter?" Wilhelm asked.

Salvarias flung his arms around Wilhelm's neck. "No, it is perfect."

Wilhelm felt a strong, very strong, punch to his ribs and grunted. "Ouch. You're getting stronger." Salvarias's laughed soared Wilhelm's spirit. He grinned and winked. "Let's get going."

Salvarias nodded, hugging him again before leaving the room, using the stick to walk.

When they entered the courtyard, Wilhelm draped an arm over his brother's shoulders. "You didn't ask for herbs in Acklar because you didn't think we had enough money." He'd caught Salvarias counting their coins yesterday.

Salvarias shrugged. "I did not know how much of our funds we would need."

"Those herbs are important. Don't go without them again. Matter of fact, promise you'll tell me when you're low."

Salvarias remained silent.

"Salv," he said sternly.

"I promise."

Once on the crowded streets, Wilhelm removed his arm, keeping it ready by his sword. The market spread across a large section of the cliff, further along the bluff and down from the estates. Shops lined one side of the spacious cobblestone street, offering clear views to the sea. Salvarias inhaled deeply, his eyes soft as he stared at the rolling ocean and gray sky. Wilhelm smiled, seeing nature lift the weight that seemed permanently mantled on his brother's shoulders.

Salvarias inhaled once more before continuing down the busy streets. "Why are you upset?"

"I'm not upset."

"Brother, you are upset with the Bellerum family. Why?"

Wilhelm shook his head. "I don't like the way they looked at you."

"I did not stop Gunder's advances and I encouraged him. They have a right to be upset. The Bellerum family is compassionate and charming. They already approve of you and it would trouble me should you turn away their affections."

"But you'd never do anything to hurt anyone. They have no right to treat you that way."

"My dear brother, you have known me for eighteen years. These people have known me less than ten days. They are reacting as they should. You must be more patient."

Wilhelm sighed and felt a punch to his ribs. Grinning, he flicked back Salv's hood and ruffled his hair.

"Here it is." Salvarias raised his hood before entering the potion shop.

Wilhelm ducked through the door and breathed in the memories. Like Falar, the store was lined with jars and potted plants, filling the small space with an earthy spiced smell. Salvarias studied the shelves and then placed an order with the shop owner.

While they waited, Salvarias examined several plants, whispering numbers the entire time. Once his order was filled, Wilhelm insisted on adding a pouch Salvarias could tie around his waist so the herbs were always available. Wilhelm paid the owner and followed Salvarias outside to join the wolf, who'd stayed in the street, and they strolled lazily along the market, slipping into the comfortable silence they enjoyed together.

A low growl issued from Adok broke Wilhelm's reverie. He glanced around the market, scanning for what had sparked the reaction. His brother didn't seem to hear and continued counting, his mind lost within itself. Wilhelm followed the wolf's gaze and saw two men in matte black armor standing in front of a smithy. He shifted his brother to the other side, shielding him from view.

"What is it?" Salvarias asked.

"Black-armored soldiers." Wilhelm made sure his brother's mage robes were covered by his cloak, pulled his hood lower, and took the walking stick. "Sit over here. I want to talk to the blacksmith once they leave and see what they wanted."

Salvarias sat on the bench, and Wilhelm put the walking stick at his brother's feet. Wilhelm faced the soldiers and gathered his cloak close, standing strategically to block his brother from view. After a few back and forth questions with the blacksmith, the men moved on to the next shop, thankfully away from the herb store. Wilhelm waited until the men had covered three stores before casually walking to the forge.

He hefted a broadsword from a display. "Hello, friend."

"Hello. Interested in a broadsword?" The smith eyed Wilhelm's borrowed one slung over his back.

"Perhaps. Fine quality," he lied.

"Thanks. That's a fine lookin' great sword," the smith said, pointing to Humar's gift belted around Wilhelm's waist.

"Thank you. I saw those men wearing black armor. Odd how non-reflective it is, don't you think?"

"Very odd indeed. I'm curious how the armor was made. And how they breathe in that bucket on top of their heads."

"I thought maybe they were seeking repairs." He lowered the broadsword and selected another.

"No, just looking for some mage boy and curious about our fortifications."

"Really? Plenty of mages about. Is there a reward?"

The man grunted. "A heavy reward. Fifty gold for information, one hundred gold for his capture and safe handover."

Wilhelm didn't need to feign his surprised look. "That's a sizable reward."

"They say he's a sneaky one."

"What does he look like?"

The man rubbed his chin. "Tall, black hair, black mark on his left hand and black eyes."

Wilhelm's heart pounded but he kept his voice even. "Shouldn't be too hard to find if he's here."

"The streets are crowded and no one taunts mages in Serinity, so it's not easy to pick them out. I'm keeping my eye open, though."

"I was curious about the fortifications myself."

The man snorted. "One of Lord Gunder's many preparations for potential attacks."

"You don't approve?"

"I'm a citizen." The man winked. "I have to complain about everything, even if I approve."

Wilhelm chuckled. "You make fine weapons. Let me think about it."

The smith's face slumped to a frown. "I'm open late."

Wilhelm bid farewell and meandered down the street, glancing back to make sure the blacksmith no longer watched him. Once he felt safe, he strode up to his brother, draped an arm over his shoulders and hurried him towards the estate.

"What is wrong?" Salvarias asked.

"They're looking for you."

A hand rested on Wilhelm's shoulder. "It will be fine, brother. I am not sure staying with the Bellerum family is a good idea. I would not want to put the family in danger."

Wilhelm barely heard the soft words over his own rampant thoughts. One thing he knew, Edium had guards and lots of them. Wilhelm would not leave the estate. "No, we're staying."

"Brother, I cannot—"

"We're staying. No discussion."

He increased his speed when he reached the less busy street leading to the estates. His gaze darted everywhere while checking the demeanor of Adok. He resisted the urge to run when the gate to the Bellerum estate came into view. His brother's breathing had increased from the quick pace, and Wilhelm lifted him in an attempt to help but refused to slow down. The guards posted in front nodded in greeting and opened the gate. Wilhelm glanced behind. No black-armored soldiers were visible.

"Edium!" he roared, entering the courtyard. "Edium!"

"Brother—" Salvarias's tone was reproving.

"No, Salv. They won't take you from me again." Wilhelm climbed the steps and strode inside the estate. "Edium!" He knew he verged on paranoid, but he didn't care.

Edium emerged from a hallway. "Here, Wilhelm. What is it? Are you all right?"

"No, I don't know what to do. I need your help." He swallowed hard against the lump in his throat.

"Anything, what is it?" Edium tried to coax Wilhelm to a chair. He refused to sit, refused to let go of Salvarias. Wilhelm loosened his hold, realizing how tightly he gripped Salvarias's shoulders.

"In the city there were two men dressed in matte-black armor. They were offering a reward for my brother and asking about the city's fortifications. They can't know we're here. Your servants have seen Salvarias and I'm worried they might turn him over or give information to the soldiers."

"I assure you, Wilhelm, my servants are loyal to me."

He shook his head. "They're offering a hundred gold."

Edium whistled and looked at Salvarias. "Still, I assure you, they won't say anything."

Wilhelm's gaze swept the bustling estate.

Edium must have sensed his concern. "I'll counter the reward and offer two hundred gold to any servant who comes forward should any black-armored man question them."

Salvarias deftly moved from under Wilhelm's arm. "Brother, you cannot ask—"

Wilhelm interrupted. "Thank you, Edium. I'll be forever in your debt should the situation arise."

"No need to worry," Edium said. "The guards at the gate have already been asked and told the soldiers they hadn't seen your brother. The incident was reported and I spoke to all. I assure you, these men are loyal to me."

"I can't thank you enough."

"I am just as concerned for my daughters. No debt is owed between us."

Wilhelm nodded and then led Salvarias to his room, settled him in a chair, and knelt in front of him. "You have to stay inside. You can't leave the walls. Please promise me. You don't understand. I can't handle it. I'll work for Edium for the rest of my life if I have to, but they can't take you."

Salvarias's eyes softened. "I promise, brother."

Chapter 26
Spring 1018 a.r.

Salvarias ate his bread and cheese alone in his room, occasionally tossing a slice to the sprawling wolf. He chose not to eat with the group even after Talura's pleas. The angry glares of his fellow companions had finally worn down his indifference, and he found he missed Lunara's lingering glances and sweet smiles.

Tonight, the attack would begin. Salvarias read his spell book in preparation for the battle. He felt confident they would defeat the beasts. Humar was an excellent leader, and his strategies for defense were carefully thought out, thorough to the tiniest detail. By breakfast, they would be celebrating victory.

Wilhelm's soft knock startled Salvarias from his thoughts.

"It's time, Salv."

He set aside his spell book and followed his brother to the courtyard of the estate. Lunara would be staying behind, though by her fiery eyes and clenched jaw, she seemed less than pleased by the decision.

Salvarias knelt by Adok and whispered, "Keep Lunara safe." He stroked the wolf's head and then mounted Mithal. Obediently, Adok padded to Lunara's side after a whimper of protest.

She smiled at the wolf, and then cast Salvarias the sweet smile he had missed.

The group headed towards the outer wall, dodging dashing squires delivering last minute orders. The city's organization impressed Salvarias, and though the citizens thought the ordeal was a drill, they moved with haste to the market. Guards were posted to ensure proper urgency and assist those with small children and the elderly. Edium seemed almost fatherly towards the city, and his glances while they rode showed a man not only intent on the overall success of their battle, but also just as focused on each citizen's safety. He often motioned to soldiers to help larger families keep track of children, and at one point, ordered a guard to help a boy who had lost his dog. Salvarias's respect for the man grew with each passing street.

When they reached the outer wall, Durak and Okulu stayed below with the ground troops while the rest climbed to the top of the city wall to stand with the other generals and Lord Gunder.

Gunder scowled at Edium. "If this is a false alarm, I won't be pleased."

Edium's curt tone spoke of his disgust for Gunder. "I'm sure it's not, my Lord. Even so, it's good for the city to perform these drills. With the increase of creatures stealing away citizens in the night, this will help us prepare for such situations."

Gunder curled his lip at Edium. "Watch your tone, Edium. I'll be part of your family in two nights' time. Odd, isn't it? We're the same age but you'll be calling me son."

The setting sun bathed the darkening sky in lavender and blood red. A breeze kissed the swaying green grasses and coaxed a formidable looking storm in from the south. Salvarias watched the deepening sky a moment before noticing the inky black clouds were rolling at an unnatural pace. He nudged his brother. After taking in the sight himself, Wilhelm grunted in understanding and passed the word.

The billowing clouds soon devoured both moon and stars. Salvarias swore he could not see more than an arm's length in front of him. The torches along the wall did little to penetrate the thick blackness blanketing the city. The air was unnaturally still and silent. Only clinking metal armor, murmuring soldiers, and crackling flames echoed through the night, creating an unsettling feeling among the men... and Salvarias. His apprehension intensified the longer he stood in silence. The soldiers shifted in restless anxiousness, and the soft murmurs turned to annoyed mutters. The snapping fires seemed to mock him, as if they knew secrets he did not. The silence became oppressive. He resisted the urge to scream in order to release his burgeoning nervousness. For the first time, he doubted his visions. Then his instincts prevailed. He was not wrong. The city would be attacked, and it would happen on this night.

"I need Okulu," he whispered.

Edium motioned for a messenger, and soon he returned with the grinning merc.

"What do you see?" Salvarias asked Okulu.

"I see a lot of black creatures out there and—oh look, there's one now!"

"Lumous!" The sparrow flittered above Salvarias.

Humar cursed. Black creatures had scaled the walls in the cover of darkness, and one had climbed over and stood in front of Salvarias. Wilhelm reacted quickly, ramming his great sword through the blackfur's mid-section. The beast's eyes widened in surprise and it slid off the blade, falling from the wall into the blackness below. Wilhelm yanked Salvarias behind the line of armored men.

The white sparrow was the only light that cut through the unnatural blackness. Whispering a word, Salvarias sent the sparrow high above the city then whispered once more. The sparrow burst into a hawk the size of the city, illuminating the entire wall as well as the meadow surrounding Serinity.

Panic struck the soldiers. The creatures overpowered the first frozen layer of men. Flesh sizzled and screams of pain erupted along the length of the wall. The blackfurs shredded soldiers with fangs and claws, ripping men asunder and sending body parts sailing into the city below. Screams rippled across the army from not only the men at the top of the wall, but also those at the base who were showered with the blood of their comrades.

The field outside came alive with crackling pops. An oppressive feeling of the entire field moving with an immeasurable force pushed against the city. What Salvarias had originally thought was an odd shadow covering the meadow turned out to be the army of blackfurs. There were too many to count.

"Oil!" Humar's voice jolted the remaining men into action.

Salvarias chanted his fire spell and sent a gigantic ball of flame hurtling into the darkness below, illuminating the crawling ground when it passed. It exploded from the impact when it struck the meadow. The fire licked over the beasts, catching its way to the farmlands. Salvarias held his breath. At the fields, the fires ceased burning.

Wilhelm gave a gentle pat on Salvarias's back and a wink. "Nicely done, little brother."

"Amazing!" Humar exclaimed.

Salvarias turned his gaze back to the fighting. Guttural screams of rage erupted from the blackfurs climbing the wall as oil cascaded over both stone and creature alike. Archers sent a volley of flaming arrows into the night and straight down the wall at any beast visible. The smell of burning fur and tar drove away the freshness of spring and caused many soldiers to be ill.

He did not cast any further spells; there was no need. Soldiers were readily taking down any creatures that successfully scaled the wall, and the barrage of fire arrows kept the masses outside the wall on constant fire. He reserved his strength and watched in satisfaction while beast upon beast fell back to the field below. The city had yet to be breached and he took comfort in his vision.

"Yesss, my pet." The presence's voice was melancholy. *"You have sssaved the city but will it sssave your sssoul?"*

He ignored the voice and lived in the moment of triumph. He hoped their victory would stomp away the fires in his nightmares.

He stood ready to assist his brother if need be, but Wilhelm swung his new great sword as if it weighed nothing. Creatures fell before him like a wave against a cliff. Salvarias caught a glimpse of Wilhelm's grin and almost laughed aloud. His brother enjoyed a good fight.

As the hours passed, Salvarias's feeling of triumph faltered. Every time they killed a blackfur, another seemed to appear. The men were tiring, and acid-dripping bodies were beginning to pile up along the wall, proving as deadly as the live beasts. He angled over the wall and focused on a group of blackfurs. Varila had launched an arrow over at one of the beasts, piercing through the blackfur's skull. It writhed on the ground and soon went rigid with death. He watched a moment longer to see the beast dissolve into the earth. One blink later, the ground sputtered tar into a sack lined by a thick membrane that simmered and sizzled, growing and expanding. Within a few breaths, a fully-grown blackfur burst through the thin film. It was such a surreal sight that none others took notice. He stared at the creatures along the wall, but none came alive. The creatures on the field could regenerate. They would never win.

Yet again Salvarias had failed. Just as he had with Tobin. When Salvarias had cast the spells over the farmlands, he had felt the alteration of energy.

"Yesss, my pet. You have failed to sssave the city. You have failed thousandsss of people." The presence's voice was now smug. *"You have killed them all and yet again have disssappointed me, my little murderer."*

Cursing himself, Salvarias paced. He had missed an important clue in his vision. As if reading his mind, white light flared before him and the vision flickered across his eyelids. Grimacing, he focused his mind and steadied the picture. A cave located at the base of the cliff behind the city housed a sphere with blue mist circling inside it. The light pulsed then faded and the darkness of the night flooded towards him. Wilhelm held him steady when the wave of dizziness swept over him. After his vision cleared, he cursed again. Wilhelm turned to the next beast. Salvarias waited until his brother was caught in a fierce fight before sneaking down the wall, knowing Wilhelm would follow if he knew. The wall could not fall, and Wilhelm killed three blackfurs to every one killed by a guard. His brother's talents were needed here, not protecting Salvarias's worthless life.

He mounted Mithal and rode a short distance before glancing back. Lord Gunder was ordering his men about, kicking those who did not move fast enough and yelling at the rest. While Salvarias watched, a creature rose behind the lord.

"Kill him, my pet," the voice hissed.

Salvarias created a fist-sized ball of fire and sent it sailing towards the creature engaged in battle with the Lord. The fire was so intense that the instant it struck the beast it exploded, raining fire down on any near, which happened to be Lord Gunder. The man flailed about the wall, screaming at people to help then tripped and fell down the stairs to the city below. His flaming body did not move again. Salvarias felt the rise of satisfaction, but it was not as sweet since he had not seen Gunder's eyes.

"Well done, my pet."

An immediate flood of self-loathing swept over him. He could not decide if he had killed Gunder or if it had been an accident. Shaking his head, he turned to see Lunara sitting wide-eyed on a white mare.

He suspected that she was also trying to determine if he had killed Lord Gunder on purpose. He did not give her a chance to contemplate. "I must get to the back of the city, to the bottom of the cliff. Do you know a way there?"

"Ye, Yes. I can take you."

Salvarias grabbed her horse's reins, stopping her from turning. "No, just tell me."

Defiance glittered in her eyes. "No, I'll show you." She snatched the reins from his hand and kicked her horse's flanks, heading up the city hill at full speed.

Cursing, he released his hold on Mithal and followed. She rode to her estate and dismounted, handing the reins to a servant, Salvarias directly behind her.

"Where is Adok?" he asked.

"I left him in my room."

"I need him."

Lunara turned to another servant. "Please open the door to my room."

Bowing, the servant left.

Lunara glided into her home, through the dining hall, then the kitchen, and down a steep winding set of stairs. She ended up in a cellar filled with wine barrels. She tested bricks along a portion of the wall and then pushed a stone, which creaked and retreated into the wall. A stone slab ground away in protest to reveal a doorway.

"Through here." Lunara ducked into a room fit for four people. "We'll wait for Adok."

As she spoke the words, the wolf trotted into the room after Salvarias. She pressed on the indented rock and it groaned flush with the wall, closing the door. They were plunged into darkness.

"Lumous." The sparrow glowed dimly. Salvarias inhaled deeply when he smelled a spring meadow, light and fresh, a slight perfume of flowers and trees. He looked around the room, but did not see what caused the alluring aroma.

Lunara groped along the opposite wall and pushed another stone. Grinding, it retreated and another door opened.

Salvarias stepped in front of her and put his body in the doorway, blocking her from following. "Stay here. I go alone."

She entered the room, forcing him back. Her eyes fixed on his. "I'm going with you. You'll not change my mind and you cannot make me stay."

He backed against the wall. "On the contrary, my Lady, I could make you stay." He seriously contemplated it.

Her body brushed against him, her eyes glowing in the faint light. "But you won't."

At her touch a strange peacefulness washed over him. His mind eased, and for the first time in his life, the dull pain disappeared. His thoughts were lazy and the images of death ceased. Shocked, he stumbled away and the flood of his normal turmoil returned, causing a dizzying feeling that made him reach for the wall. It passed and he turned down the tunnel, confused. It must have been a passing relief. Coincidence.

The tunnel allowed him to stand upright, but the width forced the trio to walk single file. He went first, followed by Lunara, and then Adok. The tunnel split and she told him to go to the left. After a short distance, he stopped at a metal box on wheels.

Lunara smiled. "We ride that down. The tunnel narrows at the bottom to stop the device. It's perfectly safe."

"Is there a way back up?"

"Yes, though more complicated."

Lunara rested a hand on his shoulder and gently pushed him to the wall so she could pass. He flinched under her touch and the peaceful feeling when she pressed by him. He shook his head.

The cart was deep and could accommodate four people. Though it was made of metal, it seemed surprisingly light. The wheels were welded under the box to keep them from the sides of the wall. Handles lined the edges inside the box and blankets were stashed in a corner. Though not cold, the underground system was cool and musty.

Lunara fumbled with the side of the box, and he heard a latch give and the door swung open. She stepped inside, followed by Adok. Salvarias entered last and latched the door closed.

"Hold onto me," she commanded.

Unaccustomed to touching another person other than Wilhelm, Salvarias's shaking hands held her waist while she bent over the side. Her feet left the ground, but she was easy to hold. She searched for what seemed like an eternity.

He could no longer blame coincidence. Her touch did not hurt but rather brought him peace. His feelings ran in a mixture of wonder at her effect on him, paired with a gut-wrenching fear. He should not be allowed to touch others, especially one as pure as her. He was evil. She was not.

Suddenly, the cart gave a lurch and then plunged down the tunnel. The unexpected lunge knocked them off balance, but he caught her, allowing her to land on him instead of the hard metal. Sitting up, he pulled her close, wrapping an arm around her waist and holding a handle with his other hand. The worries of his mind eased, and the breeze through his hair was invigorating. The ride was surprisingly smooth. The walls began to narrow, causing the cart to slow, screeching to a halt, sparks flying.

Lunara looked over her shoulder with a huge smile. "Fun, wasn't it?"

He could not help but smile with her. Her hair was windblown and excitement shone in her eyes. He had indeed found the ride to be fun.

When she pulled from his grasp, the thoughts and fleeting images surged forward, and it took him longer to rise.

She giggled, opening a latch on the front of the cart, and exited after Adok. The wolf could not get out fast enough and let it be known that he was less than pleased with the descent method.

She started forward, but Salvarias inched past her. He did not know if the creatures had found the tunnel, but he did not want to chance stumbling into a mass of the beasts. Quick but cautious, he made his way down the remainder of the tunnel until he came to a dead end. She reached past him and pressed on another rock.

"Rulose," he whispered, ending the light spell.

They were plunged into darkness. When a hand rested on his arm, he instinctively pulled away, braced for the normal fluttering images, but none came.

"Please," she whispered.

He reached out and found her hand, placed it on his arm, and allowed her to maintain her hold, living in the moment of his lazy mind and pain-free head.

He heard the door grind open, and the light from his giant eagle above the city brightened the entire area. He preferred to wander this part in darkness. He glanced at the sky and saw that the conjured storm had dissipated somewhat. The soldiers would be able to see without the eagle. He ended the spell and darkness masked the rocky shore. He inched his way forward, feeling along the wall, and found the exit. He stepped through the door and waited until his eyes adjusted. Getting his bearings, he found the correct direction and crept toward the cave. Lunara still gripped his arm, although he was sure she could see.

The sea spray drenched them and he shivered along with her. The hazy moon broke free from thinning clouds to reveal the cave entrance. A chill tingled along his spine while he stared at it. No activity bustled about and no guards stood close. Adok remained relaxed. Salvarias pulled the hood of his robes closer, concealing himself in as much darkness as possible.

The cave floor was somewhat level compared the rocky shore. The walls were jagged and he moved to the right side, allowing his scarred hand to be sacrificed instead of his spell hand. He reached out the aspen staff, feeling the sides of the entrance, and determined they were in more of a tunnel. Thankful to have close walls, he made his way forward, probing along the ground with his staff and keeping his balance as best he could with his hand.

A faint light grew in the distance. When they drew closer, he saw it came from a room at the end of the tunnel. His uneasiness doubled when no guards stood watch. Surely whatever evil sought to claim Serinity did not think itself unstoppable.

Peeking into the room, he found the sphere from his vision, no larger than a human head, resting on a pedestal; a blue mist swirling inside its crystal walls. Two torches flanked the entrance and shadows lurked in the back of the room. Glancing at Adok, the wolf remained tranquil.

"*Lumous.*" The sparrow flittered around the cave, checking crevices and corners for any lurking creatures. Content that they were alone, he commanded the light to cease and turned his full attention to the sphere.

Indeed, it was powerful. He found a pebble and tossed it at the sphere. The rock sizzled and turned to dust before even reaching the blue orb.

"What is it?" Lunara whispered.

"This sphere is bringing dead blackfurs back to life. I must destroy it or Serinity will fall." Salvarias felt traces of evil, the same evil within himself that mirrored the evil spreading through Arden. Unnatural power mixed with the magic, but how to destroy the orb eluded him.

A low growl from Adok broke his concentration.

Glancing around the room, he ordered the wolf to a deep corner hidden by shadow. Salvarias positioned himself in front of Adok and pulled Lunara in front him, turning her back to the room, and bowed his head to hide his face. She put her hands on his chest and lowered her head while she pressed close.

The aroma of a spring meadow filled his nostrils, and he could not help but inhale deeply, realizing it was her that smelled of light breezes and fresh flowers. The peacefulness of his mind at her touch was so relaxing that the guard of his mind dropped and the memories of their dreams flooded him. He rested his cheek on her soft hair, inhaling her intoxicating smell. Sliding his hands under her cloak, he gathered her body to his. It was just as he remembered in his dreams. Her warmth, the supple feel of her against him. He inhaled her again, burying his face in her hair. She felt right, familiar, comforting.

"Everything looks fine. This orb thing gives me the creeps."

The voice jolted Salvarias from his thoughts. Her chest heaved and she trembled in his arms. He snatched his hands back and raised his head. He flung up the guard of his mind, pushing her with force to the surface.

Two armored soldiers had entered the room. Salvarias nearly fainted when he saw wet footmarks on the floor leading to where they stood.

When one of the soldiers spoke, his voice echoed as if he were in a vast cavern instead of the small cave they occupied. "Dethal gives me the creeps."

Salvarias heart skipped. If Dethal was near, he would be able to sense Salvarias's presence.

"Let's get out of here. I don't want to be around when he comes. The sooner we take this city the better. I'm anxious for Dethal to return to Zeeas," the other soldier said, his voice carrying the same echo.

The men left the room.

Lunara stepped aside, her eyes remaining downcast. Salvarias hoped both could move past his lapse.

He forced in a steady breath and approached the sphere. He ignited his magic. *"Thoughts?"*

The comfort of his magic warmed him in an instant. The tone, however, was one of confusion. *"It is not solely magic, my wizard. Energy is sustaining it and working with whatever other force lives within. If it was purely magic, I could help. I do not understand this object."*

He whispered an oath and paced. Lost in his thoughts, he did not see Lunara approach the orb until it was too late.

"No!" he cried.

She dodged his lunge and grasped the orb. She screamed when her hands sizzled, but she lifted the sphere and threw it against the wall. The glass shattered, turning to a fine dust that hung in the air like morning fog.

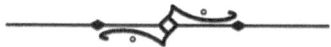

Humar cursed. Blackfur bodies were accumulating along the wall, causing soldiers to lose their lives over a careless stumble. He grabbed the arm of a passing messenger. "We need shields that we can use to shove these bodies over the wall. Get a battalion of men and see to it."

"Yes, Sir Knight." The man bowed and hurried down the stairs.

Humar paused in the fighting to ascertain their progress. The field below was aflame with flailing bodies, yet the numbers seemed to have doubled. The beasts continued to scale the wall in masses, and the defenders were thinning. Burning creatures flung their bodies against the gate, and it was only a matter of time before it would crumble. He cursed, wishing Mafarias would've responded to one of the letters by now. Humar desperately wanted his friend's advice; and power.

"Something's wrong!" Humar called to Wilhelm after dodging a charging beast. "Salvarias said it wouldn't be this difficult." Humar brought his sword down hard and was grimly satisfied to hear bone breaking. "Where is he?"

Wilhelm looked behind him and his face drained of color. "He was right here!"

Humar wheeled to the closest guard. "Where is Lord Gunder?"

"Dead, Sir Knight. He caught fire. Lord Bellerum is ruler over the city."

Humar, Wilhelm, and Varila shared a shocked glance. Humar couldn't help but wonder if Salvarias knew. The confidence of the mage's actions spoke of a man receiving step-by-step instructions.

"Find the mage!" Humar yelled to a guard. "And get me Edium!"

Varila rested a hand on Wilhelm's trembling arm. "He might have gone back to the estate. Maybe he was tired."

Wilhelm shook his head. "Salv wouldn't run from a fight. Humar, what if the black-armored soldiers got to him? What if—"

Humar offered up his most comforting voice. "Salvarias's talent has grown. He can fend them off."

Edium stormed up to the group, his face blotchy red. "Have you seen Lunara?"

Varila jerked her gaze to her father. "What?"

"A guard told me she's missing!"

Humar cursed. "I guarantee those two are together."

"Who?" Edium asked.

"Salvarias is missing as well."

Edium spewed several oaths. "Damn! Movement and lights have been spotted at the base of the cliff! I've sent archers, but I have no idea what's down there."

"Have Unbril check on it," Varila said.

Edium looked away. "Unbril's dead."

Varila marched down the wall a few feet and went on a mini killing spree. Humar felt his own pang of loss. He'd spent hours conversing with Unbril while preparing the city and had grown fond of the general.

"My Lord!" a guard cried. "We're stopping them! Look!"

They ran to the edge, and for the first time, it seemed the beasts were dying, their numbers dissipating under many fires.

Humar turned to Wilhelm. "This has Salvarias written all over it."

"He's quite talented."

Humar patted Wilhelm's shoulder. "I wish he'd share his plots with the rest of us." Humar looked along the wall at the dying creatures. It was no longer a war but a slaughter of blackfurs. "Let's see if we can find him. We'll go back to the estate and coordinate a search."

Humar glanced at Edium while they descended the stairs. The man looked pale. Humar tried to use his most respectful tone. "Do you need to stay at the wall?"

Edium's scowl could turn any man's blood to ice. "My daughter is missing in a city being attacked by acid-covered creatures. I'd abandon Zerana herself in order to find Lunara."

Lunara leaned against Salvarias until the lightheadedness faded. He turned over her hands, revealing angry red blisters.

"How? What?" he stammered.

"We should leave." She stared at her hands, shocked they hadn't dissolved. Though the skin was red and swelling, she felt minimal pain.

The mage ripped off a portion of his sleeve and tied the fabric around her oozing hands. She offered him a smile and was steady on her feet when he released her.

Obviously stifling his questions, Salvarias led her from the tunnel. Outside, she stumbled behind him over the undulating rocks towards the tunnel that would take them home. Halfway there, Salvarias froze.

He grabbed her, pulled her back against his chest, and wrapped his arm around her shoulders. Adok issued a low growl, hackles raised. Salvarias chanted a spell in the language of magic that Lunara found seductive, and she couldn't fight the shiver that ran up her neck. He drew in the air and a white film cascaded over the trio.

Salvarias's lips were close to her ear when he whispered, "You must not move."

A ball of white light illuminated a rock that jutted up from the ocean. She trembled at the evil presence and pressed close to Salvarias.

A man's voice carried over the crashing waves. "Salvarias. Of course I'd meet you here."

The mage's red hair and beard glowed like fire in the light, and she knew him to be Dethal. She shuddered, remembering Salvarias's maimed body. Even while she stared at the man capable of those atrocities, she didn't hate him. Her lack of anger towards others unnerved her. The man in front of her was evil to his core. She sensed nothing in him but hatred, fury, and greed. She should hate him, should despise one so corrupt, but she felt only pity for him. One day he'd be left with nothing but his evil, and on that day he'd beg for mercy and receive none. In the minuscule moment before death, he'd know regret, remorse, and true sorrow over the pain he'd caused, yet no amount of pleading would save him. She could see it clearly, and that was why she pitied him.

"How is my star pupil?" he asked.

Salvarias stood rigid and didn't answer. Lunara gasped when she saw red eyes gleaming behind the old mage. The blackfur towered over Dethal and its gaze was fixated on Salvarias and her.

Dethal's voice rose. "A protection spell? You think that will stop me? You can't hold the spell forever, Salvarias. Release it and I won't kill the woman."

Still, Salvarias didn't answer. A ball of fire shot across the ocean separating the two mages, flying towards her face. She cringed against Salvarias.

"Do not move!" Salvarias hissed.

She froze and could only watch her death approaching. But when it enveloped them, she felt nothing.

"I see you've unlocked your gift. I knew you had. They didn't believe me. They said no one could endure what you did and not talk. However, I saw your defiance. I'm curious exactly what your gift is, my pupil. Would you like to tell me? It must be some kind of prediction, seeing future events?"

Salvarias remained silent.

"Sansis was displeased to learn of your escape. He punished me. Do you remember my master's punishments?" Dethal rubbed his stomach.

Salvarias shuddered.

Dethal sent lightning followed by ice crashing against them. Each time, she couldn't help but flinch, yet each time she felt nothing. Dethal sneered and continued to cast a myriad of spells. Still, Salvarias held although his muscles flexed and twitched against her.

"I will kill you! Surrender!" Dethal ordered.

Two men in black armor managed their way across the rocks and stood with Dethal. She couldn't hear the men's words, but the mage flung his arms and his stance leaned threateningly forward. He must've been less than pleased by whatever they'd told him. After a yell of frustration, a distortion appeared on the rock next to a black-armored soldier.

"Swine!" Dethal screamed at Salvarias, shooting a final spell of fire.

This time, an intense heat washed over her face.

Cries erupted from the top of the cliff and arrows descended around them. Dizziness threatened to claim her, and her strength was draining.

"This isn't over, Salvarias. I will see you again, and it's you who'll lie dead at my feet!" Dethal and the two armored men walked through the distortion. The air shimmered and then the blemish vanished. The red eyes remained. With great agility, the beast leapt from rock to rock and made its way to Lunara and Salvarias. Bending, the beast opened its mouth and tried to bite her, but it couldn't touch her.

Salvarias's sank to his knees, pulling Lunara to hers. He rested against her, his head hung over her shoulder, his body shaking, and his hands limp at his sides. The creature grinned and squatted. It swiped at them and acid sizzled on the ground at her knees. The shield was failing.

Salvarias raised his head, eyes barely open, blood dripping from his nose. He groaned when he reached in the sleeve of his robe, and, as the creature tried to bite her, Salvarias rammed a dagger into the beast's throat. The blackfur gurgled a cry and fell at her knees. The rock sizzled when acid blood spilt from the beast. She ripped off a piece of her dress and withdrew the dagger, wiping off the blood. She lifted Salvarias's sleeve and sheathed the weapon.

Another barrage of arrows splintered around them.

"We must get back," she whispered.

She wrapped Salvarias's arm around her shoulders and helped him crawl on his hands and knees towards the tunnel leading to her home. The jagged rocks scraped her skin and she saw that he was bleeding as well.

Salvarias coughed. Blood trickled from his mouth. He groaned and paused. More arrows rained on the shield, and she swore she felt one poke her. Another pool of deep red blood mingled with the ocean in a puddle. She closed her eyes and focused on him, sensed the strain his magic put on his mind, and as she'd done before, she offered him strength. The blood running from his mouth eased and he lurched forward. An arrow whizzed by and her hair blew aside. They were close to cover. Salvarias twitched. Another arrow flew down and penetrated the shield, pricking his shoulder. She flicked it off him.

When the overhang of the cliff finally sheltered them, she mumbled, "We're safe."

"Rulo, rulose." Salvarias toppled to the ground.

She collapsed on the rocks, shivering, and fought to stay awake.

She sat while the wolf retrieved Salvarias's walking stick and tucked it away safely near the entrance to the tunnel.

The ocean pounded the rocks and seemed to be rising. Not wanting to chance waiting any longer, she gathered her strength. She lifted Salvarias's upper body while Adok wiggled under his back. They dragged him toward the door in the cliff. When Lunara pressed a hand to the cliff face to open the door, a wave crashed into the rock, drenching her and knocking her off balance. Both she and Adok scrambled to their feet and hauled Salvarias into the tunnel. After Adok snatched up the aspen staff, she closed the door, and darkness enveloped them. Feeling along the floor, she found Salvarias and curled up next to him in the oppressive blackness. She drifted to sleep, smelling the calming scent of lavender.

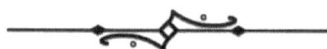

Salvarias woke and immediately regretted it. His head throbbed, and he fought bile rising in his throat. He lay still, getting his bearings, and although his brain thumped his skull, the images were missing and his thoughts were lazy. He called for light. Lunara slept peacefully in his arms.

He brushed her wet hair from her face and stared at her in the soft, white light. Sighing, he whispered her name. She stirred and slid her arm across his chest, pulling closer to him. He allowed himself a few moments of her touch, her comfort, and the unfamiliar contact with another person. He caressed her arm and whispered her name again. She moaned and opened her eyes, offering him a sweet smile.

Relief was in her voice when she whispered, "You're all right." She stood, giving him room to rise.

He wobbled to his feet and then stumbled to the wall. Darkness crept into his vision and the tunnel spun. He was near frozen, and his body ached as though he had battled an army. He wanted sleep.

Lunara rested a hand on his chest. His pain was replaced by desire. Never before had he bothered to look at a woman. His evil made him unable to experience a touch of affection, so he had blocked out the thoughts, the longing that had forever dwelt deep in his heart. However, this woman of remarkable beauty had tamed his evil soul, touched him without causing pain.

"Tisssk, tisssk, my pet," the presence said. *"Remember your mother'sss ssscreams, remember your father'sss body."*

Salvarias did. He removed her hand and opened his eyes.

"I am fine." He picked up his walking stick. "May I see your hands?"

She presented them palm up and he carefully peeled away the strips of his robes. Her hands were red, puffy, and blisters had swelled. He reached into the pouch belted around his waist and withdrew a milky green leaf. He broke it open, dripped the liquid onto her palms, and rubbed the mixture into her skin.

She smiled at him. "Thank you. That feels wonderful."

"How do we get back?"

"Follow me."

She led him down the tunnel, stopping to get the blankets from the cart they had ridden down. She veered to the left and entered another passageway he had not noticed on their descent, and eventually ran into a cart.

She unlatched the door and, after considerable coaxing, Salvarias persuaded Adok to enter, listening to the complaints that wolves were not meant to fly.

It was an artful pulley system utilizing a counterweight to propel the cart up the cliff. In no time, they were at the top.

After a short distance, the tunnel merged with the other one they had taken on the way down. At the end, Lunara opened the door and they entered the small room. She closed it and turned to open the other door but he stopped her.

"Thank you for your help tonight."

She smiled. "Thank you for saving our home, and my life, yet again."

Salvarias took a moment to collect his emotions before entering the cellar. He climbed the stairs, eager to see how the battle fared, and to find his brother. When they entered the dining area, Salvarias was surprised to see their group gathered wearing worried expressions and pacing the floor. Wilhelm gave a cry of relief and scooped Salvarias up in a warm hug.

"You're freezing! What happened?" Wilhelm asked.

"There was a magic sphere causing the creatures to regenerate. Lady Lunara destroyed it. I assume the battle has taken a turn for the better?"

Wilhelm released him and cast a crooked grin. "Yes, it's almost over. Sad news though, Lord Gunder is dead."

"Quite disturbing indeed." Salvarias glanced at Lunara, who was wrapped in her familys' embrace and watching him.

Chapter 27
Spring 1018 a.r.

The evening after the battle, Lunara strolled through the lush gardens of her family's estate in search of Salvarias. The chilly night breeze played with her hair and she pulled her cloak over her shoulders.

She smiled to herself while she wandered under the thick canopy of trees, thinking of her time alone with Salvarias. She could still smell lavender when he rustled by, hear his whispered numbers in her ear, see his deep black eyes, and she shivered at the memory of his touch. When he smiled after exiting the first cart was when she'd admitted she loved him, just as she'd loved the mage in her dreams. In that one smile, she'd seen a man she wanted to be with no matter what happened around them. Her dreams confirmed a softer side to Salvarias, an unguarded and sensitive man that existed behind the stern gaze. So often had she awakened wishing the man in her dream was real, that such a person could intrigue her, challenge her, and ignite her passion. Now, he did exist, and her love grew beyond what she'd felt in her dreams.

She didn't confess her feelings to another, including Varila. Her sister had reservations about Salvarias. Furthermore, what Lunara had shared with Salvarias was special; his smile was a privilege to witness, not something to giggle about in the night.

She caught sight of him resting on a blanket in an open, grassy area with a plate of fruit and cheese. The sparrow illuminated a book in the growing darkness. The wolf, habitually at Salvarias's side, raised his head and stared at her. Salvarias looked her direction.

She walked over and held up her book. "May I join you?"

"Of course." He motioned in front of him.

Smiling, she sat next to him, as close as possible without touching, knees drawn to her chest. He shifted in discomfort.

He moved his plate of food next to her and she picked a blackberry from the assortment.

"How are you feeling?" she asked.

"Fine. And you?"

"Fine."

Salvarias took her hands and turned them palm up. The blisters weren't so red and her skin was still soothed by whatever he'd applied yesterday in the tunnel.

He reached into his pouch and handed her another leaf. "You should use this tomorrow."

She took the leaf, thanking him. They sat together for a moment in silence before she spoke. "How did you know about the orb and the attack on the city?"

He turned his black gaze on her and she fell victim to his intense eyes. "How did you know you could touch the orb?"

She didn't want to tell him yet the words came out. "I heard a voice calling to me. It told me I could destroy it."

"How did you know the voice did not mean you harm?"

"I... I just knew." Her breath increased under his stare.

"Has this voice spoken to you before?"

"Yes." She stopped. The figure had warned her not to tell anyone about it.

"When?"

She tried to turn the conversation. "I... Did you kill Lord Gunder?"

"Perhaps. Does it matter?"

The question confused her. She cared for all life, evil or not. It was why she didn't kill, why she refused to fight. Life is precious and should be revered. However, even if Salvarias killed a man in cold blood, she didn't feel it would change her love.

"No," she responded.

Salvarias released her from his gaze and stared at the stars. Her response seemed to trouble him.

Lunara didn't take her eyes from him when she lowered his hood, purposefully running her fingers through his hair. His hair was soft for a man, thick, wavy, and the blackest of black.

He shifted again but didn't raise his hood.

She leaned forward to catch his gaze. "How did you know about the attack on the city?"

"I suspect that neither of us understands exactly what is happening to us. Therefore, we both are reluctant to reveal information. These back and forth questions could last all night."

"You could trust me."

Salvarias arched his eyebrow. "As could you, my Lady."

"I do trust you. I, I don't understand sometimes."

"You cannot possibly trust me, my Lady. We have only known each other for a short time."

"Have we? I feel we've known each other for years. Our dreams were real, shared together, and our conversations did occur. I know you, Salvarias, more than I know many people."

"I have told you before, dreams are different from reality."

She smiled. "Perhaps for you. I didn't lie in our dreams; I didn't tell you anything that wasn't true. Are you telling me you lied?"

He brow furrowed. "No."

"Then what is different?"

Salvarias's eyes softened and he turned his attention to the stars.

She reached out and twirled a lock of his hair. He pulled away. It would take an extreme amount of patience to break down his wall, but she wouldn't give up. She rested her hand on his cheek and turned his face towards her so she could see his eyes. He still flinched as if she'd struck him. "I understand times are difficult, that not all is as carefree as our walks in the gardens, but I meant each word I told you." She smiled at him. "My wish has come true."

She plucked up another blackberry from the plate and turned to lie on her stomach, elbows propping her up, her book resting on the ground. A moment passed before Salvarias lowered himself on his back by her side.

They read in silence for hours until the moon was high in the sky. Lunara shifted and nestled her head on the mage's arm and drifted to sleep. He didn't flinch from her touch.

Salvarias stood in a red fog so thick he found it hard to breathe. A soft light illuminated his mother's burnt body.

A voice hissed in his ear, "Thisss will be her fate. Remember their lesssson."

Salvarias jolted awake, gasping. The sun peeked over the wall of the estate. He realized he had spent the night in the gardens. Lunara lay on her side next to him, back towards him. Desire welled in him again. He scooted closer and inhaled her smell.

"My ssselfisssh little pet, what have you done?" the voice scolded.

He had allowed himself to be close to her, allowed her to be close to him. He had seen it in her eyes last night, a longing he desperately wanted to return. But indeed his parents' murderer had taught Salvarias a valuable lesson. Mages put others in danger, just by being in their company. Combined with his evil, it was all the reason he needed. He could never be with her. Heartache pierced through him.

"You mussst drive her away. Think of the pain ssshe would endure near you. Remember your mother's ssscreamsss, Tobin's blood."

Salvarias remembered. He had been weak last night. He should drive her away. Protect her from his evil. Resolve set, he cleared each memory of their dreams from his mind and then wiped his feelings for her from his heart.

He asked Adok to stay with Lunara and rose, taking his staff, and left her in the gardens along with the deep care he had once felt for her.

He needed no one.

Note from the Author

Thank you for taking the time to read my story. I hope you enjoyed it. If you'd like to contact me with questions, comments, or just to say hi, you may do so by emailing booksbylkevans@gmail.com, or visit my website, www.booksbylkevans.com.

www.ingramcontent.com/pod-product-compliance
Lightning Source LLC
Chambersburg PA
CBHW030542260626
47157CB00006B/2147